Finders
Keepers

Books by Fern Michaels

Books by Fern Michaels (Continued)

Eyes Only
Kiss and Tell
Blindsided
Gotcha!
Home Free
Déjà Vu
Cross Roads
Game Over
Deadly Deals
Vanishing Act
Razor Sharp
Under the Radar
Final Justice
Collateral Damage
Fast Track
Hokus Pokus
Hide and Seek
Free Fall
Lethal Justice
Sweet Revenge
The Jury
Vendetta
Payback
Weekend Warriors

The Men of the Sisterhood Novels:

Hot Shot
Truth or Dare
High Stakes
Fast and Loose
Double Down

The Godmothers Series:

Far and Away
Classified
Breaking News
Deadline
Late Edition
Exclusive
The Scoop

E-Book Exclusives:

Desperate Measures
Seasons of Her Life
To Have and To Hold
Serendipity
Captive Innocence
Captive Embraces
Captive Passions
Captive Secrets
Captive Splendors
Cinders to Satin
For All Their Lives
Texas Heat
Texas Rich
Texas Fury
Texas Sunrise

Anthologies:

Home Sweet Home
A Snowy Little Christmas
Coming Home for Christmas

Books by Fern Michaels (Continued)

FERN MICHAELS

Finders Keepers

KENSINGTON
PUBLISHING CORP.

www.kensingtonbooks.com

KENSINGTON BOOKS are published by

Kensington Publishing Corp.
119 West 40th Street
New York, NY 10018

All Kensington titles, imprints, and distributed lines are available at special quantity discounts for bulk purchases for sales promotion, premiums, fund-raising, and educational or institutional use.

Special book excerpts or customized printings can also be created to fit specific needs. For details, write or phone the office of the Kensington Sales Manager: Kensington Publishing Corp., 119 West 40th Street, New York, NY 10018. Attn. Sales Department. Phone: 1-800-221-2647.

The K with book logo Reg US Pat. & TM Off.
First Kensington Hardcover Printing: August 1998

ISBN: 978-1-4967-3931-5
First Trade Paperback Printing: January 2023

ISBN: 978-1-4201-2307-4 (e-book)

10 9 8 7 6 5 4 3 2 1

Printed in the United States of America

Finders
Keepers

Prologue

Atlanta, Georgia 1957

Barnes Roland looked around the elegantly appointed medical office, then at the man in the white coat sitting behind the polished desk. He felt guilty and disoriented and wasn't sure why. He had been friends with Sloan since they were five years old.

Totally ignoring his wife sitting across from him, he concentrated instead on trying to understand the anger in Sloan's eyes. Anger directed at him. Never at Thea because, way back when, Sloan Simpson had been in love with her. Well, the best man had won, and the South's most powerful merger of cotton and tobacco had been forged with their union.

"For God's sake, Sloan, just write a prescription so we can get out of here. What's the big deal?"

"The big deal, Barnes, is your wife. When was the last time you *looked* at her? When was the last time you paid attention to her? She's been through hell. By herself, I might add. You wouldn't be here now if she hadn't collapsed. I suggest we put Thea into the hospital and run some tests. My God, man, she can't weigh more than ninety pounds. I trusted you to bring her for her checkups on the schedule we worked out and that you agreed to."

Barnes's hands flapped in the air as he grappled with his friend's words. "Look, what was I supposed to do? She locks herself in her room and cries all day long. She even cries in her sleep. I believed you when you said our daughter's death was not my fault, but I am still consumed with guilt. That is never going to go away. Every day, every chance she gets, Thea tells me it was my fault. Do you have any idea what that's like? I can't force her to eat. I can't force her to bathe and get out in the fresh air. I gave up. Millions of women miscarry, and millions of women lose a child. They don't go off the deep end." He paused, then went on, his voice barely above a whisper, "Sloan, I can't take it anymore."

"Thea needs psychiatric help. I don't want to hear any of that crap about your position in Atlanta society either. Half the women in this town go to psychiatrists. In my opinion you could use a little help yourself. I know all about your lifestyle, my friend. You clip coupons by the bushel, you drink your breakfast, you play a round of golf, then you drink your lunch, take a nap, wake up, drink some more, then it's time for dinner and more drinks. One of the stewards from the club drives you home around midnight and pours you into bed. Read my lips, Barnes, I'm blaming you for your wife's condition. I am not nor have I ever blamed you for your daughter's death."

"What the hell is that supposed to mean?"

"I told you to look at your wife. Now, do it and tell me what you see."

Both men stared at Thea Roland.

The object of their scrutiny spoke. "Stop talking about me like I'm not here. I want a cigarette and a drink."

"You don't smoke or drink, Thea." Barnes's voice was strangled-sounding.

"How do you know what I do and don't do?" To prove her point, Thea pulled out a cigarette and lit it with a flashy gold Dunhill lighter. A matching gold flask appeared in her hand as if by magic. She took a long pull and smacked her lips, after which she blew a spectacular smoke ring. "I'm a drunk like you, Barnes. The only difference is I do it in the privacy of my room. It's the only way I can get through the days. I'm never going to have a child, Barnes. I've had three miscarriages, two stillborn children, and then, when God finally blessed me with a baby girl, He decided I wasn't worthy enough and took her away. I'm empty. There's nothing left. Do you think I don't know how I look? I do. I simply don't care anymore. If I had the guts, I'd commit suicide to be with my little girl. Maybe someday I'll wake up and I will have the guts and I'll do it. I want to go home now. I collapsed because I hadn't eaten. I'll take some vitamins and do some gardening. That was your prescription, wasn't it, Barnes? Or was it yours, Sloan?"

Sloan Simpson rubbed at his temples, his eyes burning. Didn't these people know how precious life was? "Perhaps a trip to the mountains, Thea. A change of scenery, cooler air. It's oppressive here in Atlanta right now. I recommend the Smoky Mountains. I have a cabin there you can use. It's rustic, but it serves the purpose. Will you consider it?"

"Here, there, wherever. Does it matter?" Thea said.

"Think of it as a challenge, Barnes. Leave your scissors and coupons behind. No liquor and no cigarettes. Go fishing and eat the fish."

"If I don't take your little trip, are you going to have me committed?" Thea asked.

Sloan ignored the question.

Thea drained the gold flask, her eyes sparking momentarily. "All right. We'll go tomorrow. Then I want to move, Barnes. After the trip, I want to move someplace else. I wanted to move after my little girl died, but you said no, we were born in Atlanta and we would die there. That's what you said, Barnes. We'll both die in that damn three-hundred-year-old relic we call a home."

"We'll talk about that later, Thea. Our lives are here."

"Your life is here. I don't have one. I'll go without you. I'll expect an equitable distribution of funds if you don't join me. I'm sorry to be putting you through this, Sloan. You've been a good friend as well as a good doctor. She would have been three years old today, Sloan. Barnes forgot." Thea's voice took on a singsong quality. "I can still see her when I close my eyes. I can hear her tinkling laugh when it's quiet. In my dreams I call out to her, but she doesn't answer me. She's gone, and I can't ever get her back."

"Thea . . ."

"I don't want to hear it, Barnes. You didn't even remember today was her birthday. I bet you know to the penny what the price of tobacco and cotton were yesterday and the day before yesterday and all the days before those two days. It wouldn't surprise me to know you have the numbers for the entire year swirling around inside your head."

"Thea . . ."

"Go to hell, Barnes."

Only Sloan Simpson heard Barnes Roland say, "I'm already there."

"We've been riding for hours, Thea, and you haven't said a word. I'm very concerned about you and your health. I want you to listen to me very carefully. What you said back in Sloan's office yesterday wasn't true. I cared as much as you did. I did feel guilty, and you rammed that guilt down my throat every day of our lives. Part of me will always feel guilty, but there was nothing I could do.

Our daughter simply stopped breathing. I wanted an autopsy, and you didn't. It might have brought a small measure of closure to our tragedy. You shut me out. I tried, Thea. A day doesn't go by that I don't think about her. But Sloan was right—we have to get our lives back. We could adopt a child, Thea. Two children if you want, a boy and a girl. I want us to get on with our lives . . . together. If you want to move, I'll move. I'll do whatever you want. I just want us to do it together."

Thea pulled her shawl tighter around her shoulders. "Turn the air-conditioning down, Barnes. Perhaps it will be better tomorrow. I meant it, though, when I said I wanted to move. If you see a filling station or store, will you stop? I'd like a cold drink."

"It's late, almost six o'clock. We should be thinking about dinner. Look, there's a service station. I can see the cooler from here. What flavor do you want?"

"Cream soda would be nice." Thea slouched lower in her seat as she hugged her chest with her thin arms.

She saw her then, a golden-haired child sleeping in her stroller, a yellow dog at her side. Thea moved faster than she'd ever moved in her life. She was out of the car and around the gas pump, the shawl flapping against her arms as she bent down to lift the child. The dog growled deep in his throat as Thea raced back to the car, the child's red sweater dangling from her shoulders.

His gaze riveted on his wife, the engine still idling, Barnes floored the gas pedal the moment he saw Thea throw her shawl over the child's head and leap in the car. The child's screams ripped at his insides. Sweat dripped down his face as he careened away from the gas station. In the rearview mirror he saw the yellow dog break his rope to race after the car.

It was all he could do to keep his hands on the wheel as

they barreled down the mountain. More sweat dripped into his eyes, making it impossible to see the road. He swiped at his eyes so he could look into his rearview mirror. In the distance he could see the yellow dog racing down the road.

Her voice hysterical and out of control, Thea shouted, "I found her! I found her! She's mine! Finders keepers, Barnes. *FINDERS KEEPERS!*"

Part 1

Part 1

Chapter One

Grace Larson leaned over to kiss her husband's cheek. "You're running late tonight, sport," she teased her husband.

"Hmmm, you smell good. How's your cold?"

"Better. Hannah felt a little feverish this afternoon. She's sleeping in the stroller. Jelly is watching her."

Ben Larson closed the ledger and placed it in the drawer. Suddenly he turned, heading for the front door. "Why in the world is Jelly barking like that? The pumps are closed, and the sign is up. You better check on him while I lock up and turn off the lights."

"You know Jelly. He barks when the wind blows." She listened for a moment. "He stopped barking. Guess your customer drove away. You look tired, honey. I hope you aren't coming down with my cold. It's terrible to get a cold in the summer. I hate it that you have to work here on the weekends, Ben."

Ben sighed. "I know you do, Grace. We've been through all this. We're saving for Hannah's college tuition. The first Larson to go to college is not something to take lightly.

You and Hannah are the most important things in the world to me."

"I love you, Ben Larson. That day you sat down next to me in kindergarten class and said, 'My name is Ben, what's yours,' was the day I fell in love with you. Do you want to know something else? I'm going to love you forever and ever."

"And I'm going to love you forever and ever, too. We're both going to love Hannah forever and ever, too. How are we going to handle it when she goes to kindergarten? What if she sits next to a boy and falls in love with him on her first day?"

"We'll handle it, Ben. We're a family, remember. As long as we stick together and present a united front, we can do anything. Do you agree?"

Ben hugged his wife. "Let's get our daughter and our dog and head home."

Grace grabbed her pocketbook and turned the knob of the door. "Hannah's *gone*! Ben, she's *gone*. So is Jelly. He broke the rope. Ben, do something."

"Take it easy, Grace. She probably woke up and had to go to the bathroom. She knows where the bathroom is. Jelly broke the rope because it was old and frayed. He would never let anything happen to Hannah Banana." This last was said over his shoulder as he raced toward the restroom at the back of the station.

"She isn't here, Ben. Where's Jelly? Oh, Ben, she's gone! Someone stole our little girl. Call the sheriff. Ben, call the sheriff right now! Oh, God, oh, God. Hurry, Ben. That's why Jelly was barking. Do you think it was your dad, Ben? That was a stupid thing to say. Jelly would never bark at your dad."

Ben slammed at the door until he remembered he'd locked it. His hands shook so badly he could barely fit the key into the lock. Within seconds he had Sheriff Evans on the phone. He blurted out that Hannah was missing. "Right now, Sheriff. I need you to come here right now. Grace is falling apart on me. I'm going to call the rectory and ask Father Mitchell to ring the bell. As soon as that bell rings everyone in town will be on the square. We have to move fast, Elmo. Don't tell me to be calm. My daughter and my dog are missing. This is a peaceful community, so don't tell me one of our town citizens walked off with Hannah. Hurry, Elmo."

"Ben . . . What if some stranger took her? I didn't hear a car, did you? Hannah wouldn't wander off. She's afraid of the road and the cars. Besides, Jelly would have herded her back to the station. Golden retrievers are very protective. That's why we got him for Hannah. Oh, God, Ben, what if we never get her back? We don't have any money, so it can't be a ransom kidnapping. Some crazy person stole her. I just know it."

"Shhh. Try to be calm, Grace. I refuse to believe someone just drove up and took our daughter. That's insane. I'm sure Hannah woke up and decided to go for a walk. Jelly got upset and broke his rope. He's with her. Try to hang on to that."

Ashton's only patrol car skidded to a stop. Sheriff Elmo Evans motioned for Grace and Ben to get into the car just as the church bell pealed three ominous bursts of sound that signaled a town emergency. Within minutes most of Ashton's seven thousand inhabitants would assemble in the small town square to do what they could for one of their own.

Grace burst into tears at the sound of the traffic on the square. People came on foot, on bicycles, in cars and trucks. Within minutes the sheriff called out a game plan and assigned areas to be covered. "We think the dog is with the little girl. He's protective and answers to the name of Jelly, as you all know. Do not, I repeat, do not spook the dog. My deputy is going to hand out flares to the head of each group. If you see Hannah or the dog, light it up. I put in a call to the state troopers, so we'll have some additional help."

"What about the FBI, Sheriff?" someone shouted.

"I'm working on that, Cyrus. Get moving. It looks like it might rain before long. We don't want that little girl shivering and getting wet."

Grace wept as she clung to her husband.

"Go with your mother, Grace. I'm going to help search."

"Will you find her, Ben?"

"Yes." He hated himself for the lie, but he didn't know what else to say.

"I'm going back to the station to wait. Jelly will go back there because Hannah's stroller is there. I'm going, Ben. I'll sit there all night if I have to."

"Do what you have to do, honey." To Emma Andrews, Grace's mother, he said, "Stay with her, Emma."

"Of course, Ben. Father Mitchell turned the lights on in the church. Roy Clark turned on every light in town. I don't know how he did that, but he did. So Hannah and Jelly can find their way in the dark, I suppose."

"Hannah's afraid of the dark, Mom," Grace sobbed.

"Shhh. She won't be afraid if Jelly is with her. He'll keep her warm, too. In case she wants to lie down somewhere to go to sleep."

Grace's shoulders shook. "Hannah's coming down with a cold. She felt feverish this afternoon. She fell asleep in the stroller, and I didn't want to wake her. God, why didn't I just pick her up and take her in the store? It's my fault, Mom, I never should have left her alone."

"Honey, this is Ashton Falls. You had no way of knowing something like this could happen. This is a peaceful, law-abiding town. It's going to be all right, Grace. God won't let harm come to Hannah."

"Then where is she, Mom?" Grace screamed, her voice rising to such a high pitch that Emma Andrews flinched.

Shortly before ten o'clock a misty rain started to fall. Grace huddled with her mother under the garage overhang. Her grip on the stroller and Jelly's frayed rope turned her knuckles white. At midnight, when thunder and lightning lit up the sky, the state troopers called a halt to the search.

A state trooper in a yellow slicker approached Grace. "Ma'am, your husband wants me to take you and your mother home. He wants you to know the roadblocks are in place, and the FBI will be here shortly."

"What good is a roadblock? It's been five hours. Whoever took Hannah is long gone. No, no, I can't leave. Jelly will come back here. He won't know what to do if he doesn't see me. I can't go home. I don't want to go home. Don't you understand, I have to stay here."

"Ma'am, I do understand. The weather is only going to get worse. Will you at least go inside? Mr. Delancy gave me the key to the garage. You can watch from the window."

"Do what he says, Grace. You have a cold as it is. You can't afford to get pneumonia," Emma said.

Inside, out of the rain, the sound of thunder was less ominous. "They aren't going to find her, Mom. I know it as sure as I know I have to take another breath to stay alive. Hannah isn't coming back."

"Grace, I refuse to listen to talk like this. I want you to stop it right now."

"Mom, if they couldn't find her in five hours, she isn't here to be found. Someone took her in a car. That's why Jelly was barking. Ashton Falls is a small town. They covered it in less than three hours. I know she isn't here, and so do you, Mom, so stop pretending. My baby is gone, and I'm never going to get her back. I don't know what to do. How are Ben and I going to handle this? Hannah was our life."

"Listen to me, Grace. God never gives you more than you can handle. I want you to remember that."

"I don't want to hear religious platitudes right now. What kind of god would let someone take my child? What kind of god would make me suffer like this? Don't tell me He's testing me either. I want my baby, Mom. Where's Ben?"

"I don't know, Grace. He's probably with his father and your dad. He won't give up."

"Mom, go home or go see Ben's mother. I'm better off being by myself. If Ben calls, tell him I'm here."

"I don't like leaving you alone like this."

"I'm not going anywhere. Mom."

The moment Emma Andrews left the service station, Grace walked outside to sit down next to the stroller, the frayed rope clutched to her breast. Every five minutes she called her daughter's name until her voice was little more than a raspy croak. She cried, great gulping sobs, her whole body shaking with agony.

Shortly before dawn, Ben, his father, and Grace's father returned to the garage. "I'm taking you home, Grace. I can see by looking at you you're running a fever. I don't want to hear another word. Jelly knows the way home. If . . . when he comes back, he'll head straight for the house."

Grace allowed herself to be led to the car.

"Ben, we're all just going through the motions. She's gone. We're wasting time combing the area. We need to go on television and radio. Too many hours have gone by. I feel it here, Ben. We're too late. I should have gone out there the minute Jelly started to bark. Why didn't I go out there, Ben?"

"Because Jelly barks at the wind. This is not your fault, Grace."

"You look so tired, Ben. I'm so sorry."

Ben wrapped his arms around his wife. "We'll find her, Grace. I know we will. Hannah belongs to us. We have to believe she'll come back to us."

Grace didn't believe any such thing. She knew Ben didn't believe his own words either. He was trying to make her feel better. For her husband's sake she nodded and prayed she was wrong.

The Larson family spent the following three days doing radio and television interviews, pleading with the person who took their child to return her to her family. Reporters wrote touching, poignant stories about Hannah Larson and her dog Jelly, to no avail.

Four days after Hannah's disappearance, Grace woke and knew she had to go to the garage. She threw on the first clothes her hands came in contact with. "I don't care, Ben. I'm going to the station. I have to wait. Forever if necessary. I can't stand being here in this house. I'll put the coffee on for you before I leave."

Ben sat on the edge of the bed, his head in his hands. He wished he could cry. He wished he could walk downstairs and hear Hannah shout, "Daddy, Daddy!" He wished his wife wouldn't stare into space, and he wished she wouldn't sleep in the chair in Hannah's bedroom. He needed to put his arms around her, needed to feel the warmth of her because he felt ice-cold all the way to his soul. He felt like he was living with a stranger, someone he'd just met who didn't particularly like him. He sighed. Maybe today would be better than yesterday. Maybe.

It's a beautiful morning, Grace thought. The birds were chirping, the air was fragrant with the scent of pine everywhere. The early dew sparkled on the grass that was greener than emeralds. Hannah had always been an early bird and would rush outside in the summer months with Jelly to run barefoot through the small fenced yard, laughing and giggling as she wiggled her bare toes in the wet grass. *Dear God, where is she?*

"Grace, what brings you to the station so early this morning?" Jonah Delaney asked, his eyes going to the pink stroller still leaning against the bright red Coca-Cola cooler.

"I had to come here, Jonah. Do you mind if I sit here? If it's a problem, I can go around to the side."

"Of course it isn't a problem. You can sit here as long as you like. I'll fetch you some coffee, Grace. Would you like a sticky bun or some toast? You're looking peaked to me."

"Coffee will be fine. I won't get in your way." She leaned over to sniff the stroller. "It still smells like her, all powdery and fresh. You know, clean. If she doesn't come back, do you think the smell will stay, Jonah?"

"I'm sure it will, Grace."

A long time later Grace looked up at the big rusty-looking clock over the Coke cooler, surprised that it was three o'clock. If Hannah was at home, she'd just be waking up from her nap. Tears blurred her vision when she moved from one bench to the other. When she saw movement out of the corner of her eye, she swiped at them with the sleeve of her dress. She was out of her chair a moment later. *JELLY!* "Jonah, come quick. Help me! It's Jelly. He's back. Hurry, Jonah. He can hardly walk."

Grace sprinted across the lot just as the golden dog collapsed. She gasped at his raw and bleeding paws. He was matted and dirty, his eyes crusty, his lips cracked and bleeding. The sound of his whimpering was heartbreaking. "Quick, Jonah, get some water and bring your truck. We have to get him to the vet right away. It's going to be all right, Jelly. Please, God, I need You to help me. Let this dog live. For Hannah when she comes back. For me for now because it's all I have. Please, God. I'm begging You. Don't let anything happen to this dog. Please. Please, help him." Grace swore later that she knew the moment she finished uttering her small prayer that Jelly felt the power of another being because he struggled to lick her hand and wag his tail.

"Just give him little sips of water, Grace," Jonah said. "Not too much. Can you get him in the truck?"

"I can get him in the truck, Jonah. I want you to drive like a bat out of hell. As soon as you hit the parking lot of the clinic start blasting your horn."

"Yes, ma'am."

"My God, Grace," Charlie Zeback exclaimed when he heard the horn and came running.

"Whatever it takes, do. I don't care how much it costs. I'm staying with him, so don't even think about asking me to leave."

Four hours later Grace said, "I'm taking him home, Charlie. He'll mend faster at home. I don't know how to thank you."

"He's not out of the woods, Grace. He's going to need constant care. I'll come by later tonight to check on him. It will be around midnight or so. Is that too late?"

"That's fine. I want to make sure I have this right. He can lick ice cubes and he gets a spoonful of boiled ground beef every hour. You hydrated him. We're putting doggie diapers on him so he doesn't have to get up and down. He's not to walk on his paws at all. I can carry him, that's no problem. I have the ointment for his mouth and the drops for his eyes. He's going to be okay, isn't he, Charlie? I want the truth."

"I think he's going to make it. Lord, I wish he could talk."

Grace started to cry. "He ran himself ragged trying to save Hannah. He must have run after a car. Can I pay you later, Charlie?"

"No, you cannot. This one is on the house. I wouldn't be able to look myself in the mirror if I charged you for this. Call me if there's a problem. Ben just pulled up. Do you want me to carry him out to the car?"

"I'll carry him, Charlie. He needs me. And I need him."

Ben offered to carry Jelly into the house. "No, I'll carry him," Grace said. "Will you cook up some hamburger for him? You have to boil it. Bring it upstairs with a bowl of ice and all that stuff Charlie gave me."

"Upstairs? Aren't you going to keep him in the kitchen?"

"No."

Grace struggled upstairs with the heavy dog. Breathing like a racehorse, she made it to Hannah's small, colorful bedroom. Holding the yellow dog securely, she sat down in the rocking chair. "Hush little baby, don't you cry . . ." Tears splashed down on the dog's head. "I know you did your best. You're going to be fine. We'll do what we can. That means we'll do our best. Sleep now, Jelly. You're safe. Thank You, God." Grace wasn't sure, but she thought the big dog sighed with relief. An instant later he was asleep in her lap. She continued to rock him, singing the familiar lullabies she used to sing to Hannah.

"Grace, it's three o'clock in the morning. Aren't you coming to bed?" Ben said from the doorway. He listened to the dog's painful whimpering—or was it Grace whimpering? It was hard to tell. He wanted to pray at that moment. The need was so strong he felt his knees start to give way.

"No, Ben, I'm not. I'm going to sit here with this dog forever or as long as it takes him to regain his strength and until his paws heal. I might be sitting in this chair for a month. This is my only link to Hannah. When he's well he might be able to lead us to the place where he lost our daughter. It's a miracle we got him back. Four days, Ben! Four damn days! Look at him! He was almost dead, but he made it back to the station. I told you he would. I knew it. I just knew it. Go back to bed. We'll talk in the morning."

They didn't talk in the morning. They didn't talk for days. Grace grew haggard and gaunt, Ben just as gaunt and haggard.

On the sixth day, Jelly wiggled and squirmed in Grace's arms. He wanted down, and he wanted the contraption wrapped around his back end off. Grace ran to the linen closet for an old towel she laid by the door. On wobbly legs, the bandages still wrapped around his paws, he lifted his leg. "It's okay, Jelly, that's what it's for. How about some food. Good stuff, hamburger and dog food mixed together." Jelly wolfed it down in seconds.

Grace howled her misery when the dog leaped into Hannah's small bed. With his bandaged paws he made a nest for himself, his eyes soulful when he stared at Grace.

"Maybe she'll come back someday, Jelly. I just don't know. Everyone is doing what they can. It just isn't good enough. In another month those same people will be saying, Hannah who? I don't pray anymore. I try, but the words stick in my throat. I asked God to keep you alive. That was my last prayer. I don't even know if I believe in God anymore. I miss her so much, Jelly. I don't know what to do anymore."

Grace slid onto the bed and stretched out next to the golden dog. She cried in her sleep, tears rolling down her cheeks. The dog licked them away, his eyes ever watchful.

It was all he could do.

The last golden days of summer fled with the tourists, some of them passing through Ashton Falls on their way home to ready the children for school and the Labor Day picnics that flourished in backyards across the country.

Ten weeks later Hannah Larson's pink stroller and Jelly's frayed rope still stood sentinel at Jonah Delaney's filling station, along with a poster-size picture of the missing toddler.

Little progress had been made in the ten weeks since Hannah's disappearance. As one federal agent put it, "It's like the earth opened and swallowed the little girl." The bureau brought in bloodhounds. Twice the agents took Jelly and the Larsons out in the car, stopping every few miles for Jelly to get out of the car to see if he could pick up the scent. The agents could only marvel when the retriever reached the point where he'd either given up or he could no longer follow the car carrying Hannah. The loyal dog had run a total of 135 miles. The AP wire service flashed his heroics around the country to no avail. He still wore booties filled with lamb's wool, the pads of his paws slowly healing with the ointment Grace applied three times a day.

One of the ladies from St. Gabriel's Altar Society presented Grace and Ben with a thick scrapbook of newspaper clippings that detailed Hannah's disappearance and Jelly's heroics. "For when Hannah comes back, Grace," she had said. "Put it away and don't torment yourself by looking at it." Grace had put it in Hannah's sock drawer and swore she would never ever look at it.

Grace was unemployed these days because the grocery store wouldn't allow her to keep Jelly with her. Sanitary reasons, the manager had said. She didn't care. Instead of working she dragged her sewing machine into Hannah's bedroom, where she sewed dresses and playsuits for Hannah, beautiful clothes with bits of lace and colorful rickrack. Often she sewed far into the night, Jelly at her side, Ben alone in their room. She didn't care about that either.

The holidays passed in a blur of misery. There was no Christmas tree, no wrapped presents, no Christmas cookies. Grace refused to attend Midnight Mass, so Ben and his parents went alone. She spent Christmas Day knitting a bright red sweater for Hannah, a sweater she knew the little girl would never wear.

By the time winter passed and the first daffodils sprouted in the front yard, Ben Larson was spending more time racing home to check on his wife than he was working. His termination slip arrived the day before Good Friday. Grace shrugged when she looked at the pink slip. She continued to sew and knit.

The day Ben's unemployment ran out the mortgage company foreclosed on the small two-bedroom house. Cyril Andrews and Nick Larson, along with Ben, carried Grace kicking and screaming from the small bedroom that had once been Hannah's room.

Later, when the townspeople spoke about Grace, they shook their heads, and whispered, "A nervous breakdown is nothing to be ashamed of." Then they would go on to say, "Time will heal Grace's wounds."

They were wrong. Two years went by before Father Mitchell took matters in his own hands and announced at early Mass that the following week was going to be dedicated to Grace and Ben Larson. Translated it meant the good people of Ashton Falls were going to build a house for the young couple on land donated by the parish. To further sweeten the deal Ben was offered the job of custodian of St. Gabriel's when seventy-seven-year-old Malcom Fortensky retired. The women from the Altar Society took it upon themselves to refurbish the Larsons' furniture, which was stored in their families' basements.

Grace, Ben, and Jelly at her side, wept when she walked through the small house that was almost a replica of the one they had once owned.

As Father Mitchell put it, it was time for Grace and Ben to join the living again.

When they retired for the night, Grace said, "I want a baby, Ben. It's been three years."

Exactly one year later, a seven-pound-nine-ounce baby boy named John was born to the Larsons. That same year, Jelly fathered a litter of six. The pick of the litter was named Jelly Junior.

Chapter Two

Charleston, South Carolina 1965

The little girl looked wistfully at her classmates as they skipped off holding hands. She wished she could run alongside them, singing at the top of her lungs the way they were doing. She hung back, not wanting to get into the limousine that dropped her off and picked her up every day after school. She knew her mother was sitting in the backseat, watching her behind the heavily tinted windows. The moment Thea Roland stepped out of the car to the curb, the other children stopped to stare. Dressed in a swirling flowered dress with matching floppy-brimmed hat and short white gloves, she handed her daughter a single yellow rose. Jessie accepted the rose because it was a ritual her mother went through every day. She hated the roses, hated the way her mother looked. Why couldn't she dress like the other mothers who came to pick up their children in station wagons, wearing jeans or slacks, their hair tied in ponytails? Jessie suffered through the paralyzing hug and sickening kiss of adoration before she climbed into the backseat of the limousine.

"Now, tell Mama what kind of day you had, sweetheart. You look tired. Do you feel all right?"

"It was a nice day, Mama. I got red A's on all my home-work. Sheila told the class she climbed a tree all the way to the top. Marcy said she went canoeing with her father. Claire Marie said her daddy built her a tree house, and she had a tea party. She invited all the girls to the tea party. She asked me why I didn't come. I told her I didn't know she invited me. I wanted to go, Mama."

"I don't want you scampering up and down trees. It isn't ladylike. You and I can have a tea party when we get home. Miss Ellie baked cookies today just for you. Won't that be nice? Now, slide over here and sit on my lap and tell me what else happened in school today."

"I'm getting too big to sit on your lap, Mama. You shouldn't hold my hand when you walk me to the door in the morning. The girls laugh at me and call me a baby."

"You are my baby, Jessie. They're just jealous because their mothers are too busy. Those mothers can't wait to get rid of their children in the morning. I count the hours until it's time to pick you up. Tell me what you want to do after we have our tea party. Do you want to ride in your electric car or do you want to ride your pony? Samuel fin-ished painting the trim on your playhouse this morning. He said it would be dry by the time you got home from school. School will be out in another week. And then it's that magical day—*your birthday*. Have you been thinking about what you'd like for a present?"

"Yes. I want a pair of blue jeans, some sneakers, and a beanie. I want one of those book bags that the other girls have. I hate this book bag. Nobody has a flowered book bag. I want a dog. Everyone has a dog."

"Darling, that bag cost a hundred dollars. If the other girls had a hundred dollars to spend, they'd have one just like it. Mama is allergic to animals, so you can't have a dog."

"I could keep the dog in the playhouse. The kind of

book bags the other girls have only cost five dollars. Why can't I dress the way they do? I want a dog." Jessie jerked her hand away and slid to the corner of her seat, away from her mother.

Thea Roland sighed as though the weight of the world settled on her shoulders. "Sweetheart, those girls dress that way because it's all their parents can afford. They think it's fashionable, but in reality it is quite tacky. Their parents are probably struggling to pay the tuition here at Miss Primrose's school. Daddy and I don't want you looking like a ragamuffin."

Jessie's voice took on a stubborn tone. "I want to look like everyone else. If I looked like everyone else, maybe the girls would eat lunch with me or ask me to skip rope at recess. They don't like me, Mama."

"I told you, Jessie, they're jealous of you. Would you like to go to another school?"

"Mama, this is school number four. I don't like starting over."

"Let's talk about what we're going to do for your birthday. Daddy wants to have a big party for you. We'll invite everyone from your class."

"Can I invite Sophie?" Sophie was the daughter of Thea's best friend in Atlanta. She was a year older than Jessie and came to visit twice a year. Jessie adored her.

"I don't see why not. I'll call her mother tonight."

"Can I talk to Sophie?"

"We'll see."

"Daddy promised to put a telephone in my room so I could call Sophie when I wanted to. He said I could have one in the playhouse, too."

"I'll talk to him."

"When?"

"At dinnertime."

"Will you promise?"

"Yes, Jessie, I promise. Now, slide over here and give me a big kiss."

Jessie inched her way over to her mother. She wanted to cry, but then her mother would think she was sick and take her to the doctor or else she'd give her a laxative and a cup of stinky tea that tasted like dirt from the backyard.

The moment the huge car stopped under the portico, Jessie leaped out.

"Change your clothes, darling. Everything is laid out on your bed. I'll arrange for our tea party. I think some of Ellie's ice cream will go nicely with those fat sugar cookies she made this morning."

Jessie slammed the door shut. If she had one wish in life it would be that the door had a lock. She looked around at the elaborate bedroom that had its own sitting room. She didn't like it at all.

The frilly playsuit beckoned with the matching socks and sandals. She felt the urge to cry again. "I just want a friend," she whimpered.

Jessie's eyes narrowed when she heard her mother call from the bottom of the steps. "Our tea party is ready, darling." Defiantly Jessie sat down on the bed. She looked around at what her father called Princess Jessie's bedroom. It looked just like Mac Neals toy store on King Street. As soon as a new toy or game came on the market, it was hand-delivered, and then she was forced to play with it with her parents. Everything was bright and shiny new because she didn't want to disturb her mother's arrangements. She knew when she was dropped off at school that her mother rushed home to arrange everything to her liking. She flopped back on the bed to stare up at the lacy canopy overhead. Belgium lace, whatever that was, hung in folds and drapes.

"Jessie, sweetheart, what *are* you doing up there?"

"I'm coming, Mama."

Jessie suffered through the tea party and the obligatory ride around the garden in her electric car. She did two turns on the sliding board, allowing her mother to push her on the swing before she was forced to ride her own personal carousel and what her mother called her pony. Raucous music filled the garden. She heaved a sigh of relief when the merry-go-round shut down.

"Would you like to play Old Maid or Candy Land, sweetie?"

"I have a lot of homework, Mama. I'm going into the playhouse to do it."

"Goodness, I'm going to have to speak to Miss Primrose. It's almost the end of the year. You shouldn't have homework now."

"Mama, please don't talk to Miss Primrose. Today is the last day of homework. I want to make sure I do it perfectly." From years of experience, Jessie knew if she hugged and kissed her mother and said, "I love you," she would allow almost anything.

"Ah, that's my girl. Mama loves you so much it hurts. I'll wait on the verandah for you. When you're finished with your schoolwork we can take a walk around the garden and perhaps pick some flowers for your room."

"All right, Mama. You won't forget to ask Daddy about the phone, will you?"

"Don't I always do what's best for you?"

"Yes, Mama."

Inside the playhouse that was really three small rooms complete with bathroom, Jessie went straight to what she called her bedroom. She tossed her books onto the built-in bunk bed. Everything was neat and tidy, the games and toys frayed and used. It was cozy here with the small white rocking chair and stacks of books. She loved the bright colors, but something was missing. She reached up to the lowest shelf for a giant teddy bear. It belonged, but it didn't belong. She sat down on the floor cross-legged and waited. She did this every day and didn't know why. She rolled over and over on the thick carpeting and didn't know why she did that either. Something was supposed to happen, but it never did. What? She forgot about her homework that really wasn't homework at all. All she was supposed to do was erase all the pencil marks she'd made in her books during the year. She hadn't made any marks, so there was nothing to erase. Her books would be perfect when she turned them in.

Jessie waited expectantly for something to happen. When it didn't, she reached for the teddy bear and started to stroke its furry head. Within seconds she was asleep on the floor, the teddy bear alongside her.

"I'm going to huff and puff and blow this place down," a voice shouted from the small doorway.

Jessie woke with a start. "Daddy!" she squealed. "Are you home early?"

"I came home early just to see my princess. Did you finish your homework?"

"All done. Daddy, you promised I could have a phone in my room and one in the playhouse. Are you going to keep your promise?"

Barnes Roland clucked his tongue. "When you come home from school tomorrow it will be hooked up. Do you want a colored one or one of those old black ones?"

"I love bright colors. Red. I love red."

"Then red it is."

"Can I call Sophie as much as I want?"

"As long as Sophie and her mother don't mind, I don't see any reason why you can't."

"Is that a true promise?"

"It's a true promise. Where's your mother?"

"She said she was going to sit on the verandah until I finished my homework."

"She wasn't there when I got home. Let's ask Miss Ellie if she knows where she is."

Moments later, Jessie's fears were realized. "Miz Thea went to see Miss Primrose."

Jessie started to cry. "Now it's going to be worse, Daddy. She's going to make Miss Primrose do something. Nobody will want to come to my party. Mama is going to tell Miss Primrose they have to come. I don't want a party."

"If you don't want a party, then we won't have a party. Shhh, don't cry. Do you want to tell me what else is wrong?"

"Daddy, I'm going to go into the fifth grade next year. Mama still walks me to the door, and the kids make fun of me. Why can't I walk to school? I don't have any friends, Daddy. Sophie is the only girl Mama likes. She said the girls at school are white trash. I asked Miss Primrose what that meant, and she wouldn't tell me. She said all her students were fine young ladies."

"My goodness, that's a long list of grievances. I'll talk to your mother this evening. I brought you a present. Your mother isn't going to like it one little bit. I put it on the steps. Get it, run to your bedroom, and unwrap it. Then come down and tell me how you like it."

"Are you sure Mama won't like it?"

"I'm positive."

"Will you wait for me at the bottom of the steps?"

"I'll wait."

"Overalls!" Barnes heard her scream. "I love you, Daddy! Wait till you see me!"

"You look like a farmer's daughter." Barnes laughed. "I don't think your mother will let you wear those in public." Jessie threw her arms around her father and gave him a smacking big kiss.

The front door slammed shut behind Thea Roland. Her gaze was venomous as she witnessed the spontaneity of Jessie's kiss to her father. She didn't miss the denim overalls on her daughter. "I want to talk to you, Barnes. In the library. Jessie, darling, run upstairs and dress for dinner. The lavender dress with the white collar will do nicely."

"No. I want to wear these. Daddy gave them to me."

"Do as I say, Jessie. We always dress for dinner."

"I'll eat in the kitchen with Ellie."

"You will not eat in the kitchen with a servant. Now go upstairs and change into the lavender dress."

Jessie dug her toes into the carpet. One hissy fit coming up. She jumped up and down, screaming at the top of her lungs. "No! No! I hate that dress. No! I'm going to wear these overalls forever and ever. I'm going to sleep in them!"

"Good God! Now look what you've done, Barnes. Our daughter has thrown a temper tantrum. What are you going to do about it?"

"I am not going to do anything. Children do that from time to time when they have overbearing mothers. You said you wanted to talk to me."

Thea stomped her way to the library. Barnes held back for a minute and winked at his daughter. "It was a hissy fit, Daddy."

"Yes, it was." Jessie heard him chuckling as he made his way to the library.

Her face gleeful, Jessie ran to the kitchen. "I'm eating

with you in the kitchen tonight, Miss Ellie, because I don't look good enough to sit at the table."

"Mercy," was all the old housekeeper could think of to say.

"What is it this time, Thea?"

"It's Jessie's birthday party. Jessie said her classmates won't come, so I went to see Miss Primrose and asked her why. I insisted she speak to the girls' mothers, and she refused. Then, Barnes, she told me I might be happier placing Jessie in another school since I'm so unhappy with her school. She was referring to the next term. I'd do it in a minute, but there are no more private schools in the area. We have two alternatives, neither of which is acceptable— public school or boarding school. Tomorrow I want you to set the wheels in motion to buy that school. We'll hire a new headmistress, and we will be the ones who say who goes and who stays. I mean it, Barnes. She told me in that flat voice of hers that I coddled Jessie. She looked down that long nose of hers at me. I was so humiliated. She said Jessie was the sweetest child but entirely too shy and that she needed to interact more with her classmates. She also said I was an *obsessed* mother. Do you believe that, Barnes?"

"There are two sides to everything, Thea. I'm sure Adele Primrose's version will be slightly different than yours. She owns the school. It's her life, and she isn't going to part with it."

"She will if the price is right. Money can buy anything, Barnes."

"Are you sure you want to open that can of worms? It could lead to all manner of things. Adele Primrose could turn vindictive and start an investigation. She's lived here all her life. Her roots are here. We've only been here a few years. She could look into that Atlanta business, our early years in California. If she doesn't do it herself, her attorney will. I'm not saying that will happen, but it is a possibility. What that means is she has a certain amount of social backing whereas we are relative newcomers to the area. Records and credentials could come under close scrutiny if you push too hard. What we have are very good, but those records aren't perfect. How could they be, they're forged. An apology would not be out of line, Thea. I would not disturb the status quo if I were you, dear."

Thea sat down with a thump. "Are you saying that old biddy would . . . go to those extreme lengths. Everyone knows adoption records are sealed."

"For God's sake, Thea, Jessie wasn't adopted. You've been using the term so long you've come to believe it. The case is not closed, nor will it ever be closed. Let sleeping dogs lie."

Thea's voice was a hushed whisper. "Eight years is a long time, Barnes. She's mine. I'll never give her up. That child is my reason for living."

"Then first thing tomorrow morning you had better start mending your fences. If that doesn't work, I'll step in."

"She wouldn't . . ."

"She would, Thea. If you try to rip that school away from Adele Primrose, she'll fight. You need to know that. There are some things money can't buy."

"Speaking of buying, Barnes, what in the world were you thinking of when you purchased those . . . those ugly dungarees?"

"The look of happiness on Jessie's face. Stop being such a fuddy-duddy. Let the child be a child. She needs friends, playmates. Let's invite Sophie for the summer."

"I don't think that's a good idea. The whole summer, Barnes! What in the world will I do?"

"Try knitting. Let Jessie be Jessie with a child she can relate to. You're smothering her, Thea. It's the last week of school. Let her walk. Take her shopping and let her pick out the things she wants. If you don't do it, Thea, I will."

"I can't believe you're saying this to me. All right, Barnes. There is one other thing we need to talk about. Jessie said you promised her a phone. I want you to tell her no."

"I will not break a promise, Thea. It will be installed tomorrow, and it will be a private number. That's so you won't listen in on her conversations. I understand how much love you have for the child, but it isn't healthy for either one of you. Loosen the reins, Thea, before it's too late."

Thea buried her face in her hands. "Barnes, I don't know what I would do if something happened to Jessie. Perhaps you're right. I have devoted every minute of my life for the past eight years to the child. How do you expect me to stop doing what I love doing?"

"You'll do it because it's best for Jessie. If you really and truly love her, you should want to do what will make her happy. When was the last time she smiled when you were with her?"

"She never smiles. She's always so solemn and obedient. Sometimes I think she remembers. I swear, Barnes, I think she does. All those bad dreams she had in the beginning had to take their toll on her. She always has the same dream. She screams for jelly. That must be all those people gave her to eat. She won't eat it for me, though. I don't know what any of it means. Every time I think about it I get a headache. Tell Ellie I'll take a tray in my room. Let Jessie eat in the kitchen in those . . . ugly trousers you bought her."

Barnes watched his wife leave the room. His shoulders

felt suddenly pounds lighter. He called the phone company. A promise was a promise. He headed for the kitchen.

"Let's have a picnic outside, Miss Ellie," Barnes said. "I'd like a hamburger, some real greasy french fries, no vegetables, and Jessie and I will each have two slices of that very fragrant rhubarb pie sitting on the counter. Miss Thea won't be joining us. She'll have a tray in her room. You can give *her* the poached fish and lima beans."

"Oh, Daddy, you are so funny."

Eleven-year-old Sophie Ashwood arrived in Charleston with a bikini, a diary complete with key that was chockfull of secrets and boys' names, the monthly curse, and *breasts.*

Immediately the girls raced to the playhouse, leaving Thea alone on the screened verandah. Barnes garaged the car, then took his place on the verandah next to his wife. He rattled the newspaper he was holding. His stomach started to tighten at the intense look on his wife's face. "Leave the children alone, Thea. You're scheming already. I can see it."

"I'm doing no such thing. I resent you telling *my friend* her daughter could stay here all summer. That was uncalled for, Barnes. Janice and that . . . *hooligan* she's been seeing went off to Europe, so we really and truly are stuck with her child until the end of August. What kind of mother goes out of the country and leaves her daughter with other people?"

"Obviously Janice trusts you implicitly. In addition, Miss Sophie has been going to sleep-away camps since she was five. She's very independent as well as intelligent. She's going to be good for Jessie. You're feeling jealous and don't know what to do about it. I don't want you interfering with the children, Thea. Jessie is growing up and needs to be around other children. These last two weeks have been wonderful. The moment she heard Sophie was coming she turned into a different child. Surely you noticed."

"She's that way with you," Thea said. "She's still standoffish with me. I do everything in my power to make her happy, and all she does is say thank you. I would give anything in the world if just once she would throw her arms around me and hug me. She will if I ask her, but she's so reserved. It's almost as if she's afraid of me. She *can't* remember, Barnes, she was too little."

Barnes folded the newspaper neatly and laid it on the table. "You do everything but breathe for Jessie, and if there was a way for you to do that, you would. Can't you see how you're suffocating her?"

"I'm doing no such thing. Why do you insist on tormenting me?"

"I'm not tormenting you. Let's go into town for lunch, Thea. Get your hat. I'll tell the girls."

"I'll tell them."

"No, Thea, I'll do it. Now, go get your hat."

Thea's eyes filled with tears. "Why are you doing this to me? And if I refuse?"

"Then, Thea, you will force me to take matters into my own hands. I will take Jessie back where we got her. I'm prepared to suffer the consequences. I'm saying this only once, Thea, so I hope you are paying attention."

Sobbing, Thea ran to her room. She returned minutes later with her floppy-brimmed hat, her face inscrutable. Her long, slender fingers with their perfectly manicured nails dug into the palms of her hands when she heard her husband's jovial shouts to the girls. "Jessie, Mama and I are going out to lunch. You girls behave yourselves and don't get into any trouble while we're gone. Ellie is in the kitchen if you need anything."

"Daddy, can we make telephone calls that cost money?"

"Sure, honey. Can I bring you girls anything from town?"

"Daddy, do you think you could get me a diary? With a key. Sophie has one. She said all the girls in Atlanta have them. You write secrets in a diary. I might get a secret someday. Sophie's is almost filled up."

"Show me what it looks like, Sophie."

Sophie ran into the playhouse and returned with a flowered book.

"I think I might be able to find one like this. What will you do if you don't have any secrets to write down?"

"Then you have to wait until you do have a secret. Sometimes I write other people's secrets when I don't have any of my own," Sophie confided.

Barnes nodded sagely. He supposed in a cockamamie way it made sense. "We'll see you later. Have a good time, girls."

"We will, Daddy."

"Good God, Barnes, the girls are in their bare feet. I cannot believe my daughter is wearing a . . . beanie. And you bought it, Barnes!"

"Sophie has one. It seems all the girls in Atlanta wear them. Those same girls all have diaries with keys. Thea, open your eyes. The girls are having fun. It's you that's miserable. I could probably pick you up a cap at Berlin's if you want. That would surely set this town on its ear. We can start socializing again, Thea. We could invite some of our old friends from Atlanta. I miss our bridge games. Dinner a few nights a week at the Yacht Club would be nice. You and I need to do things together for a change."

Thea dabbed at her eyes. "I feel so lost. I even feel sick to my stomach."

"Get over it, Thea. Think about how that mother and father in Ashton Falls must feel."

"We agreed never to mention places and things like that aloud, Barnes."

"That was then, this is now. I had another reason for wanting you to leave the house. Lunch was just an excuse. Let's sit here by the water and talk. No one can hear us."

"I'm not up to any more bad news, Barnes. If this little talk has something to do with Jessie, I'm not interested. Miss Primrose accepted my apology, and Jessie will return for the fall term. I groveled, and I'm not proud of it. Miss Primrose did not apologize. I had to accept that, too. I was never so humiliated in my life."

"Do you want to move back to Atlanta?" Barnes asked.

"Good God, no. Perhaps when Jessie is older. I'll give it some thought. Charleston is charming and the perfect place for a proper young lady to grow up. Now, Barnes, what is so important that we had to leave the house to talk about it?"

"Have you noticed a change in Ellie?"

"What kind of change? She's certainly grumpy lately. She's been very short with me of late now that you mention it. I assumed her arthritis was bothering her. She is sixty-eight years old, Barnes. She's worked for my family all her life. Does she want to retire and go back to Atlanta? Is that what you're trying to tell me? What will we do without her?"

"I think she overheard our little discussion a few weeks ago. Her attitude toward both of us changed after that. She is a fine Christian woman. Knowing a secret like ours will not be something she can accept. I believe she's searching for a way to do something about it."

"Searching? Barnes, you know as well as I do that Ellie can neither read nor write. She has no family left except a few distant cousins five or six times removed. To my knowledge she has never been in touch with any of them. She never gets mail or phone calls. I understand what you're saying, though. What should we do?"

"We need to keep her with us so we can be aware of

any . . . change. She adores Jessie. She won't do anything knowingly that will hurt her. Which brings me to another point, Thea. What did you do with that religious medal Jessie was wearing when we . . . took her?"

"I have it locked safely away. I would never throw away a religious item. Why are you asking?"

"I'm asking because Jessie was a Catholic. We are Baptists. We robbed her of her religion among other things."

"What has gotten into you, Barnes? None of this ever bothered you before. Why now all of a sudden?"

"I don't know, Thea. I have these awful guilty feelings. I haven't slept well since . . . that day."

"Get over it! That's what you tell me all the time. Don't even think about asking me to give her up. Did you set up that trust fund for her?"

"I did that last year. She will inherit from both of us. The trust fund is doing nicely. When she's eighteen she can draw from it if she wants to. It doesn't seem right. I wish there was a way to send money to her parents. You didn't read the papers after the . . . afterward. I did, but not right away. Later on there were updates on the anniversary of the kidnapping. That's when I started to pay attention. Her parents are simple, hardworking people. They lost the house Jessie was born in. The church they belong to built a house for them. The mother had to be dragged away from the house they lost by her husband and parents. She didn't want to leave because she believed Jessie would somehow find her way home, and if they weren't there, she wouldn't know what to do."

"Stop it, Barnes. Stop it right this minute. I don't want to talk about this. I never, ever want to talk about it."

"She might remember one of these days. She might see something, experience something that will trigger a memory."

"Who will pay attention to a two-year-old's memory? Be realistic, Barnes. I told you, I don't want to talk about this. How much money is in Jessie's trust fund?"

"Five million dollars."

"Is that all?"

"In another eight years, when she turns eighteen, it will have doubled. I don't consider ten million dollars shabby."

"We have so much," Thea said. "Do you think you could find a way to send some money anonymously to . . . those people?"

Barnes leaned across the bench, his eyes boring into his wife. "How much money do you think their child is worth, Thea?"

Thea burst into tears. "There isn't enough money in the world to make up for what I did. I know that. We could try, though. A lot of money, Barnes. We could wrap it up securely, put enough postage on it so we don't have to go to the mail window. You could go to another city and mail it. You could also return the religious medal. This way they . . . will know the child is safe and in good hands."

Barnes's voice was a hoarse croak. "How much, Thea? We won't feel any better. You know that, don't you?"

"Of course I know that. The money will . . . maybe it will make things easier for them. You said they were young. They probably have other children. A million dollars. More if you like. Or, half that amount. How much money do you have in the wall safe?"

"Four or five hundred thousand."

"How long has it been in there?"

"Five years, ten? I'm not sure. Why?"

"Because, Barnes, you can't go to the bank and take out that kind of money without raising suspicion. They have a way of tracing bills. If you've had the money for a long time, it will be all right to use it. You can go to the bank and get a new batch of money after we . . . mail it. Then in a few years we can send some more. I don't know their name, Barnes. Do you?"

"God, yes. I know the address, too."

"Go to Richmond to mail it, or Chattanooga. You could drive up one day and come back the next day. Stop in one of those cheap motels. People remember strangers. Why are we going through this after eight long years? Why, Barnes?"

"Because we both feel guilty, and both of us are afraid Jessie will remember. We're hoping this will make us feel better. It won't, but we're going to try. By keeping Jessie busy and happy she will have less time to think. Maybe if she has friends and keeps doing things, the bad dreams will stop. Are we in agreement then, Thea?"

"What else can we do?"

"Then let's go home and get to it. I'll leave tomorrow. We'll tell the girls and Ellie I'm going to Atlanta. But first we have to go to the stationer's to get Jessie a diary."

"Good Lord."

"Did you have a diary, Thea?"

"Yes."

"Did you write secrets in it?"

"Sometimes. It can be comforting to write down one's thoughts."

"I wonder what Jessie will write in hers."

Chapter Three

"Morning, Grace. Got a package for you this morning. Didn't know you knew someone in Chackago." The old postmaster handed her a package the size of a shoe box. "You don't have to sign for it, Grace. Seems to me you get one of these just about every year."

Grace's stomach muscles curled into a tight knot. Hiram was right. For the past eight years, a package just like the one she was holding in her hand arrived at the end of summer. Usually the day the tourists started to leave. One year it even arrived on the anniversary of Hannah's disappearance.

"How does it feel to be back in your own little house, Grace?"

"It feels right, Hiram. Moving back into the house and setting it up the way it was turned out to be one of my best days. It's sad, though. I can't get used to the room Ben built onto the back of the house for the boys. He did a real good job. She would be getting ready to go off to college this month, Hiram."

"I know, Grace. Marie and I pray every night for your little girl. So does this whole town. Someday, when you're least expecting it, that child will walk through your front door. You have to have faith, Grace. Now, tell me, how's Jelly doing?"

Grace's shoulders started to shake. She fought the burning tears that were building behind her eyelids. "I'm going to take him home when I leave here. Charlie is going to come by later and . . . and . . . put him down. The poor thing is so crippled with arthritis, he can't get up and down. His heart condition worsened these last six months. I've been carrying him around, but my back can't take it anymore. He's eighteen, Hiram. The same age as Hannah. We got him the day after we brought her home from the hospital. I know what I have to do. I just don't know if I can do it."

"You have to do what's best for Jelly, Grace. Charlie told me yesterday he was in constant pain. Hard as it is, you have to do it. It's his time. If there's anything Marie or I can do, just holler. Take care of that mystery package now, you hear."

Grace bit down on her lower lip. She knew what was in the mystery package: money. Thousands of dollars. Each year when the package arrived, always mailed from a distant big city, she was forced to call the FBI, who would take the money, test it, check for fingerprints, check the serial numbers and whatever else they did in their lab with no results. Eventually they returned the money and then she would put it in Hannah's toy box, one Ben had made so lovingly with his own hands. The toy box was the first thing he'd ever made for their daughter. It had a padlock these days; Ben had insisted. As if they would ever spend one dime of that hateful money. They would have returned the money, but there was never a return address on the mystery packages.

Grace tossed the package into the back of Ben's battered pickup truck. Right now she had more important things to do. More important things to care about than a package of money that would never be spent.

Ten minutes later, Grace pulled into the parking lot at the rear of the vet clinic. She struggled to bring her breathing under control. *I can do this. I will do this. I have to do this. Me. No one else.*

"For God's sake, Grace, let me carry this dog for you. He's too heavy. You might drop him."

"Charlie, shut up. I might be capable of a lot of things. The one thing I would never do is drop this dog. This dog is . . . Just open the damn door, Charlie, and then open the car door. I'll do the rest."

On the short drive home, Grace babbled to the whimpering dog so she wouldn't break down and cry. "Another one of those stupid boxes of money came today, Jelly. What do you think of that? About as much as I do, I suppose. Those people who took Hannah are trying to buy off their guilt. Each year they send more and more. I hope they never spend a restful moment. I prayed so hard, Jelly, that somehow, some way, she'd find her way home before it . . . was your time. I'll never give up the way you never gave up. No one cares anymore. Even when I call the FBI they just say oh, you got another one. They don't care. I thought the FBI always got their man. That's bullshit, Jelly. In sixteen years they didn't find one clue. Not one.

"Listen, big guy, we're home. This was the best thing Ben and I ever did. I feel more peaceful now that we're back in our old house. I know you want to . . . you know . . . go to that place that's waiting for you. The room is exactly like it was that day they carried me out screaming and kicking. Every little thing is exactly where it was. It was like it was stamped on my brain, so I would never forget. You know what else, Jelly. There are forty-two red sweaters in her room. I made another one last night. Not a whole one. I did the two sleeves. I'll probably stay up tonight and finish it.

You can never have enough sweaters. I think my mother told me that, but I'm not sure.

"I'm going to go up to the house and open the door. I'll carry you up the steps. It will be like old times, Jelly. Just you and me. Your pup who really isn't a pup any longer is waiting for you. He lies outside the door just the way you taught him. Today, though, the kids aren't here. I wanted everything to be like it was for both of us. It was such a bad time back then. Now you have Jelly Junior and I have John and Joseph. You can . . . go . . . knowing we're all in good hands. I believe that somehow, if things change at some point in time, you'll know. Just a little while longer, Jelly."

Grace raced into the house and up the stairs to Hannah's old room. It only took a second to make sure everything was the way she'd left it. She raced back to the kitchen; all she had to do was get Jelly upstairs and the rest would fall into place. Tears rolled down her cheeks. She wiped at them with the sleeve of her T-shirt.

He wasn't as heavy as the last time she'd carried him up these steps. She choked back a sob, knowing she would never carry him anywhere ever again. "Look, there's JJ waiting for us." Jelly whimpered. Jelly Junior whined, the hair on the back of his neck standing on end. *He knows*, Grace thought as she laid her best friend in the whole world on Hannah's small bed. Jelly closed his eyes as he struggled to breathe. Where was Ben? He promised he'd be here when she brought Jelly home. She turned to see her husband standing in the doorway. Even from where she was standing she could see how wet his eyes were.

"Oh God, Ben. I can't do this. I love this dog. He's my best friend. He was our daughter's protector. Eighteen years, Ben. First God takes Hannah, and now He's taking my dog. Dogs can live till they're twenty. Charlie said so.

We should have taken him to that specialist in Atlanta we heard about. We could have used that damn money."

"It's Jelly's time, Grace. We have to accept it. He's leaving us his son."

"JJ has never, ever come into this room, Ben. Never. Somehow he knew this was one place he couldn't go. It's amazing when you stop to think about it."

"He's in now, Grace. Look." Both Larsons stared at the young dog as he bellied his way into the room until he was at the side of the bed. He whimpered and whined, not knowing if he was permitted on the bed with Jelly or not.

"Go ahead, JJ," Grace said.

"Should I call Charlie, Grace?"

"No, Ben. I need more time. Just a little bit longer. Go downstairs and wait for me. I'll call you."

"How can I leave you here like this?"

"Because you love us both and you want what I want. Please, Ben, I have to do it my way."

When the door closed behind her husband, Grace dropped to her knees to stroke Jelly's head. His eyes opened briefly, then closed. JJ moved slightly so Grace could stretch out next to Jelly. She started to croon the old lullabies. Jelly's tail fluttered in recognition. When she finished she leaned closer to the dog. "I have this feeling, Jelly, that you're waiting for something. I just . . . don't know what it is. Yes, I do know. I know, Jelly. Don't move."

Grace leaped from the bed and ran down the hall to her own room where she snatched at the blown-up poster of Hannah and Jelly that had been taken on Hannah's second birthday. She ran back to the room and dropped to her haunches. Her voice was a hushed whisper. "Jelly, look. Open your eyes. It's Hannah and you. Look how manly you look. It was such a wonderful day. Can you see it,

Jelly? When she comes back, and I know she will someday, I'm going to tell her how valiant you were and . . .and I'm going to tell her about this . . . moment. She's going to remember, I know she will. She loved you as much as Ben and I love you." Grace's voice turned fierce when she said, "Don't you ever forget it, Jelly. Never, never, never."

The golden dog struggled. JJ at his side used his muzzle to help Jelly lift his head. The beloved golden dog's tail gave one mighty swish as he used the last of his strength to emit one loud, resounding woof in his struggle to paw at the picture of the little girl he'd protected so long ago. Grace cradled him in her arms as he took his last breath, a sound deep and raw and so full of pain it ricocheted through the house. Ben dropped the coffee cup in his hands as he took the steps three at a time. His own grief and pain echoed his wife's. JJ leaped from the bed to take up his position outside the door.

A long time later Grace stirred, Jelly still in her arms. "What should we do, Ben? Should we bury him or should we ask Charlie to cremate him. We never talked about it. I don't want to talk about it now, but we have to. We could keep the ashes here in the room for . . . me, for us, for Hannah if she ever comes back, and for JJ. It would be like he's still with us. But then maybe that isn't good. I don't know what to do, Ben."

"Let's do that. I think it's what we both want. We'll make a special place for him. He'll always be with us. Who cares if it's good or not. It's what we want, what we can handle. I'll call Charlie to make the arrangements. We'll have to explain to the kids what this is all about."

Grace nodded. "This is the second most miserable day of my life, Ben. I simply don't understand. We're good people. Why is God doing this to us?"

"I don't have the answer, Grace. Are we going to leave things just the way they are?"

"I think I would die before I'd move a stitch of anything. Ben, another one of those boxes of money came today. I threw it in the back of the truck. You need to call the FBI."

"The hell with the FBI. They couldn't find a pile of dog crap if they stepped in it. Forget about calling them. I'll put the money in the toy box and lock it. One of these days we need to discuss that money."

"I don't want to discuss that money. Not now, not ever. Leave it there till it rots."

The following day, Jelly's ashes were placed in Hannah's room on a small ornate shelf that Ben Larson spent the night making in the garage. JJ watched the proceedings, his head on his paws. He waited until Grace and Ben walked through the door before he got to his feet. He tilted his head to look at them before he walked into the room and took up Jelly's position on the old, worn blanket at the foot of the bed. As one, the Larsons nodded.

There was a new caretaker guarding Hannah's memory in the Larson household.

Charleston, South Carolina 1973

Jessie Roland waited until she was certain the house was completely silent. It was one-thirty in the morning. Surely her parents were asleep by now. Her steps were stealthy as she tiptoed down the winding staircase, out through the dining room to the kitchen, and then outside. She clutched her small flashlight tightly. The dew on the spiky grass felt wonderful on her bare feet. Her destination was the playhouse and the built-in storage room where she secreted everything she didn't want her mother to see. She thanked God every day that neither her mother nor Ellie could enter the little house. She herself had to get down on her knees and crouch her way through the little rooms. She was careful to hold the flashlight downward so there would be no trace of light filtering out through the tiny windows.

From long years and nights of practice, Jessie moved silently until she was in the room with the storage cabinet that had once held toys. Now it held her diaries, her cosmetics, her secret stash of money, notes from different boys when she was in high school, and, the prize of all prizes, her acceptance letters to New York University.

Jessie sat down and hugged her knees. Tomorrow she was going to be as free as her friend Sophie. Together they had come up with the plan, a year ago, after her parents refused to allow her to go to college out of state. They had insisted she attend the College of Charleston so she could live at home and walk to class. For the first time in her life the temper tantrums she excelled in refused to work. She had agreed because she had no other choice. It was Sophie who said she needed a game plan and time to prepare, and that's what she had done. Tomorrow morning she was driving to Atlanta for Sophie's party in her BMW, her high-school graduation gift. There she would sell the car and purchase a new one to drive to New York. The car would be registered in Sophie's name. Sophie had secured an apartment for her on her last trip to New York and paid the rent for six full months. Another debt she owed her best friend. Starting in September all correspondence would be sent to Sophie's apartment while she attended classes at Tulane. It was an intricate system of subterfuge, one Sophie insisted would work.

For starters, her best friend had not only lent her the money for the apartment, but also for the first year's tuition. She had also said she was taking care of the school-transcript requirements, so her parents couldn't trace her through the university. Sophie was so worldly. Sophie could do anything. Sophie was her friend. The Rolands thought Jessie was going to Georgia Tech, where she had also been accepted. With a 4.0 average she could have named the college of her choice. She knew in her heart the moment she left for college her parents would start making plans to move back to Atlanta. She wouldn't be the least bit surprised to find out they had already done just that. Weren't they going to be surprised.

Plain and simple, Jessie was going to disappear. With Sophie's foolproof plan she would have a week's head start. The first thing she was going to do before she left for Atlanta in the morning was to go to the bank and take a healthy hit from her trust fund. Sophie said she needed to take enough to live well for the first year. "Your parents won't realize what you did for at least a month or until the next bank statement comes in," Sophie said in her authoritative voice. She'd gone on to say, "Trust me."

It all came down to planning. For days now she'd been shopping, buying clothes that students were wearing in New York, according to Sophie, who was knowledgeable on every subject in the universe. "No matter what, Jessie, you can count on me." It was all Jessie needed to hear. The plan moved forward. Tomorrow phase one, as she thought of it, would go into effect.

Jessie stretched out her legs. It was going to be so wonderful to get away from her obsessive, domineering mother. She would miss her father, though. She would miss Ellie, too, but she wouldn't miss her mother at all. In fact when she drove away she knew she wouldn't look back. Nor would she ever return. She was young, strong, healthy, and she could make it on her own. It was her plan to work while attending college. One way or the other she was going to make it on her own. She had a brain and had proved it by skipping the ninth grade and going straight into her sophomore year. She was on par with Sophie now, who was also a sophomore at Tulane.

Life was going to be wonderful, but if she didn't start moving, something was going to go awry. She shoved her treasure trove to the small doorway and pushed it through. Then she backed out and closed the door. Within minutes she had her things secured in the trunk of the BMW along with all the new clothes she'd purchased, still in their shopping bags. The trunk was full. The best part of everything was, she wasn't taking a thing her parents had bought her. She was going to make a clean break and never look back.

Back in her bedroom, Jessie took a shower and dressed for the morning. There was no way she would sleep tonight. She would sit up and read and perhaps go downstairs to make a cup of tea. Bright and early she'd be ready for her trip to Atlanta.

Instead of reading, Jessie found herself rocking in her favorite chair. An overwhelming feeling of sadness swept over her, and she didn't know why. Just earlier she'd been elated at the prospect of her freedom. Maybe it was the picture of her parents on her dresser that had appeared one day right after her tenth birthday. When she opened her eyes in the morning it was the first thing she saw. When she was younger she'd wished that someone would steal it, but it was such a ridiculous wish she knew it would never happen.

By most standards she had a wonderful life. Doting parents, albeit obsessive, everything worldly that money could buy, a beautiful home, a generous allowance, a fantastic trust fund, her own car, one friend, and no pet except a tired old goldfish who swam aimlessly in his small tank. She hadn't even bothered to name the fish because she wanted something more alive, something to *breathe* on her, something to cuddle with.

Jessie continued to stare with unblinking eyes at the picture of her parents. Her father was a kind man who

seemed dedicated to making her life as worry-free as possible. He was also a wonderful arbitrator where her mother
was concerned. She would miss him but not enough to make
her want to return. It was her mother that was driving her
from the house. She roll-called all the years of her life and
the misery she'd endured at her mother's hands. She re-
sented everything about her mother—right down to her
flowery afternoon dresses, floppy hats, and pristine white
gloves. She hated the sickly smell of her perfume and the
pressed powder on her cheeks. She hated being called
sweetheart, darling child, and precious love. She realized
in that one brief second that she hated her mother. There
was a darkness about her she couldn't explain, a certain
tone in her voice that reminded her of something she could
never name. She hated the sensation that her skin was
crawling when her mother wrapped her in her arms to
smother her with hugs and kisses. She couldn't breathe
then. Even now she felt the darkness, and her breathing
was uneven.

Just a few more hours and she would be free of it all.

Barnes watched Jessie walk across the yard. He wouldn't
have seen her if it wasn't for the moonlight. He felt a tight-
ness settle between his shoulder blades. A cigar found its
way to his mouth. Here in this room he'd been relegated
to he was permitted to do whatever he pleased. Thea had
banished him from the room they shared several years ago
when his restlessness prevented her from sleeping. "You
reek of cigar smoke, and your snoring is loud enough to
wake the neighbors." He'd welcomed the move because he
spent half the night pacing and worrying. Guilt was such a
terrible feeling. He longed for the days when it was time to
send another package of money to the Larsons. For a few
hours he was able to almost wipe the guilt away. He was
toying now with the idea of sending a graduation picture

of Jessie with the next box. His insides started jumping around when he thought of the FBI tracking the picture. Better to let sleeping dogs lie.

In a few hours Jessie would be driving alone to Atlanta for Sophie's yearly party. Sophie's parties were the envy of all the proper young ladies in Atlanta because they were never chaperoned. Janice Ashwood removed herself from the steaming city to flit wherever the spirit moved her when Sophie's party loomed on the horizon.

Thea had taken to her bed when Jessie announced she was attending the party. She'd literally turned blue with anger when Jessie announced, just days earlier, that she was not returning to the College of Charleston. In his life he'd never heard such a screaming match as he heard that day. Jessie's words still rang in his ears. "You lied to me. You said if it didn't work out for me, you would allow me to go to Georgia Tech. You promised, Mother. Now you're breaking that promise. I knew this would happen, so I took matters into my own hands. I registered and paid my tuition. I'm going. If you persist in fighting me, I will never come back here. I need a life. I'm eighteen. I'm a year ahead of myself because I studied all my life. I wanted you to be proud of me. I don't want to be shackled to you any longer. I feel like I can't *breathe* when I'm around you. I did what you wanted. I always did what you wanted because you taught me to be obedient and respectful. My life is your life. You drove me to this point, Mother. I have to take charge of my life."

Barnes blinked when he remembered how Thea had stretched out her arms, trying to grapple and paw Jessie, who nimbly stepped away. "Don't touch me!" she'd screamed. "I hate it when you strangle me with your arms." Thea had collapsed into a heap on the drawing-room floor. Jessie had stared at her, then walked away. It was over. She would start to remember soon, he was sure of it. He was so sure that he was actually considering taking Thea to some South American country where the FBI would never find them.

Barnes frowned as he watched Jessie carry boxes from the playhouse to her car parked at the back of the house. He moved quickly then, running down the steps to the library window, where he would have a better view of his daughter's activities.

He'd known for a long time that Jessie kept things in the playhouse she didn't want him or Thea to see. He hadn't minded, and he kept quiet because Thea never suspected. He knew for a fact that she went through Jessie's room every single day. What she hoped to find would always be a mystery. Perhaps some clue that Jessie was starting to remember.

Barnes waited until he heard Jessie creep up the steps before he poured himself a tumbler of bourbon and lit a new cigar. When he finished both he walked over to the wall safe and opened it. Thea's heirloom jewelry, the religious medal he'd never sent the Larsons even though he'd told Thea he had, and bundles and bundles of cash. Two days ago he'd replenished the currency when he mailed off a box of money to Jessie's parents from Chicago. He lined up the bundles of money on his desk the moment he closed the safe. He needed to write a note. He needed to say something to the young woman he'd come to love with all his heart. He knew in his heart, in his mind, in his gut, that Jessie was never going to return to the Charleston house. He thought of his wife and what it was going to do to her. So much money. He poured another tumbler of bourbon and fired up a fresh cigar. He needed other papers from the built-in file cabinet. His hands were unsteady when he shuffled through the bank folders until he found the ones that pertained to Jessie's trust fund.

Barnes drained the glass of bourbon before he clamped

his teeth around the fat cigar. He penned off a short note to include in the box. He was an expert at wrapping tidy boxes. He nestled all the cash from the safe, the small jeweler's box with the medal, and the papers inside the box. He wrapped it securely with paper and twine before he used a thick black marker to write Jessie's name on the outside. Where the return address would normally go he wrote DAD.

He rummaged in his desk drawer for the spare key to Jessie's car. He used up more minutes telling himself he was doing the right thing before he summoned up all his guts to walk outside. He felt like a sneak when he rearranged Jessie's boxes in her car. He was careful to put his own box next to the accordion-pleated carton so that she would see it when she unpacked her car.

Back in the house Barnes stomped his way to the filing cabinet. His face twisted into a grimace when he recalled words from a movie he'd seen. When you want to hide something, hide it in the open, which was exactly what he'd done.

The folder was thick and full of clippings from the AP wire service. Words like complicity, reciprocity, kidnapping and accomplice ricocheted around inside his head. He had been a willing participant. His hands were clumsy as he shuffled the clippings in the folder. He read them all, but then he'd read them before on nights like this when his guilt threatened to consume him. He wondered if the day would ever come when he would show the folder to *anyone*. At some point he knew he'd destroy the file. He just didn't know when that time would be.

The file drawer closed at the exact moment Jessie poked her head inside the doorway. "You are an early bird today. Aren't those the same clothes you had on last night? You didn't sleep, did you?"

Barnes did his best to smile. He thought he was finally drunk. He must be—the bourbon bottle was empty. "No,

I didn't sleep. It's only seven o'clock. I thought you weren't leaving till nine. You don't look like you slept either."

"Would you like me to make some coffee? We can let Ellie sleep in this morning. It was nice of you to get her that hearing aid, Daddy."

"Coffee sounds good." Food, drink, and Ellie were safe subjects. Barnes followed Jessie to the kitchen. He watched her, marveling at her wholesomeness. Thea was going to throw a fit when she saw her jeans rolled to mid-calf and her sockless feet clad in dirty white sneakers. The baggy T-shirt was tied in a knot at her waist and topped off with a cherry red sweater wrapped around her slim shoulders. She wore a leather strap watch with a big face. He wondered where the Rolex was, the one Thea insisted he buy for her. Probably thrown in a drawer upstairs. To his knowledge the dress watch Thea had given her several years ago, encrusted with diamonds and emeralds, had never been seen. It was probably in a drawer somewhere, too, along with all the other pricey baubles Thea bought on a monthly basis. He doubted if Jessie's real family even knew what a Rolex watch was. From his position next to the kitchen window he had a clear view of his brand-new cream-colored Bentley, Thea's Mercedes sedan, and Jessie's year-old BMW. One of the articles said the Larsons drove a ten-year-old pickup truck. He felt sick to his stomach.

"I don't think I've ever seen you in a red sweater before, Jessie."

"That's because Mama hates red sweaters. I just bought it the other day. Actually I bought two of them. They look so cheerful. I don't know why, but I love the color red."

Barnes felt his stomach heave. There had been a red sweater in the pink stroller that day when Thea grabbed the child. To his knowledge he'd never seen it since.

Barnes glanced in the dining room; Thea was already seated at the table, dressed for the day, complete with makeup. He felt his stomach start to knot up. "Jessie and I are having coffee in the kitchen, Thea. Do you want to join us?"

"In the kitchen!" She made the three little words sound like her husband and daughter were drinking with the devil in hell. "Jessie is leaving in a little while. Don't you think the dining room is more appropriate? Good grief, Barnes, is this the thought you want to leave with Jessie? Drinking coffee in the kitchen is so tacky. She'll be back in a few days. It isn't like she's going away forever. I packed our bags, Barnes. We'll drive a discreet distance behind her to make sure she arrives safely. Then when she leaves, we'll follow her home. Why are you looking at me like that, Barnes?"

"Because we aren't going to Atlanta. At least I'm not. You can do whatever you please. I warn you, though, I will tell Jessie of your intentions."

Thea's hands fluttered in the air. "Jessie has never gone away on her own before. She'll be driving alone. Things happen."

"Jessie is a responsible adult. She will rise to any occasion except possibly where you are concerned."

"What does that mean, Barnes?"

"It means whatever you want it to mean. Furthermore, I am not moving back to Atlanta. You can do whatever you want."

"If you think for one minute I'm going to allow my child to be in that city alone and unchaperoned, you are mistaken. She has no idea what the real world is like."

"Then it's high time she found out. Get that thought right out of your head."

"I'll go alone."

"I'll cut off your funds, Thea. Or, I will do what you consider the unthinkable."

"Don't threaten me, Barnes. I have enough to endure as it is."

"Coffee's ready, Daddy," Jessie called from the kitchen.

"It's your choice, Thea. Join us or stay here."

Jessie's voice was flat and devoid of all emotion when she said, "Oh, Mama, I didn't see you at first. Aren't you up early?"

Thea took a deep breath before she replied. "I wanted to be ready to see you off. Daddy and I are going to miss you. This will be your first trip alone away from us. Give her some money, Barnes." She sidled closer to her daughter, who inched away from her. It was so obvious Barnes had to turn away so he wouldn't see the tears in his wife's eyes.

"I don't need any money."

"That is an absolutely horrendous outfit you're wearing. I've seen ragpickers who look better. Where did you get that sweater? Red is not your color, Jessie. It washes you out. I don't like red sweaters. Take it off."

"I like red sweaters, Mama. When I was little I had a red sweater."

"You certainly did not," Thea screamed.

Jessie's jaw dropped as she gaped at her mother.

Barnes's voice was gentle. "I think perhaps you forgot, Thea. Sophie's mother gave Jessie a red sweater once."

"Oh. Well, perhaps you're right. You never wore it though, Jessie. Anything red on blond-haired people looks garish."

"Move past this, Thea, before it gets out of hand," Barnes hissed in her ear.

Her mother's voice was so controlled, so tight-sounding, Jessie could only stare at her when she said, "Tell us about the party. How many people will be attending?"

"A hundred or so."

"Good heavens," was all Thea could think of to say.

"It's time for me to go. It won't be so hot and sticky this early. Do you want to say good-bye here or out by the car?"

"I don't want to say good-bye at all. You're just going to Atlanta for a party. Promise me you'll call the minute you get there."

"Mama, stop worrying. I'll call."

"Where are your bags?"

"I put them in the car earlier."

"What are you wearing to the party? You didn't even tell me, Jessie. We used to share everything. If this party is so important, why didn't you show me your dress?"

"I didn't buy a dress, Mama. I'm going to wear one of Sophie's. It seemed silly to spend the money on a dress I'll only wear once. Sophie and I are the same size. You should drink your coffee before it gets cold."

"When will you be home?"

Jessie gritted her teeth. "I don't know."

"Call us when you're ready to leave."

"Sophie wants me to stay for the week. I might."

"A whole week," Thea gasped. "But that means you'll only be home one day, and then it's time to leave for college. You left everything to the last minute. You need new clothes, bed linens, a new trunk. . . ."

Jessie shrugged.

"What is that . . . *thing?*"

"It's a knapsack," Jessie said, slinging a heavy, green-twill bag over her shoulders. The red sweater stayed in place.

"Come along, ladies, and I'll escort you to the car."

"Come here, sweet love, and give Mama a big kiss and hug."

Jessie suffered through the obligatory kiss and hug. She pretended not to see the tears rolling down her mother's cheeks.

"Daddy, have a nice weekend. Take Mama for an ice-cream cone. She thinks that makes everything better."

She felt herself flinch when her father whispered in her ear. "You aren't coming back, are you?"

Jessie looked in her father's eyes. She couldn't lie to this man who had intervened so many times on her behalf over the years. "No, Daddy."

"I'll miss you."

"Bye," Jessie called from the driver's seat as she backed up her car.

Today was the first day of a whole new life.

She didn't look back.

Chapter Four

Jessie sighed with relief when she finally parked the BMW under the Ashwoods' portico behind Sophie's sporty Mercedes coupe. She looked at her watch. Five hours exactly from the moment she left the bank parking lot.

"God, I was starting to worry, Jessie," Sophie said, throwing her arms around her friend. "Did you have any trouble? What you need is a drink. You look ghastly. I do like your 'don't give me any shit' outfit. Your mother must have had a fit. Did you hit the bank? Did you bring all your worldly possessions? How long are you going to stand there?" It was all said in one breathless rush.

Jessie laughed. "Smooth as silk. Everything worked out, so far, just the way you said it would. Daddy knows, though. He asked me point-blank, and I didn't deny it. He won't do anything. For whatever it's worth, he understands. I think he even sympathizes with me. I made it to the bank as soon as it opened and took a generous hit on my money. I brought everything that means anything to me. Oh, I bought two red sweaters, and my mother freaked out. Lord, it must be a hundred degrees."

Sophie laughed. "Put your suit on and take a dip with me. Everything is ready for the party. We don't have to do a thing except sell your car and get you a new one. It will only take us thirty minutes to do it. I called ahead, and all the paperwork is done. I ordered you a Jeep. A real Jeep. Bright red."

"You didn't!"

"I honest to God did!"

"I love you, Sophie Ashwood."

"And I love you, Jessie Roland. I think we're going to be best friends all our lives."

Jessie stared at her friend without a trace of envy. To say Sophie was beautiful would be the understatement of the year. She had a golden wealth of hair she wore piled high on her head for height, so curly it was unmanageable. She had inherited her dimples and chocolate-colored eyes from her father. Her patrician nose and high cheekbones were her mother's. Her perfectly proportioned body was pure Sophie. She exercised, swam, played tennis, and basically was a vegetarian. With her infectious personality she had the rare ability, on meeting someone for the first time, to put them so at ease they became instant friends. From kindergarten on she had always been in the top three percent of her class. If Sophie had any faults, it was that she loved to curse for shock value and had a hair-trigger temper.

"My mother would skin you alive if she saw you in that bikini," Jessie said.

"Your mother isn't here. I got you one just like it but in green to match your eyes. I laid it out on the bed. Go ahead, do your thing. I'll be out by the pool waiting for you."

"Did you get a wrap for the suit?" Jessie asked.

"Nope. You will have to parade through the house showing all that skin. Wait till you see the dress I picked out for tonight. Slits, bare shoulders, no back. Did I say tight? You can't wear underwear."

Jessie gasped. She could hear Sophie laugh all the way to the pool.

She was doing the right thing. She really was.

Jessie eyed the skimpy bikini and the sheer wraparound skirt wadded into a ball that wasn't supposed to be there.

She'd been here before, in this very room that was next to Sophie's with a connecting door. The first time she'd come here for an overnight stay, along with her parents, was when she was eleven or so, and Sophie had complained to her mother that there should be a connecting door between the rooms. The very next day there was a door. What Jessie really liked was the fact that there were locks on all the doors in the Ashwood house. Perfect for keeping overbearing mothers at large. Or in Sophie's case, a neglectful mother. Jessie only remembered seeing Janice Ashwood a couple of times.

The room was extra large for a bedroom, and so luxurious Jessie had a hard time imagining the amount of money spent on the costly furnishings. Ankle-hugging carpeting tickled her bare toes as she walked around touching costly figurines and crystal accent pieces. The room was decorated in champagne-colored brocade, imported lace, and satin. A film director would have been hard-pressed to come up with a room that looked half as luxurious. A flowering deep pink dogwood in a Ming urn complemented the priceless paintings in soft summer colors that adorned the walls.

The big question was, how did one turn this room into a sanctuary? One didn't, she decided. It was just a perfect room like all the rooms in the Ashwood mansion, except for Sophie's room, which was such a mess you had to kick stuff out of the way just to walk through to the bed.

The magnificent room boasted three telephones with three separate numbers, just like Sophie's room. The white phone was for parents' calls and never answered. The blue phone was for friends and answered all the time; the beige phone was for any young man who had the desire to call. She really should call her mother, Jessie thought. A promise was a promise. It would be her last phone call. She could rehearse her conversation while she changed into the bikini. From past experience she knew it wouldn't work because her mother went off on tangents she had to respond to.

"I need a tan," she moaned when she viewed her slim figure in the long, gilt-edged mirror hanging on the bathroom door.

Sophie poked her head in the door. "What's taking you so long, Jess?"

"I'm trying to make up my mind if I should call home now or wait?"

"What do you feel like doing?"

"Not calling at all. I did promise, though."

"Then do it and get it over with. The water's great since we put in the heater. I do like that suit. Maybe we can all go skinny-dipping tonight when the party winds down."

"You wouldn't!"

"I would. I've done it. Believe it or not the girls aren't shy about it, but the boys kind of flinch and hold their hands in front. It's worth it to just watch them. Everybody checks everybody else out. I say if you got it, show it. You don't have to do it, Jessie, but it is fun. So, are you going to call or not?"

"I guess I might as well. Don't go. Stay and listen."

Sophie perched on the edge of the bed. "How many times do you think your mother will call while you're here?"

"Every ten minutes. You were such a genius for coming up with the three phones. Isn't it expensive, though?"

"My mother doesn't care. We have so much money we could probably burn a pile of it and no one would notice, especially the bankers. My mother's favorite expression is 'Send me the bill.' "

"It's a good thing she married that rich Greek the first time around."

"You're not kidding. She inherited everything he had. My father was so poor my mother had to buy him a suit to get married in. She said he was good in bed." Her voice turned flat when she said, "And then he drank himself to death a year after I was born."

"We are two misfits. You realize that, don't you, Sophie?" Sophie nodded. "I don't know which is worse, a mother like mine or one like yours. Have you seen her at all this year?"

"She came home for Easter and managed to rustle up an Easter basket she left by my door Easter morning, then she was off again. She spends all her time these days getting cosmetic surgery in Europe. She looks younger than I do. You wouldn't recognize her. Hell, I didn't recognize her, and she's my mother. The last time she called she said, and this is a direct quote, 'Darling, youth is fleeting so enjoy it while you have it. Buy what you want, do what you want, and have the bills sent to the attorneys.' So, I do what she says." Sophie's voice turned so fierce her eyes started to water. "I don't ever, ever want to end up like my mother. Right now as we speak she's traipsing around Europe with some guy who is only three years older than me. When he works he paints houses. When my mother gets tired of him she'll settle some money on him and he'll live out his life in luxury. She's incredibly generous to the men in her life."

It was nothing new to Jessie. She'd heard it all before. The only thing that changed was the name and occupation of the man in Janice Ashwood's life. "Do you have money of your own, Sophie? Like a savings account or checking account?"

Sophie hooted. "I have a trust fund that gets replenished every year. Mother sold off a couple of those Greek shipping tankers and put all the money in my fund. I think she has seventy-three more to sell off. It's disgusting, isn't it?"

"What are you going to do with all that money?"

"Spend it as fast as I can."

"On what?"

"Something will come to me. Do you need money, Jessie?"

"No. You've already put out a lot of money for me. When I'm settled I'll start to pay you back. Sophie, what would you do if you weren't rich?"

"Look at me, Jessie. The money has nothing to do with my abilities. I have a brain. I'm a quick learner. I have a wonderful memory that serves me well. I'm fortunate in that respect. I think I will make an excellent architect someday. Who knows, you might want me to design a house for you when you decide to get married. The plans will be my wedding present to you. Spending my mother's money . . . my money, however you want to look at it is . . . my way of punishing my mother. In the beginning I thought she'd take notice when the bills started rolling in. She didn't even flutter her artificial eyelashes. I started spending more and more until there wasn't a damn thing left to buy. She still didn't notice. To answer your question, I would persevere and then I would prevail. That's what it is all about, my friend. We're alike in so many ways and unlike in others. You have persevered in your own way. As of today you are prevailing. I envy you because I don't know when it will be my time to prevail. It will happen, though."

Her voice turned dreamy. "I'm going to build a bridge someday that will be so magnificient the whole world will notice. Do you know why I want to build a bridge?" Not waiting for Jessie's response, she rushed on. "You start with nothing. Then you build a bridge that will take you someplace you wouldn't have been able to go. When it's done and you cross it you have the option of going on to that wonderful place or going back. Do you think that's sad?"

Jessie nodded. "Swear to me, Sophie, that no matter what road you or I take or whatever happens in our lives, that we will always be friends. I don't mean that we have to call each other incessantly or write every week. I want to know that you will always be there for me the way I will always be there for you. I want you to swear, Sophie."

Sophie's face turned solemn. "I swear, Jessie. Look, let's scratch the swim and go to town so we can turn your car in. Are you still planning on leaving in the morning?"

"Yes. There will be less traffic on a Sunday. I have to unload the car first, though."

"First you are going to call your mother and get that out of the way. Want a cigarette?"

"Sure." Smoking was something they used to do in the playhouse with the windows closed. "She's sitting there with her hand on the phone. I'll bet you ten dollars she picks up before the first ring is finished."

"Hey, Jess, this is me. That's a sucker bet. Just do it!"

Jessie rolled her eyes when the phone in Charleston was picked up the moment it started to ring. Sophie flopped back on the bed, her hands laced behind her head.

"I got here about an hour ago. For heaven's sake, Mother, why did you do that? Do you have any idea how embarrassing it's going to be when the police come knocking on the door? I said I would call. I'm calling. Why are you crying, Mother? If you don't stop, I'm going to hang up. We're going swimming. Right now we're drinking beer and smoking cigarettes. Yes, the police officer will smell it on me. That doesn't make me trashy. All right then, it makes me trashy. I don't care, Mother. You can call as often as you like. We probably won't hear the phone with the party and everything. I didn't look at the dress. Would you like to talk to Sophie so you can ask her? She said you don't wear underwear with it."

Sophie buried her face in the pillow, her whole body shaking with laughter.

"Mother, you had better not show up here. I will not allow you to humiliate me like this."

Sophie reared upward when she heard the silent scream building in Jessie's voice. She made a violent move with her hand for Jessie to cut off the conversation. "It's time to go, Jessie," she called loudly.

"I have to go now, Mother. Sophie is waiting for me. We are talking, Mother. Actually, no, Mother, I don't want to talk to you. I'm on a holiday. I thought we agreed that this was my time. Do some needlepoint or go out with Daddy. I left my room tidy. Why did you have to do anything to it? I know you love doing it, but you just made work for yourself. I don't know why the room looks like no one was ever in it. Maybe it's because you wouldn't allow me to do anything but sit and sleep in it. Mother, I am much too old to blow you kisses over the phone, and I will not say all those gushy things either. I'm eighteen. You're crying so hard you can't hear a word I'm saying, so I'm going to hang up. Good-bye, Mother."

"Good God! How do you deal with all that. You, Jessie Roland, have the patience of a saint. Did I hear you right? Is she coming here?"

"She called the state police when I didn't call after five hours. They're going to show up at your door. Is that sick or what? I think she might come here. I'll call back in half an hour. If there's no answer that means she's on her way, which means I have to leave. Let's do the car thing right away."

"First we have to change," the ever practical Sophie said. "I'll meet you downstairs in ten minutes."

Forty minutes later, Sophie said, "So, what do you think? This is a one-of-a-kind vehicle. They aren't going to go on the market for some time. I wheeled and dealed," she said proudly. "Don't you just love the candy-apple red color? All the guys at school are going to love you. Do you think you can handle it?"

"Absolutely. Thank you so much, Sophie. Let's get this straight now. The car is registered in your name. So is the insurance. You typed up a letter saying you loaned me the car and I'm to keep the letter with all your papers in the glove compartment."

"Right."

"I cash the check from the BMW and take cash, which I give to you. By taking cash, I can't be traced."

"Right again. So, let's head for the bank. I'll stay outside in the parking lot. Cashing a check for that amount will be something the teller will remember. I don't want her to put our two faces together when your mother calls in the Feds. She will, Jessie, so be prepared. Remember now, the world revolves around your social security number. Forget your old one and remember the new one I got you. I don't even want you to think about asking me how I did it. I got all your transcripts fixed with the new number. As of today, you are a new person. You're sure now that you can handle all this?"

Jessie's face was grim. "I'm sure. Someday when we're old married ladies and bored to tears I want you to tell me how you did all this."

"It's a deal. Let's go. I want to see if your mother answers the phone. We might have to switch to Plan B."

"What's Plan B?"

"I'm going to work on that while I sit in the parking lot."

*   *   *

Thea Roland stared at the pinging phone in her hand, then turned to see her husband watching her. "I've been sitting here for hours, Barnes, waiting for her to call, and she said she'd been there an hour before she called. How could she do that to me? She said I humiliated her by calling the police. She didn't even sound like our daughter. This is what happens when I listen to you, Barnes. You said give her freedom, latitude, let her experience things. She's a stranger I don't even know. Sophie and that slut of a mother of hers are to blame, too."

Barnes sat down across from his wife. "That slut of a mother was your best friend all your life. Sophie is a wonderful person with opinions and ideas. That young woman was the best thing that ever happened to Jessie. This is all your fault, Thea. Whatever happens in regard to Jessie, you are the one who must take full responsibility."

"How dare you say such a thing to me. I've given up my life for that girl, and this is the thanks I get. I'm going up there as soon as I can get myself together. I'm going to bring her home."

Barnes clipped the tip of a cigar and lit it with a gold lighter.

Thea stared at him with unblinking eyes. "I forbid you to smoke that smelly cigar in the house. The drapes will smell, and so will the carpets."

"Get used to it, Thea. This is my house, and I will do whatever I damn well please."

"What's gotten into you, Barnes? Did you hear anything I said?"

"I heard every single word. You are not going to Atlanta to spoil Jessie's weekend."

"I'm going, and that's final. I didn't ask you to drive me. I'll drive myself. And when I return our daughter will be with me. The biggest mistake of my life was listening to you."

"*No!*" The single word was a thunderbolt of sound. "The biggest mistake of your life was the day you kidnapped that child."

Thea sobbed. "You hush, Barnes. We said we weren't ever going to talk abut this."

"Damn it, Thea, we have to talk about it. We have to get used to the idea that Jessie is not with us anymore. This is her time now. We talked about this before. I'm not going to put either one of us through that again. It's over and we have to get on with our lives. You are not going to Atlanta, and that's final. If you try to leave, I'll truss you up like a turkey at Thanksgiving."

"I'm going, Barnes. With or without you. You're my husband and not a warden. Like you said, get used to it."

"I'm warning you, Thea. It will be the last straw where Jessie is concerned. She will never forgive you. Do you want to live with that? More to the point, can you live with that?"

"Stop saying such ugly things to me, Barnes. Jessie loves me. It's Sophie's influence that is causing all these problems. We have to find a way to get that young woman out of our daughter's life. Think, Barnes, what can we do?"

"We aren't doing anything. How many times do I have to tell you that?"

Thea stood up, her eyes glazed, her jaw slack. "I'm going to Atlanta. Come with me or stay here. It doesn't matter anymore."

Barnes stared at the mangled cigar in his hand. He sighed. "Get in the car, Thea."

"Thank you, Barnes. I knew you'd see my way is the right way. We'll open up the house in Atlanta. Jessie can come home weekends. We can even take her to dinner in the middle of the week. I'll hire a new cook, and she can take food to Jessie to make sure she doesn't eat all that starchy, fatty food the cafeterias serve. We'll decorate her room or perhaps get her an apartment of her own. Jessie will be so grateful. We need to start planning for the holidays. A cruise, Barnes, just the three of us. The Greek islands will be nice. The three of us will have such a wonderful time. We'll take our meals together, sightsee together. We'll be a happy family again."

Barnes held the door of the car for his wife. He heard the phone ring just as he climbed behind the wheel. He wondered who it was. Not that it mattered.

"Dial it again, Jessie. You're all wired up. Maybe you dialed the wrong number."

"I dialed the right number, Sophie, but I'll do it again. I know my mother. They're on the way. At best I'll have a four-hour head start if I leave now. I hate missing your party. Will you take pictures and write me a long letter?"

"Of course. I'll help you load up the Jeep. Don't drive too far today, Jessie. Stop somewhere for the night. Get an early start in the morning. Don't worry about anything here. I'll carry the ball. I'll be waiting for your call first thing in the morning."

"I'm doing the right thing, aren't I, Sophie?"

"Does it feel right, Jessie?"

"Yes. Yes, it does."

"Then you're doing the right thing. Come on, let's get to it. It's a good thing we had the Jeep gassed. You're ready to go. Do you have the map I outlined for you?"

"I have everything. Sophie, thank you for being such a good friend."

"My pleasure."

"What is that?"

"I don't know. It looks like my father's writing. I want

to open this before I leave. Why would my father . . . What is this?"

"Your future," Sophie said, scanning the papers Jessie held out to her. "I have stuff just like this. It's for your trust fund. Your father turned it over to you. That means you can do whatever you please with it, and you don't have to ask for permission. When you get settled you call the bank and set up mailing instructions. Your father signed all the release papers so things are in order. The bankers will do whatever you want. If you want, use my address until you're comfortable with things. From the looks of this you are one wealthy young woman. What does the note say?"

Jessie choked back a sob. "It just says he wishes me luck, and if I ever need him, to call and leave a message at his club. He said he loves me and wants me to be happy and to think of him once in a while. He also said he will never interfere in my life, but he can't promise the same for my mother. He even gave me a medal. It looks old and worn. I wonder why he would do that."

"Do you want me to keep this stuff for you?"

"Do you mind?"

"Not at all. When you're settled we can discuss it. I'd like to read through it all again and then compare it to my trust fund. Mother had the 'best of the best' draw up mine. I don't want anything coming home to roost on your shoulders at some point in the future. With that mother of yours you need all the edge you can get."

Jessie hugged her friend, her eyes filling with tears. "Thanks, Sophie. I keep saying that, don't I?"

"Yeah, but it's okay. Start that engine and do the speed limit. Don't pick up any hitchhikers and don't drive after dark."

"Yes, Sophie."

"Go on, get out of here before I start to cry."

"Are you really going to go skinny-dipping?" Jessie called over her shoulder.

"You bet. Have a good life, Jessie Roland," Sophie whispered, a catch in her voice.

Barnes felt his nerves stretch to the breaking point as Thea rambled on and on about the future. Defiantly he opened the window all the way and fired up a cigar. Thea ignored the obnoxious smoke as she continued to prattle about buying Jessie a new designer wardrobe. He knew she would wind down eventually. He waited.

Ninety minutes later, Thea took stock of the scenery outside the car window. "We aren't on the interstate, Barnes. Where are we?"

Barnes stalled for time. "On the road. I'm driving, Thea. I know where I'm going. Why don't you take a nap?"

"I don't want to take a nap. Exactly where are we, Barnes? This is not the road to Atlanta. This isn't even the scenic route."

Barnes heard the scream start to build in his wife's throat. "I never said we were going to Atlanta. You assumed that's where we were going when I told you to get in the car."

"What do you mean we aren't going to Atlanta? Where are we going?"

"I'm taking you back to the scene of your crime. After I do that you can damn well do whatever you please. I don't give a good rat's ass anymore. I can't take it, Thea."

"Stop this car right this minute! How could you do such a thing? I refuse to go back to *that place*. Do you hear me, Barnes? I refuse. If you don't stop this car, I'll jump out."

Barnes's response was to press harder on the accelerator. A glorious cloud of smoke filled the car. Thea started to cough and sputter. "Go ahead, Thea, jump. I'm doing eighty miles an hour. You'll break every bone in your body. You'll be in the hospital for *years*. No one will come to visit you. You alienated all your friends with that sick devotion you foisted on Jessie. Jessie will never know. Listen to me, Thea. She isn't coming back. Not now, not ever."

"Stop it! Stop it!" Thea shrieked. She huddled into the corner of the car, her entire body shaking with the force of her sobs. Barnes ignored her.

Hours later, Barnes slowed the powerful car. On his right was a small green sign that said, YOU ARE NOW ENTERING THE HAMLET OF ASHTON FALLS. The cigar clamped tightly between his teeth, he said, "Look alert, Mrs. Roland. We are approaching the scene of your dastardly act. I'm going to get gas. Would you like that cold drink now?"

"Shut up, Barnes."

"It looks the same. Imagine that. Sixteen years, and it still looks the same. Let's see, it was a cream soda you wanted when we were here last. Get out of the car, Thea."

"I will not."

"You will get out, my dear. Otherwise, I will put you out. Walk over to the cooler and get your cream soda."

Whimpering, Thea climbed from the car and on rubbery legs walked over to the cooler. Instead of looking down into the red ice-filled cooler, she raised her eyes to see a rusty pink stroller nailed to the wall next to a frayed and tattered rope. She reached out for the edge of the cooler before she dropped to the ground in a dead faint.

Barnes took his time walking over to where his wife lay on the ground. He dipped his snowy white handkerchief into the ice water in the cooler and let it dribble down her face. She sputtered to wakefulness.

"Time to get up, Thea. Here's your cream soda. They're deposit bottles, so you have to drink it here and leave the bottle. How much do I owe you?" he asked the elderly man who had pumped his gas.

"Eight dollars and twelve cents will do it and a quarter for the pop. You folks just passing through?"

"You could say that."

"I seen you lookin' at that there stroller hanging on the wall. A little girl was kidnapped right here at this station, a long time ago. That there rope belonged to the dog that tried to save the little girl. The dog died a little while back. They never did find the little girl. The case ain't closed. Don't 'spect it ever will be closed. Them FBI fellers come by once or twice a year to check on things. Nothing like that ever happened in Ashton Falls before and probably won't ever happen agin. Is your missus feelin' better now? Looks a bit peaked."

"Female problems," Barnes said in a low voice as he fired up a fresh cigar. "Where do you put the empties?"

"Jest sit it on top. I cleaned your windshield. They tell me city folks like to get their windows cleaned. No charge."

"Thank you very much," Barnes said.

"Yes, thank you," Thea managed to say as she staggered to the car where she hunched herself into the corner.

"Why did you do that, Barnes? You were never a cruel man. Why?"

"I did it for you, Thea. I know it was a shock. Now we are going back home and pick up our lives. The next time those 'FBI fellers,'" he said, mimicking the old man, "come around, he's going to remember the lady that fainted under the stroller and mention it. I am as guilty as you are, Thea. I'm not trying to absolve myself. I simply don't understand how I allowed you to do the things you did all those years. I guess I was a coward. I saw how happy you were, but I also saw how unhappy Jessie was. I wish I could tell you how many times I wanted to take her out of her bed in the middle of the night and return her to Ashton Falls. Sending all that money to her family didn't make the guilt go away. We are both miserable excuses for human beings. I want some semblance of a normal life now that Jessie's gone. With or without you, Thea. By the way, we're going home now."

Her voice quaking with fear, Thea whispered, "What did you mean when you said Jessie wasn't coming back? Did you mean after the party or next week?"

"I mean she isn't coming back. Period. She's had enough of the both of us. I think sometime soon she's going to remember what happened that day. I know I've said it before, but the feeling grows stronger each day. We should start to think about moving so if that day does happen, we won't be around to be arrested. Neither one of us would do well in prison, Thea. I've been thinking about Spain."

"I think you're losing your mind, Barnes. Jessie would never leave us. We're her parents."

"She left us. She's not going to Georgia Tech, I'll bet my last penny on it. When she said good-bye it was good-bye in every sense of the word."

"I don't want to hear talk like that, Barnes."

"The reason you don't want to hear it, Thea, is because you know it's true. You've been in a state of denial for so long you don't know what the word truth means any longer."

"She's in Atlanta. When we get home we can call her, and I'll ask her point-blank." Thea's voice was pitiful when she said, "I finally figured out why you're so cruel to me. You've never forgiven me for not being able to give you children. You need to blame God for that, not me."

"That's the most ridiculous thing you've ever said to me."

Thea ignored him and spent the remainder of the trip home crying into soggy tissues. Barnes winced at the litter on the floor.

It was almost dawn when Thea tiptoed into her husband's

room. He was snoring lightly. Satisfied that he wouldn't hear her, she crept downstairs and out to the parked car. She was going to Atlanta.

Twice she almost fell asleep at the wheel. Most of her energy gone, Thea pulled off the highway for strong black coffee three different times. Her adrenaline kicked in when she approached the Buckhead area where Jessie had gone to visit. When she parked the car behind Sophie's racy sports car, she was still trying to figure out why Barnes had said such ugly things to her. Jessie's car was nowhere to be seen. A quick glance at her watch told Thea it was a little after eleven. All the stopping and starting had delayed her by an hour and a half.

She knew this house as well as she knew her own. She let herself in the unlocked front door and made her way up the steps. The sickening smell of flowers and stale alcohol and cigarette smoke followed her. No one seemed to be stirring. She wondered if her old friend Janice was in residence or was off on some jaunt.

Thea opened the door to the room Jessie had always stayed in, a huge smile on her face. The room was neat and tidy, with no sign of an occupant. She moved to the connecting door and opened it. Sophie was sprawled across the bed in her underwear. Thea checked out the bathroom. Her daughter was nowhere to be seen. Her eyes started to burn. Was Barnes right?

"Sophie, wake up," Thea said, shaking the girl's shoulder.

"Mrs. Roland! My God, what are you doing here?"

"I'm looking for Jessie. Where is she? I didn't see her car."

Sophie yawned elaborately. She detested this wild-eyed woman standing in front of her. "The reason you didn't see her car is because Jessie isn't here. She left after she talked to you yesterday."

"Left? Where did she go? Don't lie to me, Sophie."

Sophie shrugged. "I don't know where she went."

"We both know that's a lie. I know all about how you two girls shared secrets. If Jessie went someplace, she would tell you."

"There's a first time for everything. You look tired, Mrs. Roland. Would you like some breakfast or perhaps a nap?"

"I don't want either one. What time did she leave?"

"I wasn't really paying attention. Noon, perhaps a little later. What time did she call you? She left right after that."

"Why? Why would she do that? She was looking forward to your party."

"I think you need to ask yourself why she left, Mrs. Roland, since she made the decision to leave after she spoke with you."

"I'm calling the state police. They'll find her and bring her back."

Sophie bit down on her bottom lip. More than anything she wanted to tell this woman what she thought of her. "Do what you have to do, Mrs. Roland. I'm going to take a shower. Stay as long as you like. I'm leaving for school as soon as I get dressed. It was nice seeing you again."

Thea Roland waited for three days before she made the return trip to Charleston. She walked like a frail old lady, her eyes red-rimmed with all the tears she'd shed. It was her husband's cold whispered words that sent her flying to her bedroom, where she stayed another three days. Over and over his words drummed through her head. "Now, Thea, you know what those people felt like when you took their daughter away from them. This is your just punishment."

A week to the day after Barnes's ominous words to his wife, the Rolands left for Spain.

Chapter Five

Jessie's gaze swept around the motel room. It was spartan but clean and neat, absolutely unlike the five-star hotel suites her parents always chose when the family took a trip. She liked the small out-of-the-way motel with soda machines on each floor and the small fragrant coffee shop off the main lobby. The towels were coarse but snow-white, the soap sweet-smelling.

Her hair still damp from the shower, Jessie finished dressing. She looked forward to ordering a hearty breakfast in the coffee shop. If she wanted greasy bacon or sausage topped off with sawmill gravy, there was no one to tell her a fruit cup and Shredded Wheat with skim milk would do nicely. She might even buy a pack of cigarettes and smoke them, one after the other, while she drank four cups of coffee. She could dawdle all she wanted as long as she left a generous tip. She could buy the local paper and read it while she had her first cup of coffee.

Freedom was heavenly.

Jessie left the motel, put her bags in the Jeep, paid her bill, and had one of the best breakfasts in her life. It was noon when she remembered her promise to call Sophie. The last road sign had said there was a rest stop thirty miles down the interstate. That was okay. Sophie would probably still be sleeping off her party.

Forty minutes later, mindful of Sophie's warning to drive the speed limit, Jessie pulled off the exit road that led to the Windjammer Rest Stop. She used the restroom, then ordered two hamburgers, french fries, and a large Coke. While she waited for her food, she dialed the number of the blue phone in Sophie's bedroom.

"How was the party, Sophie?"

"Never mind the party, Jess. Your mother is here. She called me a liar. She knows I know where you are. Don't worry, I didn't say a thing. I'm out of here as soon as I finish packing. She's going to call the police to be on the lookout for you. Pile your hair on top and jam a hat on top of your head. Be sure to wear your sunglasses. They won't spot you in a million years. For whatever this is worth, I don't think I've ever seen your mother look so ragged. Your father isn't with her. Where are you? Is everything okay?"

"Everything is fine. I slept like a baby last night. I ate this monster breakfast, and I'm going to eat a huge lunch. I'm in some little town right on the border between Virginia and North Carolina. I stopped when I got tired. I'm going to drive to Washington, D.C., and spend the night there. Tomorrow I'll start out for New York. I'm in no hurry." Jessie's voice turned wistful. "Was the party a success?"

Sophie picked up on the wistful sound of Jessie's voice. "It was like all the other parties. We danced all night. The food was all gone. No one drank that much, so there were no fights. I think it broke up around three or so. No, we did not go skinny-dipping in case you're wondering. Listen, Jess, call me tomorrow when you're ready to leave Washington. Maybe you should stay on an extra day or so

and do some sight-seeing. You'll love Washington. It's another way of saying the trail will grow colder if you aren't
on the highway. Kick back a little, Jess. You earned it. Are
you nervous?"

"Not at all. I wish you were with me, though."

"If you ever really need me, Jess, send up a flare. I belong to your old life. You have a new life now, so don't
look back. I'll handle things here. Don't forget to call me
at my apartment back at school. I want you to promise to
check in every day until you're settled in New York."

"Okay, Sophie. Drive carefully. Do the speed limit and
don't pick up any hitchhikers."

"That's my line. I'll talk to you tomorrow."

Jessie paid for her lunch and ate it in the car as the Jeep
tooled down the interstate, the radio blasting at full volume.

Next stop: the nation's capital.

She'd done it all, seen everything the most famous city
in the world had to offer. She'd taken tours with other
tourists, walked neighborhoods to get a feel for the real
people versus the politicians of the city, and then she'd
taken the Jeep to drive around the city and the outlying
areas on her own. She'd gotten lost more times than she
cared to remember. She'd even treated herself to a picnic
lunch in Rock Creek Park. Twice she'd gone to Georgetown University to walk around the campus and talk to
the people in the admissions office. There was no doubt in
her mind that she could enroll in the prestigious university
for the next semester if she wanted to. The big question
was, did she want to? The game plan called for New York;
switching at this late date probably wouldn't be wise.

She loved the power and history of the city. She toyed
with the idea of getting a job and taking night courses.
Was that wise? Probably not. Better not to disturb the sta-

tus quo. But instead of paying attention to her concerns, Jessie turned to the classified section of the *Washington Star.*

While her knowledge of the city was limited, she at least had a vague idea of the different areas as she searched out apartment rentals and job opportunities. All the job ads required experience. How was one supposed to get experience if no one would hire you? Sophie would know. Without stopping to think, Jessie placed a call to Sophie, who picked up on the first ring.

"Sophie, it's me. I want to switch plans but I need your help. Tell me what you think of this idea." Fifteen minutes later, Jessie wound down as she waited, hardly daring to breathe, for her friend's response.

"I think it's a great idea. I knew you were going to love Washington. Let me get my thoughts together. I think, Jess, that you should work on the Hill. My mother knows some very influential people in Washington. When I was little, our senator used to come to our house. Mother went to school with him. I could call him and ask if there are any jobs available. In this world it's not what you know but who you know. If you're really interested, I can get you a resume that will blow their socks off. We can fudge a little here, hedge a little there. No one really checks those things anyway. If Senator Timrod vouches for you, you are in, my dear. Do you think you would like working for a senator or a congressman?"

"Would I ever. Yes, I would."

"Okay, this is what you do. Go shopping. Buy some nifty clothes while I work on this. Don't stint either. Get a new hairdo and make sure it's fashionable. You're sure, Jessie, this is what you want?"

Was it? "Yes, Sophie, it's what I want."

"All right but this is going to take a little time. I have to switch everything from New York. What about school? Our educations are paramount."

"I'll go nights."

"Be sure you do. Working and going to school isn't going to be easy. I'm glad we didn't do anything with your trust-fund monies. Check out the banks and let me know which one you want to use. I'll call you the day after to-morrow. My decks are clear here. I registered yesterday, so my time is my own until Monday. I bet I could do this for a living if I wanted to. Hanging out my first year at college with what my mother called 'undesirables' gave me a slight edge on how to get things done when you don't want other people to know your business. My father might not have been a driving force in my life, but he knew how to wheel and deal. I guess I inherited his instincts. Too bad I want to build bridges."

Jessie's voice grew jittery. "I don't want to do anything illegal."

"There's illegal and then there's illegal. I'll keep it in mind. I know exactly how to do this. If anyone wants to run a background check on you for any reason, I'll fix it with one of my mother's companies to cover for you. I'll set up a whole file. It's not as though you're assuming a new identity or anything like that. You're still going to be Jessie Roland. That isn't going to change unless you get married. As long as you pay your taxes and don't cheat the government, I don't see anything wrong with what we're contemplating. The social security number now is . . . a tad iffy. People do this all the time I'm told. I read *True Crime Reporting* on a monthly basis. You would be amazed at the helpful hints they give out for just this kind of situation. If you want to change your mind, now is the time to do it before I get this all under way."

"No. I'm okay with all of it. My parents will never suspect I work for the government. Right now that's all I care about. If you work for a senator or a congressman, what do you do?"

"I don't have the foggiest idea. You're talking to a girl who has never held a job in her life. I'll find out when I call Senator Timrod. Whatever it is, you can handle it. Probably social stuff, you know, making appointments to get their hair cut, arranging luncheons, sending flowers to their wives. Opening the mail. Maybe some typing. Junk like that. You have wonderful social skills, and you're an excellent typist. That report you typed for me last year didn't have one mistake. Working on the Hill probably pays very well, too. When a scandal breaks you'll be one of the first to hear it. Make sure you call me right away if you hear something because I love political gossip and scandals. You get off for all the government holidays and when it snows. It's got to be a breeze of a job. Give me a yes or no right now."

"I love this city, Sophie. I feel very comfortable here. Yes, yes."

"Okay, hang up so I can get started. Whoever would have thought you, Jessica Roland, and me, Sophie Ashwood, were into subterfuge? If your mother could only see us now."

"I don't want to talk about my mother, Sophie, not now, not ever."

"Okay, I hear what you're saying. This is the last time I'll bring up your mother's name. I called home, and the housekeeper told me your mother stayed three whole days before she finally left. She didn't eat a thing the whole time, and she didn't sleep in any of the beds. There weren't any wet towels, so I have to assume she didn't take a shower either. That's pretty sad, Jessie. Wouldn't it be nice if we had mothers we could call Mom. I always wanted to do that. I know you did, too. Listen, there is one other thing before we lay this to rest. Why did your father give you a Catholic St. Christopher's medal? I only know that because it says so on the medal. The medal bothers me, and I don't know why. Southern Baptists do not buy Catholic medals. Maybe you were left on someone's doorstep, and it was around your neck. Think about that one, Jessie Roland!"

Jessie hooted with laughter. "Call me when you have things all set. I'm going to go out to look for an apartment. Thanks for everything, Sophie."

"My pleasure."

Five days later, Jessie Roland moved into a three-room furnished apartment at 1755 Kilbourne Place in Mount Pleasant, within walking distance of Rock Creek Park. The small, cozy apartment was only a few blocks from the bus line that with transfers would take her anyplace in the city. She also registered to take six credits in the evening at Georgetown University. The only thing she didn't have was a job, but according to Sophie it was just a matter of days until Senator Timrod could line something up for her.

The call arranging the interview came on a Tuesday morning just hours after Jessie's phone was hooked up. The voice on the other end of the phone sounded old and querulous. The reedy voice said an interview was scheduled with Senator Angus Kingsley himself, the senior senator from Texas, in his offices in the Rayburn Building promptly at two o'clock.

Jessie looked at the clock. She had less than three hours to prepare. She was a whirlwind then, picking and choosing from her new wardrobe. Should she drive herself, take the bus, or opt for a taxi? She finally decided on a taxi since she was unsure of the transfer route and she needed to be on time.

Mindful of Sophie's admonition that less is more, she

carefully applied her makeup. The object, according to Sophie, was to look like you weren't wearing makeup. Would the day ever come when she could do things on her own and not depend on Sophie and her special brand of wisdom? Of course it would. She just needed patience.

Jessie stood back from the long mirror she'd purchased at Woolworth's to examine her appearance with a critical eye. The hunter green suit was the perfect color to complement her eyes. The white-silk blouse with the narrow tie at the throat was definitely feminine. Small pearl earrings, also from Woolworth's, along with her Timex watch, were her only jewelry. The small black-leather purse matched her shoes, which she knew were going to give her a blister on her little toe before the day was over. She took a deep breath. *I know I can do this. I want to do this. I will do this.*

"If I'm lucky by this time tomorrow, I might be a working girl in this city. An independent working girl. I can learn to be frugal, to make it on my own." Sophie said talking to oneself was a dangerous pastime. Jessie stuck her tongue out at her reflection. Then she giggled. "Please, God, let this work for me."

He was a tall, pleasant-looking man with clear blue eyes that crinkled at the corners when he smiled. He was impeccably dressed, his crisp shirt whiter than milk. Jessie thought she could see her reflection in his shiny black shoes. When he folded his hands in front of him, she noticed that his nails were clipped short and manicured.

It's going well, Jessie thought halfway through the interview. Some of the tenseness eased between her shoulder blades. She tensed again when the senator asked if she would have a problem working late. "I would of course compensate you for late hours. I might need you occasionally on the weekends if we're working on an important bill."

"Weekends won't be a problem, Senator Kingsley. However, I'm enrolled for evening classes at Georgetown. On Mondays I have a class at eight. On Wednesday my class is at five thirty. I can return after class on Wednesday. Mondays I can work till seven-thirty. Tuesdays, Thursdays, and Fridays I'm free."

The senator frowned. "When will you do your studying?"

"On my lunch hour and on Sundays."

"The job is not hard, but it is a demanding one. Do you think you can handle the duties I outlined as well as the hours, Miss Roland?"

"Yes, Senator Kingsley, I think I can handle it. When would you want me to start?"

"Mrs. Prentis will be leaving officially in two weeks. She's been on a short leave of absence this past month." The senator's voice dropped to a soft whisper. "Mr. Prentis is in failing health and Agnes wants to spend more time with her husband. I hired her the day I came to Washington, and she's been with me ever since. She's agreed to come in to show you how things are done. She's here now if you would like to meet her." Jessie nodded. "If you have no other plans for the rest of the day, you could stay on now and get a feel for the way we do things. Mrs. Prentis will discuss your salary and your benefits. Paperwork takes time. I like my coffee strong and black with just a smidgin of chicory. You make a nice appearance. I like that, Miss Roland."

Jessie flushed. "Thank you, Senator Kingsley."

Jessie liked Agnes Prentis the moment she was introduced to her. She was white-haired, pink-cheeked, and buxom, and she wore sensible shoes with a pair of worn felt slippers hidden beneath her desk.

At six o'clock, Agnes Prentis leaned back in her chair. "Now, do you have any questions before we leave this zoo?"

"At least a million, but they can wait until tomorrow. Do you want me to come in at eight or eight-thirty?"

"Seven-thirty would be better. We have a lot of ground to cover. If we're lucky, we might get out at five. Senator Kingsley works most nights till midnight. Don't panic now. That doesn't mean you have to stay that late. Do you mind if I call you Jessie?"

"Not at all."

"I'm going to be very blunt about something. If you want to keep this job, and I think you will, be very cordial to Mrs. Kingsley. The senator's wife has a very sharp tongue, and she wants what she wants yesterday. That's another way of saying everything has to be done instantly. Mrs. Kingsley and Tanner, their son, live in Texas. The senator goes home weekends, or at least he tries to. That's not to say Mrs. Kingsley and Tanner do not come here to Washington; they do, but over the years their visits have dwindled to one or two trips a year. Mrs. Kingsley calls the office five or six times a day. Tanner rarely calls. If possible, put the calls through. You'll need to use your best judgment where that is concerned. If you let her, she'll run you ragged traipsing all over town for what the senator calls 'her piddly-diddly nonsense.' You'll need to stand firm, or she will walk all over you. Please understand. I'm not being disloyal to the senator. I just want you to be prepared. You'll like Tanner. He's a bit of a rogue, and he does like the young ladies. After one of his visits, all I do is take calls for him. He doesn't like to say good-bye, you see."

Jessie drew a deep breath as she tried to digest all the information Mrs. Prentis was offering.

"There is a staff of four, but you'll be in charge. Scheduling will be the biggest problem, but with time you'll make it all work out. Delegate whenever possible, especially on the nights when you have to work late. The senator likes a full coffeepot at all times. Don't be concerned if it looks like mud after sitting for hours. He likes it that way. He waters his own plants early in the morning and trims the leaves himself. He loves raisin-filled cookies." She paused, smiled warmly. "Now I say we go home and get a good night's sleep. Tomorrow will be a long, full day. I've kept personal logs I'll leave with you. When you feel more confident about how things are going you can return them."

"That's very kind of you, Mrs. Prentis. I appreciate it."

"Call me Agnes. When my husband Gerald is feeling better and you have things under control, perhaps we can have lunch."

"I'd like that, Mrs. . . . Agnes."

The older woman smiled. "I think, Jessie, you are just what this office needs. In case you don't know it, Senator Kingsley is one of the most influential members of the Senate. There is talk of his becoming Majority Leader next term."

Jessie hoped she looked suitably impressed as she followed the older woman from the office.

Her first job.

She was a working girl in the most famous city in the world.

An independent working girl. Oh yes.

Part II

Chapter Six

Ashton Falls, Tennessee July 1976

Grace Larson stared at the glass of lemonade in her hand. The ice had melted long ago, so why was she still holding the glass? She wondered why she hadn't at least sipped at the tart drink. As she leaned over to set the glass on the floor of the front porch JJ eyed the glass and flopped down under the swing.

"I've never seen heat like this, JJ," Grace said as she wiped at her brow with her apron. "I think I might ask Ben to bring down some bedding, so we can sleep on the porch tonight."

"Grace!"

"I'm on the porch, Ben. I think we should sleep out here tonight. It must be a hundred degrees upstairs."

"At least," Ben said as he sat down next to his wife on the swing. "Is something wrong, honey? You seemed out of it all day."

"I guess it's the heat. Maybe it's my hot flashes. I watered all the plants on the porch twice today, and they're still wilting. Why is that, Ben?"

"Have you been thinking about Hannah all day?"

"Yes, and I don't know why. Why do you think they stopped sending the money, Ben?"

"I was thinking about that the other day. Maybe they ran out. Maybe they died. Maybe they had a figure in mind when they started to send it and in their mind, they're all paid up. We should think about doing something with that money, Grace. Nobody in their right mind keeps money like that in a trunk."

Grace patted her husband's hand. "I haven't been in my right mind since the day Hannah disappeared. The best thing that could happen to us is someone breaks into our house and steals the money. I wouldn't even report it to the sheriff."

"We could give it away."

Grace reached down for the warm lemonade. She gulped at the sour drink until her eyes watered. The sleeping dog opened one eye to watch the proceedings. "If we do that, Ben, then we're admitting it's over. It will be like . . . we're giving up."

"I gave up a long time ago, honey. So did you in your own way when you stopped knitting those red sweaters."

"That was different, Ben. It's hard to knit with the arthritis in my hands. I guess I should have told you I've been buying red sweaters."

Ben's tone of voice changed. "Yes, you should have told me. Why, Grace?"

"Because I won't give up. Those red sweaters give me a sense of peace. I don't know why that is either."

"I think we need a vacation. Sometimes these mountains close in on me. You've always liked the beach. Let's just pack up and drive to Florida."

"There's no money for a vacation, Ben."

Ben stood up and jammed his hands in his pockets. "I'm tired of all this, Grace. All we have to do is go upstairs and open that damn trunk. We could pay for the kids' college education. They deserve it. I'm damn sick and tired of living hand-to-mouth. We live like hermits. We never have ten extra dollars that doesn't have to be accounted for. You need new clothes. I need new shoes. The boys can use a lot of things. Before long we're going to need a new refrigerator. I can't fix that old thing one more time. Are we going to use an ice chest when it finally goes? And what about your arthritis medicine? I choke every time I see that bill from the pharmacy. We can't keep handing out money to our parents and eating macaroni seven days a week. We could make life so easy for them. Look at me, Grace. Do you have any idea how tired I am? How much longer do you think I can continue to work two jobs? There are some days when my back is so bad I want to cry. I've had it, Grace. We need to make some changes here, and we need to make them real soon or I'm out of here. I'll leave you with this whole mess we've created. Notice, Grace, that I said, we've created."

"What are you saying, Ben?"

"You know damn well what I'm saying, so don't pretend you don't. This stupid bullshit is over."

Tears rolled down Grace's cheeks. "I wouldn't know what to do without you, Ben."

Ben's voice was so cold, Grace shivered. "Then don't bring it to a test."

"How much, Ben?"

"The amount doesn't matter. We have to move on to a better life. I'm not saying we should buy a big fancy house or a sports car. All I want is for all of us to be more comfortable, and be able to pay for the kids' college. I'm giving you five minutes to make up your mind. At the end of the five minutes I will either go into the kitchen and sit down with the calculator or I will go upstairs to pack my things. The clock is ticking, Grace."

"All right, Ben. Do whatever you have to do."

"Grace?"

"What?"

"Do not ever serve me macaroni again. I want you to go into the house right now and throw out all the peanut butter. I will never, ever, eat it again either. Tomorrow you will go shopping for all of us, your parents, my parents, for the boys, and us. I'm going to make a list of things for you to do tomorrow. You are going to handle this, Grace, and you will not fall apart. If you do, I will leave you with your parents. I will not look back."

"All right, Ben. Don't beat it to death. I said to do whatever you have to do."

"After dinner tomorrow night you will pack our bags, I'll load up my new truck, we'll park the kids with your mother, and we'll start on our vacation."

Grace's voice dropped to a bare whisper. "When did you stop loving me, Ben?"

"The day you told John we couldn't afford to pay for his college education."

"Will the money make it right, Ben? Will it help you to start loving me again?"

Ben refused to meet his wife's pleading eyes. "I don't know."

"I never stopped loving you, Ben."

"You don't even know who I am anymore."

"You're my husband."

"It's nice of you to remember. For years now I thought I was just someone who took up space here and paid the bills."

Grace started to cry. "I guess you were in a way. I'm sorry, Ben. I don't know what else to say."

"Sorry is a good place to start. We'll work on it from there."

Ben watched his wife from his position at the kitchen table as she cleaned out the kitchen cabinets. It wasn't true what he'd said about not loving her. He loved her so much he ached with the feeling for what they'd both lost. He was glad now that his wild gamble was paying off. He would not allow himself to think of the alternative if Grace hadn't agreed to use some of the money in the trunk. Already his shoulders felt lighter, and he thought he could see a glimmer on the horizon.

"The trash men are going to love me this week," Grace said. "I have two dollars and fifty cents in the sugar bowl, Ben. Let's go down to the store and get ice-cream cones. JJ hasn't had one for a long time. You can work with your calculator when we get back."

"Two dollars and fifty cents! Did you hear that, JJ. Come on, boy, get your leash and let's take Mom out for ice cream."

Washington, D.C. December 1976

Jessie slid her overnight bag under her desk and hung her garment bag on the hat rack. In just a few hours she would be leaving for New Orleans and Sophie's graduation. Five whole days with her old friend she hadn't seen in over a year. They would do graduation, the Thanksgiving they missed, and Christmas all in one shot, Sophie had promised.

Jessie was early that morning, purposely so because she had last-minute details to see to so the office would run smoothly until her return. She turned on the coffee machine, then replaced the wilted flowers with fresh ones she purchased on her way to work every other day. Sometimes she wished she wasn't so conscientious. However, that conscientiousness had earned her the title of right hand to Senator Angus Kingsley, a job she took very seriously. In the past three years she'd learned what she had to do and what she could have others do to free up more time for her studies and to make herself indispensable to the senator. She could do two things at once while she was thinking and planning ahead to her next project. Once she'd danced a jig in her office when she overheard the senator tell someone he couldn't function without Jessie Roland. Shortly afterward she'd been given a healthy raise.

Jessie looked around the four rooms in which she'd spent the last three years working. She loved the rich, warm paneling, the vibrant Oriental carpeting, and the one-of-a-kind works of art adorning the walls. Works of art personally selected by the senator's wife. More than anything, though, she loved the mahogany floor-to-ceiling bookshelves crammed to overflowing with law books and handsome leather-bound rare first editions as well as glossy *New York Times* best-sellers. The furnishings were old, worn, and comfortable, something she particularly liked. The plants the senator trimmed and watered were healthy and added a homey touch to the otherwise masculine suite of rooms. She sniffed, wrinkling her nose. The scent of power was everywhere in the office suite, and she was part of it. She thought about the secrets she knew and the other secrets Agnes Prentis had told her. She clamped her lips shut as she shook her head to clear her thoughts. She crossed her fingers that the day would never come when someone would ask her under oath about those secrets. Breakfast deals, cloakroom deals, golf-course deals. When she returned, she'd think about those things. Today was hers, and she wasn't going to give Senator Kingsley and Washington a second thought.

Mentally, Jessie ticked off the small chores yet to be done. Fill the senator's candy jar with licorice sticks, check to be sure the "munchies" drawer was filled with fresh bags of chips and pretzels, the refrigerator full of soda and juice. She eyed the portable bar in the senator's private office. None of the bottles was past the halfway mark. Was there extra ice? She opened the small under-the-counter refrigerator. Plenty of ice. Everything was neat and tidy, no sign of dust anywhere. The coffee, filters, and bottled water were ample. Now, on to the appointment book and the senator's schedule.

Jessie took a long moment to stare at the two family photographs all senators kept on their desks. Angus Kingsley was no exception. Smiling faces in happier places. She wondered how she knew that. Possibly through her predecessor Agnes Prentis's logs, or else little hints she'd dropped during her first year on the job. She had to wonder if the rumors she'd heard about the senator and Mrs. Kingsley were true. It was hard to imagine the shaggy senator she adored being unfaithful to his wife.

Alexis Kingsley reminded her of Sophie's mother, elegantly beautiful, always dressed to the nines, with cold eyes and a colder heart. From what Agnes Prentis had said, her assessment of the senator's wife was accurate. According to Agnes, the only time Alexis Kingsley came to Washington was when she wanted something. Jessie shivered when she looked in the appointment book. Alexis and Tanner Kingsley were coming to town next week. They would arrive the day after Jessie returned from Louisiana.

During the past year she had fantasized about Tanner Kingsley. Each time she dusted the silver-framed picture, a different fantasy would surface. She couldn't help but wonder if the young man was as handsome in real life as he was in his photograph. Unlike his mother, he sat astride a horse, and was dressed in denim with well-worn boots. His Stetson was pushed back on his head as he smiled into the camera. Agnes said Tanner had charisma, which according to Agnes, was another way of saying he could have any woman he wanted. She'd gone on to elaborate by saying Tanner had the same kind of charisma his father had when he first came to Washington, years ago.

Jessie blew an imaginary speck of dust from the ornate silver frame. Next week she'd see the Kingsleys in the flesh and make her own assessment.

The door to the outer office slammed shut. Angus Kingsley never closed a door. He slammed it shut to announce his arrival. Jessie waited for the bear of a man to trundle into his office, demanding coffee.

"Damn, Jessie, I'm glad you're early today. There has been a change of plans. My wife and son moved up their visit from next week to today. You'll have to pick them up at the airport and take them to the hotel. Damn, you do make the best coffee, Jessie."

Jessie gasped. "Senator, I can't pick up your family. Did you forget? I'm leaving for Louisiana in an hour. I penciled it in your appointment book last month."

"You know I never look at that damn thing. I rely on you to get me to where I have to go and to remind me of things."

"Senator, we discussed my time off back in September. I told you how important this visit is to me. You said it was fine with you. Those were your exact words, Senator. I didn't take a vacation this year because you needed me. I need this time off."

"I'm sorry, Jessie, you'll have to cancel your plans. I'm going to need you this week. I promise to make it up to you. Long weekends and a nice raise. You can't let me down."

"Senator, I can't cancel my plans. Sophie is graduating. We talked about this so many times. You cannot reschedule a graduation."

The senator stared at her, his bushy eyebrows meeting in the center of his forehead.

"Your wife and son could take a taxi, Senator. People do that all the time. Or, you could engage a car service. The staff is needed here all day today. If you pull someone, things are going to get fouled up. You know how you like things to run smoothly. More coffee?"

The senator held out his cup. "Alexis in a taxi. By God, I'd love to see that. I suppose I could send the chauffeur and my car."

"I don't think you should do that, Senator. Victor Grimes is on that watchdog committee for government waste and he's been in here three different times asking questions about your field trips and your personal car usage. As I see it, a taxi or a car service are your only options. I have to leave now, Senator, or I'll miss my flight."

"Do you have time to make another pot of coffee before you leave?"

"No. Diane will make it when she comes in. I hope you have a lovely visit with your family. I'll see you next week and don't worry about anything. The staff, if they follow all my notes and my instructions, will have no problem. Don't forget you have a dental appointment this afternoon at four o'clock." She waved an airy good-bye before she left the office.

Jessie was in the hallway when she remembered her personal log in the top drawer of her desk. She set the suitcase down to return to the office for the little book with her scribbled notations. It would never do for someone else to find it or look at it. Rule Number One, Agnes Prentis had said, was never to leave the log unattended and to be sure to take it home at night. She'd obeyed Rule Number One to the letter.

Jessie arrived at Dulles Airport with fifteen minutes to spare. She checked her overnight bag with her garment bag before she headed for the restroom. A shrill shriek of childish laughter made her turn to see a set of identical four-year-old twins barreling down the concourse as they sought to elude their harried mother. She had only a moment to try to sidestep the shrieking twins or be bowled over. She turned too sharply and lost her footing, her handbag flying across the floor as her high heels sought for traction. A heartbeat later, she felt strong arms under her own arms, and then she was right side up. She turned to see the white knight who had rescued her and found herself staring into the bluest eyes she'd ever seen. Familiar eyes. Summer blue eyes. Then she almost fainted when the young man held her at a distance. "I think you're okay, just shaken up. Kids can be rambunctious. I wish you'd say something, so I know you're okay." His tone was light, teasing, almost bantering.

She wanted to say something, she really did, but her tongue felt like it was three sizes too big for her mouth. She felt her head bob up and down as she tried to force her facial muscles into a smile. She failed miserably.

"For heaven's sake, Tanner, the young lady is fine. Stop *hovering* and let her catch her breath. Obviously she needs to catch a flight. Can you tear yourself away so we can be on our way?" It was all said in one long breath, in a tone that could have chilled milk.

Tanner Kingsley, his back to his mother, winked at Jessie, and said, "She doesn't know that I thrive on saving damsels in distress. Is that your purse over there? Hold on. I'll get it for you." His hand touched hers when he held out the leather purse. Jessie felt an electric current shoot through her body. "Have a good flight." She nodded. A moment later mother and son were gone from her sight.

Jessie Roland was aware of two things at that precise moment. One, she had just met her destiny, and two, there was no time to use the restroom because her flight was boarding.

* * *

Her legs wobbly, Jessie boarded the airplane. Seated next to the window, she buckled up and leaned her head back on the headrest. She closed her eyes as she tried to conjure up Tanner Kingsley's face behind her closed lids. What she'd just experienced was such a strange fluke it had to mean something. The question was, what did it mean? A coincidence? Coincidences happened all the time. Fate? Was she meant to meet Tanner Kingsley in such an unlikely manner? Would she ever meet him again? She had the advantage over Mrs. Kingsley and her son since she'd seen their picture every day for three long years while they knew nothing at all about her.

She felt herself squirm when Alexis Kingsley's image surfaced behind her closed lids. She'd had only one brief glimpse of the senator's wife before her attention focused on Tanner. She'd been impeccably dressed and coifed. Sophie would have known to the penny what the woman's outfit cost. Where did the Kingsley money come from? The ranch? The senator's pay wasn't all that much, and he had to pay his living expenses in the city. She balanced his personal checkbook every month, and there was very little left at the end of the month. As far as she could tell, he had never sent any money back to Texas, which made her assume the ranch was self-supporting. Sable coats and Chanel handbags like the ones Mrs. Kingsley had cost a lot of money.

Jessie gave herself a mental shake. The Kingsley finances were none of her business. Balancing the senator's personal checkbook was just part of her job. She sighed. Moments later she was asleep. Hours later the flight attendant had to tap her shoulder to wake her. "We're about to land, miss. Fasten your seat belt and return your seat to the upright position." Jessie did as instructed. A quick glance at her watch told her the flight was landing on time. She would have enough time to visit the restroom, comb her hair, and freshen her makeup before heading for the university. Sophie had said her apartment was on the way to the university, so she should have the driver leave her bags on the front porch.

Sophie was graduating *summa cum laude* six months ahead of schedule, and, to boot, was valedictorian. It was mind-boggling.

Sixty minutes later, ticket in hand, Jessie followed the throngs of parents entering the auditorium. Front row, center. Now how had Sophie managed that? She took her seat, aware of the empty seat next to hers. She looked up and down the row. Couples. Fathers and mothers. The empty seat must have been reserved for Janice Ashwood. In her heart, Jessie knew Sophie's mother would be a no-show. How awful for Sophie. She would be forced to stare at the empty seat when she gave her speech.

Did Jessie dare ask someone to remove the chair? Should she volunteer it to someone who didn't have a ticket? Was it her place to do anything? No, no, no to all of the above. Where Sophie was concerned, hope would always spring eternal. Jessie folded her bulky coat and purse and placed them on the chair. It was all she could do.

The auditorium lights dimmed as the graduates marched down the center aisle. Jessie craned her neck to see Sophie. Her heart swelled with pride when she saw her friend take her seat. *She looks different,* Jessie thought. This last year had obviously wrought changes in her friend. She hoped they were all to the good. The insane desire to smash the empty chair next to her was so strong that Jessie clenched her fists and bit down on her lower lip.

Jessie's mind drifted as the dean took the podium and droned on and on about the graduating class and how hard they had all worked to arrive at this day. She was back in the airport staring into Tanner Kingsley's summer blue eyes, eyes all the more startling because of his bronzed complexion capped off by sun-bleached blond hair. He had seemed incredibly tall and muscular. A bronze Adonis. She felt a curl of heat work its way up to her chest and neck at the thought. She wondered if she looked as flushed as she felt.

"Sophie Marion Ashwood."

Jessie jerked herself back to reality as Sophie walked to the podium. Where was her speech? There had been nothing in her hand. Trust Sophie to wing it. She sucked in her breath when she saw her friend, her eyes bright with unshed tears, stare at the empty seat next to Jessie. Her gaze swiveled to Jessie, who mouthed the words, "It doesn't matter. I'm here. Get on with it." Sophie smiled and nodded.

"I hate your stinking guts, Janice Ashwood, for doing this to Sophie. I hate you as much as I hate Thea Madeline Roland," Jessie muttered under her breath.

Jessie listened in awe to Sophie's passionate speech about building bridges to the future, her voice ringing through the auditorium. With a five-second pointed stare at the empty seat in front of her, Sophie finished and walked from the podium before the audience could grasp that she'd finished her speech. The applause was polite. Sophie deserved more.

Jessie had to do something, and she had to do it now before the moment passed. Without a second's hesitation and in the blink of an eye the bulky coat and purse were on the floor and she was standing on Janice Ashwood's reserved chair. She was probably going to make a fool of herself. It didn't matter. Whatever it took to make this day memorable for Sophie she was willing to do, even if she made a fool of herself in the process. Her clenched fists beat the air as she yelled at the top of her lungs, "Yay, Sophie! Yay, Sophie!" Then she turned and shouted. "That's my friend Sophie. She completed the program in four and a half years instead of five to graduate first in her class. She deserves more than that polite hand-clapping you did a few minutes ago. Now, let's hear it for my friend Sophie!" She whistled between her teeth the way Sophie had taught her when they were little, her arms pumping up and down as she shouted, "Hoo, hoo, hoo!"

The audience laughed in delight as they followed suit. Sophie ran across the stage and leaped downward, her gown flapping around her legs as she made her way to Jessie. "I'll be damned. You are a serendipity if I ever saw one." Tears streaming down her face, Sophie climbed up on the chair, and shouted, "Thank you. Thank you."

To Jessie she said, "C'mon, we're out of here. I can't believe you did that. Where in the damn hell did you get the guts to do something like that? You hate speaking in front of people, you hate being on display."

"I didn't want them to forget you. I wanted this to be a memorable day. I know how hard you worked. I also know what that empty chair meant to you. Look at it this way, if someone had been in the chair, I wouldn't have been able to do it. I didn't think about it. I just did it."

"You sure as hell did. Did you see me bound off that stage?"

"Yes, and I saw your underwear, too. And to think I had to twist your arm to even attend this graduation. You wanted them to mail you your diploma."

Outside in the clear evening air, Sophie turned to Jessie. "Do you have any idea how much your friendship means to me, Jessie Roland? I've been in a dither for weeks worrying about the senator giving you the time off. If there had been two empty seats in that auditorium, I would have cut and run. I just want you to know that."

"I do know that, Sophie. Your friendship means as much to me as mine means to you. So, how are we going to celebrate?"

"Let's go home and drink some good wine and catch up. It's been over a year since we've been face-to-face. Tomorrow we can start doing things. I'm leaving next week for Costa Rica."

"Sophie! That's a world away. Why? For how long?"

"Three years. It's my internship. I couldn't pass it up. You can come and visit."

"God, I miss you already."

"Jess, it was a hell of a night. Thank you."

"I'm sorry about . . ."

"Don't be. I knew she wouldn't come. She did send a letter with a check that would have fed a third-world country. I tore the fucking thing to shreds. It was an exercise in futility. She won't even notice. I don't know if you want to know this or not but your parents are still living in Barcelona, Spain."

"I don't want to know. I don't think about them. At least I try not to. Let's get an ice-cream cone and see who can lick it the fastest. For some reason I feel like a little kid tonight."

"You're on. Want to race? Loser buys."

Jessie kicked off her high heels and stuffed them into her pockets. Both girls dropped to a sprinting position the way they used to do when they were little. "Two blocks, make a right, then a left, and the ice-cream parlor is something you can't miss."

Huffing and puffing, Jessie pulled up short. "That was a sucker bet. You don't have any money. My stockings are in shreds, and you're still wearing your cap and gown."

"I owe you, okay? You never used to be that fast. I'm in love, Jess."

"No kidding. There must be something in the air. I think I met my destiny today at the airport."

"Let's go home and talk unless you want to go down to Bourbon Street to listen to some jazz."

"Tomorrow night. I think we should pick up some good Creole food and just hang out. It's been a long day. I hope you changed the sheets on my bed."

Sophie shrugged. Jessie laughed.

It was three in the morning when Sophie rolled the three empty wine bottles across the living-room floor. "We probably should call it a night," she mumbled.

"Why?"

"Because, that's why. Are you sure you don't want me to run a check on the Kingsley family? It would be my pleasure. This will be a com . . . com-pre-hen-sive report. If you're even thinking about getting involved with the son, then we need to know everything there is to know. Even if you aren't going to get involved, it won't hurt to know what makes the family tick. I met this guy last year, and he can do *anything*. I really learned how to network these past two years. You said something earlier that's been tickling my brain."

"Your brain is on overload, Sophie."

"Be serious, Jessie. Remember when you told me Agnes Prentis died a month after her husband passed away?"

"Yes, it was sad. She was really a nice lady, and she worked for the senator for over twenty years. I went to the funeral with the senator. There was hardly anyone there. I felt so bad for her. I still have all those logs she gave me for reference."

"That's what I'm talking about. I think you should pack them all up, even the ones you started, and mail them to my house in Atlanta. Don't ask me why because I don't know why. It's just a gut feeling. Each time you finish a log, send it to the house. Just mark Sophie's Books on the outside and the housekeeper will store them for me. Will you do it?"

"Are you into some kind of spy stuff? You're making me nervous, Sophie. They're just logs about what went on on a daily basis. Mostly they were Agnes's observations. That's what mine are."

"Does anyone know you keep a log, Jessie?"

"I didn't tell anyone if that's what you mean. I keep a log for the office. It's more like a detailed appointment book. It's very succinct."

"Then why do you keep a private one?"

"Because . . . because Agnes Prentis told me to keep one. It's a habit now more than anything. Are you suggesting something I'm not picking up on?"

"Washington is a shitty place, Jessie. All those lobbyists and power brokers. I've heard stories about how deals are cut and the way votes are bought and sold. Your guy has been in there a long time. There is no reason to believe he doesn't have a few skeletons. When the dark brown stuff hits the fan, it splatters everyone. In Washington innocent people get branded all the time. Angus Kingsley is a powerhouse and powerhouses get blown down from time to time, and it usually isn't their own doing either. There's always going to be fresh meat snapping at his heels. I don't want to see you caught up in something out of your control."

Jessie felt the fine hairs on the back of her neck start to bristle. Sophie was always right, always on the money, and she had never been an alarmist. "Okay, I'll pack them up and send them off as soon as I get back. Go ahead and do the check. It can't hurt anything. It will be discreet, won't it?"

"Attagirl, Jess. Of course it will be discreet. Forewarned is forearmed. A girl has to be careful these days."

"What about you, Sophie? Did you do a check on your guy?"

"Didn't have to. He's exactly who he says he is. Which is another way of saying he is a civil engineer with the firm that I'm going to intern with. Douglas, Doheny, and McGuire is one of the top firms in the country. They have forty-four engineers and fifty-three architects on their payroll. That doesn't count the office staff. Jack comes from a stable, normal family. I met him through a friend last year. Both his parents are schoolteachers. He has two brothers and two sisters. He's the third child. He worked his way through school waiting tables and making pizza deliveries. He has a mountain of student loans. His parents helped, too, but there are two sets of aging grandparents that have to be taken care of. He took me home to meet his parents in August. They're rowdy, boisterous, and very, very loving. Mr. Dawson holds Mrs. Dawson's hand, and he kisses her on the cheek all the time. The siblings adore each other, and they know what everyone else is doing. The family is very sharing. If one of them needs help, the others drop what they're doing and pitch in. They have an old dog named Mandy, who poops in the same spot every day. No one gets excited. Whoever sees it first cleans it up. The dog is old but a real love. His parents love me. They're a *real family,* Jess, the kind of family you and I hungered for but never got. I want to belong to them so bad I can taste it. Jack's dad told him not to let me get away. I told a lie, though, Jess. I told him I went to school on loans, too. I made up this whole new identity for myself. Actually, it's pretty pitiful that I would do such a thing. Now I regret doing it. I have to give it a lot of thought before I make a serious commitment. Jack is big on being up front and truthful. In a million years he would never understand my mother and the way it was. Never, ever. By the way, his name is Jack Dawson. My toes curl up every time I see him."

"Why didn't he come to your graduation?"

"Because he's working in Memphis. He starts with the firm I'm going with on Monday. He'll be here sometime later this week. He's going to Costa Rica, too. You'll get to meet him. He didn't have the money for the trip. Do you know what his favorite saying is? Poverty builds character."

Jessie cut to the chase. "So, tell me, how is he in bed?"

"In a word, *spectacular!*"

Jessie rolled on the floor laughing as Sophie uncorked a fourth bottle of wine. "We're blitzed, you know."

"So what! This is your day. Well, yesterday was your day. It's a new day now. How am I going to meet Tanner Kingsley? Did I tell you he has summer blue eyes? Remember those bluebells that used to grow by the playhouse? Same color. He's all golden bronze, and his hair is bleached. He has a cleft in his chin and one dimple. Only one. Isn't that strange?"

"You noticed all of that in five seconds! I'm impressed," Sophie said dryly.

"It was longer than five seconds. I couldn't talk, so I stared."

"Invite yourself for the holidays. Pull that lonely stunt and maybe the senator will feel sorry for you. We can rehearse tomorrow so you come off naturally."

"I could never do that."

"Like hell you can't. If you can stand up on a chair in an auditorium packed with people and hoot and holler you can do anything! We'll rehearse tomorrow. My mother got married again."

"Really," was all Jessie could think of to say.

"Some Polish count. He has a lot of z's in his name. The card and check were mailed in Argentina. Imagine that," Sophie said bursting into tears.

"Shhh, don't cry, Sophie. Someday when you're least expecting it she'll show up and want to act like a real mother. You'll see. I think she's afraid to grow old, and having a beautiful, brilliant daughter like you makes her realize her life is empty. Even you must realize jealousy plays a big part in the way she acts. She's trying to fill her life with all the wrong things. Don't hate her. If anything, you should feel sorry for her. You have everything going for you, Sophie. Don't let her get to you. The chair wasn't really empty. I put my coat and purse on it. Nobody paid any attention to the damn thing until I stood up on it."

"You're right. Especially the part about me being beautiful and brilliant. You have so much common sense it's downright scary. What do you think she'll do when I have my first child?"

"She'll get another face lift, a tummy tuck, and buy herself a twenty-year-old husband no one else wants. Then she'll start to think about your child and want to be part of his or her life. It will be up to you what you do at that point. Sophie, you can't start a relationship on a lie. That goes for marriage, too. If your guy doesn't understand, then he's not the one for you. If you need me for backup or verification, just call."

Sophie nodded. "What about you, Jess? Do you still hate *them?*"

"Sometimes I think I do. I don't like them. Sometimes I think I'm the only person in the world who doesn't love their parents. I'm not talking about you, Sophie. In your heart you love your mother. I don't. I wish I could understand my feelings, but I can't. They meant well I suppose. It's me. I don't *feel* anything for them. I don't even miss them. I rarely think of them. I haven't touched the trust fund at all. I doubt if I ever will. I'd rather borrow money from you and pay you back."

"We're at a turning point in our lives right now. You know that, don't you, Jess?"

"I was thinking the same thing myself earlier today. How strange that both of us are on the same wavelength. It's kind of scary but exhilarating at the same time. We'll make it. Guess what. By the time you're back, I should have my degree. Do you mind if I sleep right here on the floor?"

"Nope. That's where I'm going to sleep. If I had a gold star, I'd paste it on your forehead, Jessie Roland." Sophie tossed two pillows from the cluttered sofa in Jessie's direction. "Night, good friend. Thanks, Jessie, for everything."

"My pleasure. Night, Sophie."

Chapter Seven

"Are you sure we have everything, Ben? I'm ready for this, but I'm not ready if you know what I mean. I said I wasn't going to cry and what am I doing? I'm bawling my head off, and we aren't even out of the driveway. What is going to happen to me when we have to drive away and leave John at Clemson?"

"We aren't losing John. He'll come home holidays and summers. In case you haven't noticed, our oldest son is all grown-up. He even has a girlfriend. All the other mothers will be crying, too, and the fathers will be just as choked up as me. We'll get through it. It's not like . . . before. We know John will come back. If you hold on to that, everything will be okay."

Grace wiped at her eyes. "Next year Joseph will be going away, too. I wish . . . Oh, Ben, I wish so many things. She should be here with us. If things had worked out, Hannah would have graduated already. I pray every night, Ben, that when our daughter turns twenty-five she'll start to remember and search for us. I don't know why I've attached so much importance to the number twenty-five. Coming of age, that sort of thing, I guess. Ben, what if she went to Clemson and is back there for Alumni Day or something like that and we see her and not realize it's Hannah. What if that happens, Ben?"

"Stop doing this to yourself, Grace. This is John's day. Let's not spoil it for him. He's having his own separation anxieties today just the way we are. We have to make this work for him. The first Larson to go to college! I'm so damn proud I could bust!"

"Speaking of busting, look at your dad, then look at mine. Two cars and a truck to get one boy off to college. It's amazing."

"It makes sense. John and I will go in the truck. All his gear and trunks go in the back. My parents and your parents go in one car, and you and Joe go in your car."

"Here comes the first Larson to go to college. Mom's got the camera. Our boy is going to be just fine. We taught him right from wrong. He's a hard worker and knows the value of a dollar. He won't disappoint himself or our family. That's a given."

Panic rivered through Grace. "Ben, what if he meets Hannah somewhere and doesn't know it's her. What if, Ben?"

"Grace, stop it! Don't ruin everything. If there is one thing we don't want, it's John feeling guilty about going off to school."

Grace choked back a sob. She nodded. If there was one thing she didn't want to do it was ruin John's day. He'd worked too hard to have her blow up and spoil things. She forced a smile.

Ben heaved a sigh of relief as he stared at his wife. The years had taken a terrible toll on Grace. It seemed like her hair had turned gray overnight, and what he had thought of as temporary frown lines were now deep grooves etched into her forehead and around her eyes. He reached for her rough, worn hand. Grace clasped his tightly.

"Here he comes!" the elder Larson shouted. The family

clapped their hands as John bowed low to the family applause.

"I have something to say," the young man said seriously.

"Hear, hear!" Ben said.

"I just want to say thanks for everything all these years. I promise to call once a week. I'll say my prayers every night, and I'll brush after each meal. I'll give it everything I got so you won't be disappointed in me." His voice choked up when he said, "I'm going to miss all of you. What I'm not going to miss is mowing the grass, raking the leaves, and shoveling snow. That's your job now, Joe," he said, hugging his brother.

Grace took a step backward. He was so handsome, this son of hers. He was also a warm, caring, sensitive boy. The day he turned thirteen she'd gone to him and asked him if he wanted Hannah's room. He'd looked so shocked and when he finally found his voice he said the only thing that could possibly have made her feel better. "No way, Mom. I'd just have to move my stuff out when she comes back." Hannah's room was still intact, but these days the door was open instead of closed.

He had her in his arms then. He whispered in her ear. "I think I know what you're thinking and feeling, Mom. It's okay. She's coming back. I just don't know when. It'll happen. You know I never lied to you. Not ever. I love you, Mom."

Grace felt herself choke up. "Get in the truck," she said as she hugged her son so tight he groaned.

As the miniparade made its way through the small town, the shopkeepers waved and shouted, "Good luck, John." Grace basked in their good wishes for her son.

If only . . .

Washington, D.C.
December 1979

The lights on the small artificial Christmas tree began to twinkle the moment Jessie turned on the switch. She frowned. For some reason the tree seemed out of place today. Maybe it was the absence of presents. The staff had taken their gifts the previous day at the senator's insistence when they left for the holiday recess.

Her eyes filled as she wondered how she would fill her time until January 3, when Washington returned to work. She was so looking forward to Sophie's return next month.

"Jessie, you're crying. What's wrong?" The concern in the senator's voice allowed the tears to overflow.

"For a moment I was feeling melancholy. I was just thinking the tree looks . . . I don't know, out of place. You know, not real. Someday I'm going to have a real tree that smells. Is there anything you want me to do before you leave?" Jessie dabbed at her eyes and blew her nose.

"My dear, you run this office so efficiently I would be hard-pressed to find anything that needed to be done. I have plenty of time. I'm not leaving until later this evening. I feel at loose ends myself. Why don't you make a fresh pot of coffee, and the two of us can sit down and talk. We haven't done that in a long time. You're right about the tree. It's sorry-looking. Spindly, too. The truth is, it's downright tacky. Where did we get it?"

"It was in the closet. I assume Mrs. Prentis bought it at some point. I think I'll throw it away when I take it down after New Year's."

"Good thinking, Jessie."

"Do you have a real tree at the ranch?"

"Lord no. Alexis has one of those god-awful white things she decorates with blue balls and blue lights. The house always reminds me of a science-fiction movie at

Christmastime. She likes to entertain during the holidays. Growing up, my parents always had real balsam, and my brothers and I would string popcorn and cranberries to hang on the tree. My mother saved all our school projects and hung them on the tree, too. On Christmas Eve my father would light these tiny candles, and we'd all sing carols. My mother played the piano. It was a wonderful time for all of us. I wanted the same kind of Christmas for Tanner, but Alexis wouldn't hear of it. She hates pine needles, and balsam makes her sneeze." He sighed as he loosened his tie. "I think we should add some of this fine Kentucky bourbon to this fine coffee. What do you think, Jessie?"

"I think you should do whatever you want, Senator, as long as you don't get behind the wheel of a car. I don't like anything in my coffee, but I'll be glad to fix yours. Carrying all those presents on the plane is going to be rather awkward. I could have boxed them for you or sent them by UPS."

The senator yanked at his tie, removing it altogether. "They aren't going to Texas." He finger combed his bushy hair, his eyes on Jessie for her reaction.

"Oh."

The senator leaned back into the softness of the leather sofa. "One of the things I like most about you is that you mind your own business. After six years, I know you know about Irene Marshall. Agnes knew, too. Hell, everyone in this damn town knows about my relationship with Irene. Alexis knows about it, too, but pretends she doesn't. Tanner looks the other way. My son is not judgmental. As a matter of fact, Tanner adores Irene. She knitted him a sweater when he was in high school. He still wears it, to Alexis's chagrin. It has holes in it, and one of the sleeves is unraveling, but he doesn't care."

There didn't seem to be anything to say to the senator's

confession, so Jessie sipped at her coffee, her eyes down-cast.

"What are you going to do over the holidays, Jessie?"

"Study I guess. Perhaps I'll do some shopping. Watch television. Sleep late. Clean my apartment."

"Are you saying you're going to be alone?"

"Yes. Sophie is still in Costa Rica. We always spent Christmas together. She flew home the last two years."

The senator reached for the bourbon bottle. He splashed a goodly amount into his cup. "People shouldn't be alone on the holidays. Why is that, Jessie?"

"Christmas is a time of sharing. Parents expect their children to come home for Christmas. It's that one time of year when everyone seems to put problems aside as they try to recapture past childhood holidays. If you knew your wife was planning an old-fashioned Christmas like your mother made for you as a child, you wouldn't be able to wait to get home instead of dreading it."

"Another time, another place, and that statement would be true. Unfortunately, today it isn't, my dear. How did you get to be so intuitive at such a young age?"

Jessie shrugged. "Sophie helped. I could have gone to Costa Rica. Even though she'll be home next month, Sophie offered to send me a ticket. I said no. I'll see her next month."

More bourbon splashed into the empty coffee cup. "Come to Texas with me."

Jessie's jaw dropped. "That would be too much of an imposition, Senator. I don't think your wife would appreciate an unannounced guest for two weeks."

"It's my ranch, Jessie. That means the house is mine. It was left to me by my grandfather. I can invite whomever I want whenever I want. I would be honored to have you as my guest. I think you might like Tanner. He could teach you to ride. I wish that boy had a yen for politics, but he doesn't. He stands up to his mother. I admire that. She has a girl all picked out for him. She's not someone I would pick for a daughter-in-law. Tanner doesn't think so either. The girl's family is socially prominent and quite wealthy. Her family's wells are still producing whereas ours dried up years ago. It's all right, we made our fortunes, and they're intact. Our only problems now are water rights." More bourbon found its way to the cup. "So, are you coming or not?"

"Senator, I'm not prepared. This is the last minute, you know." It was working out just the way Sophie said it would, and she hadn't done a thing to promote the situation. Perhaps it was meant to be.

"Are you telling me you can't pull this off? Jessie Roland who can do the impossible. The same Jessie Roland who can fend off the ghouls with one look. The Jessie Roland who makes this office hum efficiently. That Jessie. How difficult is it to pack a bag and pull the plugs on appliances? I can drop you off and wait till you pack. Then we can deliver the gifts to Irene and head for the airport. Sometimes you need to do spontaneous things. This is spontaneous. Well?"

Did she really want to do this? Did she want to spend two weeks wandering around an empty apartment? Did she want to cry herself to sleep on Christmas Eve? The bottom line was did she *really* want to be alone? "All right, Senator. I accept your invitation. Will I need party clothes?"

"I expect so. Jeans, too."

"I picked up your cleaning and laundry today, Senator. You might want to freshen up if you're going to be delivering presents. A fresh shirt makes all the difference. A cup of strong coffee with nothing in it will also help."

The senator's head bobbed up and down. "I never spent one holiday with Irene in all the years I've known her. God knows I wanted to. Did you buy me a present, Jessie?"

"It's under the tree, Senator."

"I bought one for you, too. It's in the bag with the family presents. Can I open mine now?"

Jessie smiled. Sometimes the senator was like a child. She handed him the small package.

The senator's shoulders started to shake when he held the small gift in his hand. "My mother gave me one of these when I was six years old. Alexis threw it out when we got married. She said it was junk. I didn't know she threw it out until it was too late. Wherever did you find this, Jessie?"

"In an antique store in Georgetown. It's not new."

The senator turned the small globe upside down. A Christmas tree in a globe with snow. "Child, you couldn't have given me anything better than this. The fact that it's old is all the more reason for me to treasure it. For all I know it could be the one Alexis threw away."

Jessie pretended not to see the older man's eyes fill with tears. "I'm glad you like it. I'll clean up here while you change your shirt."

As Jessie tidied up the office her gaze kept going to the beribboned stack of presents on the senator's desk. She wondered what was in the exquisitely wrapped packages. Baubles, bangles, jewels? What would a man like the senator buy his paramour? What did she look like? Was she a long-legged beauty with a golden cascade of hair and a shape to die for? How did the presents on the desk stack up to what he bought his wife? What would a father like the senator buy his son Tanner? New riding boots? A horse? A new car? The thought of seeing the surprise on

Tanner Kingsley's face when she walked through the door with his father set her body tingling. Would he remember seeing her at the airport?

Angus Kingsley emerged from the lavatory and shrugged into his jacket. His hair was freshly combed, but the moment they went outdoors it would be all over his head like a wild bush. He'd obviously run the razor over his face, too. Jessie held his topcoat for him.

"Why aren't you married, Jessie?"

Taken by surprise she smiled. "I guess my white knight hasn't found me yet. I have things to do and places to go before I take a step like that. I'm not finished with school yet. I want my degree in hand. I think I can finish up next semester."

"Will you leave me then?"

"I don't know, Senator."

"I don't think I'm going to run again next term. Campaigning is becoming too dirty to suit me, and I'm not getting any younger."

"I think the season is getting to you, Senator. You belong here. In many ways this is your home. You still have a lot of things to do for your constituents. You'll feel differently when you return from recess."

"No, I won't. I'm an old warhorse who has seen his time come and go. It's a wise man who knows when it's time to stop and smell the roses."

Jessie didn't know how to respond to the senator's statement. He seemed lost, sad, and very melancholy. The way she'd been earlier. By most standards sixty-six was still considered young. Strom Thurmond was old. He even *looked* old. Claude Pepper was old. He looked *ancient*. "I have some shopping bags someplace," she muttered. "Do you want me to call Clarence to come for the bags, or do you think we can manage?"

"We can manage. They do look pretty, don't they?"

"They're gorgeous, Senator. Will Miss Irene think you wrapped them yourself?"

The senator made a sound that was supposed to be laughter. "She knows better. She saves all that folderol. She has boxes and boxes of it. I pay extra for the wrapping just to see the smile on her face. I think she likes the trappings more than the gifts. I want you to know, Jessie, I did my own shopping this year. You were right, my dear, it isn't the gift but the thought that counts. We'll see if that axiom is right when my wife opens her gift."

"I think this is the last of it. It's going to be a wonderful Christmas for Miss Irene."

"Oh, these aren't all for Irene. Two are for her son Andrew and two are for Connie. They're twins and in their last year of college."

"I'm ready, Senator. Will we be going to my apartment first?"

"I'd like you to meet Irene and the twins, Jessie. They live right off Dupont Circle, so it's on the way to your apartment. That's if you don't mind. Irene makes her own eggnog, and I know she'd like us to share a cup with her. If it makes you uncomfortable, I understand."

He's looking for approval, Jessie thought. *God, why me?* He was holding his breath waiting for her answer. She could tell he really wanted her to go with him. She smiled. "I'd like that, Senator. You're sure she won't mind."

"Irene loves young people. She won't mind at all. Did you call Clarence?"

"He's waiting for us. I think it's going to snow. A white Christmas would be nice."

"I haven't seen one of those for a long time. We aren't even out the door, and I miss this place."

"Didn't you just say you weren't going to run again?" The senator laughed ruefully. The sound sent chills up Jessie's arms.

There was little traffic in the middle of the afternoon, so the driver made good time before he stopped at a small Tudor house set on a well-landscaped lawn. Jessie could see Christmas lights sprinkled among the fragrant outdoor evergreens. A large, fresh pungent wreath with a giant red bow adorned the front door.

Before the senator could ring the bell he turned to Jessie, and said, "Jessie, I will never apologize or defend my relationship with Irene. This might sound dated and corny to your ears, but this wonderful lady is the wind beneath my wings. I do not like judgmental people. People fail to see that things are not always black or white. Enough said."

"Angus! How wonderful! And you must be Jessie. My dear, Angus talks about you so much I feel like I've known you forever. She's just as pretty as you said she was. Would you listen to me. Come in, come in. It's cold out there."

Jessie stared at the woman and hoped her surprise wasn't etched on her face. This was no glamorous, long-legged beauty. This lady was probably the same age as the senator, perhaps a year or two younger. She was plump, pink-cheeked with springy gray curls and wore wire-rimmed glasses. *She laughs a lot*, Jessie thought.

"I wasn't sure if you'd make it or not, Angus. I'm sorry, but the twins aren't here. They went ice-skating with some of their friends. They'll be sorry they missed you. Shall we have our eggnog in the kitchen or the living room? The tree is up and decorated, and I do have a nice fire going."

"Then it's the living room. Jessie and I were talking earlier about people who have real trees that smell up the whole house. It's a beauty this year, Irene. I wanted Jessie to see how you decorate for the holidays."

"It's . . . heavenly, Mrs. Marshall."

"Stop right there with the Mrs. Marshall business. My friends call me Irene."

"It must take you a very long time to do all this," Jessie said looking around.

"I start early. I'm a collector, and this is the time of year I get to put out all my treasures. A lot of my things were passed down to me by my mother and my grandmother. My daughter will carry on the tradition someday. I just love this time of year," she bubbled. The senator smiled indulgently.

"I love a fireplace with a roaring fire," Jessie said, sitting down on the hearth. "It sort of brings a room together. I like cozy rooms."

"One of my neighbors brought me a load of cherry wood and some birch. It burns slow and steady. It doesn't smoke up the room." Irene's voice turned fretful when she said, "Lately, I can't seem to get warm. The twins fuss at me to turn the thermostat down. Of course they're wearing two sweaters, and I'm in short sleeves." Jessie took that moment to look across the room at the senator. There was so much pain etched in his face she was dumbfounded. Something was happening here she didn't understand.

The senator's voice was gruff and unsteady-sounding when he said, "Irene, do you have any of your famous cookies? I'd like Jessie to taste them."

"Of course I do, Angus. I made them this morning when you said you would stop by." The tense moment passed when Irene bustled out to the kitchen. She returned a moment later with an elegant silver tray loaded with fat raisin-filled cookies.

The hour-long visit passed pleasantly, but there was an undertone of something Jessie couldn't define. When it was time to leave it was her suggestion the driver take her to her apartment and pick up the senator on the way back. He agreed.

"Would you excuse us a moment, Irene."

"Of course. I need to check on my pot roast."

The senator's jaw dropped. "You're making pot roast?"

"That's what I said, Angus. The twins love it as much as you do. Potato pancakes, too." Angus groaned.

"Jessie, my dear, I have something to tell you. I'm afraid I brought you here under false pretenses. I'm not going to Texas."

"I don't understand, Senator. You invited me to go with you. Do you want me to leave? Should I call your family?"

"Jessie, I don't think I've ever seen you so frazzled. I think you'll understand when I explain. I've never spent a holiday with Irene and her children. This will be . . . this will be . . . Irene's last Christmas. She's terminally ill. I thought I could leave, but I can't. I want you to go to Texas. You will tell my family exactly what I tell you to say, which is I've been detained. It is doubtful if I'll make it to Texas at all. Beyond that you know nothing. Alexis knows you would never discuss office business with her. You can call me here if you need me. Irene plans to tell the twins about her condition after New Year's. She wants this Christmas to be special. If I could turn the clock backwards, I would do things so differently. I don't know what I'm going to do when she's gone, Jessie. I truly do not know. I realize I'm asking you to lie in a manner of speaking. By the same token you are merely following instructions. In this case I can only hope the end justifies the means. Tanner will entertain you while you're there. It's going to be good for you to mix with young people. All you do is work and study. I know you can handle this, Jessie. The twins are going to need me. Will you do it, Jessie?"

"Of course I'll do it."

"Good girl. My gifts for you, Tanner, and his mother

are in the car. Put them under the tree when you get to the ranch. I'll call you tomorrow." He handed her a small card. "This is Irene's number. Don't let Alexis get hold of it. There's a private line in my study with no extensions. Use that phone if you want to call me. I think you're going to like my son, Jessie. I know he'll like you. Tolerate Alexis for both our sakes."

"I'd like to say good-bye to Irene, Senator."

"Of course you would. Irene!" the senator bellowed.

"Good grief, Angus, I was just in the kitchen. You aren't on the senate floor, you know."

"Jessie wants to say good-bye. I won't be saying good-bye. I'm staying until January 3, when Congress reconvenes."

Irene's eyes filled with tears as she hugged Jessie. She whispered in her ear. "This is just a guess on my part, but I think Angus is playing the role of matchmaker. You will adore Tanner. You are exactly what he needs. Have a safe trip, and thank you for making this holiday so very special for me. Merry Christmas, Jessie Roland."

"Merry Christmas, Mrs. . . . Irene. Merry Christmas, Senator."

"Thank you for making this easy for me, Jessie. Have a safe trip. Clarence has your ticket."

Outside in the crisp December air, Jessie drew a deep breath as she tried to clear her head. She could think about this past hour when she was on the plane. Her heavy purse banged against her leg as she climbed into the car. When she got to her apartment, if she had time after packing, she'd write the day's events in the log and hide it under her mattress. Or was this one of those things that were better left unrecorded? Agnes Prentis had said, "Write down *everything* regardless of what it is or how personal you might consider it and *never, never*, make light of your own part in the day-to-day operation. When the chips fall, and they will fall, you have to be in the right position to catch some of them." Whatever that meant.

The small glossy shopping bag on the floor of the car caught her eye. Three presents sat on the bottom of the bag. Two of the three were wrapped in wrinkled green tissue paper with shiny red ribbons. The third was professionally gift wrapped in shiny gold foil with a shimmering red bow. She knew without question the senator had wrapped two of the gifts himself. She rather thought it was the senator's way of making a statement. She smiled when she closed her eyes to envision the exquisitely wrapped presents she'd helped to carry into Irene Marshall's small comfortable home. She crossed her fingers, the way she had when she was a small girl, that the senator and Irene's Christmas would be all they wanted it to be.

Jessie looked around the crowded terminal for some sign of Tanner Kingsley. Baggage in hand, she waited next to the baggage carousel as the senator had instructed. Fifteen minutes later she was still waiting. The milling crowds had thinned a little, offering her a better view of the harried travelers. The senator had said Tanner would be waiting in the baggage area. This trip was a mistake. Maybe what she should do was find a messenger to deliver the gifts to the ranch and take the next plane back to Washington. She detested inconsiderate people. Especially inconsiderate rich people. A curl of anger circled her stomach when twenty more minutes went by with no sign of Tanner Kingsley.

"That does it!" she muttered. There was no excuse for someone being thirty-five minutes late. There had been no page for the senator either. Inexcusable. Absolutely inexcusable.

Dragging her bags, her purse, and the shiny shopping

bag, Jessie made her way to a bank of telephones, where she dialed Irene's number. "This is Jessie. I'm sorry to bother you, but I need to speak to Senator Kingsley. No, everything is not fine. The senator can explain it to you when he hangs up. Senator, this is Jessie. I'm at the airport, and your son is not here. I've been waiting for over forty minutes. I'm angry and as soon as I can find a messenger to deliver these gifts to your ranch, I'm taking the next plane back to Washington. I'm sorry I allowed you to talk me into this. Yes, I'm very angry. I'm glad you never saw me angry. I'm not a nice person when I'm angry. I deplore inconsiderate, thoughtless people. I'm referring to your son Tanner, not you, Senator. Of course I listened to the pages. They did not call your name or mine. No, Senator, I will not hire a car service or take a taxi. I told you, I'm taking the next plane to Washington. I'm hungry and I'm tired. My friend Sophie would call your son a shit. I think I agree with that assessment. Have a nice holiday, Senator. Good-bye." Jessie slammed the receiver so hard into the cradle it bounced out and hung drunkenly on its curled metal cord.

Seething with anger, Jessie slammed it again. This time it stayed in place. She turned to see a pair of summer blue eyes laughing at her. "I can truthfully say I've never been called a shit before."

"Really," was all Jessie could think of to say. Her backbone stiffened. "A shit is someone who keeps someone else waiting for fifty minutes without a word of explanation. Here, the senator asked me to deliver these. Merry Christmas."

"Hey! Wait just a damn minute."

"Don't tell me to wait just a damn minute. Get out of my way."

The laughter in Tanner's voice only made her more angry. "How did you know I was the shit in question?"

"I see your stupid picture every day, that's how. I even have to dust it. Guess what, I won't do that again."

"Look, I don't even know who the hell you are. I came here to pick up my father. When I didn't see him I went to the bar. I was on time. I didn't know I was supposed to pick *you* up. I knew Pop would come into the bar. I just assumed he met someone and lost track of time. He holds meetings in the john, on sidewalks, in the rain, in the snow, and sometimes on horseback. You're his secretary, I presume, so that means you should have taken your job seriously and called ahead. Did you do that? No, you did not. I'm a victim here. How long are you going to stay mad? We should go to the bar and talk this out. Then if you don't want to stay, you can leave. Do you really think I'm a shit?"

"You look like one," Jessie snapped.

"Pop said you were one of a kind. He said I would like you. I hate it when he's right. That means I like you. Are we going to have that drink or not?"

"What time is the next flight?"

"Probably an hour or so."

"Probably isn't good enough. I need to know exactly when the plane leaves, so I can change my ticket."

"I guess that means you want me to check it out."

"Since it's your fault, I'd say that's an accurate assumption."

"You want to know something? My mother isn't going to like you. Not even one little bit."

"Ask me if I care," Jessie said, her voice ringing with sourness. "No manners either."

"I heard that."

"You were supposed to hear it. I don't talk just to hear myself, and I never say anything I don't mean. Run along and don't make a mistake on the time."

"Run along! You're telling me to run along! No one has said that to me since I was in the first grade. Where the hell did Pop find you?"

"In the Rose Garden at the White House," Jessie shot back. "Insufferable."

"I heard that, too. Makes sense, in and about the thorns. Prickly as all hell."

"I heard that."

Tanner threw back his head and roared with laughter. People turned around to stare at him, amused expressions on their weary faces. "My mother is definitely not going to like you."

"I really don't care, Mr. Kingsley, what your mother thinks of me. Since I'm not going to your ranch, I don't see that it matters. What time is the next flight?"

"Two hours and ten minutes. I guess that means we have time for that drink after all. Hemlock, Miss Jessie?"

"For two," Jessie shot back.

In the dimly lit bar, Jessie ordered a gin and tonic. Tanner ordered a Coors.

"We should make a toast," Tanner said, holding his beer bottle aloft. "Let's make it to meaningful apologies and new beginnings."

"Okay." Jessie's glass clinked against Tanner's bottle.

"I'm Tanner Kingsley, and you are?"

"Jessie Roland."

"Obviously you feel the need to place blame, and I can't fault you for that. It's Pop's fault. He should have told you I'd be in the bar. Obviously he had other things on his mind. How is Irene?"

"Irene who?"

Tanner swallowed a mouthful of beer. "Ookayy. Is Pop coming home for Christmas?"

"Your father said to tell you he's been detained. He sent a gift for you and your mother."

"That's it, he's been detained. Would you care to elaborate?"

"No."

"Is he coming at any point during the season?"

"He said it was doubtful."

"My mother isn't going to like this. She must have scheduled at least two dozen parties. No, she is not going to like this at all. I meant it when I said she won't like you. I'm not trying to be brash and unkind. You'll pick up on it in five seconds. My mother is one of those people who can make you feel like hell just by looking at you."

"Since I won't be there to give her the chance, what difference does it make?"

"I thought we went beyond that. Speaking strictly for myself, I'd like the opportunity to show you around the ranch and take you into Corpus Christi. My mother's parties are boring, and she's forever trying to fix me up with one of her friend's daughters. She does the same thing with my sister, Resa. You'll like Resa. She teaches school. It's the only profession my mother thought was fit for a proper young lady. She doesn't come home much and prefers to live in town. Christmas is pretty much a command performance if you know what I mean. Then there's Pop. Whatever he has going for himself right about now is going to be spoiled if you return. I think he was counting on you to take up his slack."

"Oh."

"Yeah, oh. What do you say? I'll keep you under my wing twenty-four hours a day so the wicked Texas witch doesn't get to you."

"You sound like you don't like your mother."

"You're right. I don't like her. I love her because she's my mother but that doesn't mean I have to like her. Resa feels the same way. Pop doesn't feel anything. I'm sure you picked up on that early on. As kids, Resa and I knew our parents were different. How could it not be different with a mother who lives in Texas and a father who lives in Washington, D.C.? I guess you know all that."

"I don't know anything about your family. Your father doesn't talk about you or your mother to me."

"He used to confide in Agnes. I guess I thought he'd do the same with you. She kept diaries."

Jessie's heart skipped a beat. "A lot of women keep diaries. I did myself when I was younger."

"So, are you staying or going?"

"It probably wasn't a wise idea for me to come here at all. I find it very difficult to say no to your father. He was concerned that I was going to be alone for the holidays and that's why he invited me. I won't feel comfortable, and obviously your mother doesn't know about me."

"Surprises are wonderful! Please, change your mind and come with me. You don't really want to be alone for the holidays, do you?"

"No, not really. On the other hand I have no desire to be abused by your mother. I've had enough of domineering mothers to last me a lifetime."

"I'm not even going to ask what that means. So, if you're ready, let's hit the road and head for the ranch. It's a good hour's ride."

Jessie finished her drink. "I know this is a bad idea. I'm only doing this so I don't let your father down."

Tanner reached for her bags. "You didn't tell me how Irene is doing."

"Irene who? How would I know how she is, whoever she is."

"She's my old man's lady friend is who she is. I know you know, and I know that you know I know. She's a very nice lady. She's the kind of mother every kid should have. I really like her. When I was in D.C. last time Pop told me she was very ill. I asked because I genuinely care how she is."

"If you know who she is, why don't you call her and ask how she's feeling? People who care do things like that. It isn't that hard to pick up the phone to make a call. It might be nice to send a Christmas plant if she isn't feeling well. Poinsettias are lovely at this time of year. You could even send more than one."

"You are tight-lipped, aren't you?"

"Is that a compliment or a criticism?"

"Actually, it's both. If anything happens to Irene, Pop will leave Washington."

"How do you know that?" Jessie asked.

"Because he told me. I always thought he'd stay until they voted him out or he died in his office. He's not big on ranch life these last ten years. He can handle it for a few days at a time. I don't think he could live here year-round."

"Why doesn't your mother live in Washington? If it's none of my business just say so."

"She won't play second fiddle to a fat little nobody with gray hair. That's how she views Irene. She totally ignores the fact that Irene was a federal judge until four years ago when she got sick. She retired three months after her diagnosis. I've known Irene since I was a senior in high school visiting Dad on spring breaks. She makes the best cookies you ever ate."

"I don't think you should be telling me things like this. Your father might not want me to know about your personal lives."

"So, what do you think of my truck?"

"It's a kidney crusher," Jessie said as they bounced along a rutted road. "Don't you have highways here?"

"We're taking the scenic route. It chops off seven miles. This truck was my father's first vehicle. I can crank this old girl up to seventy and zip right through the pasture and not miss a beat. I bet you're wondering if I take my dates out in this."

"I wasn't wondering any such thing." He was just like his father in the sense that he could read her mind.

"I do it once. If they balk, I don't ask them out again. My wheels shouldn't be important. What's your opinion, Jessie Roland?"

"If I was dressed up, and you showed up in this manure-smelling vehicle, I'd tell you to go fly a kite. If I was dressed for pumpkin picking or cow tipping, I might consider driving in it. Then again I might not. I'm really hungry."

"Why didn't you say something?"

"Why didn't you ask?"

"Are you always so prickly? Do you ever smile? Are you engaged or dating anyone? Do you like making slow love for hours at a time, or do you like that wild, animal stuff?"

Jessie felt herself cringe. Virgin that she was, she wasn't sure how to respond. Damn, Sophie would have turned on a dime and given him a shot he wouldn't forget.

"Well? Cat got your tongue?"

"No. I was thinking how best to respond so you would understand. I like a man with slow hands who knows what to do with those hands and who follows instructions to the letter. Anything less is totally unacceptable. Sex in my opinion is an *event*." *Sophie, you would be so proud of me*. The fact that her body felt like it was on fire was something else.

"An *event*?" Tanner's voice sounded nervous.

Jessie's head bobbed up and down. "An event. You gotta measure up." She hoped the laughter bubbling up in her chest wasn't obvious to the handsome man sitting next to her.

"Measure up?"

"Hmmnn. Yes, measure up."

"What does that mean *exactly?*" The voice was jittery-sounding now.

"What do you think it means?"

"Hell, it could mean any number of things."

"Like what? Name me something."

"This is a stupid conversation," Tanner said.

"Yes it is, considering you just met me."

"I was just trying to put you at ease by being friendly."

"Why didn't you just ask me what color my underwear is."

"What color is it?" She'd never heard a strangled voice before.

"Yellow."

"Yellow is a nice color. I like yellow."

"What color is yours? Do you wear those baggy things or those tight cotton ones?"

"Why do you want to know?"

"I want to put it in my memory sampler. Well?"

"The tight white ones, only they aren't *really* tight."

"Tsk, tsk," Jessie clucked her tongue. "I just read an article in a leading health magazine that said underwear like that reduced men's sperm count to zero."

"You better not talk like that in front of my mother."

"You started it."

"Then I'm finishing it. Have you been to the Washington Monument?"

"No. I don't think I'm going to like your mother."

"At least you'll start out even. Is there anything else you think I should know?"

"Like what?"

"You know, size, weight, size. I said that, didn't I?"

"Yes. 34-23-34. Perfect size eight. Weight 110. And your measurements?"

"Have you seen the Lincoln Memorial?"

"Yes."

"Me too. Nice evening, isn't it?"

"You're avoiding my question."

"No, I'm not. I'm not answering it."

Jessie grinned in the darkness. "Why?"

"I just met you, that's why."

"Okay. I lied about everything."

"What?" he squawked.

Jessie laughed. And laughed. She'd never had this much fun in her whole life.

Maybe this trip wasn't a mistake after all.

Chapter Eight

"Time to wake up, Jessie Roland." Tanner nudged Jessie's shoulder lightly. "We're home!"

"What time is it?" Jessie did her best to marshal a smile as Tanner opened the car door for her. She felt incredibly tired, and the prospect of meeting Alexis Kingsley was making her heart pump faster. She looked around, but everything was in total darkness except a dim yellow light over what appeared to be the back door.

"I think my mother is waiting up. She doesn't usually do that. She has a sleep routine she adheres to. It's twenty past one in case you're interested. You said you were hungry earlier. I think I can rustle you up a sandwich." It was all said in a flat, emotionless voice that caused Jessie to raise her eyebrows. This definitely was not a happy occasion.

"Don't worry about the sandwich. I think I'd just like to go to bed. It's been a very long day. By the way, I'm sorry I fell asleep."

"Me too. Our conversation was just starting to get interesting when you nodded off. Not to worry, we have ten whole days to finish it. The conversation I mean." Tanner's tone of voice changed. It became light, almost playful with an undercurrent of something she'd never heard before. "Ready to beard the dragon lady?"

"I . . . guess so."

Tanner laughed. The fine hairs on the back of Jessie's neck started to prickle, and she began to get a sick feeling in the middle of her stomach.

They were in a dimly lit kitchen that looked homey and smelled heavenly. "I think this is my favorite room in the whole house," Tanner whispered.

"Mine too. I mean I like kitchens, too. Why are we whispering?" Jessie asked.

"Because Mattie's room is off the kitchen. She's the cook. I thought I might whisk you up the back staircase so you can avoid meeting my mother until morning."

"Why don't we just get it over with. If your mother hates me as much as you seem to think she will, you can turn around and take me back to the airport."

"I expected you to come in the front door, Tanner," a voice said from the darkened hallway outside the kitchen. "Please, keep your voices down. I swear, Angus, you'll do anything to irritate me, won't you?"

"Pop isn't here, Mother. He sent his secretary instead." They were in the dark hallway. Jessie heard rather than saw Tanner fumble for the light switch. She wished the floor would open up and swallow her.

Alexis Kingsley was dressed in an ice-blue satin pegnoir with matching feathered mules. Her makeup, even at this hour, was as flawless as her elaborate hair. Huge diamond studs twinkled in her ears. There was no welcoming smile on her face.

The sick feeling inside Jessie's stomach crawled up to her chest. She worked at a smile but knew she wasn't successful. "Mrs. Kingsley, it's nice to meet you. I apologize for the late hour. The senator asked me to tell you he's been detained." When Alexis Kingsley made no move to take her outstretched hand, Tanner reached for it and squeezed it. His cold voice when he addressed his mother sent chills up Jessie's spine.

"I assume you're having a bad night, Mother, so we'll leave you with your bad manners and head on up to bed."

Alexis ignored her son's frosty tone. "When *will* the senator be arriving, miss, what did you say your name was?"

Jessie's back stiffened as did her facial features. "Jessie Roland," she said coolly. "The senator said it's doubtful he'll be coming for the holidays."

"Why is that?" Alexis snapped.

"I don't know, Mrs. Kingsley."

"Aren't you his secretary?" She might as well have said, aren't you the one who does the pooper scooping? "Secretaries are supposed to know everything, or is this one of those need-to-know issues Angus is involved in."

For the second time, Jessie said, "I don't know, Mrs. Kingsley."

"Then why are you here?"

"Mother, that's enough."

Jessie's back stiffened more. "Right now I'm wondering the same thing myself, Mrs. Kingsley. I merely followed the senator's orders. Here," she said, thrusting the wrinkled shopping bag with the small presents nestled on the bottom. Alexis had no other choice but to reach for it. Diamonds sparkled on her fingers. Jessie turned on her heel and headed back the way she'd come.

"Jessie, wait!" To his mother Tanner hissed, "That was uncalled for, and Pop is not going to appreciate it. I don't think you want to irritate him, do you? An apology is definitely in order."

"I do not apologize to secretaries, Tanner. Your father is doing this deliberately to humiliate me. He knows how important my Christmas party is. *Everyone* will be here. Washington shuts down for the holidays. This is unforgivable."

"I'll apologize for you, Mother, since your good sense seems to have left you. I for one wouldn't want to be standing in your shoes when Pop hears about your rude behavior. He adores Miss Jessie. He trusts her, and he depends on her."

"Don't threaten me, Tanner. I will not tolerate that sort of behavior from my daughter, and I will not tolerate it from you. Do what you want. I'm going to bed."

Tanner's shoulders slumped. His long-legged stride took him into the kitchen. "Jessie, I apologize for my mother. Tomorrow she'll react differently. She gets like this every year before the party. I don't know why it's so important to her, but it is. Please stay. I want you to stay. How else can I get through that awful party? I promise to stick by your side every single minute of the day. The night, too, if you want. I hate to admit this, but I'm not really up to a ride to the airport again. I get up at four-thirty. If I crash now I might get a few hours' sleep. Please, reconsider."

"For now. I will want to leave tomorrow, though. I'll call the senator and explain."

"Let me do that. Come along, you look dead tired."

Jessie followed Tanner up the kitchen staircase. The house was tomb quiet and just as dark. Tanner turned on switches as he went along. "I'm putting you in Resa's old room. She decorated it herself. I think you'll like it. It's right over Pop's study and has a wonderful view of the gardens. Mattie cleans and freshens up the room once a week. She keeps hoping Resa will come home. Mattie is the one who really raised Resa and me. I guess by now you more or less figured out we aren't like those television families you see every week at eight o'clock."

"I'm sorry this has become such a problem. Good night, Tanner."

"Good night, Jessie Roland. For whatever it's worth, I'm glad you're here. Sleep well. We'll talk in the morning."

It was a pretty room, Jessie thought as she closed the door. She stared at the shiny brass lock for a moment, a puzzled look on her face. Without thinking, she snapped it home. Locks were for security. She couldn't help but wonder if the other bedrooms had locks or just Resa's. She looked at her bags. Should she unpack? No. She wouldn't be here that long. It would be one less thing she had to do in the morning before leaving for the airport. Instead she peeled off her clothes and slid into the high four-poster with the lacy canopy.

Jessie was treading the fine line between wakefulness and sleep when she heard harsh voices that seemed to be coming from behind her night table. Maybe she was already asleep and was dreaming. She punched at the pillow under her head. She didn't want to listen but she had no choice. . . .

"What are you doing down here, Tanner?"

"I was going to ask you the same thing, Mother. If I remember correctly, you said you were going to bed."

"Your father doesn't answer his phone. That tells me he's with *that woman.*"

"*That woman,* Mother, used to be your best friend. *That woman* is my father's ex-wife. *That woman* is the woman you betrayed by having an affair with her husband and getting yourself pregnant. *That woman* is the woman who divorced her husband so you could give your child her father's name. You never loved Pop. You married him for his money and the power you thought he had. What you did has eaten at your soul every single day of your life, so don't deny it. You hated Irene's unselfishness for giving you what you wanted. You hated her abilities, and when she became a federal judge your hatred doubled because she wasn't the nobody you claimed she was. Everyone loves Irene Marshall. By everyone, I include Pop, Resa, and myself. If you're looking for her number, it's unlisted."

"Give it to me, Tanner."

"Never in a million years, Mother."

"I'll call Resa."

"She won't give it to you either, so don't waste your time calling her in the middle of the night."

"That snippet you brought here must have it. She'll have to give it to me. I'll take the first flight out in the morning and go to her house. I do know where she lives, Tanner. She still lives in that silly little cracker box she lived in with your father."

"Jessie is following Pop's orders. Even if she knows the number, she would never go against Pop's orders. Now, if I were Pop, I'd head for some warm South Sea island and celebrate Christmas under a palm tree. He knows how you think and operate, Mother. Anticipating that you will do exactly what you just said, he would not take a chance and stay in that 'silly little cracker box.' Do what you like, Mother. For starters, I'd cancel your party. I heard a rumor in town last year that you pay people to attend." A crash, the tinkle of broken glass, and Tanner's harsh laughter curled up through the heating vents and into Jessie's ears as she burrowed into the nest of pillows.

Jessie rolled over and laced her fingers behind her head. Wasn't anyone happy? What should she do? Did she dare creep downstairs to call the senator? Would Alexis Kingsley leave for Washington in the morning? The senator had once been married to Irene Marshall. That fact alone was mind-boggling. She wondered if Agnes Prentis had known that and why, if she had, she hadn't told her. Maybe she needed to read her predecessor's diaries from cover to cover. She realized a moment later she couldn't do that. Following Sophie's instructions, she'd mailed the diaries off to Atlanta. Besides, the senator's private life, past and present, was none of her business.

When she was no longer able to hold her eyes open, Jessie slept, her dreams full of rosy-cheeked ladies serving her raisin-filled cookies by the dozen as a cold-eyed regal-looking woman tried to snatch them from her.

Jessie woke with a start when she heard someone knock on her door. She was about to call out when she remembered she'd locked the door. She was sleeping in the buff, so it wouldn't do for her to run to the door. "Just a minute." She ran to the bathroom and found an old terry robe hanging on the hook behind the door. She slipped into it.

"I'm Mattie, miss. Mr. Tanner told me to bring you some coffee. He said he would wait to have breakfast with you. He said to tell you to wear old clothes because he's going to take you riding. You best skedaddle, miss. Mr. Tanner don't have much patience this early in the morning."

Skedaddle. It must be a Texas word. Obviously it meant get a move on. "Tell Mr. Kingsley I'll be right down. Oh, thanks for the coffee."

Jessie wondered what had happened to her good intentions as she stood under the needle-sharp spray. Tanner assumed she was staying, at least for today. One day wasn't so bad; she could leave tomorrow. If she stayed on a day or so, she wouldn't feel so guilty where the senator was concerned.

Dressed in creased jeans, ankle boots, and a red-plaid cotton shirt, Jessie was ready to head downstairs. At the last second she dabbed some delicious-scented perfume, a birthday gift from Sophie, behind her ears. She looked then at her unmade bed and her open suitcases. She made the bed and closed the suitcases. Decisions made before breakfast were usually less than satisfactory.

It was a pretty room, a girl's room. Daffodil yellow walls with crisp white curtains on the windows made it all girlish somehow. When exactly had Resa left this house? Jessie frowned as she stared at the quilted spread that was a splash of color with bright spring flowers dancing across the diamond squares. It matched the two tufted chairs and ottomans to perfection. The meadow of apple green carpet felt new and unused. Was this room Resa Kingsley's sanctuary or was it like her old room back in Charleston—just a place to sleep. There were no mementos, no old clothes in the closets. There should be something that said Resa once lived here and spent time in this room curled up in the pretty chairs. Was the old robe Resa's or did some other person leave it behind? "I think I'm going to like you, Resa Kingsley," she murmured as she left the room.

Jessie entered the kitchen to see Tanner sitting in the breakfast nook that offered wraparound windows with a spectacular view of the gardens and brick courtyard. He smiled, and the room became lighter and brighter. Dressed casually, much the way she was, he exuded confidence and charm. "Name it and we have it. If we don't, Mattie will find a way to get it for you. So, what will you have?"

"Toast, juice, and some coffee."

"No, no, that will never do. This is a ranch. You have to order steak, potatoes, and eggs with a side order of flapjacks. Then you walk away chewing on an apple with a banana in your pocket."

Jessie laughed. "If I ate all that I wouldn't be able to get up. I don't plan on working the north forty or whatever you call it." She looked pointedly at the table set for two.

"My mother left an hour ago for Washington. If you know how to reach my father, I suggest you do it now. We have a one-hour time difference, so it's barely six in D.C.

I'll give Mattie your order. How does one egg, bacon, toast, juice, and coffee sound?"

"Wonderful. Where is the study?"

"Go out through the dining room, down the hall, and it's the second door on the left."

Jessie closed the door of the study, her gaze searching for the heating vents. Would Tanner go to her room to listen? Did the vents carry to other rooms? Did he know voices carried to the second floor? She was so nervous she was shaking as she fumbled in her back pocket for the card with Irene's phone number on it. She dialed the number, her fingers tapping the glass topped desk. The phone was picked up after the third ring. "Irene, it's Jessie Roland. Can I speak to the senator, please. In the shower? Will you give him a message? Mrs. Kingsley left an hour ago for Washington. I heard her talking last night to her son. The voices carried up through the vents. She said she knew where you lived and she was going there. When I came downstairs this morning Tanner said his mother had left for D.C. He seemed to think it was imperative I call you. I gather this all has to do with a Christmas party Mrs. Kingsley is having. I'm so sorry, Irene. Is there anything I can do?"

"No, child. I'm sorry you're involved in this messy affair. I'll give Angus your message the moment he gets out of the shower. Thank you for calling. It will give me time to arrange something for the twins so they aren't here when Alexis arrives. Don't worry about any of this, Jessie. Angus and I can handle it. We've been doing it for more years than I care to remember. Give Resa and Tanner my love."

"I will, Irene. Good-bye."

"What did Pop say?" Tanner asked when Jessie took her seat at the table.

"Your father was taking a shower. I left a message."

"That's it. You left a message."

"Yes. What . . . what will happen now?"

"God only knows. Pop won't come back with my mother if that's what's worrying you. In my opinion they only have two options. Either they go somewhere or they don't answer the door. The twins will be home, so they have to consider them. My guess would be they'll pack up and go to Irene's family's horse farm in McLean. She goes there in the summer to get out of the heat in Washington. The acreage is fallow now. Irene rented it out for a few years to some foreign diplomats when she needed money for the twins' college tuition. Her husband left her with a mountain of debts. Mostly bad investments. It took her years to pay them off. The diplomats paid some very high rent and installed a high-tech electronics fence that surrounds the entire house. You can't get near the place because it's riddled with barriers and split-rail fences. You need passwords and all that junk. If they go to the farm, they'll be safe. I don't even know if my mother knows Irene still owns it. It's not our problem, Jessie. I say eat hearty so I can show you around the house, the grounds, and then we'll go riding. After that we'll head for town and have lunch with Resa. I called her, and she's going to take the afternoon off."

Jessie ate the food she didn't want just so Tanner would smile. He did. "Okay, get your apple off the sideboard and stick a banana in your pocket. Jesus!" Tanner said slapping his forehead. "I forgot to ask, do you ride?"

"I do. I haven't ridden in years, though."

"We have plenty of liniment. You won't be doing any dancing this evening. I'm glad you're staying, Jessie."

"How did that happen? Me staying?"

"You saw the error of your ways. No one wants to be alone over the holidays, and I think you took pity on me."

"Do you know anyone whose family is happy?" Jessie blurted.

"When I was in college I used to beg my buddies to invite me to their houses for breaks. Resa did the same thing. The best times in my life were the years I went to Bluefield, West Virginia, to my best friend's house. Jack had nine brothers and sisters and they all came home for Christmas with their kids and dogs and cats. I slept on the floor in a sleeping bag with everyone else. I'd wake up in the morning and there was a dog, a cat, and a toddler in my sleeping bag with me. Each year it was a different kid and each year he or she would wet his or her pants and I would be full of dog and cat hair for a week. They had wonderful neighbors. Bob and Miss Liz and their son Rand. Their last name was Henry. It was a pretty little town with wonderful people. We ate Polish food the whole time. The kind that sticks to your ribs. Every single holiday I gained ten pounds. Every Christmas the whole kit and caboodle went out to cut down the Christmas tree, and we all decorated it. The dogs and cats stepped on the ornaments and broke them. No one got excited. We sang carols. Off-key of course. I will treasure those holidays until the day I die."

"Are you still friends with Jack?"

"Jack died on his way back to school his last year of college. January 17. The time of his death was listed as 3:11 P.M. He died of massive internal injuries. A tractor trailer went out of control on an icy road. Jack didn't make it. I almost didn't make it either. I took that entire semester off and just bummed around. I still dream about him, especially at this time of year. I went back one year loaded down with presents. The family welcomed me with open arms, and so did the Henrys, but it wasn't the same. Nothing is ever the same. You get one shot, and it's up to you not to screw it up. Pop had a second chance with Irene, and he grabbed it. If Jack hadn't been in my life, I probably wouldn't be so tolerant of Pop's relationship with Irene."

Jessie digested the information. It was obvious Tanner was waiting for her to make a comment. "I don't know what I would do if something happened to my best friend Sophie. I don't know how I would react to death. Not well I'm sure. You said you were going to show me the house."

"That in itself is a downer. My mother calls in this agency every year to set things up. It's . . . it's different."

"It certainly is different," Jessie said later as she looked around the huge drawing room. "It reminds me of a science fiction layout. Does your mother like the color blue?"

"I think the decorator told her she liked blue and pearl white. She was really put out when none of her friends copied her theme, as she put it. Most of my parents' friends use the traditional red velvet and live evergreens. I'm partial to colored lights myself. Irene decorates her house every year. It always smells so good. At least that's how I remember it. I personally consider this an eyesore. Every room pretty much looks like this one, right down to the bathrooms. White tree, blue lights, and blue balls. All the flower arrangements are blue and white with white candles. Even the gifts are wrapped in white paper with blue ribbons. I go to Resa's on Christmas Eve and sleep over. She has a small tree that's artificial because she lives in an apartment. At least it's green. We give each other a present and drink some wine. We share old times and talk about the future. Together we cook a big dinner just for the two of us. We do the same thing for Easter. Resa will do anything to avoid coming out to the ranch."

Jessie listened, unsure if she should say something or not. Was he testing her? If so, why? Who would he report back to, his mother or his father? "Your sister isn't married then?"

"She came close but no, she isn't married. My mother

stuck her nose into things, and before either Resa or I knew what happened, Michael was gone. Resa had a breakdown of sorts and has never forgiven my mother. I thought my father was going to bodily throw my mother out of the house over that incident. If he had, I would have helped him. I tried to find the guy on my own but didn't have any luck. Resa and I both think he was bought off. If so, he wasn't the one for Resa. It was years ago. Irene helped her through the worst of it. A science-fiction scene, huh?"

Jessie laughed. "Uh-huh."

Tanner reached for her hand. "Come on, we're going riding. You can ride Tulip. She's Resa's horse and very gentle. Just say 'Whoa' when you've had enough, okay?"

"Okay." She hated to let loose of his hand. A warm, tingly feeling spread throughout her body as she waited for Tulip to be led out of the barn. "When is the big Christmas party?"

"Saturday. The day after tomorrow. You're staying then?" Jessie squared her shoulders. Either she was making the biggest mistake of her life, or she wasn't. Only time would provide the answer. She nodded.

It was almost noon when Jessie called a halt, and said, "Whoa, Tulip."

"Had enough?"

"For today. Is all this land yours?"

"Five thousand acres. See that outcropping of rocks? That's our southern boundary."

"Who owns the land beyond the boundary?"

"The Holts. The Kingsleys' archenemies."

"Like in the Hatfields and the McCoys?"

"You could say that. We don't talk about the Holts, and we don't socialize with them either. It's just the way it is." There was grudging respect in Tanner's voice when he said, "Luke owns most of Corpus Christi."

"Who's Luke?"

"He used to be a friend. Living on a ranch so far out doesn't allow for too many friends. Luke lived next door, figuratively speaking. As kids we were inseparable. Things went wrong. What say we head back to the ranch and get duded up so we don't smell, as Resa puts it, horsey. Want to race?"

"Sure."

He rode like the wind. The best Tulip could do was a slow canter. Jessie reined in the horse ten minutes after Tanner handed his horse over to the groom. She slid from the saddle to land in Tanner's arms. "I am going to feel this tonight," she told him.

"The Jacuzzi might help. We can do that after dinner along with a good bottle of wine."

"I didn't bring a bathing suit."

Tanner grinned. "I don't remember saying anything about a bathing suit. Thirty minutes, casual dress."

Jessie laughed as she made her way to the second floor. She was surprised to see that her suitcases had been unpacked, her clothing pressed and hung neatly on hangers inside the spacious closet that was scented with lemon verbena, as was the dresser drawer where her underwear and other things were aligned neatly. She frowned. She hated people doing things like this for her. It reminded her of the conditions she'd lived under back in Charleston where housekeepers and maids, not to mention her mother, saw to things on an hourly basis. She was halfway to the bathroom when she turned and made her way back to the dresser with its sweet-smelling pomanders. First she messed up her underwear and took out her pajamas to throw them into the second drawer. Her stockings, gloves, scarves, and wool socks went into a third drawer. Everything was messy now, just the way it was back in Washington.

Standing under her second shower of the day, Jessie let her thoughts drift. When would Alexis Kingsley return?

Today, tomorrow? Would it really be possible to stay out of the cold, arrogant woman's way? She shuddered under the warm spray when she recalled the science-fiction Christmas decorations. Christmas parties were supposed to be festive. How could such a gloomy atmosphere downstairs make for a festive party? What difference did it make? It wasn't her party. All she had to do was attend. If she didn't want to attend, she could plead a headache or she could return to Washington. The big question was, did she want to return? A niggling voice reminded her of Irene's whispered words and her own recollections of the first time she'd seen Tanner Kingsley. Her destiny. Anything was possible.

Jessie toweled herself dry, her thoughts still on Tanner. He seemed to like her. He was certainly gallant, and she loved his sense of humor. But more than anything she loved his defense of Irene Marshall and his feelings for the older woman.

A quick glance at her watch told her she had seven minutes until it was time to meet Tanner downstairs. Since she'd brought little in the way of clothing, it was easy to pick an outfit. Sophie had taught her about mixing and matching using accessories so one didn't have to travel with five suitcases. She slipped into a Jonathan Logan cranberry-wool dress she particularly liked. A single strand of pearls with matching earrings completed her outfit. A lightweight white-wool jacket graced her shoulders. She was ready with two minutes to spare.

"Right on time," she laughed as Tanner tapped his foot with pretended impatience

"You look good, and you smell even better. What is that stuff you're wearing? Send me a gallon so I can sniff it after you've gone. I'll sprinkle it everywhere."

"It's French. It's *Amour*. Sophie gave it to me several

years ago as a gift. It's outrageously expensive; I only use it sparingly. A whole gallon! It would cost *thousands*. "

"Okay, half a gallon. A quart will do. Even a pint."

Jessie laughed again. "How about if I sprinkle some on a tissue and you can keep it in your sock drawer?"

"It's a deal."

"Miss Jessie, there's a phone call for you."

"For me!"

"It's probably Pop. You can take it here or in the study."

Jessie nodded as she made her way down the hall to the study. Her greeting was cautious. "Hello, this is Jessie Roland."

"Jessie, Angus Kingsley here. I want to give you a new phone number. Are you in my study?"

"Yes, Senator, I am. I have a pencil." Jessie repeated the number to make sure she copied it down right.

"This number is just temporary, Jessie. We'll head back to Washington on Saturday if things go right. My wife will return to Texas for her party. I want you to call me when she returns, so I can take Irene back to her house. She was doing so well until this cropped up. She wants to go home. I do, too. I don't know why I didn't anticipate this."

"I understand. I'll call you as soon as I can. Tanner is waiting for me, and he's going to want to know why you called. What should I tell him?"

"Tell him it's need-to-know. He'll understand. Are you enjoying yourself, Jessie?"

"Yes, Senator, I am. We're going to town to have lunch with Resa. I'm looking forward to meeting her."

"Give her a big kiss and hug for me. Tell her I love her. I think you're going to like her as much as you like Tanner."

"I'm sure I will, Senator."

"Irene sends her best."

"And mine to her. I'm so sorry this happened."

"It's not your fault, Jessie. It's mine. Enjoy your luncheon."

Jessie folded the small piece of paper and slipped it into the toe of her shoe before she left the study. She'd entered carrying nothing, and she should exit carrying nothing.

"Please tell me that call wasn't from my mother."

"It wasn't your mother. It was your father."

"Is everything okay with Pop?"

"I think so. He said, should you ask, it's need-to-know. He also told me to give Resa a big kiss and hug and to tell her he loves her."

"Pop adores Resa. Always has. She's shy and doesn't make friends easily. Growing up it was just us two and Luke Holt. She's never outgrown her shyness. When you get to know her she's very verbal. My mother never let her be a kid or a young girl. I was the rebellious one, and Resa was the obedient one. She used to cry herself to sleep at night. The day she went off to college was the happiest day of her life. She's the brainy one. Did I tell you that?"

"No. Shouldn't we be leaving? We don't want to keep your sister waiting. Can we stop at a florist so I can get her a Christmas plant?"

"Of course. Now, why didn't I think of that? I'm supposed to bring the wine, so that's two stops we have to make. Resa doesn't eat meat. Did I tell you that? It makes my mother nuts."

Jessie laughed. "No, you didn't tell me that. What else didn't you tell me?"

"That about sums it up. When are we going to talk about Jessie Roland? You know, all that stuff about where and how you grew up. What colors you like, what you like to eat, that kind of stuff."

Jessie sucked in her breath. She had known this question was going to come eventually. Damn, she hoped she could remember everything Sophie had written down about her phony background. "Let's see. How about when we run out of things to talk about, and you want to be put to sleep. My past is incredibly boring. I was born, I grew up, and here I am. That's about it. I'll fill in the blanks later."

"Tell me about your friend Sophie."

"Sophie Ashwood was born and bred in Atlanta. She should be a Southern belle, but she isn't. Her mother is either the second or third richest woman in the world, which means someday Sophie will step into that position. She's an architect and is in Costa Rica finishing her internship. Her main goal in life is to design and build a bridge. We more or less grew up together. She's my friend, my confidante, the sister I never had. She's engaged to be married to an engineer who also wants to build bridges. She can do anything she sets her mind to. I cannot imagine my life without Sophie in it. It's probably the way you felt about your friend Jack. End of story."

"End of story? I don't think so. I sense there's more. I want to hear it."

Jessie debated a full second before she blurted out what she'd done at Sophie's graduation three years ago. Tanner laughed so hard he had to pull over to the side of the road. He laughed even harder when she said, "It's on film. Sophie paid someone to film it because she knew her mother wouldn't be there. I don't know if she sent it to her mother or not."

"Did you ever see it?"

"God, no!"

Tanner pulled into traffic. "When we get married will you ask Sophie to show it to me?"

When we get married. Jessie's heart started to pound inside her chest. It was a joke. Well, she knew how to handle a joke even one like this, thanks to Sophie.

"Absolutely," she said. "I'll even reenact it for you."

"So, when would you like to get married?"

"When you give me an engagement ring, and it better not be one of those itsy-bitsy little things you need a magnifying glass to see."

Tanner pretended shock. "Are you saying you're one of those material girls?"

"No. I want something I'll be able to leave my oldest daughter, assuming I have a daughter. I never understood why a girl needs a ring just because she's engaged. A plain gold wedding band, a wide one, will do nicely, thank you. You aren't writing any of this down. Why is that? I also do not believe in divorce." Jessie giggled at the panic on Tanner's face.

Tanner's voice was so strangled-sounding Jessie could barely make out the words. "I can't hear you," she sing-songed. "You started this, you know."

"I said I have total recall."

"I'm not living in that house with your mother either." My God, did she really just say that?

"Huh?"

"You heard me. Your mother doesn't like me. Guess what? From what I've seen I don't like her either. I said I'm not living with her when we get married. You're turning white. Want to quit now?"

His color restored, Tanner pulled to the curb. "I'm going to get the wine. Do you have any preferences?"

"It's up to the guy to choose the wine. Sophie told me that. Get two bottles."

"Two? Why?"

"I dance on the table after two." *Sophie, Sophie, Sophie, you should just hear me.*

Tanner leaned into the open car window. "You're a smart-ass, too, aren't you?"

"Uh-huh."

"What do you do after three bottles?"

"I've never gotten that far. I imagine I would be creative."

Tanner squawked something that sounded like, "I'll be damned."

Jessie doubled over laughing. Her whole body felt hot. She wondered how Tanner's felt. Maybe she should ask. As Sophie always said, you'll never learn anything unless you ask questions. Sophie also said some things were better left alone and unsaid.

Tanner was breathing like a long-distance runner when he returned to the car with *three* bottles of wine, a smug expression on his face. Jessie laughed. And laughed. The smug expression became uncomfortable until he also laughed. "Touché, Jessie Roland."

Where Tanner was tall and muscular, Resa was petite and fragile. But their summer blue eyes and golden brown hair matched. Resa had a nimbus of short golden curls circling her doll-like face. Tanner's wide, sweeping grin and her happy smile made Jessie feel welcome. "Welcome to my humble abode, Jessie. It's small, but it's all mine. One paper, one magazine out of place as Tanner will tell you later, makes the place look cluttered. I'm so happy to meet you, Jessie. The last time Pop was here all he did was talk about the 'marvelous Jessie Roland.' I guess you know he adores you. Come in, come in. My goodness, are all these plants for me? Thank you so much. Ohhh, it looks so . . . *Christmasey.*"

Jessie smiled. She liked this wide-eyed thirty-three-year-old moppet immediately as Resa linked her arm with hers. "I know *you* picked out these plants, so you're going to have to place them. Strategically of course. So, what do you think of my tree?"

"It's lovely," Jessie lied.

Resa's laughter tinkled around the small room. "I'm big on truth here."

"The ornaments are pretty."

"My kids at school made them for me. I even have some of Tanner's, and a few of my own that I snitched from home. Actually I didn't snitch them at all. My mother threw them in an old box because they didn't go with her elegant tree, and I just scooped them up. I remember so clearly the day we made them in school. Oh, well, that was a long time ago. Tell me, why did Tanner bring three bottles of wine? Are we having an orgy, and you guys forgot to tell me?" Her laughter tinkled again.

Jessie whispered, "I told him I dance on the table after two bottles. I think he thinks three could be *anything*." This time Resa hooted.

"So, what's for lunch?" Tanner asked.

"Stouffer's macaroni and cheese and somebody else's fish sticks. I thawed a frozen apple strudel and some Cool Whip for dessert. Did Mattie send me a CARE package?"

"Yes, and I forgot to bring it in. Two frozen casseroles and some homemade bread. I'll get them."

"Mattie feels sorry for me. She knows I can't cook worth a darn. Most times I eat out or have soup and a sandwich. I don't eat red meat. My parents consider me a traitor in that respect. My mother does. Pop doesn't care. What did you think of the ranch?"

"It's wonderful what I saw of it. It's so . . . sprawling. All those cattle. I never saw so many cows in my life."

"Shhh, we never say the word 'cow' aloud. Steers. Don't let one of these Texans hear you say cows. And my mother?"

"I didn't much care for her," Jessie said truthfully.

The wide eyes widened even more before Resa laughed with delight. "That's more or less how I feel. It's terribly sad, don't you think?"

"Yes. I like to be around happy people. My own childhood wasn't all that great. Life is just too short to be unhappy."

"I knew I was going to like you, Jessie Roland. Are you all set for the big as in 'big' party? My mother always refers to it as the social event of the year. It isn't. It's just one of those obligatory things certain people feel they have to attend. I find it downright gruesome. I'm not going this year. I have a date!"

"With a real man!" Tanner challenged as he plunked down the frozen casseroles on the kitchen table.

"Yes, a real man. You're on your own this year, little brother. His name is Josh Kelly. He joined the faculty in September. I've been seeing him since the first week in September, and I really like him, so don't mention it to Mother. If she asks where I am tell her I have the flu or that I went to Australia. I don't ever want him to meet Mother. By the way I saw Miss Bippity-Bop the other day. She told me she will be attending the party." To Jessie she said, "She's the girl Mother picked out for Tanner. Her real name is Barbara Bendix. She's a man-hungry tiger."

Tanner groaned. "I have an idea. Why don't Jessie and I join you and Josh on Saturday. A double date. We haven't done that in years, Resa. Do you think Josh would mind?"

"Josh won't mind. He's dying to meet you. Are you sure you're willing to face Mother's wrath?"

"Of course I'm sure. I wouldn't have suggested it otherwise."

"That means no family member will be at the party. She'll make you pay dearly for it, Tanner."

"Then I'll just take a page out of Pop's and your book and move out. Don't think I haven't thought about it. What's on the agenda?"

"Dinner and a movie or the movie first and then dinner. Josh usually takes care of the arrangements. Don't show up in that damn truck, okay?"

"Okay."

"We go dutch. You pay, and he pays. No problems when the bill comes."

"I can handle that. Do you really like this guy?" Tanner demanded.

"Like him? I worship him. This is the man I've been waiting for all my life. If he asked me to marry him tomorrow, I'd say yes."

A worried frown settled on Tanner's face. Jessie found herself holding her breath "Does he worship you?" he asked.

"Uh-huh. Look!" Resa extended her left hand. "We're engaged," she chortled.

"You got engaged and didn't tell me! How could you do that, Resa?" Tanner demanded.

"Two days, Tanner. I wanted to savor it all to myself for just a little while. I'm telling you now. I met his parents the first of December. God, they are so nice. His mother reminds me of Irene. His dad is bluff and hearty. They are so down-to-earth, so *real* it's scary. Josh and his parents are a little puzzled that I didn't take them to the ranch. I can't take the chance *she'll* do something, Tanner."

"She'll never hear it from me. You know that, Resa. Jessie isn't going to say anything. For God's sake, don't tell anyone until you're . . . when are you getting married?"

"Valentine's Day."

"How wonderful, Resa. Congratulations." Jessie reached for her left hand. "It's beautiful."

"Thank you for saying that," Resa said shyly. "I know it's small, but it's perfect. I am just so thrilled. There are no words."

"I told Jessie you were shy and withdrawn. I never heard you talk so much in my life. This calls for a toast!"

"That's because I'm in love. It means I'm not ugly, I'm not worthless, and I'm not a nobody. Josh says I'm beautiful inside and outside. He said I'm a valuable human being and I am somebody because I am going to be Mrs. Joshua Kelly. Mother was wrong!" Tears glistened in her eyes. Tanner reached for one of his sister's hands and Jessie reached for the other. "Why does she hate me so much, Tanner?"

"We aren't going down that road today. We're celebrating. Who cares what she thinks. You proved her wrong so many times I lost count. Get it through your head, she doesn't matter."

"Guess what! Josh doesn't eat red meat either. You know what else? He's never grumpy or out of sorts. He has the best disposition."

"On that happy note, let's eat lunch. Here's the toast. To my sister Resa. May she always be as happy as she is today Wait, wait, I'm not finished. And to Jessie, who is going to entertain us after we finish all three of these fine bottles of wine!"

"Hear, hear," Resa said holding her glass aloft.

Chapter Nine

Alexis Kingsley cursed the wet snow that seeped into her sling-back heels the moment she stepped from the Yellow Cab. She thrust a twenty-dollar bill through the window of the taxi, not knowing if it was too much or too little. She simply didn't care. Wet, swirling snow covered her as she picked her way up the flagstone path that led to Irene Marshall's house. She jabbed at the doorbell, still cursing under her breath. She jabbed again and again with no response. "Damn you, Angus, open this door!" She banged on it with clenched fists, then kicked at the shiny brass plate at the bottom of the door. Words she hadn't used since her racy youth spewed from her mouth.

She looked around to see if her movements were being observed. The falling snow made visibility almost zero. She bent down. People in the movies always left keys under planters or doormats or over the doorframe. She shook out the doormat that was covered with a quarter inch of snow. No key. By standing on her toes she could reach the ledge over the door. The fragrant evergreen wreath tickled her face, making her sneeze. No key. She looked inside the milk box. Two quarts of milk and a pint of cream. The milk and cream had to mean no one was home at the moment but would return; otherwise, the milk and cream would freeze. No key. She tilted the box and there it was, taped to the bottom. "You are just so damn predictable, Irene." Alexis pocketed the strip of gray electrical tape so she could replace it and the key when she left the premises.

Inside it was warm, the thermostat set at seventy degrees. She called out, knowing there would be no response. Where had they gone? Was Tanner right, and Angus was sunning himself on some South Sea island? Or had Tanner called his father and warned him she was coming? It would be just like Tanner to do something like that to spite her. She kicked off her shoes and slid out of her fur coat. She'd never been in this house. It was tacky, small, and cozy. Angus liked cozy things. The furniture was worn, the carpet comparatively new and cheap-looking. Everywhere she looked there were framed pictures of the twins. Angus would be in his glory with a fire blazing, his feet up on the worn ottoman. The chair that matched the ottoman was oversize and would hold two comfortably. Irene and Angus. She sat down on the beige-and-brown chair. It was extremely comfortable. Broken in.

Alexis stared through narrowed eyes at the evergreen nestled into a corner nook on the right side of the fireplace. The tree fit the room as did all the other Christmas decorations. Having an eye for antiques, she knew some of the things she was looking at were priceless. She leaned her head back into the softness of the double chair. Once when she was little she'd been in a room like this with a Christmas tree just like this one. That tree had been decorated with stale popcorn and wilted cranberries. There were no presents under the tree, though. She moved out of the chair and walked over to the tree to check out the carefully arranged presents. How elegantly they were wrapped. Were the contents costly? Who had bought them? Irene?

Angus? She compared them to the two sloppily wrapped presents in the shopping bag that Jessie Roland had handed her earlier.

Alexis dropped to her knees. She shook the gifts, rattled them, and then looked at the name tags. All of them were for Irene and her children and all of them were from Angus. "Damn you, Angus. Damn you to hell!"

Her vision blurred as she stared at an oversize ornament directly in front of her. She knew it was expensive because she'd seen ornaments just like it in catalogs. She reached for it and crushed it in one hand. The fragile glass fell into a hundred pieces, to scatter in and about the exquisitely wrapped gifts. She reached for another and then still another. She raised her eyes to stare at a delicate porcelain angel on top of the tree. The fire tongs found their way into her hand. With one swipe the angel shattered into the branches of the fir tree. She was angry now, angrier than she'd ever been in her life.

The fire tongs whipped across the tree again and again until there was nothing left of the beautiful ornaments. One last swipe sent the tree reeling into the corner. Alexis replaced the fire tongs and walked out to the kitchen. It smelled like cinnamon and lemon, much like that house she'd been in so long ago. She savored the smell for a moment. Irene loved to cook and bake. The refrigerator was full, without an inch of spare space. A succulent pink ham was on the first shelf. Two roasted chickens sat on a platter on the second shelf. The remains of a pot roast, Angus's favorite food, were on the third shelf. Fresh vegetables filled both bins. Bottles of wine along with milk and juice were on the high top shelf. Instead of closing the door to the refrigerator and freezer, Alexis let both of them hang open. She couldn't help but wonder what was in her own refrigerator back in Texas. She should know but she didn't.

A rum cake sat under a cut-crystal dome. Angus adored

rum cake. She pinched off a piece. It was delicious. The cut-crystal dome crashed onto the tile floor. Alexis stepped over it as she lifted a second dome to stare down at a mince pie. Another one of Angus's favorite desserts. It, too, found its way to the ceramic floor. Overhead a luscious emerald fern hung over the sink. Irene had always loved green plants. She probably trimmed this one with manicure scissors. There wasn't a brown or yellow leaf anywhere on the exquisite plant. A flower store would show this plant off or display it in a window. Angus had plants like this in his office that he tended himself. Alexis reached for a long-handled carving knife from the rack near the stove. She whipped it across the plant twice until it toppled into the sink, the rich black potting soil scattering everywhere.

The red-checkered cushion covers on the scarred-oak chairs with the matching place mats matched the checkered curtains on the window and looked handmade. Irene had always liked to sew. The hooked rug by the sink looked handmade, too. In the movies women always did homey things like that in the winter when they were waiting for their husbands to return. Alexis scooped them up and carried them to the living room, where she tossed them into the fireplace. She reached for a long matchstick. Within minutes flames shot upward.

Alexis moved on through the dining room, where she opened the antique breakfront to stare at the array of fine, heirloom crystal. She had nothing half as beautiful back in Texas. She pushed and shoved until the breakfront toppled over the dining-room table. The sound of the shattering crystal was melodious.

She walked down the short narrow hall to the main bedroom. The king-size bed was made neatly. It was a plain room, half-masculine and half-feminine. The colors were earth tones with splashes of color on the walls. The carpet was soft and a dark chocolate. The small fireplace looked like it was used. A lot. How cozy. Logs stood upright in a wicker basket. It was an intimate, warm bedroom, with two comfortable matching chairs and a television set in the corner.

Blind rage coursed through Alexis as she conjured up a picture of her husband and Irene sitting side by side or making love in the big king-size bed. She stomped about the room, her body shaking with rage. The wet towels hanging side by side in the cramped bathroom intensified her rage.

Alexis prowled the room like an angry stalking tiger as she emptied dresser drawers and ripped into closets that held her husband's clothes right next to Irene's out-of-style clothing. The sewing box on the top shelf yielded a pair of scissors to help in her destruction. She gouged and ripped, her face a mask of rage. When she was finished she entered the bathroom, where she proceeded to shred the wet, worn pink towels. She opened the medicine cabinet, intent on destroying it, too, when she noticed all the medication bottles on the bottom shelf. Something alien tugged at her heart as she picked up one of the bottles, praying it didn't have Angus's name on it. It didn't. The breath left her body in a loud *swoosh* of sound. She scrutinized the nearly empty medication bottle carefully. Take for pain as needed. Take one every four hours for pain. The thought that Irene Marshall was in pain pleased her. In the small vanity under the sink she found a stub of an eyebrow pencil. She copied down the drug names and would check them out later. Unpronounceable drug names had to mean Irene had a serious condition. "How nice," she muttered. She left the medication intact and closed the door to the medicine cabinet.

Alexis meandered down the hall to the twins' bedrooms. She stood in the doorway to stare at total disarray.

She should know the twins' names, but they eluded her at the moment. A picture of Irene, Angus, and the twins that had been blown up to poster size took center stage on one wall along with a smaller poster of John Lennon. Beneath all the junk, clothes and books scattered everywhere, there were indications it was a girl's room.

She wrinkled her nose. College students were young adults. She herself would never tolerate a room like this in her house. The boy's room was worse, with sports equipment everywhere. The poster in this room was different. This one was of Angus, Tanner, and the boy with a baseball glove on his hand. Angus had one arm around the boy's shoulders, and Tanner had his other arm around him. The raging fury she'd felt before returned with such force she had to sit down on the edge of the bed. "How dare you bring our son to this . . . this place! How dare you, Angus!" She sat that way for a long time until she felt the rage dissipate.

Why in the name of God had she come to this hateful place? Why was she torturing herself like this? She didn't belong here in this nest of sin. In the living room she looked around for a phone. She flipped through Irene's address book until she found the number for the taxi company. While she waited for the call to go through she plucked the small white card from a monstrous poinsettia sitting next to the phone. For one brief moment she thought she was going to faint. *Have a wonderful holiday. Resa and I both send our love.* It was signed Resa and Tanner. When the dispatcher, his voice crackly and hoarse, came on the line, Alexis gave Irene's address and was told it would be at least an hour before a cab could be dispatched because of the snow. She pitched the poinsettia in the general direction of the fire that was now just smoldering ashes.

How was she going to pass the time for a whole hour?

She decided to make coffee. While it perked she gouged out a piece of the rum cake with her fingers. It really was delicious. She ate a second piece; the remainder of the cake she tossed into the sink with the green fern.

As she sipped at the coffee she wondered if she could be charged with breaking and entering. She decided it was very likely. She had to leave as soon as possible. It was snowing harder now. Would her flight take off on time? She might have to go to a hotel. She drank more coffee. She rinsed the cup before she pulled out the plug. She also needed to find a pair of shoes or boots. Her open-toed, open-heeled shoes were worthless in this kind of weather, and she didn't want to catch a cold.

The hall closet held an array of outer footwear. She dithered, finally choosing a pair of ankle-high boots that were a size too big and a size too wide. They would serve the purpose. She shuffled to where she'd thrown her fur coat and purse. She slipped into the coat and clomped her way back to the closet for a small canvas bag hanging on the door. She stuffed her dress shoes into the bag. She was ready now to go back to Texas. The last thing she did after she closed and locked the door was replace the key exactly the way she'd found it under the milk box. The cab arrived five minutes later. If the snow continued, any footprints she left would be obliterated.

She hated this town. She really did.

Jessie woke slowly as she savored the toasty warmth of her bed. She stretched, her thoughts going to Tanner and the two hours they'd spent in the Jacuzzi sipping wine. It had been one of the nicest evenings of her life. So nice that she wanted many more just like it. She'd looked good in Resa's bathing suit. Tanner had even commented that Resa never filled it out like she did. She curled deeper into the covers, her face flaming when she thought about the wine she'd consumed. One more glass and she would have dragged Tanner here to her bed. She wondered what today would bring. Was he ever going to kiss her? She'd certainly given him every opportunity. For some reason she'd thought he would be all over her. Maybe his restraint had something to do with her working for his father. On the other hand, maybe she wasn't his type, and he simply wasn't interested.

Then there was Resa and the words she'd whispered in her ear when they were leaving. "Tanner has *never* taken any girl, not even Bippity-Bop, into the Jacuzzi. He must really like you." She thought he did. She hoped he did. She prayed that he did.

She knew she was falling in love, and there wasn't a thing she could do about it. She wished Sophie was close enough to call. She needed to share her thoughts and feelings.

God, she felt wonderful.

Tanner's booming voice thundered into her room. "Hey, Jess, it's eight-thirty. Up and at 'em!" He gave the door two sharp whacks. "Ten minutes!"

She loved it when he called her Jess. "Fifteen!" she shouted back.

"Not a minute longer." Two more sharp whacks and then silence.

Jessie beelined for the shower.

She literally skidded into the breakfast room, her eyes on her watch, fifteen minutes later.

"I do love a lady who is on time," Tanner grinned.

"The table is no place to be boisterous, Tanner. Where are your manners? Good morning, Miss Roland."

Jessie's good mood shattered in an instant. "Good morning, Mrs. Kingsley."

"When did you get back, Mother? How's Pop?"

"Late last night. I didn't see your father. In fact, I didn't get out of the airport at all. I called at least a dozen times, but there was no answer. I finally gave up. All I did was waste time. They're having a snowstorm up the whole East Coast. I was fortunate I got a flight back when I did. Did your father call while I was gone, Tanner?"

Tanner bit into a piece of toast. "Not to my knowledge. Jessie and I are going into town and won't be home for lunch or dinner. Everything here is taken care of. We had lunch with Resa yesterday. School's out for the holiday, so she's going shopping with us. Is there anything we can bring you from town?" Jessie flinched at his cool, polite voice.

"No. It's just as well. I'm redoing the house today, and you'd both be underfoot."

"What does that mean, you're redoing the house?"

"I'm changing the holiday decorations. You should be happy, Tanner. For years you and Resa have complained about my themes. This year it will be a traditional Christmas."

Jessie didn't think it was possible for Tanner's voice to get colder but it did. "It doesn't matter anymore, Mother. Resa and I are all grown-up now. It was important when we were kids. I won't be here anyway. I'm spending Christmas with Resa. In case you've forgotten, I've been doing that for the past five years. Jessie will be joining us this year. So, what that means is, don't go to the expense and time of doing it for us."

Alexis sat tight-lipped, her eyes narrowed to mean slits. "I see."

"I doubt it," Tanner said. "Come on, Jessie, let's leave. We can catch something to eat in town. You'll see us when you see us. Have a nice day, Mother."

Jessie rose from the chair. "Good-bye, Mrs. Kingsley." Alexis's nostrils quivered. "Just a moment, Miss Roland. Were you in my bedroom sampling my perfume?"

Jessie stopped in her tracks. "I beg your pardon."

Tanner turned, his face murderous. "What are you implying, Mother?"

"I want to know where this . . . this . . . secretary got perfume that sells for $400 a quarter ounce. Not very many people can afford expensive French perfume, especially on a secretary's salary."

"Are you saying I went into your room and used your perfume, Mrs. Kingsley?" Jessie asked in a choked voice.

"That's exactly what I think unless you can come up with a better explanation."

"No, no, Jessie. Let me be the one to explain," Tanner said. His eyes were steely cold, his jaw jutting forward as he stared his mother down. "Jessie's best friend Sophie gave the perfume to her. As a matter of fact we were discussing it yesterday. Miss Sophie can probably buy a gallon of the stuff and splash it all over the house if she wants to. You owe Jessie an apology, Mother. Since you are so arrogant and merciless, I know you won't do it so I will do it for you *again*. Sometimes, Mother, you disgust me. Let's go, Jessie."

"Will you wait for me one minute, Tanner?"

"All the minutes you want," Tanner said.

Jessie flew up the stairs. She raced into her room and grabbed the small elegant gold-and-crystal perfume bottle. She flew back down the steps and plopped the bottle on the table in front of Tanner's mother. "Keep it!" she said in a choked voice as she ran from the room.

"Sometimes, Mother, I absolutely detest you. This is one of those times. Keep this up, and I'll be moving in with Resa. I hope you're ashamed of yourself."

"Don't be ridiculous, Tanner. Anyone would have assumed what I assumed. No, I am not ashamed. Another thing, don't ever make the mistake of threatening me again. That was a threat, wasn't it?"

"You know what, Mother, it's whatever you want it to be."

Outside, Tanner took great gulps of air. He knew Jessie was crying. Damn it to hell. Resa would know what to do and say. "Jessie, I am so sorry that happened. I spend too much time apologizing for her. I don't know why." He wrapped his arms around her, murmuring words she couldn't hear.

"I can't stay here. I need to go back to Washington. Why doesn't she like me? Good Lord, she doesn't even know me."

"Shhh, it's not important."

"Yes, it is important. I'm starting to like you too much. It can't work."

He kissed her then because he didn't want to hear what she was going to say next. A long time later he said, "I don't want you to go. You could stay with Resa."

Jessie sighed. The kiss was her undoing. She felt like a wounded puppy. "No, I cannot stay with Resa. I will not infringe on her privacy. She's in love and wants to spend all her free time with Josh. I guess I could stay on and get a hotel room if you really want me to stay."

"Give me Pop's phone number. Don't pretend you don't have it. This is too serious a matter to let go."

"He'll be upset if I give it to you."

"No, he won't. Not when he knows what Mother has been doing."

"I'm sorry, Tanner, I can't do that. I gave your father my word. He asked me to call him when your mother returned. Can I do that from Resa's apartment?"

"Sure. Let's go. Are you okay?"

"I think so. That was some kiss. We should do it again." Be bold and brassy when the occasion warrants, Sophie had said.

Tanner laughed. "Don't worry, we will."

* * *

It took all of ten minutes to bring Resa up to date on her mother's behavior.

"Jessie, how awful for you. She does things like that all the time. Sometimes I don't think she realizes what she does. I don't want to believe my own mother would deliberately hurt someone the way she hurt you. But then she's done the same thing to me so many times over the years. Sometimes I think she hates me."

"She does not hate you, Resa. I think she hates herself."

"And Pop," Resa said.

"Can Jessie use the phone in the bedroom?" Tanner asked.

"Of course. Look, Tanner, this package came from Pop this morning. It's my Christmas present. I wonder why he sent it here?"

"Sometimes you are so dumb, Resa. He sent it here because he knew you wouldn't be going to the ranch. Jessie hand-delivered mine and Mother's," he said smugly. "Don't forget, I want to talk to Pop before you hang up."

Jessie looked around the small bedroom as she dialed the senator's number. *Now this*, she thought, *is a sanctuary*. The spread on the double bed was full of bright red tulips and so cheerful, Jessie blinked. The same color red was used in corduroy to cover the cushions on what looked like an antique white rocking chair. Crisp white Priscilla curtains covered the windows. Cozy. Feminine without being girlish. Bright red rugs dotted the shiny hardwood floors. Children's artwork adorned the walls, each drawing signed with a hand print. "Yes, Senator, it's me. Mrs. Kingsley returned late last night. She said she didn't get out of the airport because of a snowstorm moving up the East Coast and was lucky to get a flight back to

Texas. I'm at Resa's, Senator. We're going shopping, and then we're going to bake Christmas cookies. I'm having a wonderful time. I love your daughter. Yes, I like your son, too. Tanner wants to talk to you. I wouldn't give him the phone number because I gave you my word. If you hold on, I'll call him. If you're driving back to town, Senator, be careful."

In the small living room, Jessie accepted a mug of hot coffee. "I have some sticky buns warming in the oven," Resa said. "It will be just a few minutes. Listen, don't let my mother get you down. After a while you learn to tune her out."

Jessie gulped at the hot coffee. From smothering love to deep hatred. Where was the happy medium?

Tanner returned to the kitchen just as Resa was taking the sticky buns out of the oven. "Drip butter over them, Sis. Be sure you turn on your answering machine when we leave. I told Pop to call when he gets back to Irene's house. He hates driving in snow, but Irene wants to go home. So do the twins."

"It's on. I screen my calls. If I don't want to talk, I don't pick up the phone. The only person I dodge is my mother," Resa explained for Jessie's benefit.

"Nobody ever calls me, so I don't have to worry," Jessie said.

"I'll be calling you, so you better pick up," Tanner said. Jessie's face turned rosy pink. Resa smiled.

"Aren't you going to tell us what Pop said?"

"He said he'll take care of it. He will, in his own way."

"I say we leave the dishes and get on with our shopping. I want to buy something absolutely wonderful for Josh. Something he would never buy for himself. Something totally outrageous so when he looks at it he says, Resa got this for me."

"Then let's go, ladies. I have a few gifts to buy myself."

"Me too," Jessie chirped.

This is so nice, Jessie thought as she gathered up her packages from the trunk of Tanner's car. *I feel like I've known these two people forever and ever. For the first time in my life I feel like I'm part of something. The best part is it's happening at the most wonderful time of the year. I will not let Alexis Kingsley spoil this for me. I will weather this the way I've weathered everything else in my life.*

"You look pensive," Resa said, her arms full of packages.

"Do I? I was just thinking how happy I am. Until this year I spent Christmas and Thanksgiving with Sophie. I cannot tell you how I dreaded the holiday."

"Then you made the decision to bite the bullet and stay at the ranch?" Jessie nodded. "Trust me, Jessie, when I tell you Tanner will not let Mother get another crack at you. Oh, oh, the red light is on. I have a message. Either it's Josh or Pop. Maybe both."

"How long are you going to stare at the blinking light, Sis? Oh, I get it. Come on, Jessie, it might be Josh whispering sweet nothings that are meant only for her ears. I'm going to make some coffee, okay?"

"Grind the beans twice, Tanner," Resa said.

"Sometimes she can be so damn bossy. Like I don't know I'm supposed to grind the beans twice. She tells me that at least once a week, maybe twice," Tanner grumbled.

Jessie smiled. "For some reason I don't think of you as a person who cooks or makes coffee."

"Jack and I had an apartment together for two and a half years. He couldn't afford to eat out, and he knew how to cook. He taught me everything he knew, which wasn't a whole hell of a lot. We didn't starve, though. He made the best damn pepper steak I ever ate. Jesus, I'd give anything if he was here. You would have liked him, Jessie. See, I told you I get like this over the holidays. I think about that guy all the time."

"I never really knew anyone who died except Agnes Prentis. I didn't know her that well. It must be awful."

"It's the realization that it's final. You are never, ever going to see that person again. You'll never hear them laugh, never hear them call your name. You'll never be able to say, Hey, Jack, what did you think of that home run?' Shit! How did I get on this subject anyway?"

"I think it had something to do with grinding beans. Resa, what's wrong?"

"Pop wants you to call him, Tanner. Something happened, but he wouldn't tell me what it is. Here's the number."

"Jesus! Is it Irene?"

"I don't think so. I could hear her in the background. The twins were jabbering, too. Whatever it is, it must be serious. I never heard Pop sound like that. They all made it back okay, so there wasn't a car accident or anything like that. Use the kitchen phone. I want to hear."

Jessie got up to go into the living room.

"Don't go, Jessie. I don't think there's anything about this family you don't know. We want you to stay. Pop might want to talk to you."

"Tanner's right, Jessie. Will you call already, Tanner. I'm a wreck just thinking about what could be wrong. Pop sounded . . . terrible."

"Shhh, the phone's ringing. Pop, what's wrong?"

Jessie and Resa watched as Tanner's face drained. "Jesus. Is Irene okay? Do you want me and Resa to come there? I'm sure we can get a flight in a few hours. I only know what she said, Pop. You don't think . . . Did you call the police? What did they say? So, who has a key? Did the twins lose their keys or perhaps lend one to someone? Of course I know they're responsible. Irene's making spaghetti. Uh-huh. What do you want me to do, Pop? Nothing? No, I do not think you should come home. Resa doesn't think so either, and neither does Jessie. Wait a minute. There was something strange Mother said this morning. She's getting rid of that science-fiction junk she's been decorating with for years. She said she was having someone come in to redo everything today so that it would be more traditional. I took that to mean a green tree with lots of red stuff and all those Christmas plants. Pop, you could call or have the twins call the different taxi companies and ask them if they took a fare to Irene's house. I think they keep logs. You could also call the different car services. Irene does have insurance, doesn't she? Christ sakes, Pop, what do you mean it lapsed? Couldn't you help her out? I thought you were on top of stuff like that. You drummed that in our heads often enough. We're okay. Are you sure you don't want Resa and me to come to D.C.? Okay, 'bye, Pop."

"What happened?"

"I think you got the gist of it. Someone broke into Irene's house and destroyed everything. The police say someone had to have had a key because the locks weren't jimmied and the windows were all locked. Whoever it was destroyed everything. All Irene's treasures and heirlooms, all that crystal in the dining room. I guess whoever it was messed up the kitchen pretty bad. They burned the kitchen carpet and seat cushions and sliced up the Christmas tree. Pop thinks it was Mother."

"Mother! She said she didn't leave the airport."

"That's what she said," Tanner agreed.

"This can't be good for Irene in her condition. Mother does hate her, though."

"Irene's making spaghetti. The twins went out to get a new tree. Once the shock wears off, Irene will handle it."

"Mother wouldn't do something like that. Would she, Tanner?" Resa asked fearfully.

"I honest to God don't know, Resa. I know it's a bit lame, but why do *you* think she's switching up all of a sudden. I am, of course, referring to her Christmas decor."

"I'd like to believe she finally realized how depressing all that blue-and-white junk is."

"One day before her famous yearly party? The very next day after her trip to Washington, where she sat in the airport and then turned around to come home? I don't believe that for one minute, and I don't think you do either."

Resa paced around the small kitchen. "Will Pop call the taxi companies? God, Tanner, what if it was her?"

"I don't think he really wants to know. No, I don't think he will call. He won't call for Irene's sake. I don't think she could handle knowing it was Mother. Random vandalism will be easier for her to deal with."

"I feel like we should do something," Resa said.

"Let's go to Washington," Tanner said. "Call Josh and ask him if he wants to go. I'll take Jessie back to the ranch to get her things. There's an eight o'clock flight. Pop used to take it all the time. We can do it if we decide right now. My treat, Resa, all the way."

"Okay. Get going. I'll talk Josh into it. Pick us up, okay? I'll stay with Jessie, and you and Josh can stay in Pop's apartment. Is that okay with you, Jessie?"

"Of course."

"Get your stuff, Jessie, we have to skedaddle."

"You Texans certainly do things on the spur of the moment," Jessie said as she gathered up her packages.

"Do you think it's the right thing to do, Jessie? The truth now."

Jessie didn't stop to think. "Absolutely. I think your father needs both of you with him at this time."

"That's good enough for me."

"How will your mother take this?"

"Not well. Not well at all."

Chapter Ten

Suddenly, thousands of twinkling, colored lights came into view even though Tanner and Jessie were just turning onto the mile-long driveway leading to the Kingsley ranch. Tanner stopped the car and rolled down the window. "What the hell!"

Stunned at the sight, Jessie climbed from the car. "They're Christmas lights, and they look like rainbows. There must be thousands of them. They're everywhere," Jessie said, her voice ringing in awe.

"It looks more like a million from where I'm standing," Tanner said joining her. "You're right, they are everywhere, even on the fencing. Jesus! The generators must be working overtime or else she's sucking kilowatts from the Holt ranch. Luke will be like a wild mustang if that's what she's doing. God damn it, everything is going to be thrown out of whack now. Obviously my mother didn't think this through. Get back in the car, Jessie. We aren't going anywhere unless I straighten this out.

"What in the hell do you suppose she was thinking of to do this? You're a female, Jessie. Am I wrong or is this *cartoonish?* If Pop is right and she . . . did all that damage back in Washington, how could she . . . I guess I want to know if she's flipped out. Get in the car, Jessie. I can't wait to see the rest of this . . . whatever this is."

Jessie took a deep breath. "First of all, Tanner, you don't know if your mother was even in Irene's house. She said she wasn't. We're all innocent until proven guilty. She did say she was going to make an old-fashioned Christmas. Maybe these lights are part of what she considers an old-fashioned Christmas. Most women don't know anything about electricity. I know I don't. I also don't think your mother was the one who hooked up all these lights. It's just a guess on my part, but I think it took an army of men to arrange a display like this. The decorators probably did exactly what she told them to do, which was plug them in. They lit up, and that was the end of it. When you explain it to your mother I'm sure she'll make adjustments."

"Is that before or after Luke Holt ruins us?" Tanner snapped.

There was no way for Jessie to respond. She climbed from the car to follow Tanner into the house.

If she was awed by the outdoor display of multicolored lights, Jessie found herself thunderstruck at the retina-searing North Pole display of elves, miniature workshops, shiny red-foil-wrapped gifts, and in the center of the floor, a monstrous Christmas tree that was so large it reached the point of the cathedral ceiling. She backed up a step and then another step. She could see that Tanner was speechless. "I'll get my things together and meet you at the car," she muttered. If Tanner heard her, he gave no sign. As she made her way upstairs to her bedroom she could hear him bellowing for his mother.

What kind of family was this? She needed to get out of here, and the sooner the better, but first she needed to clean up a little and change to a less wrinkled-looking sweater. She was in the bathroom waiting for the water to warm up from the faucet when she heard Tanner's voice searing up through the heating vent next to the enclosed shower. She increased the water pressure, hoping it would drown out the voices. When it didn't, she flushed the toilet, then turned on the shower. She could still hear the voices. She had no other choice but to listen as she washed her face and applied fresh makeup.

"Just tell me one thing, Mother, who hooked up all these Tinkertoys? Are you using the emergency generators?"

"How should I know? The decorator did everything. It's part of his job. Do you like it?"

"It's not important if I like it or not. What's important is your decorator better not have tied into the Holt electric box. Get Mackie up from the barn and tell him to switch everything to the emergency generators unless you want Luke Holt to shut off *everything*. We have a deal with the Holts, and you cannot go back on it. I don't have time to fool around with this right now. I'm going to Washington with Jessie and Resa, and I don't have much time. Cut off the power and do it *now!*"

"I will not! What do you mean you're going to Washington? Why? You and your sister had better be here for the party, Tanner. You can send that secretary packing. She'll be no loss."

"Fine, Mother. Have it your way. When Luke turns off the power think about how you're going to explain that to the people who attend your party. Are you going to use flashlights? How will those fancy caterers warm up all that gourmet food you plan to serve? Pop told me something pretty terrible today. He said someone broke into Irene's house and destroyed it. He thinks you did it. Did you?"

"How dare you accuse me of such a thing. I told you I

didn't leave the airport. If Irene chooses to leave her doors open, she should expect things like that to happen."

"You better hope that's the truth, Mother, because Pop is calling all the taxi companies and car services in the city to see if anyone drove a fare to Irene's house."

"I forbid you to go to that woman's house. This is all Resa's doing. Resa and that damn secretary. And you follow along, Tanner, just like Pavlov's dog."

The phone rang at the same moment the house turned dark.

In the darkened bathroom Jessie heard Tanner laugh. "This is just a wild guess on my part, Mother, but I'd say that's Luke Holt calling you to tell you he turned off the power in case you didn't notice. I'll leave you to do the explaining. Enjoy your party, Mother.

"Jess, are you ready?" Tanner shouted. "The power's out, so be careful. Stand still till I get there. I have a flashlight. I keep a bag packed for emergencies like this, so I'm ready to go. Watch your step and stay close behind me."

"Did all those lights blow a fuse?"

"Something like that."

"Is your mother upset?"

"More or less. Climb in, Miss Roland."

"I'm in, Mr. Kingsley."

"Next stop after Resa's house is Washington, D.C. It looks like we'll be spending Christmas together after all."

"If the snow doesn't melt, it will be my first white Christmas."

"I thought you came from Michigan. They have snow all the time."

Jessie's heart thumped in her chest. She had known she'd get tripped up eventually. "We always spent the winters in a warm climate. We had snow, but it never snowed on Christmas Eve like it does in the movies. Christmas was always balmy," she lied. "That's why I went to so many different schools." *That's it, Jessie, keep it up and dig yourself deeper into a hole.* She felt relief when Tanner didn't seem to be paying attention to what she said.

"Listen, Jessie, I'm sorry my mother treated you so shabbily. I hope you don't think any less of me. I'm sure you've never come across a family like ours. I could apologize from now till tomorrow, but it won't change things. It is what it is. I think what I'm trying to say is I really like you, and I don't want anything to go wrong. Do you understand what I'm trying to say?"

Did she? "Yes. Believe it or not, I do understand about families being strange. We're starting out with honesty. Your mother doesn't like me, and I don't much care for her. If we can get past that, I think things will be all right. I don't know if long-distance relationships work."

"We could make it work if we wanted to. I do. How about you?"

Jessie's voice was breathless. "Oh, yes," she said. "I do, too."

"Then it's settled. We're going to have a whole week to get to know one another. I can fly to Washington on weekends and we can talk on the phone during the week. I have things under control at the ranch. Mackie is aces when it comes to running things. I can take off days at a time if I want to. I'll get to see Pop more often, too."

Jessie grew light-headed. It sounded like he was asking her to go steady. Such a strange word for a relationship. Did people her age still go steady, or was that something only high-school youngsters did? Sophie would know. She tucked the thought away for future reference. She was saved from any kind of response when Tanner said, "Would you look at that. They're on the curb waiting for us, baggage and all. Jessie, don't say anything about my mother. I don't know how much Resa wants Josh to know.

I guess she's afraid he might get spooked. I thought you would, too."

"I don't spook easy. I won't say anything. Your father is going to be surprised."

"I don't think so. He knows me pretty well. What will surprise him is Resa and Josh."

"It's kind of sad that your mother will be alone for Christmas."

"Pop won't be there for her to badger. I guess it was meant to be. Hey, are you guys ready? What the hell do you have in all those bags, Resa?"

"Presents," she said, her voice ringing with happiness. "I knew you wouldn't think about it, so I did the shopping."

"Thanks, Sis. We can shop over the weekend."

"What Tanner means, Jessie, is you and I can shop while he and Josh do guy things."

Jessie laughed. If she could somehow manage to erase Alexis Kingsley from her thoughts, she might have a wonderful holiday after all.

"Mother called, Tanner. She was upset that we're going to miss the party."

Jessie noticed that Tanner clenched and unclenched his jaw. "How upset?"

"Luke Holt turned the power off. I didn't ask for details. I said good-bye and hung up. I knew she would call back, so Josh and I waited outside for you. I'm really looking forward to a whole week in Washington. Are we going to stay for New Year's Eve?"

"What do you think, Jessie? Can you see yourself ringing in the new year with us?" Jessie did her best to hide her smile. When Tanner reached for her hand she squeezed it.

Fifteen minutes later, Tanner pulled to the curb outside the airport. "I'll let you out here. Check us in, and I'll meet you at the gate. Don't leave without me."

Only Tanner heard Jessie say, "I'll wait for you forever."

"I'm going to hold you to that," Tanner shouted as he drove off to the long-term parking area.

As Jessie trailed behind Resa and Josh she realized she meant exactly what she said. She would wait forever for Tanner Kingsley because she was falling in love with him. How long was forever?

It was twenty minutes to midnight when Tanner rang Irene Marshall's doorbell. It was opened almost immediately by Angus Kingsley. In the light from the foyer that spilled out the door, Jessie could make out Irene's puffy eyes and drawn face. "Happy holidays!" Tanner boomed.

"That goes for me, too," Resa shouted.

Not to be outdone, Jessie and Josh Kelly shouted the same greeting.

"Bless your hearts. Come in, come in. Angus, take their coats. You must be starving. We have a lovely fire that hasn't burned down yet and a freshly stocked refrigerator. This is so nice, so wonderful of you all to come. Isn't it wonderful, Angus?"

"It's damn wonderful," Angus said as he clapped his son on the back, then hugged Resa. "Jessie, Josh, I can't tell you how happy this makes us."

Their coats hung in the closet, their bags settled by the door, Irene ushered her guests into the living room. Jessie was stunned to see how different yet how tidy the room looked. "It smells heavenly," she said.

"We've been burning pinecones for ambience. Angus, open some wine while I rustle us up some food."

"We'll help," Jessie and Resa said in unison.

"Now that's what I like to hear. You men sit here and put your feet up and enjoy Angus's fire while we take care of the food."

In the kitchen, Irene sagged against the counter. "Thank

you so much for coming. Angus is taking this so very hard. A terrible thing happened, but between the two of us we made it right. The twins helped, of course. Earlier we sent them off with some of their friends so our doom and gloom wouldn't rub off on them. We're over the worst of it now. At least I think we are. Your arrival makes it all right. What do you think of my drugstore decorations?"

How tense and jittery her voice sounds, Jessie thought. "I think they're beautiful. The tree smells heavenly. I think there are more lights on this one. Everything seems to, I don't know, sparkle more. The spirit is inside you, Irene. That's what makes all the difference. Whoever it was that did this can't take that away from you. That person is the loser, not you. Do you agree, Resa?"

"Absolutely. Compared to the ranch this is magnificent. It doesn't make a bit of difference where the red bows and the shiny Christmas balls came from. The best part is we're all together. Jessie and I are going shopping tomorrow. Would you like to join us?"

"Let's see how I feel in the morning. Now, what will it be, hot roast beef sandwiches or cold ham and cheese with even colder pickles?"

"Hot roast beef," Resa and Jessie said in unison.

The three women worked in companionable silence until Irene burst into tears. "I don't care about any of this but that dastardly person destroyed all those beautiful packages Angus brought over. He was so proud of them. He was devastated at the total destruction. It's not that I want them replaced. I don't. I can't bear to see him so unhappy."

"If Pop is unhappy it's because someone tampered with your happiness, Irene. For Pop himself, he couldn't care less. Everything is going to be all right. Pop will make it right. Moving right along to the really important stuff, tell the truth now, do you love Josh Kelly?"

Irene wiped at her eyes and smiled. "I think he's a fine young man, and you need to snatch him up before someone else gets him."

"I already did. Look!"

"Oh, Resa, I am so very happy for you. Does your father know?"

"Josh is probably telling him right now. Mother doesn't know. Tanner and Jessie are the only people I've told so far. Josh told his family, too. I am so happy, Irene."

"You deserve all the happiness in the world, my dear. I'm so glad you shared it with me. What about you, Jessie? Christmastime is such a wonderful time of the year to fall in love. It looks to me like Tanner has stars in his eyes. I think I see a noticeable sparkle in yours, too. Forgive me, I shouldn't be trying to play matchmaker."

Jessie's face turned a rosy pink.

"Jessie, we're embarrassing you, aren't we?" Resa laughed.

"It's all right."

"Soup's on!" Resa called from the kitchen.

"It's a midnight feast!" Angus chortled.

"Grace first, Angus," Irene said.

Angus bowed his head, his voice a somber whisper. "Thank you, God, for this food and for allowing my family and friends to share it with us. May all our holiday seasons be as wonderful as this one. Amen."

Everyone started to talk at once to cover Angus's choked voice and at the same time pretending not to see the tears in Irene's eyes.

It was two in the morning when Angus handed the keys to his small apartment to his son. "Irene said you can use her car to take the girls to Jessie's apartment. Irene is tired and should be in bed. We'll talk more tomorrow. I'd like you to do something for me, Jessie. I've written it all down. Drive carefully, Tanner. The weatherman said the roads are treacherous. There are chains on Irene's tires, but you still need to drive defensively. We'll meet up for dinner. Irene plans to cook all day tomorrow. Good night, everyone, and thank you all for coming."

"I'm sleeping till noon tomorrow," Resa said, climbing into the backseat of Irene's car.

"Me too," Jessie said.

Josh and Tanner agreed. "We'll pick you up at noon, have lunch, then do whatever you want."

"Sounds good." Resa yawned.

Later, outside her apartment, Tanner waited while Jessie opened the door for Resa. "You can have the bed on the right and the thermostat is in the hall."

"The roads really are bad, and everything is freezing. Please drive carefully. Are you going to kiss me good night?" Jessie asked boldly.

Just as boldly, Tanner said, "No."

"Oh."

"Not because I don't want to. When I kiss you I'll do it right. I don't like to start things I can't finish. Our day is coming."

"Are you talking about sex?" Jessie blurted.

"I'll let you know about that, too." Tanner grinned. "Sometimes anticipation is better than the actual event."

"I never heard that. Even Sophie never said anything like that, and Sophie knows *everything*. "

"We'll discuss Sophie's knowledge at some point in the future. Good night, Jessie."

"Good night, Tanner."

Tanner was halfway down the hall when he turned and walked back to where Jessie was standing. "Your expectations weren't met, is that right? Tell me what it was you expected."

"Bells, whistles, rockets, heavy breathing. A little ravishing and a little plundering. I was more or less prepared. I didn't get too far in my thinking."

"When I get back to Pop's place I'm going to write that all down. Do you want it in that order?"

A devil nipped at Jessie's tongue. "Absolutely. Do you think you can handle it?"

"Oh, I know I can. The big question is, can you?"

"I guess we'll both have to wait and see, won't we? Why are you sweating? It's cold out here in the hall," Jessie said, her voice ringing with sweetness.

"I'm sweating because I'm bundled up."

"Oh. Good night."

Jessie smiled as Tanner stalked his way to the stairwell. The devil nipped again. She ran down the hall and then skidded to a stop. "Sex," she said, her voice ringing in the empty hallway, "is a participatory event. I just want you to know I'm prepared to *participate*. However," she said wagging a finger under his nose, "it might be wise to set some sort of timetable. You really are sweating. I hope you don't catch cold. You better hurry or Josh will freeze out there in the car."

"You get me all riled up and then tell me you're worried about Josh. Women!"

Jessie smirked all the way back to her door. She scurried inside in time to see Resa dive under the covers.

"Is he a good kisser?" Resa asked. "I always wanted to know that about my brother."

"You'll have to ask someone else. I practically threw myself at him. No soap. He's not shy, so I can't use that as an excuse. Tell me about Bippity-Bop."

"The girls at school gave her that name because she bopped from one guy to the next. I think she had every guy in Texas. Tanner went with her during his senior year in high school. He dated her off and on when he came home for breaks during college. She's been married and divorced twice. No kids either time. She is absolutely mouth-watering gorgeous. She has a figure to die for and all the money in the world. All the girls were jealous of her. Loose as a goose. I think the only guy that didn't fall for her was Luke Holt. My mother would give up everything she holds dear if Tanner would marry Bop. She couldn't care less about her hot-pants reputation. Her parents feel the same way. You know guys. Bop was okay to play with but not to get serious with. Mother was furious when Tanner told her nothing would ever come of it. Bop's going to the party with her parents thinking Tanner will be there. She won't give up. She wants him. She's always wanted him. You know that old adage, you always want what you can't have. Picture a Barbie doll in your mind, and that's Bop. Her female friends call her Barbie, too. My mother calls her Barbara."

Jessie pulled a warm flannel nightgown over her head. "What does she do?"

"Do?"

"You know, a job, what? How does she spend her time?"

"She shops. She got millions from her two divorce settlements. Plus, her family is very, very rich, and she's an only child. Big oil family. The teachers at school tell me she drives a racy sports car and lives in a fabulous condo in town. In a way, Jessie, she's your competition. For some reason, from time to time, Tanner seeks her out. I think it's only fair you know that. Tanner is a great guy, and I love him with all my heart, but he does have his flaws, as I do, and I have to assume you have a few yourself. Even Josh has a flaw or two."

Jessie's heart fluttered in her chest. "Do you know her personally, Resa?"

"Everyone knows Bop. She's outgoing, friendly, she can laugh at herself. She can be charming, and, like I said, she's gorgeous with a figure to match. She lives to party and she can hold her liquor. For some guys that's a winning combination. I should tell you she does a lot of volunteer work. She doesn't actually do the work, she lends her name to different worthwhile projects. In all fairness, anything she involves herself in raises money. I don't think you have a thing to worry about. My brother's falling for you in a big way. Irene didn't look too good, did she?"

Tanner was falling for her. Jessie punched her pillow to get it just right, a smile on her face. "She looked very tired. I'm sure tomorrow will be better. I mean today. I'm so tired I can't think straight. Good night, Resa."

"Night, Jessie. I like your little apartment. It's cozy, rather like a nest. I tried to make my apartment into my own nest . . ."

Jessie waited for Resa to continue but her light, even breathing signaled that her roommate had fallen asleep in mid-sentence. Jessie climbed out of her cocoon of blankets and dropped to her knees. She said her prayers the way she did every night, adding an extra prayer for Irene Marshall. She was almost asleep when she got up a second time to pad out to the living room, where she withdrew the leather-bound logbook from the small bookshelf nestled under the window. She wrote steadily for thirty minutes before she placed it under the sofa. The last thing she did before sliding into bed was to look at the list the senator had handed her. She was to go to two speciality shops in Georgetown and replace the items listed. The postscript to the note said she was to get the fanciest, prettiest gift wrap available and to charge everything to the senator's account. She slipped the list into her purse. Now she was ready to go to bed.

Shortly before dawn, Jessie's restless sleep took her to a familiar dark, dizzying place that left her struggling for breath. She cried out, her legs and arms beating and twisting the covers. Her body was soaked with perspiration, her curly hair plastered to her head when she finally shed the heavy quilt she was wrapped in. Coughing and sputtering, she swung her legs over the side of the bed just as Resa crawled over her bed to take her into her arms.

"Jessie, what's wrong?"

"Nothing. Just a bad dream."

"It must have been a doozie. You were screaming."

"I'm sorry if I woke you."

"That's okay. Do you want me to make you some tea? Tea always seems to make things less intense. I don't know why that is. Do you want to talk about it? I'm a good listener."

"It's the same dream I always have. I'm in this very dark place, and I can't breathe. I try to scream, and sometimes I do. Sometimes I can't. I get dizzy like I'm being pushed or something. Whatever it is it's going very fast, and then I wake up. I always wake up coughing and choking. For some strange reason I feel like I have a cold when I wake up. It's weird."

"You were screaming jelly, jelly. At least that's what it sounded like to me. I might not have heard you right. How often do you have this dream?"

"When I was little, almost every night. As I got older it was less and less. Sometimes months go by, and I won't have it. My friend Sophie is the one who figured out that I have the dream when I'm extremely tired or something has upset me. I have no idea why I would scream for jelly. It's not something I normally eat. My mother used to try and force it on me, and I always balked. Too sweet I guess. Go back to sleep, Resa. I'll go out to the kitchen and make a cup of tea. There's no point to both of us losing sleep. When I calm down I'll go back to bed."

"Are you sure?"

"Yes, I'm sure."

"You should buy one of those dream books and see if you can figure out what the dream means. It's strange that you should have the same dream for so many years. It must mean something. Something really traumatic must have happened to you when you were a small child."

"That's what Sophie said. Maybe when we're shopping I'll see if I can find one. Pleasant dreams."

"Don't drink too much tea, or you won't be able to fall asleep again."

In the kitchen, Jessie made coffee instead of tea. She'd lied to Resa. After the dream she could never go back to sleep. Her insides were quivering, and her head felt like it was going to explode right off her shoulders. Resa was right. She should try to find out what the dream meant. Sophie had said dream books were hocus-pocus. According to Sophie there was a simple explanation to the dream, which was when she was an infant she probably got tangled up in the covers and couldn't get untangled. Fear and terror took over, making it impossible to scream. The more you struggled, the more frightened you became, and that's why you started to perspire. The only explanation she could offer for the jelly was the apple quince kind she hated and her mother made her eat every morning when she was little.

It made sense to a point. But, if Sophie's reasoning was right and they talked it out and she accepted it as fact, why was she still having the same dream years and years later? What in the world did jelly have to do with anything?

"Jelly, jelly, jelly," Jessie muttered, her heart racing so fast she could barely catch her breath. When she calmed down sufficiently so that she could think clearly she started to mutter again. What she was experiencing and feeling now was something new. Nothing like this had ever happened in the aftermath of the dream. Was something so simple and so sweet as jelly the clue to unlocking the secret of her awful dream? If there was an answer it eluded her.

Her sunny, yellow kitchen was almost too warm now. She looked around, marveling at what she'd done on weekends to turn the drab apartment into something cozy and comfortable. She'd always been partial to the color yellow and all the gold and earth tones. She'd drawn on that partiality when she decorated the apartment. The small kitchen was her favorite room, though and she'd spent more time trying to find just the right accent pieces. Herbs in yellow-painted pots rested on the extra wide windowsill. The trailing grape ivy had to be trimmed at least once a week or the tips grew into the herb pots. She loved to pinch off a leaf from one of the herbs when she felt domestic and cooked soup or a savory stew. Young couples got married and started out in apartments like this. When she got married she wondered where she would live? Her thoughts carried her back to the house in Charleston where she'd grown up. Was her playhouse still standing? Did her parents sell the old house with the polished banister and wide verandah or was it standing empty? Did they ever go back there? She didn't miss them or the cold, unwelcoming house at all. Sophie's house was no better with all the marble, chrome, and glass. Neither house had ever been a home in the true sense of the word. This minuscule apartment was her home, and it was hers and hers alone.

Tears welled in her eyes and then overflowed. She rubbed at them with a paper napkin and blew her nose.

Maybe I wasn't supposed to be happy. Maybe God put me on earth to . . . what? To be miserable? To cry myself to sleep at night? What?

What do you want, Jessie? an inner voice queried. "I want a family. The kind of family Tanner's friend Jack had. I want a husband, children, and pets. I want my own little house, and I want that house to be the kind of house where my family can't wait to get back to at the end of the day. I want to make meat loaf and cookies and take the animals to the vet. I want to juggle children's schedules and know my husband appreciates it when I ease some of his burdens. I want a verbal family, and I want all of us to respect each other's opinions. I want my children to grow up strong and independent. Do I want too much? Are my wants impossible dreams?"

As always when there were no answers to her questions, Jessie reached behind her chair to pull her sketch pad out of the kitchen drawer. She slouched in her chair, her pencil flying over the paper. She was still sketching at eight-thirty when the phone rang. Thinking it was Tanner, she worked a smile into her voice when she said hello.

"Sophie!" she squealed. "I was just thinking about you. Where are you? San Francisco! You're back early! Is Jack with you? He's winding things up and will be back January 3. How awful for you. Where are you headed? Atlanta. Of course I will. If I leave this morning, I'll get there at the same time you arrive by plane. I can pick you up at the airport. God, Sophie, I missed you. I can't wait to see you."

Jessie stared at her sketch pad. Did she just volunteer to drive to Atlanta when she had a houseguest and a possible romance that was just getting off the ground? Life was full of surprises.

"Did the phone ring?"

"Yes. It was my friend Sophie. She's in San Francisco. She called to invite me to Atlanta. I'm going to pack and leave as soon as possible. You're welcome to stay as long as you like. I'll be back the day after New Year's. I made coffee, so help yourself."

"You're leaving! But what about Tanner . . ."

Jessie smiled. "What about him?"

"I thought . . . you seemed . . . he . . . Never mind, it's none of my business."

Jessie reached for her purse on the kitchen counter. She handed over the senator's shopping list. "I think Tanner will be able to direct you to Georgetown. I have to hurry, Resa. I told Sophie I'd meet her at the airport."

"Can I help you do anything?"

"No. I'm not packing that much. Sophie and I are the same size, and she has closets full of clothes. Just the essentials. I'll have to have my car looked at. Air, gas, oil check, that sort of thing. However, it takes time. I am so excited. I haven't seen Sophie in almost a year."

"Don't worry about the beds or anything. I'll take care of everything. Are you sure you don't mind me staying here?"

"Not at all."

"What should I tell Pop and Tanner?"

"Tell them what I just told you. Resa, I just work for your father. I'm not part of your family. You all made me feel comfortable but uncomfortable at the same time. Do you understand what I mean?"

"Of course. We've taken advantage of you. Yes, we have. You've been bounced around like a rubber ball, and my mother didn't help matters. This might be good for Tanner. No one has ever stood him up. At least not to my knowledge. He's one of those guys who if he stands still for five minutes women will flock to him."

"So what you're saying is I'm just one of many women on his list."

"That's not what I meant. What I meant was when he

sees you aren't just waiting for his call he'll start thinking about you more seriously. I'm probably not expressing my thoughts right. The bottom line is it will be good for Tanner. It will be good for Pop, too. He depends on you too much. This is after all your vacation, and all of us have infringed on your time. Holidays or not, it isn't right. Don't give anything a second thought. I'll take care of everything. Do you have a phone number you want to leave with me?"

Jessie's mind whirled. Which number to give her? She grinned when she thought of the three phones lined up in Sophie's room and in the room she always slept in. She rattled off a number, uncertain which phone number she was giving out.

Forty minutes later, Jessie walked out the door of her apartment. Her destination: Atlanta, Georgia.

"I'm stuffed! I haven't had food like this since last Christmas! I bet I can pack on twenty pounds between now and when Jack gets back. He won't know me. Oh, Jess, I love him so much! But you know that, so let's talk about Tanner Kingsley. Oh, there goes the phone. Is it him, Jess? Do we let it ring or what?"

Jessie squirmed in her chair. "I don't know."

"Answer the damn phone, Jessie."

Jessie's arm snaked out to pick up the ringing phone. Her hello was cautious sounding.

"Jessie, it's Tanner. You deserted me. A good-bye would have been nice. I had all these wonderful plans for this week. I miss you."

"I . . . it was early. I knew everyone was tired, and I didn't want to wake you. I'm sure you'll all have a wonderful time."

Jessie rolled her eyes at Sophie and mouthed the words, "I don't know what to say."

"Tell him you want to get laid. That should make him nuts!" Sophie mouthed in return.

"How long are you going to stay in Atlanta?"

"I'm going to leave on the second."

"How about a date for New Year's Eve. I'll fly down there, and we'll do the town. Yes or no. We did have a date you know."

"I . . . I'd like that. You would really fly to Atlanta for New Year's Eve?"

"I really would."

Sophie crawled off the bed and left the room. "Talk all night," she whispered from the doorway. "I'm going to catch a catnap." Jessie nodded.

"That's so nice. It will give me something to look forward to."

"Do you think you and your friend will be talked out by then?"

"No. We can talk forever. She has a wedding to plan for. That alone will take days and days. You only get married once."

"Not in this day and age."

"For Sophie it will only be once. I feel the same way. To me marriage is forever."

"What if one or the other falls out of love? You can't make someone love you."

"That's why a person needs to be sure when they take that final step. I can't imagine loving someone and then falling out of love. I can't see that ever happening to me. Can you?"

"Sure. I didn't mean that the way it sounds. What I mean is I've seen it happen with some of my friends. The wife becomes more of a mother to the kids and less and less like a wife. She lets herself go and doesn't care how she looks. It might not sound nice, but it happens."

"Are you trying to tell me something, Tanner?"

"I don't know. Maybe. It's just my personal opinion."

"Motherhood is a full-time job. A serious job if it's done right. Are you saying a woman has to be *all things?* Like super mom, super wife, super career woman."

"Forget that career part. Wives shouldn't have to work."

"That sounds nice, Tanner, if we lived in a perfect, rich world. Everyone isn't as fortunate as you. Some women, actually a lot of women, have to work to make ends meet. That alone would make for a pretty frazzled woman. Speaking strictly for myself, I didn't go to college just to go. I went to get an education. I hope to put that education to use someday when I finish, which will be this semester. What that means to you is I do not agree with what you're saying."

"I didn't mean to rile you up. How did we get on this subject anyway? When you finish are you going to leave Pop?"

"Well, guess what, you did rile me up. You brought up the subject and yes, I probably will seek a job elsewhere when I have my degree."

"Wait a minute. Let's back up to the part where I asked you to go out New Year's Eve and you said yes."

"Fine. Once words are spoken they can't be taken back. Just so you understand."

"Okay, I understand. Pop and Irene were really upset that you won't be with us for Christmas."

"I'm not part of your family, Tanner. I don't belong at Irene's house with her family and your family. I'm not comfortable knowing as much as I know about your families."

"If you'd talk more about your family, then we would be even."

"There's nothing to tell," Jessie said, her heart thumping in her chest.

"So you say. I bet your family is riddled with secrets just like everyone else's family."

"I'm sorry to disappoint you, but there are no secrets."

"If you say so. Do you miss us, just a little bit?"

"A little bit. How is Irene today? Did you all go shopping?"

"Irene says she's fine. Pop said she didn't sleep all night. He found her in the living room crying when he got up. He explained it this way. Some person came into Irene's house and decided parts of her life weren't worth anything, so that person destroyed those things. Irene will turn it around. She has Pop, Resa, and me for whatever good we are. And the twins, of course. Resa bought out the stores. You should see your living room. By the way, I like your apartment. It's you, and that's a compliment. In a way it reminds me of Jack's and my first apartment when we were in college. Jack's mother fixed it up for us. You know, she hung curtains and decorated the bathroom. Hell, we even had towels that matched the shower curtain. She brought tons of green plants, but they all died. She'd just look at us and replace them. It was really bare without the plants. I'm babbling here. I can't believe you left."

"Why is that so hard to believe?"

"I wanted you to stay. I thought you wanted to stay, too. Did you leave because I wouldn't kiss you?"

"How old did you say you were? That was a ridiculous thing to say. If I wanted to kiss you, I would have kissed you. I would have knocked you down, sat on top of you, and kissed you till your teeth rattled. I'm aggressive. Write that down. I think I'll hang up now and spend some time with my friend. It was nice of you to call. I'll look forward to New Year's Eve. Give my regards to your family." Jessie thought she heard a sputtering sound and something that sounded like, "I'll be damned."

I'll be damned is right, Jessie thought. She was so light-headed she had to drop her head between her knees. She was trembling when she raised her eyes to see Sophie lounging in the doorway, laughing hysterically.

"Baby, you have certainly come a long way from that shy little girl from Charleston. I couldn't have done it better. You're really falling for this guy, aren't you?"

"Yes. There's a part of me that's shooting off warning signs, though."

"Always pay attention to the warning signs. How about I run a check on him and his family? The mother sounds like a witch from hell. I bet she has secrets that would blow our minds."

"I don't think so, Sophie. We need to go on trust here. A relationship is only as good as both people. Look at me, with that bogus identity you created for me. What do I do when he wants to meet my parents?"

"We'll worry about that later. Let me run the check. We won't look at it. I'll put it in the safe in my closet. No one has the combination but you and me. If the time ever comes when things get sticky, and, Jessie, you know things always get sticky, it will be there. The flip side to that is the report might be so boring it will put us both to sleep. I promise you I will not open it. I'll have them red-wax seal it. Okay? That witch of a mother of his is probably running a check on you as we speak. That's the bad news. The good news is she doesn't have my talented resources. You don't have a thing to worry about where she's concerned. She'll come up dry."

"Would you have run a check on Jack?"

"Yes, Jessie, I would have if I hadn't met his family and friends. I'm dreading the day I have to tell him everything."

"Are you going to do it before or after you get married?"

"Before. I have to give him the chance to back out. Jack is big on truth and honor."

"Tanner's best friend was named Jack. It doesn't mean anything. I don't know why I even mentioned it. Okay, run the check."

"We want everything, right?"

"I guess so."

"Consider it done. All it will take is two phone calls. I'll meet you downstairs in the kitchen. I'm starving. We need to talk about what you're going to wear for your big date on New Year's Eve. It has to be spectacular. All glittery and shimmery. You can wear my diamonds. If you're sure you really, really want this guy, we have to set up his seduction. He's already planning yours. That's a given. You really think this is the guy for you?"

"Oh, yes. I'm sure, Sophie."

"We have a lot of work ahead of us tonight, my friend. I want sauerkraut, mustard, and relish on my hot dog."

Jessie laughed. It was like old times with a new twist. "I can handle it, Sophie."

Chapter Eleven

Jessie did her best to hide her dismay. She thought about Irene Marshall's tasteful, warm living room with the fragrant fir tree compared to Alexis Kingsley's retina-searing horror. This room, though, would win the prize.

"It's pretty dismal, isn't it?" Sophie asked.

"The tree is beautiful. The household staff did what you asked them to do, which was set up the tree. This room is too large for the tree. Even if you had a tree in every corner, it still wouldn't be enough. These spindly antique chairs, marble floor, and the ugly windows do not make for warm and cozy. The fireplace is working. It's cold outside the way it's supposed to be for Christmas. I have an idea, Sophie. Let's go out to your old playhouse and bring in the bean-bag chairs and the little table to pile our presents on. We'll drag some blankets down from upstairs and make things cozy while we wait for Santa to arrive. Wonderful things are supposed to happen on Christmas Eve. We'll decorate the tree and hang up our stockings."

Sophie's smile was sad, but she agreed. "There's an echo in this room. A carpet might cut down on it."

"We don't have a carpet, so it doesn't matter. Our nest

will be by the fire. If you like, we can move the tree closer
to the fire so we can appreciate it while we snuggle. I'll
push the stand from the back and you pull from the front.
There won't be anyone to see it but us, so it doesn't make
a difference where we place it as long as it's not too close
to the fire. We need to get into the spirit, Sophie. Just think
about this time next year. You'll be married, and it will be
your first Christmas as a couple. You might even be pregnant by then. Everything is going to be so wonderful for
you, Sophie."

Two hours later, Jessie dusted her hands dramatically.
"It's beautiful if I do say so myself. Our nest looks cozy
and warm, the fire is blazing and we have a buffet fit for a
king. There's just one thing left to do. We have to hang up
our stockings!" With a wild flourish, Jessie whipped out
two oversize red-felt stockings from a shopping bag next
to her pile of presents. "I even had our names stenciled
with silver glitter on them. I know they're tacky, but that's
okay. You hang them, Sophie. I got those sticky things to
hang them with."

"Jess, you are too much."

Jessie sat down cross-legged in front of the fire. She was
up a minute later when she saw Sophie's shoulders start to
shake.

"She isn't coming, is she, Jess?"

"No, Sophie, she isn't coming."

"I hoped. I really did. I thought for sure she'd come this
year. I called everyone under the sun to try to get a message to her. For weeks I called the last number she gave
me, but there was never an answer. I wrote letters, hundreds of them, hoping one or two would catch up with
her. I called her bankers, her lawyers, her accountants, her
business manager. They all promised to get a message to

her. I think my mistake was telling her I was getting married. A daughter old enough to get married and have a child probably wasn't something she wanted to hear. She wouldn't have come anyway. It's just you and me, Jess."

"It's okay, Sophie. We have each other. It's your mother's loss, not yours. To date both of us have not only persevered, but we have prevailed. Look at us, we're here. We did this," Jessie said waving her arms about. "We're together. We are going to drink this fine wine, eat this fine food, stare at the fire, reminisce, talk about Jack and Tanner and then we're going to go to sleep. In the morning we're going to open all of these gorgeous presents and then go to church. I'm okay with this, Sophie. Are you?"

"God, Jess, what would I do without you?"

"That's my line. Those stockings are pretty awful."

Jessie suddenly felt a chill run up her arm. She moved closer to the fire. The chill stayed with her. A premonition? Of what? Trying to shake the ominous feeling, she said, "Want to sing some carols? We could start with 'Jingle Bells' to put us in the mood."

Sophie slid her bean-bag chair closer to Jessie's. With their arms around each other's shoulders, the young women sang happily but off-key, until they finished all the carols they could remember.

Hours after Sophie fell asleep, Jessie was still wide-awake, her insides quivering. She tossed and turned in her nest, but sleep eluded her. She listened to Sophie's even breathing for a few minutes before she got up to rummage in her shopping bag for the stocking stuffers she'd bought the day before. She jammed and crunched trinkets, candies, and essentials until the stocking was filled to the brim. The remaining items were dumped any old way into her own stocking. Maybe she could sleep now. She squeezed her eyes shut and thought about her upcoming date with Tanner Kingsley. She had to find just the right dress, just the right shoes, just the right hairdo. Lord, what would she wear on top? Her camel-hair coat? Absolutely not. Sophie's long sable coat or her white-ermine cape? She grimaced as she scrunched her face into the pillow. Obviously she needed a lot of work when it came to the art of seduction. Well, she had six whole days to practice. With Sophie's help anything was possible.

It was midafternoon, two days before New Year's Eve, when Sophie held the door for Jessie. "I swear, girl, you bought out the store. Hurry up, let's spread it all out on the bed and look at it before your friend Tanner gets here."

Giggling like schoolgirls, they emptied the bags and boxes, placing everything neatly on the bed. Hands on her hips, Sophie stared at the bed. "That's some kind of underwear, Jessie. It's so . . . so . . . *ethereal*-looking. It's just strings and gauze. Emerald green is definitely your color. There must be ten thousand sequins on that gown. Jess, you will sparkle and shimmer all night long. Are you sure you're going to be able to walk, never mind dance in those stiletto heels? I still cannot believe you talked that woman into gluing all those sequins on those shoes."

"I can believe it. I spent almost a year's pay, Sophie. For one night! I think my brains must be scrambled. What time is it?"

"Almost three."

"Tanner said he'd be here between three and three-thirty. I want to change and freshen my makeup. What are you going to do, Sophie?"

"I'm going to take a walk. I'll meet you in the library later. You don't need me hanging around when Tanner gets here. Besides, I want to check the mail. That investigative report was due today. Don't worry, we are not going to read it. It's going in the safe as soon as it arrives."

"Sophie, what did you do with your mother's Christmas present?"

Sophie's face closed up tight. "I didn't do anything with it. It's still on the dresser. What am I supposed to do with it? What kind of parent gives her only child a deed to a Greek island for a Christmas present? Not only that, it didn't get here until the day after Christmas. All right, all right, I'll put it in the safe."

Ten minutes later, just as Jessie was about to step into the shower, Sophie called to her. "Everything's in the safe, Jess. I'm going out now. I'll be back in about an hour."

"Okay."

Jessie emerged from the shower and slipped into a thick terry robe. The phone rang as she was padding into the bedroom for her clothing. Thinking it was Tanner calling to say he was on his way, Jessie playfully said, "I'm counting the minutes and the seconds." She was taken aback when the voice on the other end of the wire asked for Sophie Ashwood.

"I'm sorry, Sophie went for a walk. She'll be back in an hour. Would you care to leave a message?"

"And you are?"

"Jessie Roland, Sophie's friend."

"Yes, I know of you, Miss Roland. Sophie has spoken of you to me many times. My name is Arthur Mendenares. I am Janice Ashwood's attorney. I'm afraid I have some devastating news. I don't know if it would be better for Sophie to hear it from me or you."

Jessie felt a lump start to grow in her throat. "Perhaps you should tell me what the news is and we can decide together. Is it about that Greek island Mrs. Ashwood gave Sophie for Christmas?"

"I'm afraid not, Miss Roland. Janice Ashwood and her companion were killed earlier this morning in a motor accident. My details are sketchy. The driver as I understand it was a race-car driver and liked to travel at high speeds. He misjudged a hairpin turn and went over a cliff. It's my understanding both Janice and her companion had consumed several bottles of champagne. Now, which one of us should tell Sophie?"

"I don't want to do it, but I think it might be better coming from me. I can't believe this. What do you want us to do?"

"I've already taken the liberty of chartering a plane. All you have to do is get Sophie to the airport. Janice's will calls for her to be cremated as soon after her death as possible. She was most explicit in her details. She did not want her remains to be sent back to Atlanta. She was most adamant about that."

"Where . . . where did this happen?" She was asleep, and this was all a very bad dream. She was going to wake up any minute now and Tanner would walk through the downstairs door shouting her name. *Please, God, make this a bad dream. Please.*

"Outside Monaco. The remains are charred beyond recognition. Before you can ask, we know for certain it was Janice and her friend because the car behind them was full of friends. They witnessed the accident. I will personally meet Sophie at Orly Airport. I am so very sorry."

"Yes, I'm sorry too. I'll . . . I'll get Sophie's things together. Do you want her to call you back?"

"No. I have to leave now. There are a million details to be seen to. Good-bye, Miss Roland."

Jessie ripped off the terry robe and dressed. She tossed things into suitcases willy-nilly and then carried them downstairs. Her face drained of all color when she heard the solarium door open. Sophie trying to be quiet because she thought Tanner was here. Jessie called out to her friend.

"Just a minute, Jess."

"Now, Sophie. *RIGHT NOW*," Jessie screamed.

Sophie arrived on the run. "Jessie, what's wrong? Did something happen to Tanner? No, not Jack. Not Jack, Jessie." Jessie shook her head.

"It's your mother, Sophie. Mr. Mendenares called while you were out. We couldn't decide who should tell you."

"For God's sake, Jess, tell me what? So she got married again. What else is new? She was probably honeymooning over Christmas. Don't look at me like that, Jess. You're scaring me. What is it?"

"Your mother . . . and her . . . the person she was with, were killed earlier this morning. I am so sorry, Sophie. I packed for you. There's a chartered plane waiting at the airport. I'm going with you. Mr. Mendenares will meet us at the airport. He said . . . what he said was . . . the bodies were charred beyond recognition."

"Then how do they know it was my mother? I don't believe it. My mother would never die like that. First she'd have a parade and sell tickets to the event. You know that, Jessie. There has to be some kind of mistake."

"There's no mistake, Sophie. A car full of your mother's friends was behind her when her car went over the cliff. Mr. Mendenares said your mother wanted to be cremated as soon as possible after her death. They're waiting for you. Put your coat on."

"It's really true then, Jessie?"

"Yes, Sophie, it's really true."

"I have to tell the housekeeper."

"I took care of all that. We'll go in my car and leave it at the airport."

"What about Tanner?"

"Tanner? God, I forgot about him. We can't worry about him now. He's all grown-up. He can handle this. Get in the car while I explain about Tanner to the housekeeper. You don't mind if he stays here, do you?" Sophie shook her head.

Jessie was backing the Jeep out from the portico when a bright yellow taxi pulled alongside.

"Whoa! Where are you ladies going?"

"Tanner, I don't have time to talk to you right now. The housekeeper will explain things to you. Go inside and make yourself comfortable. I'll call you tonight."

"Okay, but where are you going?"

"France."

"Like Paris, France?"

"Yes. I'll call you."

"Are you going to be back for our date?"

"I don't know. I'll call you."

"What should I tell my father?" Tanner shouted.

Jessie didn't think he could hear her response, but she shouted it anyway as she leaned out the window. "Tell him I quit!"

"What's today's date, Jessie?"

"It's the seventh of January. You need to eat, Sophie. This shrimp is wonderful. Please, I'm starting to worry about you. You aren't sleeping. Have you looked in the mirror?"

"I'm not sleepy. I'm not hungry. When I look in the mirror I see my mother. When your parents die there are no buffers between you and mortality. I have no other family. It's just me."

"You have me, Sophie. I consider you my sister. I hope you look on me the same way. We always said that's the way it was. This tragedy will put it to the test. You have to be strong."

"I can't handle all this bullshit, Jessie. It's all so fucking complicated. There are corporations within corporations. There are holding companies and shipping companies and all kinds of stuff. A person would have to be a wizard to have a handle on all of it. Furthermore, I don't want to handle it."

"Then appoint someone to handle it for you. Everything seems to be running smoothly with the people in charge. Hire one of those big-name law firms to oversee everything. They'll send you financial reports every month. You shouldn't have to deal with all that right now. Your mother didn't concern herself with the working end of things. I assume she had a bank account she drew on. It will pass on to you and . . ."

"And?"

"You bank the money I guess. There's a lot of good you could do with the fortune you just inherited. Now isn't the time to dwell on all of this."

"Now is the time. How in the hell am I going to explain all of this to Jack?"

"My advice would be to tell him rather than explain. You can't change things, Sophie. It is what it is."

"Your favorite saying, it is what it is. I'll never know if I spooked her or not by telling her I was getting married."

"That had nothing to do with her death. It's not your fault. Do not try to assume the blame, Sophie. I will not allow you to do that. Do you hear me?"

"Of course I hear you. I don't even know what she owned. I don't know anything. How can I go back to the States and leave things in the hands of strangers?"

"You have to go back because Jack is waiting for you. You have bridges to build."

"I guess that means you want to return to Washington."

"Only if you want to go back, Sophie. The only thing waiting for me in Washington are my classes for the last semester. Classes don't start for another two weeks. I quit my job, remember?"

"What about Tanner?"

"He calls every day. That surprises me. The senator

called yesterday and asked me something that was so silly I snapped at him. How am I supposed to know where he left his galoshes? I think he just wanted to see how I was. Resa called twice. I'm surprised that Irene hasn't called."

"Let's go home. You go back to Washington, and I'll go back to New Orleans."

"See, you made a decision. It wasn't so hard after all."

"Let's go to Spain first so you can see your parents. Don't look at me like that, Jessie. I would give anything to have been able to see my mother one last time. I didn't see her for five years. That's not right. Life is very fragile, as I just found out. I don't want you to have any regrets later on. We'll stop, say hello, have a meal with them and leave. It is the kind, decent thing to do, Jessie."

Jessie's stomach knotted itself into a tight fist. What Sophie said was true. The difference was, Sophie had loved her mother whereas she had never loved hers. The kind, decent thing to do. She nodded. "A few hours. That's it. Do they know about your mother?"

"Not to my knowledge. I'll tell your mother. They were best friends at one time. For some reason I think my mother worked hard at staying in touch with your parents. This is just a wild guess on my part, but I think she viewed your mother as a respectable, genteel, Southern lady. I think she might want to know. As most people age they tend to mellow out. For both our sakes let's hope it's true in regard to your parents. Did you ever touch the trust fund?"

"No."

Sophie sighed. "Let's make arrangements and pack. I've had it with all this sunshine, and these goddamn flowers are starting to make me ill. You're right, this is good shrimp. I'd kill for a nice juicy hot dog right now. I have some calls to make. We'll be back in the good old U. S. of A. by tomorrow night."

Jessie's heart fluttered in her chest. Sophie was back among the living. Maybe Tanner would travel to Washington to see her. On the other hand, he might be fed up with her by now. She would not think about her parents. She absolutely would not. Instead she would think about throwing herself into Tanner's arms and what would come afterward.

"We have"—Sophie looked at her watch—"exactly two and one half hours until we have to leave for the airport. We can cut that down to an hour and a half if it looks like it's getting to you. Just tug on your ear, and I'll pick up the ball. We'll walk around to the back. The housekeeper said both your parents are in the garden. I wonder why they picked Barcelona to live. It doesn't compute."

Jessie's face was grim. "I know." What was she doing here? "I should have brought something. I was taught never to go anywhere empty-handed."

"Pick a flower," Sophie snapped. Jessie did.

"That's Jack Daniel's and Bombay gin on the table. They're drinking. It's only ten o'clock. My mother doesn't drink. She sips sherry on Christmas Day."

Sophie wrinkled her nose, then rolled her eyes. "They'll be wasted by noon and take a nap for the afternoon. Everyone takes a nap in the afternoon to get ready for a heavy dinner and more drinking. According to my mother that's the European way. That's what my mother used to do. Give them a memory to hold on to, Jessie. It can't hurt since you'll be leaving, and they'll be staying on."

Jessie stared at Sophie. No matter how sharp her tongue, no matter how angry her eyes, Sophie Ashwood was grieving. She realized at that moment she would do anything to make Sophie happy. She nodded.

Jessie took a moment to view the surroundings and compare them to the garden back in Charleston. She finally decided there was no comparison. She inched her sunglasses down over the bridge of her nose and immediately shoved them back into place. The sunshine was blinding. The rainbow of flowers in hanging baskets, in clay pots, and crawling up trellises made her gasp. Intricate, lacy, wrought-iron furniture nestled under umbrellas as multihued as the array of flowers. A knee-high deep green hedge separated the patio from the rest of the garden. She looked down to see her reflection in the Italian marble. *It must be a sturdy tile*, she thought crazily, knowing Sophie's house in Atlanta was full of the shiny Italian marble. She sniffed at the fragrant air from the colorful blooms. The intoxicating scent made her feel light headed. She stared at two fat bumblebees sipping at the center of a luscious crimson bloom. Iced tea, the ice melted, sat in an exquisite cut-glass pitcher on one of the little tables, along with a plate of cookies. A clear crystal dome protected them from insects. Neither looked like they'd been touched. On another table was a bottle of Jack Daniel's and one of Bombay gin along with several packages of cigarettes.

Six steps down from the patio a magnificent blue-crystal pool shimmered in the blazing sun. Beyond the pool a tennis court beckoned. Jessie blinked behind the dark sun glasses. Who used these things? As far as she knew her parents neither swam nor played tennis.

"Mama? Daddy?"

"Jessie, is it really you? Barnes, our sweet baby is here. Jessie, love, come here and give Mama a big kiss and hug. Say hello to Daddy. I knew you'd come to us. I knew it. Didn't I say she would come, Barnes? I prayed every day. Oh, you sweet child, Mama loves you so much. Kiss Daddy and then come and sit with me. I want you next to me. You won't leave again will you? Oh, is that flower for me? Did you pick it from the garden? Did it remind you of me? You were always a thoughtful child. Dear God, I missed you so much."

Jessie felt her entire body stiffen as Thea's clawlike hands reached for her, dragging her down to the chair where she smothered her face with wet kisses. The sour smell of gin and her mother's cigarette breath made her gag. "I can't breathe, Mother. Please, you're smothering me. Let me go. *LET ME GO!*" Jessie struggled as she forced herself backward, her breathing ragged, her face full of panic. Thea started to cry, the tears making trails through the thick powder on her cheeks. Panting, Jessie continued to move backward until she was standing next to her father's chair. She bent over to kiss him lightly on the cheek as she tried to bring her breathing under control.

"Calm down, honey. Your mother just got carried away for a moment. I was just thinking about you yesterday, Jessie. You look well. Are you happy?"

"Yes, Daddy, I am happy."

"What brings you to Spain? Sophie, sit down. It's so nice to have you two girls here with us. Thea, ring for some iced tea for these pretty young women."

Sniffling, Thea reached for a tiny silver bell on the table next to her chair.

"Mrs. Ashwood passed away. She was killed in an auto accident right before New Year's. I didn't want Sophie to have to go through that alone, so I came with her. We're on our way home now."

"You've been here since before New Year's, and you just now came to visit?" Thea whined. "Come here, Jessie, sit by Mama so I can tell you how much I missed you. Give us your phone number and tell us where you live."

"No, Thea. Hush now."

"Mama, did you hear what I said? Mrs. Ashwood *died.*"

"Of course I heard you. She was here right before Thanksgiving. She had some young man with her who hadn't even shaved yet. She looked ghastly, didn't she, Barnes? She was wearing one of those short leather dresses. *Leather*, mind you. At first I thought the boy was her chauffeur, but it turns out he was her lover. He kept pawing her all through dinner. It made me ill. I'm sorry, Sophie, but your mother was a slut."

Sophie wilted in front of Jessie's eyes.

"That's enough, Thea!" Barnes barked. "Not another word," he barked a second time. Thea shriveled into the padded lounge chair.

Sophie finally gathered her wits about her. She turned to address Barnes. "Mr. Roland, did my mother say anything about me?"

Never a liar by nature, Barnes correctly interpreted his daughter's imploring gaze. "My dear, she talked about you all through dinner. She was so excited about giving you a Greek island for a Christmas present. She told us you were getting married and she thought it would be a wonderful place to honeymoon. She told a little fib, though. She told the young man she was with that you were only seventeen. She had every intention of going to Atlanta for Christmas, Sophie. She was looking forward to it. Then it was around the tenth of December I believe, she called and said she wouldn't be going to the States after all. She said she had to have some serious, as she put it, female surgery. She did recover because she called us Christmas Day. She said she tried for hours to call you, Sophie, but she couldn't get through."

Jessie hugged her father and whispered, "Thank you for doing that."

Sophie wept openly.

Thea was out of her chair and heading for Jessie, her arms outstretched in a pleading gesture, tears streaming down her cheeks. Barnes was on his feet a second later. He stiff-armed his wife. "I'm going to show the girls our garden, Thea. Have Dolores prepare something tasty for lunch."

Thea sat back down. "Will you sit next to me, Jessie? You've grown even more beautiful, hasn't she, Barnes?"

"Yes, Thea, she has. Jessie and Sophie are the two prettiest girls I've ever seen. I am so sorry about your mother, Sophie. If I had known of her passing, I would have gone to the funeral. Janice loved life."

"And men. And boys," Thea snapped.

Sophie ignored Thea. "There wasn't a funeral. Just a service. Mr. Mendenares said Mother wanted to be cremated, so that's what we did. I have to figure out a way to handle all . . . everything."

"For the time being, child, let things be. The people on your mother's payroll are the best of the best. She always said her holdings were in capable hands. Those hands will not change with you at the helm. That's why Janice was able to travel and do all the things she did. She trusted everyone, and that trust, as far as I know, was never abused."

"Daddy, what's wrong with Mama? Why does she look like she does?"

"She drinks too much. She doesn't eat properly. She doesn't sleep, but she does take catnaps. All she does is cry and look through the photo albums. She refuses to do any kind of exercise at all. I can't even get her to take a walk. Her arthritis is getting worse. She's done all this to herself. I don't want you blaming yourself, Jessie."

"She doesn't look well."

"She isn't well, Jessie. Tell me, did you finish school and do you have a job?"

"I only have one semester to go and I'll have my degree. I had a nice job, but I had to quit to come here with Sophie. I can get another one. I've been going to school at night. I met a nice young man recently."

"It's about time. Is he from a good family?"

"I think so. I like him a lot. Thank you, Daddy, for not asking specific questions."

"I just want you to be happy, Jessie. How are those dreams? Do you still have them?"

"Yes, but they're changing. The . . ."

"I think I hear Dolores ringing the lunch bell," Barnes said hastily. "Come along, girls."

Jessie took her seat next to her mother. Thea reached for her hand and squeezed it. It felt hot and dry. Her chair was so close to hers she could feel her mother's hot breath on her cheek. "Mother, please. If you hold my hand, I can't eat. Look, I can't stand this. I don't understand it but when you're close to me I feel like I can't breathe, and I get this panicky feeling. You need to move your chair, Mother. You make me feel like I'm in one of those awful dreams. It's the same kind of feeling. I know it sounds . . . weird, but it's the only way I can describe it. That's what I meant, Daddy, about things changing."

Jessie stared at her father's white face. "Daddy, is something wrong? You look ashen."

"It's gas."

Jessie laughed. She cringed when her mother's shoulder touched hers, but she didn't move.

"How long are you staying, sweet love? There are so many things we can do. You can have the room right next to mine. There's even a connecting door. We can shop and dine out. We can take some little trips by car. It's wonderful, isn't it, Barnes? Our daughter has finally come home. We bought this house because of the pool and the tennis court. We know you love things like that. I had this patio garden designed with you in mind. I pictured the two of us sitting here playing chess or reading and sometimes listening to music. It's almost as beautiful as you are, sweet love. Tell me how much you missed your daddy and me."

"Everything is lovely, Mother. I'm not staying. I have to get back and look for a job. I want to finish school. I couldn't come all this way and not stop to see how you and Daddy are doing. Sophie and I are leaving right after lunch. If you cry, Mother, I'll leave right now."

"Jessie, darling, sweet love, don't you love me? You are being so cruel. Ask her, Barnes, how she can be so cruel to me when all I do is love her."

"Excuse me, I need to use the bathroom," Sophie said.

"Mother, I have tried so often to explain to you. You refuse to listen to me. You frighten me. Right now my heart is pounding in my chest just sitting here next to you."

"Sweet child, that's just because you're home with us. You're excited. I know you love us. Every girl loves her parents. Look at Sophie. She loved that worthless mother of hers."

"That's enough, Thea."

"You hush, Barnes. Jessie needs to understand these feelings. I don't want her to leave thinking she doesn't love me. Or us. Barnes, why don't you buy Jessie a Greek island, too?"

"Mother, for God's sake, I don't want a Greek island. I think it's time for us to leave now. Are you feeling better, Daddy?"

Barnes forced a chuckle. "It was gas. If you eat bread, it makes things right."

"I'll have to remember that." She turned to see Sophie standing in the doorway. "Are you ready, Sophie?"

"Yes."

"Then I guess it's time to say good-bye."

"We didn't show you the house, Jessie. I fixed a room for you. It's been waiting for you since the day we moved here. Please, let me show it to you. It's exactly like your old room back in Charleston. When you see it I know you'll change your mind and stay."

"All the more reason not to want to see it. I hated that room, Mother. I truly hated it. I don't want to argue or fight with you. Can we just say good-bye and leave it at that?"

Thea wrung her hands as tears flowed from her eyes. "Will you come back?"

"I don't know, Mother."

"Barnes, I want to go back to Charleston."

"Good-bye, girls. Have a safe trip. I'll have the minister here say some prayers for Janice."

"Good-bye, Daddy. It was a nice lunch."

"Mama, take care of yourself. Please, Mama, don't do that. No, I don't want you to . . . Mama, don't."

"Go, Jessie. I'll take care of your mother."

"Run, Sophie. Fast. Can't you go faster?"

"Jessie Roland, what the hell was that all about?" Sophie demanded as Jessie pushed her into the backseat of the car. To the driver she screamed, "Hurry, get away from here. Take us to the airport."

Struggling to take deep breaths, her face whiter than Sophie's blouse, all Jessie could say was, "I don't know." She started to cry then. "What's wrong with me, Sophie? Why can't I love her?"

"God, I wish I knew, but I don't, Jessie. Now I *really* understand what you went through with her. Before I just saw bits and pieces. Jessie, she was fucking scary. Your father acted a little weird, too. He didn't have gas. You don't go white in the face from gas. He acted a little strange in the garden, too."

"I know, and I don't want to think about it. I wish we had never come here."

"I'm sorry, Jess."

"No, you were right to make me come. It's me. I don't ever want to see them again. Do you think God will punish me for feeling this way?"

"Nah. He probably doesn't like them either."

Jessie smiled. "You're probably right and that's okay with me."

"Me too, Jess. Me too."

"If there's anything I can do, Sophie, call, okay?"

"I'll work through it, Jess. There's no point in me going back to Atlanta. I can catch a flight to New Orleans in an hour. I want to see Jack. He's probably sitting in the apartment chewing his nails as we speak. I'm glad I kept the apartment. It gave me a home base."

"You didn't 'just keep it,' you bought the building."

"I did. Three years is a long time to expect a landlord to hold an apartment. Listen, don't worry about your car. I called ahead to arrange with this company to drive your car back here to D.C. You'll have it in a couple of days. I know you're dying to get back to your apartment, so you can call Tanner. Be happy, Jess."

"You too, Sophie. God, the third richest woman in the world. That's going to take some getting used to."

The sudden grip on Jessie's shoulders was almost as fierce as the look on her friend's face. "Look at me, Jessie, and listen to me. All of that won't make a difference. I am who I am, and that's never going to change. I'm going to get on with my life just the way you're going to get on with yours. Don't forget, you promised to be my maid of honor. I'll call you when I set the date. Remember what I said. Be happy."

"You too, Sophie."

Still wearing her coat and gloves, Jessie dialed Tanner's private number in Texas. She shrugged out of her coat and was pulling off her gloves when Tanner's voice hummed over the wire.

"Hi. I'm back. I was wondering what you're doing this

weekend. I have this outfit I bought for our New Year's date, and I'd hate to see it go to waste. We could go to the Shoreham and dance the night away or we could stay here at my apartment and . . . *do other things."*

"Tell me more." Jessie shivered at the huskiness of his voice.

"A little of this, a lot of that. You know what they say about anticipation."

"Tell me," he whispered.

Jessie lowered her voice till she was whispering, too. "You'll have to wait and see."

"Are you going to stand me up again?"

"No."

Jessie curled up on the sofa and snuggled into the corner. There was so much she wanted to say to this young man who made her blood sing.

They talked for hours before Jessie called a halt. "It's the jet lag, and I can't keep my eyes open."

"Will you promise to dream of me?"

"I'll do my best. Will you promise to dream about me?"

"Jessie, I've dreamed of you every night since I met you. You are the first person I think about when I wake up and the last person I think about before I go to sleep. Does that answer your question?"

"I think so."

"Are we falling in love, Jessie Roland?"

"I wouldn't be surprised, Tanner Kingsley."

"Good night, Jessie."

"Good night, Tanner."

Jessie managed to stagger into her bedroom, where she peeled off her clothes and slipped into her nightgown. She debated about washing her face and brushing her teeth. The world probably wouldn't come crashing down if she missed one night. Two minutes later she was sound asleep.

Chapter Twelve

Jessie walked to the window to stare out at the dark, stormy night. Where was Tanner? Was his flight delayed? Was he sitting on a runway waiting for the maintenance men to de-ice the wings of the plane? She risked a glance at the small bedside clock. He was three hours late. She might as well take off her glamorous dress and the spike-heeled shoes that were making her feet cramp. Should she call the Shoreham and cancel their reservation? She parted the curtains again. Sleet slammed against the window in hard-driving sheets. Startled, she backed away. Only a fool would venture outdoors on a night like this. If there was one thing she knew, it was that Tanner Kingsley was no fool. The urge to cry was so strong she bit down on her lower lip.

A phone call would have been nice.

Jessie looked around at her neat, tidy apartment. She'd spent hours cleaning and polishing. For what? So she could sit here decked out like a princess to stare at the gas logs that were burning so brightly. Alone. She eyed the expensive bottle of wine she'd purchased. She didn't have to look in the ice bucket to know the ice had melted an hour ago. She marched to the window again to part the curtains. The wind was still howling, the sleet still beating at the windows. She craned her neck for a sign of a car. No headlights could be seen anywhere on the street.

She kicked off her shoes and watched in dismay as tiny green sequins flew in all directions. Damn. She might as well take off the costly dress and put on her old woolly bathrobe. She was struggling with the zipper when her doorbell rang. Her face as radiant as the summer sun, she ran to the door and pulled it open. She gasped. "Tanner! You're soaked! I didn't hear a car. How did you get here?"

"I walked. It was the lesser of two evils," he croaked. "I need to get out of these clothes."

"You walked! From where? Why? Of course you need to get out of those clothes. Come in. Sit by the fire . . . no, no, go into the bathroom. I'll find something for you to put on. Hurry before you catch cold."

"From Fourteenth Street. The roads were too treacherous and the cabbie refused to go any farther. We had a date, remember? I always keep my dates. I already had a cold when I started out earlier this afternoon, Jessie. I probably have pneumonia by now. Can you make me something hot to drink?"

"Yes, yes, of course. Just . . . just throw your stuff on the floor and take a hot shower. Yes, yes, that's good. Do that. I'll . . . I'll . . . what I'll do is make you a hot toddy and find something warm for you to wear. You don't look good, Tanner."

"I feel like I look, too. Do you have any aspirin?"

"In the medicine cabinet."

"I'm okay, Jessie. Wipe that look off your face."

Jessie forced a smile. "Okay, Tanner."

Jessie forgot about the sequined dress as she rummaged in her small closet for something that would fit Tanner and afford him some warmth. The only thing she could find was her woolly oversize bathrobe and a long baggy, flannel nightgown. She cringed when she tried to picture the handsome young man in her nightclothes. She hung both on the bathroom doorknob before she raced to the kitchen.

She'd never made a hot toddy in her life and only had a vague idea of what went into one.

When the teakettle whistled, Jessie scooped, dumped, and poured, adding a tea bag as an afterthought to the large soup cup. She carried the steaming brew into the living room and almost dropped the cup when she saw Tanner dressed in her clothing, standing by the fire. His face was flushed a bright red and even from where she was standing, she could see he was shaking.

"I have chills." His teeth chattering, his hands trembling, he reached for the cup. In her eagerness to help him and alarmed at the same time, Jessie found her own hands trembling as she held out the heavy cup. Tanner's shaking hands allowed the contents to shoot upward and then downward onto the sequined dress. Jessie yelped with pain as the hot liquid soaked the dress. The cup safely in Tanner's shaking hands, she tugged and worked the zipper of the sparkling dress until it dropped to her feet. Tanner seemed oblivious to her near nakedness as he gulped at the fiery liquid. "What the hell is *this*?"

Jessie took a second to realize he wasn't referring to her or her skimpy attire. "Tabasco, whiskey, brandy, mint, and tea. Maybe you should get into bed. The fireplace doesn't really throw off any heat, and the windows are old and drafty."

"That sounds good. I took six aspirin."

"Six!"

"Yeah. Show me the way. You should get dressed before you catch cold."

Jessie looked down at what Sophie had called her ethereal underwear and flushed the same color as the bricks on the fireplace. "I will as soon as you get into bed."

"I like garter belts," Tanner said as he grappled with the quilt and spread on Jessie's bed. "I like to hear those things *snap*." Jessie flushed a deeper pink.

"I have some extra pillows."

"I'll take two. How about extra blankets?" he said, his teeth chattering like castanets.

"I'll get them. Did you finish your drink? Would you like another one?"

"I finished what you didn't spill. Yes, I would like another one."

It was on the tip of Jessie's tongue to say he was the one who spilled the drink, but she bit her tongue instead. Men were such babies when they got sick.

In the bathroom, she shook her head in dismay at the mess Tanner had left behind. It took her twenty minutes to wipe up the water and hang up his wet clothes. She used up another few minutes changing into her regular underwear, slacks, and a pullover sweater.

Whiny and fretful, Tanner called out, "What's taking you so long, Jessie?"

A frown built between Jessie's eyebrows as she made her way to the kitchen. This time she used a smaller cup to make the toddy.

Still flushed but propped up in a nest of pillows and quilts, Jessie could see that her houseguest was still shaking with chills. A devil perched itself on her shoulder, "Don't spill it this time," she said sweetly.

"I liked you better in your underwear. What do you call that stuff you were wearing before?"

"Underwear."

"The last time I was this sick I was ten years old. Do you think I have the flu or something?"

"Or something. I'm sorry there's no radio or television here in the bedroom. Maybe you should try to sleep."

"I can't sleep when I'm cold. I know I have a fever. My skin feels hot and dry, and yet I'm freezing."

"The aspirin should start to work soon, Tanner. Finish the drink. It will help you sleep."

"Will you stay here and talk to me?"

"If you want me to. Do you want me to call your father or Irene?"

"God, no. By the way, Pop asked me to plead with you to take back your job. He said he understands about you having to go with your friend to her mother's funeral."

"I'll let you know. I want to finish up my classes and graduate in the spring. It's only a few months. If I don't work, I can study during the day. I might think about going into the office one or two days a week. Right now I'm just not sure. Sophie's wedding is looming out there. I don't think she's set a date though. I'll need time for that. At least a couple of weeks. For now the answer is no."

Tanner burrowed deeper into the covers. "Pop isn't going to like that. I feel like a wet noodle. I saw this movie once where a nurse saved a soldier's life by getting into bed with him and keeping him warm."

"I saw that movie, too. They were in the snow in an igloo. You're in a warm bed with three quilts and a chenille bedspread. You're wearing flannel and wool, and you've had whiskey and aspirin. That poor man had nothing. You'll sleep better alone."

"Was that a no?"

"Yes. I mean yes, it's a no. You're fighting sleep. Try to relax. I'll stay here with you. I could read you today's paper."

"I read it on the plane. Tell me about you. From the day you were born. Don't leave anything out. I want to hear everything. Then I'll decide if we should get married or not."

"Married! We hardly know each other."

"I'm in your bed. I saw you in your unmentionables. I rest my case."

"Are you saying, assuming I'm interested, that you wouldn't accept me as is? That you need to know *everything* about me from the day I was born?"

"I have a feeling that you harbor deep, dark secrets, Jessie Roland. I want to know what they are. I don't like things rearing up out of nowhere to slap me in the face."

Jessie felt herself cringe. "Then, Mr. Kingsley, you need to rattle someone else's cage. My past, as you call it, is of no interest. I am what I am. That's another way of saying take me or leave me."

"Will your parents come to the wedding?"

"What wedding are you talking about? If you mean ours, the answer is no."

"My parents won't like that."

"Ask me if I care, Tanner. It is what it is."

"You are tough. Pop likes that trait in you. I don't."

"That's too bad, Tanner. What you see is what you get. When and if I get married, I intend to work. I don't have any objection to sharing my money with my husband, but I will not account to him for what I spend. I'm independent now, and I don't plan on changing anytime soon."

"The women in our family don't work."

"Resa works. She's independent. Why should I be different?"

"Resa left the fold. If we get married, I don't want you to work."

"I guess we won't get married then. Are you *that* wealthy?"

"We were. At this point in time I think the saying would be, we keep up appearances. I'm more than capable of supporting a wife."

"Did something happen so that your fortunes were reversed?" Her words sounded so Victorian she flushed.

"You could say that. Bad land deals, water rights, and we had to cut back on our herds because of the water. Luke has us over a barrel. He's waiting for us to grovel, and Kingsleys do not grovel. Not ever."

"I see," Jessie said.

"No you don't, but that's okay. Our heads are above water. For now. Too bad you aren't rich like your friend Sophie, Jessie. I'd sweep you off your feet in a heartbeat."

Jessie thought her heart would pound right out of her chest at Tanner's words. Sophie was right. Sophie was always right.

"Living paycheck to paycheck has its advantages," she finally managed to say.

Tanner snorted. "Name me one thing. Just one."

"It builds character."

"Banks don't recognize character as a deposit. They like cold, hard cash."

Jessie watched as Tanner's head drooped, and his eyes closed. He was finally asleep.

She sat in the small rocker, her hands folded, for a long time. She played their conversation over and over in her mind, liking it less and less as the minutes wore on. She stared at the sleeping man, her brow furrowed in thought. Yes, she was attracted to him. Yes, she was clearly infatuated with him. The truth was, she lusted for him. Was attraction, infatuation, and lust enough to build a foundation on? Sophie would say no, and she had to agree. Was she falling in love with Tanner Kingsley? More than likely. Maybe what she should do was move on before she became really involved. She nibbled on her thumbnail as she continued to stare at the man sleeping in her bed. She didn't know how she knew, but she knew: Tanner Kingsley was capable of breaking her heart. The big question was, did she want to take that chance? Yes, yes, a thousand times yes.

Jessie tiptoed from the room, closing the door behind her. In the kitchen, she dialed Sophie's number from memory, hoping she wasn't interrupting anything.

It took a full three minutes before Jessie realized Sophie's voice didn't have the usual lilting tone she was accustomed to. "Would you listen to me! I'm just babbling here. What's going on, Sophie? You sound different. Are you still overwhelmed with all your mother's affairs? Did you and Jack decide on a date yet? You would make a beautiful June bride. Something's wrong, Sophie. I can hear it humming over the wire."

"Jack isn't here, Jessie. He's off on a three-week job. We more or less set the date for June. We aren't planning anything big. Just a simple wedding with a few friends. I'll probably wear a suit and a small veil. It's iffy right now. My mother's affairs are running smoothly. Everything is in order. I did quit my job, though. I'm thinking of opening up my own offices."

"That's wonderful, Sophie. I can see you running your own business. Now, tell me what's really wrong, Sophie? Did you tell Jack?"

"No. I think he knows, though. If he doesn't know, then he suspects something. Remember when I told you he changed? It's that, and something else I can't put my finger on. This is just a rumor, and I can't pin it down no matter how hard I try, but a friend told me that Jack was in France when we were there."

"What!" The single word exploded from Jessie's mouth like a gunshot.

"That was my reaction."

"You could come right out and ask him, Sophie. You were never one to beat around the bush with anything, or is it that you don't want to know? If he was there, what does it mean? You said he was an honorable, honest man. Besides, what reason would he have to go to France? You said yourself it was a rumor."

"It could mean anything, Jessie. It could mean he knows. It could mean he was checking up on me. One thing is certain, if he was there then he lied to me about staying on in Costa Rica. I hate a liar as much as he said he did. He *said* he was going off on a three-week job. I don't know if it's true or not. What I do know is I've never been so miserable in my life. I was going to call you earlier, but I wanted to get it all straight in my head first. Why me, Jessie?"

"Take the bull by the horns, Sophie. Call out all those investigators you use all the time. Ask all the right questions. Get in his face and look in his eyes. Depending on what you see and hear will help you to make the decision to tell or not to tell. If he loves you, Sophie, being rich won't make a difference. Tanner told me a little while ago if I was as rich as you, he'd snap me up in a heartbeat. *That*, I didn't like. I'm sure you're overreacting to . . . all your new responsibilities and your mother's death."

"What if it was all a lie, Jessie? What if he sought me out *because* of who I was? Men marry rich women all the time. They're no different from women who want to marry rich husbands."

"It sounds to me, Sophie Ashwood, like you've already made up your mind that he's guilty. That's not fair to Jack, and you know it."

"No. My problem is I didn't live by my own rules. By obeying those rules it got me to this point. I was so blase when I told you I didn't have to run a check on him. That was my first mistake. Jessie . . . I . . . won't know what to do if . . ."

"Jessieeeeee." The muffled call came from the bedroom.

"Sophie, hold on for a minute. Tanner's awake."

"How long did I sleep, Jessie?"

"Several hours."

"I thought you were going to sit here with me."

"I did for a while. I'm talking to Sophie on the phone. Do you want something?"

"Some more aspirin and some tea. A smile would be nice. Get rid of your friend and sit here with me."

"I can't do that, Tanner. Sophie has a problem, and we need to talk it through."

"Sophie is the problem," Tanner said. "When we get married there won't be a Sophie in our lives. Why do you let her run your life? Is it because she's rich?"

"I beg your pardon," Jessie said, her voice turning cold and frosty.

"Forget I said that. It must be this damn fever. About those aspirin, Jessie."

"I'll get them."

"Don't forget the tea."

"I won't." She had to remember he was sick and feverish. Sick, feverish people were usually cranky and out of sorts.

In the kitchen, with the phone to her ear, Jessie put more water on to boil as she continued her conversation with Sophie. By stretching the phone cord, she was able to close the kitchen door. Even so, she lowered her voice to a hushed whisper. "Listen to me, Sophie, you need to calm down and look at things with an open mind. You are not totally blameless here. Remember that. You had to know that sooner or later, no matter how many precautions you took, somehow, some way, little things would leak out. If you love Jack and he loves you, then things will work out. You're the one who always told me things aren't always black or white, that sometimes there are shades of gray.

You need to think things through, Sophie. I'll call you first thing in the morning. I'll probably be up most of the night, so if you want to talk later, call me."

"Jessieeeee."

Jessie slopped the remainder of the liquor into a clean cup, added the boiled water and tea bag. As an afterthought she gave two hearty splashes of Tabasco sauce to the cup before she stirred it. She blinked when the mess foamed and bubbled. She stopped in the bathroom for the aspirin bottle.

"I think I feel a little better," Tanner said. "I still have the chills, but they aren't as intense. I'm actually starting to sweat. I think that's good."

Jessie sat down opposite the bed, her thoughts with Sophie.

"I'm sorry about tonight, Jessie. You looked so beautiful. This is some date."

Jessie smiled. "I can truthfully say I never had a date like this."

"Me either. So, do you want to get married or not?" he teased, his voice coarse and raspy.

"Someday," Jessie said lightly, uncomfortable with the conversation.

Tanner chuckled. "I would imagine being married to you would be the ultimate challenge. How do you think we'd do as a married couple?"

Jessie felt her heart skip a beat. "Off the top of my head I'd say the word challenge is apt. This is just a guess on my part, but I have the feeling you're a control freak. I would never allow *anyone* to control my life."

"Is that what you think of me? Taking charge is different from controlling someone. If one or the other person doesn't take charge, things usually go to hell. I've learned that from past experience."

"Then there's that part about your mother not liking me

and me not liking her. That has to count for something. Since we're playing this game, where would we live?"

"At the ranch until I find something for us or we could build. We still own a lot of land. There are a few acres that would be perfect for us to build on."

"No."

"No what?"

"No to living at the ranch. I'd rather live in a tent."

Tanner frowned. "It takes time to build a house. Months actually if the weather is good, and even then all kinds of things go wrong. It could be as long as a year."

"Aren't you kind of old to be living at home with your mother? I would think a young, virile man like yourself would want his own place."

"My father called the shots on that one. He wants someone in the house with Mother. You never question Pop. You just do what he says. Marriage now would put a different spin on everything."

"I see. You want to get married so you can get out of the house." Jessie's stomach started to churn.

"That would be a plus, but no, that's not the reason. I find myself extremely attracted to you."

"More than Bippity-Bop?" Jessie said, a sour note creeping into her voice.

Tanner threw his head back and laughed. "Resa's been talking, I see. We had our day in the sun. I moved on, and so did she. It was a long time ago. Would you care to share some of your past . . . what shall I call them, indiscretions?"

"No."

"There you go. It's my feeling that whatever happened before is over and done with and can't be changed, so why dwell on it. One or the other of us will get our feathers ruffled and then we'll have a fight and not speak for days, maybe months. Let sleeping dogs lie, I say."

"You're just riddled with clichés, aren't you?"

"It sums it up, doesn't it?"

"I'd say so. Would you like a sandwich?"

"My throat is sore. Thanks anyway. It's nice of you to put up with me. I really am sorry about tonight."

"I guess it wasn't meant to be. Things always happen for a reason. I think you should try to sleep now."

"What are you going to do?"

"Sit in the living room and read. I want to stay up in case Sophie calls."

"Is something wrong with her?"

"A few problems. I think she'll work them out."

"I didn't mean what I said earlier."

"Yes you did. You wouldn't have said it otherwise. Sophie is my friend."

"Is that another way of saying she comes first?"

"It has to be that way for now. I'll say good night. Do you want me to turn off the light?"

Tanner's raspy voice sounded more petulant than before. "You might as well. This is a big bed. If you get tired, you can sleep here with me. On top of the covers or under them. Your choice."

"I'll remember that. Sleep well."

In the living room Jessie curled into the corner of the sofa. The landlady always turned the heat down at ten-thirty, and it was chilly in the apartment now. She shivered when she remembered there were no extra blankets or quilts. She wished she'd taken an extra sweater when she left the bedroom. For a few seconds she debated going back into the bedroom but decided she'd feel foolish since she'd turned off the light and closed the door with such finality. She finally opted for her all-weather coat in the tiny hall closet. She snuggled beneath the coat with the shearling lining. The moment she stopped shivering she let her mind race as she replayed Tanner's conversation, word for word, in her mind. She knew she should be thinking about Sophie and her problem, but Tanner was here, just yards away, and it was hard to concentrate on Sophie, who always came up with the right solution to every problem imaginable. This time would be no different. She knew that Sophie would manage to stifle her grief and get on with the business of living and planning her wedding. Sophie was a survivor.

Jessie moved restlessly in her warm cocoon, a sign that the hateful dream was ready to invade her subconscious. As she thrashed about beneath her coat, the dream took her to a place she feared and dreaded. A moment later a bloodcurdling scream ripped through the apartment just as the phone in the kitchen shrilled to life.

Tanner leaped from the bed, his hair literally standing on end at the loud screaming coming from the living room. In his haste to get to Jessie he tripped on the belt of her robe, his feet tangling themselves in the hem of the baggy nightgown.

"Jesus Christ! What the hell happened?" he roared in his raspy voice. "Jessie, wake up! Wake up, Jessie!"

Jessie reared back and could only see the tall figure cast in the dark shadows of early dawn, looming in front of her. A second bloodcurdling scream whipped through the apartment. She lashed out, her arms flailing as both her legs shot forward in a wild kick to Tanner's midriff. Tanner lost his balance and toppled backward. "No! No! Jelly, Jelly!"

"The damn phone's ringing. Wake up, Jessie, you're having a nightmare. Jesus, I could have broken my arm. I had no idea you were so strong. Will you wake up for God's sake. Your landlady will be up here in a few minutes if you don't shut up. Come on, Jessie, enough is enough. Get up! That's a goddamn order! Look, I'm not going to touch you. Just get up and calm down, okay?"

Jessie moved then as she focused on Tanner. Her heart thundering in her chest, her body wet with sweat, she bolted for the bathroom. Inside, she locked the door and sat down on the edge of the bathtub. She struggled to take deep, even breaths to calm herself. Outside the door, Tanner pleaded with her to open the door.

"I'm . . . fine. It was a really bad dream," she whispered until she realized he couldn't hear her. On shaky legs she walked to the door and opened it. "You . . . you scared me standing there like that. You reminded me of . . . of . . . "

"In this getup I'm wearing I'm surprised you didn't faint. Did I look like the Wicked Witch of the West or something?"

"A woman. You looked like a woman, but I couldn't see your face. Sometimes I have bad dreams. Some are worse than others. I'm sorry if I woke you."

"Hey, that's okay. Like I should complain. If you were sleeping in your own bed, you probably wouldn't have had the dream. It's only five-thirty. Come into the bed and relax. I think I hear the heat coming up through the radiators. We can talk."

"I don't want to talk about the dreams. I hate them. I'll be fine. Are you feeling better?" Her voice was more shaky sounding than ever.

"Now that you mention it, yes. My fever seems to be gone. My throat is still sore, but my sexy voice is the same. Come on, we'll cuddle and talk about the weather and your friend Sophie."

Jessie allowed herself to be led into the bedroom. "Did you say the phone rang?"

"It did. They'll call back. It was probably Pop. He gets

up at five and thinks everyone else should, too. He knew I was coming here, and he might have wanted to talk. For some reason he likes to start the day by talking to me. Relax, Jessie."

Relax. How could she relax after that horrible nightmare and being so close to this handsome man? She was strung tighter than banjo wire, and they both knew it.

Snuggling beneath the covers, Jessie found herself being pulled closer to Tanner. She didn't object. His nearness left her feeling breathless.

"You smell good," Tanner murmured against her hair. "Are you calming down?"

"No. How can I be calm when I'm lying next to you in my bed?"

"I'm calm."

"Men are always calm. Women are jittery about things like this. You are wearing my clothes you know."

"I can take them off if it bothers you."

"That isn't necessary."

"You must be pretty warm with all the stuff you're wearing and all these quilts."

"Actually, I feel . . . just fine."

"Liar. I can see the perspiration on your forehead."

"It's these quilts and the spread. We could take some of them off."

"Done!" Tanner chortled as he kicked the spread and two of the quilts to the bottom of the bed. "Howzat?"

"Ah, better. Yes, a lot better. I hear the heat rattling in the pipes. This apartment gets really warm during the day. Really warm. The truth is it gets hot. Sometimes I have to open the windows. Even in the winter. The bathroom gets like an oven. The kitchen is worse." She was babbling but couldn't seem to help herself

"You talk too much."

"That's because I'm nervous."

"Because of what we might do or what we might think about doing?"

"Both."

"Sex is what two people do when they're together in bed. Out of bed, too. In cars. On the grass, sometimes in kitchens. The shower is good. Chaise lounges are great. See, you have me babbling, too. Do you want to get to it, or are we going to talk it to death?"

Worms of fear crawled around inside Jessie's stomach. Was she ready for this? In her eyes sex was a commitment. "Why don't I make us some breakfast. I could cook you some oatmeal. It won't bother your throat. Breakfast is a good way to start the day. See, it's getting light out. That means it's a new day."

"I don't want any breakfast, and I don't think you do either. I want you. Period. Maybe it's this getup I'm wearing that's putting you off. Well, we can remedy that right now."

Jessie blinked when she saw her robe and flannel night-gown sail across the room. She could feel the heat from his leg when it brushed against hers. She tried to shake down her pant leg to no avail.

"Your turn," Tanner grinned.

Jessie peeled off her thick socks.

"I was thinking more along the lines of your sweater." His bare toes grappled with her bare toes. Jessie wondered if toenails could burn. Hers felt like they were on fire.

"Need some help?"

"No! I can do it myself."

"Are you always this . . . shy with guys."

Guys. He thought she was experienced, and it was her own fault for letting him think that. Damn. "This might be a good time to tell you I . . . what I mean is . . ."

"Yes," Tanner drawled.

"I don"t . . . I should have . . . you see . . ."

"Don't tell me it's that time of the month? I don't want to hear that, Jessie."

"I beg your pardon."

"You know, your period. Do you have it?"

It was an out. What if he was bold enough to want to check? She shrank into the bedding. "No, I don't have my period."

"That's a relief. What's our problem here?"

Jessie bolted upright. "The problem is I'm a virgin," she blurted.

"Shit!"

"That's it, shit!"

"You led me to believe . . . you said . . . all kinds of things. What it means is I now have to change my . . . *approach*."

Approach meant a strategy of sorts. She couldn't help but wonder if he would whip out a map from somewhere. She wished then for worldliness and sophistication. Right now she felt like an overage Girl Scout. "I know, and I'm sorry. I wanted you to think I was worldly. I really hate to admit this but what little I do know about . . . all of this is what I've read and what Sophie told me. I really did lead a sheltered life. Would you rather I'd slept around?"

"Hell no. I believed you. That doesn't say much for my intuitive powers or my observations."

"Does that mean it's soft now and you can't or don't want to do it? I just need some time to . . . you know, work up to taking my clothes off. Furthermore, I never thought, expected to do this until I got married. I'm breaking one of my own rules here. This is very important to me. Men never seem to respect women in the morning when they do . . . have sex and aren't married."

"You're putting me on, right? You can't be that archaic

in your thinking. Jesus, you are. Okay, let's go back to square one. You go into the bathroom and take your clothes off. Come back to bed with a towel wrapped around you. Securely. Then you get into bed and when you're ready to take the towel off, you tell me."

"Are you making fun of me?"

"Yeah. But in a nice way. Get moving before I change my mind."

"I always thought you needed candles and . . . oil, wine and you know—"

"Move!"

Jessie scampered to the bathroom. As she stripped off her clothes she eyed the shower. She should be fresh and clean for *the event and the approach leading up to it.* A shower would only take a few minutes.

"I'm waiting!" Tanner bellowed.

"Shut up, Tanner," Jessie bellowed in return.

"What the hell are you doing in there?"

"Taking a shower."

"You're what?"

"I told you, I'm taking a shower. Maybe you should take one, too. I had one last night but you must have taken one over twenty-four hours ago. Okay, I'm done. I'll leave the water running. I have lots of hot water. Gallons and gallons of it. You can stand under the shower all day and it will still be hot."

"Shut up, Jessie Roland," Tanner said as he stomped his way to the bathroom. "Don't look."

Jessie looked, then turned away. For some reason she thought it would look different. She didn't say anything. She didn't need to. Her expression said it all. She heard Tanner groan as he yanked at the shower curtain. Where was the fun? The exhilaration? It all seemed like such a chore. She eyed the messy bed. In the blink of an eye she straightened the sheets and the light blanket. Taking a deep breath, she let the towel drop to the floor. Her heart hammered in her chest as she lay back against the pillows, the sheet pulled up to her chin. When she heard the shower curtain rip across the rod, she took a second deep breath. She squeezed her eyes shut when she heard the bathroom door open.

"Well!"

Jessie cracked one eyelid. Then she cracked the other before she yelped when Tanner in all his naked glory started to beat on his chest with his clenched fists, at the same time emitting a bull roar. She let her gaze shift from his face to the quivering mass between his legs. She didn't need Sophie to tell her this was one magnificent specimen of manhood. A curl of heat began to form in the lower part of her stomach. She liked the feeling.

"Say something," Tanner said.

What was she supposed to say, for God's sake? Jessie whipped the sheet down and away from her naked body.

"Come here," she managed to croak.

"I'm there." Tanner crossed the room in two steps and bounded into the bed, driving Jessie backward, his naked body covering hers. Instinctively, she held herself rigid as she bit down on her lower lip.

At best it was a weak resistance and then no resistance at all when his tongue licked at her lips, his hands searching, probing, then finding those secret places only lovers knew. Her lips parted ever so slightly, allowing just enough room for his tongue to spear into the warm recesses of her mouth. A low moan of surrender escaped her lips.

She gave as good as she got, molding her body against his, her own hands as busy as his. He played with her then, his lips nipping her earlobe and then her lips. She wanted more, always more. Using all her strength she toppled him over until she was on top of him, her breasts mashing against his broad, sweaty chest. She moved against him, her own body slick with sweat. With his head between her hands she held him steady, her lips eating his, her tongue working furiously, searing them together.

And then she was on her back again, her legs pried apart. Her subconscious told her this was the moment and she welcomed it. The tiny cry of pain went unnoticed by both of them as she relentlessly clung to him, helping him, guiding him, and then the finale as she soared to heights she never thought possible.

Gasping and struggling for breath, her body a silken sheath of wetness, she allowed herself to be drawn into Tanner's arms. "I liked that. I really liked that. Let's do it again."

"Whoa. Easy does it here. We need time to . . . to rebound. At least I do. Just lie here and talk to me. Lovers call it pillow talk. The magazines say women love pillow talk. Do you?"

Did she? "Yes. There wasn't one part of my body you didn't touch or kiss. I didn't know I had so many nerve endings. They were all twanging at once. It was beautiful. I want to do the same thing to you."

"You have my permission, but later. Did I hurt you?"

"Only for a moment. I don't even remember it now." She cuddled deeper into his arms, her fingers playing with the fine furring on his chest. "How are you feeling?"

"Exhausted. I think a nap is in order. Don't move, just lie here next to me."

It would take a dragon to move her, Jessie thought. She had no intention of going anywhere. She said so.

"That's good. You feel good next to me."

"Did you hear the phone ring?" Jessie asked sleepily.

"Yeah. It was probably Pop. He never gives up. The next time one or the other of us gets up we should take the receiver off the hook."

Jessie's last conscious thought before drifting off to sleep was that she would do whatever this man asked of her because she was in love with him. "Okay," she murmured.

Chapter Thirteen

Jessie stared across the Tidal Basin, marveling at the glorious array of cherry blossoms that were so spectacular they took her breath away. Would she be here next year to see them? Would they be as pretty, or was this year special? Did she even care? Probably not. The only thing she cared about right now was the piece of paper in her hand. She'd read it a hundred times during the past few hours. Maybe a thousand. That didn't matter much either, since the words were seared into her brain. She was pregnant. That was what mattered. The *only* thing that mattered. It was all her fault. Sophie had warned her that women had to take responsibility for themselves. She hadn't done that, and her pregnancy was the result. Tanner said having sex using a condom was like washing your feet with your socks on. He'd adamantly refused to wear protection. She'd been just as adamant about not going on the pill. It was her fault because she hadn't paid attention to her menstrual cycle. Abstaining a few days a month wouldn't have been so difficult. Why hadn't she done it then? *Because, for some reason, I can't deny Tanner anything. He mesmerizes me. He has me in his control, and I was afraid to rock the boat. I was afraid he wouldn't come back. I lived for those long weekends and our days and nights of sex.*

Dear God, what would Tanner say when she told him? Would he walk out on her? He didn't seem to like children much. Right now she wasn't even sure how she herself felt about children. In fact, just recently, he'd referred to a child on the street who had been skipping rope as a snotty little bastard. She recalled how his lip had curled in distaste. That's how Tanner felt. The big question was, how did she feel about being pregnant? What exactly were her feelings for Tanner Kingsley? Was she in love with him? Was it a sick kind of love? Was she obsessive about their relationship? Right now she didn't feel anything where he was concerned. That was strange in itself. Until yesterday her heart skipped a beat at the mere mention of his name. Today she thought she hated him.

A strong wind whipped across the Tidal Basin, bringing with it a thousand fragile, pink blossoms. Jessie reached out to cup her hands for the falling petals. How pretty they looked, how delicate. She shivered inside her spring coat. Maybe she should go back to the apartment. And do what? She couldn't even call Sophie since she had no idea where she was. It had been months since she'd heard from her. She'd called everywhere and left messages to no avail. She'd even called Arthur Mendenares, but he seemed to be missing, too. On a business trip, his office said.

Tears trickled down Jessie's cheeks as she let her mind travel back to January. She'd been so caught up in her own little world back then she'd ignored Sophie, put her off, forgetting to return her calls, taking the receiver off the hook when Tanner was in town, which was every Thursday, Friday, Saturday, and Sunday. Monday, Tuesday, and Wednesday were spent in class or at the library. There had been no time for Sophie.

A fat pigeon waddled up to the bench Jessie was sitting

on. She fed it bread crumbs. Another pigeon appeared. She fed it, too. Would others appear or were these two friends like she was with Sophie? "We still are friends. I didn't mean to make it sound like past tense," she said to the pigeons, who seemed to be listening to her words. She threw more crumbs.

The trickle of tears turned into a waterfall. A baby. She was going to have a baby. And she wasn't married. Motherhood. Marriage? Would Tanner marry her? Did she want to be married to Tanner for the rest of her life? She had to do something, and if she wasn't ready to do something, then she needed to *think* about doing something.

Jessie crunched the lab report into a ball and stuffed it into her pocket before she got up to walk aimlessly around the basin.

Three long months since she'd begun her affair with Tanner. Three long months of waiting for the phone to ring, waiting at airports to pick him up and drop him off. Three long months of lust. It was all about sex. Tanner thrived on sex, but then so did she. It was the off hours, the hours when they weren't sleeping, eating, or romping and rolling in the bed that bothered her. Those hours were spent in silence, reading or watching television. More often than not hours would go by before either one said a word. Love wasn't supposed to be silent. Love was supposed to be joyous with each party sharing and confiding things that didn't even matter. Tanner didn't like to take walks or go for rides in the country. Tanner didn't particularly like going to the movies. Oh, he would go, but he never seemed to enjoy the picture and never wanted to discuss it afterward. He wasn't crazy about eating out but he did that, too, on occasion. He much preferred for her to cook elaborate dinners with sweet desserts after which he would sleep for hours while she cleaned up. When he woke he was ready for sex. It was those times she waited and hungered for. It was those times she didn't want to give up. Sick, obsessive love. A strangled sound escaped her lips. She was turning out like her mother. Now that she was pregnant and it was too late, she was forced to recognize the signs she'd chosen to ignore all these months.

She didn't know how she knew, but she knew that Tanner would have no patience with a pregnant woman. Knowing that, accepting that, where did it leave her? Nowhere, that's where.

Her life was one big mess, and she had only herself to blame.

Jessie turned for one last look at the beautiful rows of cherry trees. She found herself shivering. It was unseasonably cool even with the trees blooming so late this year. Another week and it would be May and then it would be June and Sophie's wedding. *If* there was a wedding. In order to have a wedding, you needed a bride. And a groom. Maybe she should go back to the apartment and try to locate Sophie's boyfriend, Jack Dawson. If nothing else, it would give her something to do to take her mind off her pregnancy. Or, she could study for the last of her finals. Who would attend her graduation? She started to cry again as she climbed behind the wheel of her Jeep.

Jessie entered her apartment a long time later. For the first time since she had gotten it to make sure she didn't miss any of Tanner's calls, she didn't head for her answering machine to see if the little red light was blinking.

In the kitchen with her coat still on, she made coffee. While she waited for it to perk, she rummaged in one of the kitchen drawers for the yellow pad she'd used when she was trying to locate Sophie. The list of numbers she'd called was endless, taking up three whole pages on the legal pad. Maybe she was wasting her time. Maybe Sophie didn't want to be found. Sophie was a master at getting lost, a trait she'd acquired when she was a teen bent on evading a mother who didn't give a whit if she was being evaded or not.

Jessie flipped open the telephone directory, running her finger down the long list of Dawsons. She patiently dialed each Dawson with the name John, Jack, and the initial J with no results. She then looked up the number for Sophie's old firm and placed a call. She did her best to make her voice warm and chatty when she said she was Jack's sister and would only be in town for a few hours between flights. She babbled nonsense about him being in Costa Rica and herself being in England. Her ploy worked. She copied down the number the personnel director rattled off. She dialed the number only to get a recording device. Unwilling to leave a message, she switched to the list of numbers she'd called over the past few months when she tried to locate Sophie.

It was dark when she hung up the phone for the last time. It rang almost immediately. For the first time in months she let the phone ring until the answering machine picked up. It never once occurred to her that it might be Sophie. No one of any importance called her these days. The few friends she'd made through school had moved on. The senator had stopped calling at the end of February and Irene was in the hospital, according to Tanner. She'd tried to visit once but was told visitors were restricted to family members only. She'd sent a card and flowers.

The urge to cry again was so strong, Jessie headed for the bathroom, averting her eyes from the red blinking light on the answering machine. A warm shower always made her feel better. A light supper and then she would curl into the corner of the worn couch and try to figure out what to do with her life. *Pregnant. Unmarried. A child. Responsibility.*

The television on low, her pad and pencil on the end table and the phone she'd dragged from the kitchen with its twenty-five-foot cord rested on the floor by her feet. Not that she would answer it. It was there in case a brilliant burst of insight occurred as to where Sophie might be. God, how she needed her friend. *Where are you, Sophie?* Tears puddled in her eyes. She brushed at them angrily. She felt a storm building inside her body. She made no move to squash it. Instead she let it surge through her, her fists pummeling the sofa cushions. Then she screamed her despair. Sometimes anger was good. It cleared one's brain. Her foot lashed out, toppling the stack of books on the coffee table. A crystal candy dish sailed across the room. A vase of early daffodils flew in another direction, the slimy green water staining the light gray carpeting. She should have thrown them away days ago. What difference did it make? The flowers were dead anyway. She howled again as she collapsed against the sofa cushions. And then the anger was gone as quickly as it had come. Her head jerked upward at the same moment her shoulders stiffened. *Get on with it, Jessie. Just get on with it.*

Her resolve was sharp when she entered the kitchen to fix herself a sandwich and a fresh pot of coffee. While she waited for the coffee she scurried to her bedroom to rummage in the small trunk under the window. The packet of personal papers along with her savings-account book was secured with two taut rubber bands so it would fit into the sleeve of one of her red sweaters. She dropped to her haunches, aware that something wasn't quite right about the contents of the trunk. Everything was folded neatly, it just wasn't folded the way she normally put things away. She'd always folded the sleeves of the sweaters the way the department-store clerks did, so the sweaters would lie flat. She squeezed her eyes shut. She crossed her fingers the way she had when she was a child that her papers would be untouched.

The phone rang, six long blasts of sound as her trembling fingers fumbled with the last sweater in the trunk. Her heart fluttered in her chest when she realized the sleeves were folded wrong. The packet looked the same, but it had been touched, gone through. Who? Her landlady wasn't the curious type. To her knowledge the elderly lady never ventured to the second floor of the building because it was difficult for her to climb the stairs with her arthritis. Tanner? She'd known it was Tanner; otherwise why was she even bothering to check the trunk. Aside from her savings-account book that was self-explanatory, the rest of the papers wouldn't mean much to anyone but her. She said a prayer of thanks then that Sophie had insisted she keep everything in the Atlanta house.

The phone rang as she walked back to the kitchen. She ignored it as she poured coffee. It stopped in the middle of the sixth ring and then rang again a few seconds later. Munching on her cheese sandwich, Jessie tuned out the ringing phone. Tanner was persistent, she had to give him that.

Snuggled back into the corner of the sofa, Jessie finished her sandwich. She could have been eating sawdust for all she cared. The coffee seemed extra strong and bitter. She gulped at it. When she finished the coffee, the phone rang again, six long peals of sound and then silence. She rifled through the slim packet of papers. She didn't bother with her passbook account. She knew to the penny how much money she had in her account; $6,714.33. The little nest egg would hold her over till the end of the year, at which point she would have to tap her trust fund. Medical bills, giving birth, supporting a child had to be expensive. Someone had told her that, but she couldn't remember who it was. She would have to find a house somewhere that had a yard and a porch. Children needed space. As she grappled with her options, the phone rang again. She paid no attention. She could go back to the house in Charleston, open it up and live there. Or, she could go to Sophie's house in Atlanta. The third option, which didn't bear thinking about, was going to Texas to live with Tanner—provided he wanted to marry her, which she seriously doubted.

Jessie smoothed the wrinkled papers from the packet onto her lap. Sophie's last report to her at the beginning of January said she had a little over twenty-one million dollars in her trust fund. On one of the small calendars that was divided into quarters, she had placed little stars, each one denoting a million dollars, plus other little squiggles that only she would be able to decipher. It was obvious that her parents had added to the fund since the day she'd left home. Twenty-one million dollars, and it was all hers to use or not use. The decision was hers alone. It would certainly go a long way toward raising a child.

A headache started to hammer behind her eyes. She had to find Sophie. She reached for the phone just as it rang. Her eyes narrowed to slits, she grappled with it as she barked, "Hello."

"Jessie, where in the goddamn hell have you been? I've been calling you all day. Didn't you get my messages?"

"No. I took a walk."

"You took a walk!" He might as well have said, "You danced with the devil!"

"Do you love me, Tanner?" She ticked off the seconds until he answered. Ten long seconds.

"That's a pretty silly question, Jessie."

"If it was a silly question, I wouldn't have asked it. Do you?"

"Why else would I fly to Washington every weekend?"

"Sex. You said our sex was the best you ever had."

"Sex is sex. I could have sex seven days a week with seven different women if I wanted to. I chose you."

"Am I supposed to be thankful or grateful? I want to hear the words, Tanner."

"Have you been talking to that *squirrely* friend of yours? That's it, isn't it? You finally located Sophie, and she's full of wedding plans and you're getting all misty-eyed. You're starting to think about getting married. Right or wrong? You're leading up to something, Jess. What is it?"

Jessie crooked the phone between her ear and her shoulder so she could massage her temples. The pain inside her head was so intense she thought it would spin off her shoulders. "I did not locate Sophie. Marriage is not something I'm thinking about right now. Since you have an aversion to saying the words I need to hear I will assume you do not love me. There doesn't seem much sense in prolonging this conversation. Why were you calling me all day anyway?"

"To tell you I'd be up tomorrow. Irene died this afternoon. I thought you would want to know. The funeral's the day after tomorrow at St. John's."

It was hard to think with the bongo drums beating away inside her head. "I'm sorry. Irene was very nice, and I liked her. But . . . I won't be here, Tanner." On an impulse she said, "I'm leaving for Atlanta tomorrow morning," she lied. "You'll have to stay with your father."

"Atlanta! What about school and your finals. I don't want to stay with my father."

"Well, you can't stay here. My landlady will not approve of you being here alone. I'm sorry. You could stay at a hotel."

Tanner's voice turned frigid. "Or you could stay here for the funeral, which would be the decent thing to do. Why are you being so selfish? Or is it that you don't want me in your apartment? Are you giving me the old heave-ho, Jessie?"

"I told you, I have plans. I only have one exam left. My professor agreed to work with me and is allowing me to take it at seven tomorrow morning. I only met Irene once, Tanner. It's not like she's a blood relative."

"She was my father's wife once."

"That has nothing to do with me."

"So you won't stay. You're going to Atlanta even though I want you to stay."

"Yes."

"If you don't know where Sophie is, why are you going?"

"Does it matter, Tanner? I don't ask you to account for your time. I'm going, and that's the end of it."

"You're damn right that's the end of it."

Jessie blinked when she heard the dial tone in her ear. The headache banging away inside her head left her almost immediately. Her eyes started to burn. "I will not cry. I absolutely will not cry," she muttered over and over as she went to the kitchen to fill her coffee cup. She stopped in her tracks halfway into the living room when she realized she felt an overwhelming sense of relief that left her feeling peaceful yet drained of all emotion.

Tomorrow morning she would check into a hotel until after Irene's funeral. She could study there, take her last final exam, at which point she would make decisions regarding her future. A trip to Atlanta wasn't such a bad idea, nor was a trip to New Orleans out of the question. She had to find Sophie.

Jessie did three things before she brushed her teeth and turned down her bed. She dialed Jack Dawson's number one last time. When the answering machine clicked on, she hung up. She then listened to Tanner's irate messages, erasing them as they ended. She unplugged the phone; then she disconnected the machine, and shoved it in a drawer.

Jessie slipped the envelope containing her check for three months' rent under her landlady's door with a note saying she wasn't sure when she would return. She left Sophie's phone numbers in Atlanta and New Orleans, with instructions they not be given out to anyone. Nor was anyone to be admitted to her apartment while she was away. At the last moment she added a twenty-dollar bill to cover any long-distance calls the landlady might have to make on her behalf.

Everything had been taken care of. She'd attended her graduation, graduating *summa cum laude,* cleaned out her refrigerator, disconnected all the appliances, had her pre-natal checkup, asked the post office to hold her mail until otherwise notified, had her Jeep serviced, and was now ready to go. The letter in her hand felt hot and dry. Should she mail it or not? It probably didn't matter one way or the other since she hadn't heard from Tanner in over a month. She'd hoped he would show up for her graduation, but he hadn't. It was all the proof she needed that Tanner Kingsley didn't love her but then in her heart of hearts, she'd known that.

Mail the letter or not? All she had to do was leave it on the hall table and the landlady would mail it for her. In the end she stuffed the envelope in her purse. Some things were better left alone.

Next stop, Atlanta, Georgia.

The antebellum house in Atlanta was tomb quiet. Jessie felt like an intruder when she let herself into the house. It took less than thirty minutes to realize that Sophie hadn't been back to the house since their return to the States following the tragedy of her mother's death. There was no waiting mail and none of the servants had heard from her. Everything was clean and polished. Sophie's room was tidier than she'd ever seen it. Tears puddled in her eyes. *"Where are you, Sophie?"* she whispered.

Jessie sat down on the edge of the bed. She wanted to

cry so bad she bit down on her tongue to stop the hot tears burning her eyes. She got up, knuckling her eyes as she opened closets and drawers, hoping for some kind of sign. There was nothing. Sophie had so much of everything it was hard to tell what was missing and what wasn't. She searched the desk and came up empty-handed.

Choking back her sobs, Jessie went outside to her friend's old playhouse. The bean-bag chairs they'd used at Christmastime were back in the playhouse. She sniffed, a smile breaking out on her face. The small rooms smelled like Sophie. This time the tears escaped and rolled down her cheeks. She allowed herself to cry then for her friend and herself for what they had both allowed to happen. Sophie was alone somewhere. She was here, alone. It wasn't supposed to be like this. For years they'd sworn to one another that they would only be a phone call away. For all she knew Sophie could be on the other side of the world. She continued to cry. In her entire life she'd never felt as alone as she felt at this moment. She knew what she was feeling was grief. It had to be grief, because nothing else could hurt this much. She likened it to the highest mountain, the endless desert, the deepest part of the ocean.

Jessie slept, curled into the bean-bag chair, awakening at midnight. She knew there would be no more sleep, so she carried her bags back to the car and set out for New Orleans. She could take her time and drive all night and be there by morning.

The long drive was uneventful. She stopped once for coffee around three-thirty and then again at six for a quick breakfast. She arrived at the house in the Garden District a little after eight in the morning. The door was ancient, the lock just as old and worn, the key from her key ring, ornate. The house smelled of mildew and dust from being closed up too long. She spent ten minutes turning on air conditioners and opening the blinds. Everything in the apartment was covered with a thick layer of dust. Sophie wasn't here and she hadn't been here for some time. The refrigerator held two wrinkled apples and a half bottle of Evian water. She slammed the door shut so hard it bounced open again. She closed it properly the second time.

Jessie searched the apartment from top to bottom but found nothing to indicate where her friend might have gone. Sophie liked to travel light. More often than not she traveled with only her purse, her passport, and a wad of cash, preferring to buy things on the run.

With nothing better to do, Jessie cleaned the apartment. She sighed with relief at four o'clock when she returned the cleaners and buckets to the pantry. She showered, washed her hair, dressed, and headed for the market, where she stocked up on enough groceries to last her a few days.

On the fifth day of her stay, Jessie woke to make a mad dash to the bathroom. The dreaded morning sickness the doctor had warned her about left her gasping for breath. She fixed tea when her stomach settled back to normal. She needed to think, to plan. She couldn't exist in this limbo forever. The last two days had left her feeling like a runaway gypsy with no roots and no future. She tried not to think about Tanner and where he was and what he was doing. It simply hurt too much to think about the man she thought she was in love with. Was she being fair in not telling him about her pregnancy? A child needed a father. A child should carry his father's name. What kind of mother would she make?

The phone behind her rang. To her ears the sound was fierce and angry. Should she answer it or not? Her greeting was cautious.

"Sophie, is that you? I've been calling you for weeks. Where were you?"

Weeks. She'd been here five days, and the phone hadn't

rung once. Who was this person? Her voice stayed cautious. "This isn't Sophie. I'm Jessie Roland. Who are you?"

"Jack Dawson. Is Sophie with you?"

"No, she isn't."

"Do you know where she is?"

"No. Do you?"

"I wouldn't be calling if I did. What are you doing in Sophie's apartment?"

She didn't care for his tone. "Why do you want to know?"

"Because I do. Well?"

The fine hairs on the back of Jessie's neck moved. "I'm visiting."

"Are you here for the wedding?"

"What wedding?"

The exasperation in his voice was unmistakable. "Sophie's and my wedding. We're supposed to be getting married in two weeks. I haven't heard from her in six weeks. She said she had things to do and places to go, and she would be in touch. It's natural to think, since you're her best friend, that you're here for the wedding. So, where is she?"

"I have no idea. I've been trying to locate her myself for weeks now. Did she go out of the country?"

"Not to my knowledge. I've been in Arizona for the past few weeks on a cleanup job. I've tried calling her, but there was never an answer. Sophie hates answering machines and refuses to own one."

Jessie's heart fluttered. "The wedding is still on? I thought . . . Sophie more or less . . . I assumed it was on hold." Her heart kept fluttering. Was this man someone Sophie *used* to know? Did she run away from him? Jessie clamped her lips shut.

"As far as I know it's still on. I ordered my tux even though it's a small private wedding. Sophie picked up her dress. That much I do know. My entire family is coming for the wedding. It better come off. I need to ask you a question. Has Sophie always been so . . . mercurial?"

Mercurial. Uh-oh. Jessie unclamped her lips. "More or less. If I hear from her, I'll have her call you." She hung up the phone. In minutes she was in Sophie's bedroom, pawing through the closet. Pushed far in the back, an ankle-length swirling creation hung on a scented, padded hanger inside a clear plastic bag. White satin shoes and a small veil were in separate plastic bags hanging on separate hangers. As she moved the shoes and veil farther back she noticed a second garment bag. Sophie's going-away dress. No, the ticket on the hanger said Jessie Roland. Sophie had picked out her maid-of-honor dress. Even through the clear plastic she could see that both dresses were exquisite. The labels inside both dresses said they were designed by Oscar De La Renta. She thought about her thickening waistline. If the wedding came off, she would have to have the seams let out. If. The biggest *if* of them all was what was she to do if Sophie didn't return in two weeks?

More mystified than ever, Jessie returned to the kitchen. She looked around helplessly. All she could do was wait. *Where are you, Sophie?*

Three days before Sophie's scheduled wedding, Jessie received a phone call from her landlady. Her heartbeat quickened as she listened to Mrs. Fisher's words. "I'm sorry, Jessie, but your young man was so persistent, I gave him your address and phone number. I won't bore you with his sad story. I really think, child, that you should give the young man a second chance. Now, I don't want to know what the problem is. I want you to think about it yourself. Real, true love only comes along once in a lifetime. I know what I'm talking about."

"Did he say he was coming here, Mrs. Fisher?"

"I believe so, child. I hope you aren't angry."

"No, Mrs. Fisher, I'm not angry. Thank you for calling."

Jessie walked out to the overgrown garden. The heat was stifling, the plants and flowers in desperate need of water. It would be something to do. Maybe Sophie was planning on getting married in the garden. She could wash down the colorful furniture after she weeded and trimmed the plants. It would be something to do and good exercise at the same time. Tanner was coming here? What did that mean? Did he realize he loved her and couldn't live without her? Anything, she supposed, was possible. She didn't believe it for a minute.

It was totally dark when Jessie finished the last corner of the garden. For the past hour she'd been working with just the tiny walkway lights for illumination. Everything smelled earthy, clean and fresh. She'd unearthed a small fountain beneath a maze of honeysuckle vines. The fat cherub with the hose in his belly gurgled happily when she turned the water on. It brought a smile to her face. She knew in full daylight the garden would be spectacular and worthy of Sophie's wedding. The iffy wedding wasn't going to come off. She was sure of it. *Sophie, where are you?*

As Jessie meandered through the house and into the bathroom it occurred to her that Jack Dawson had not called. Nor had he stopped by. With the wedding a mere three days away he should be a basket case of nerves, with his entire family arriving and no bride in sight. *Sophie, where are you?*

Jessie carried her coffee out to the garden. She'd been right last night. In broad daylight the garden was spectacular. She particularly loved the moss growing between the old bricks. She sniffed appreciatively. She was going to sit here all day long in this wonderful yellow chair and drink coffee. As she looked around she knew she would be able to make concrete decisions she could live with in this serene walled garden. If Sophie didn't return for the wedding, she would pack up and leave on Sunday. She would write a long letter and leave it under the pillow, the same kind of letter she'd left in the house in Atlanta. She would not think about Tanner Kingsley today or tomorrow or the day after tomorrow. Tanner Kingsley was just someone she used to know. *My mind knows that,* she thought, *but my heart has trouble accepting it.*

Hours later, when the sun was high in the sky, Jessie picked up the rainbow-colored dress to let the side seams out. How like Sophie to pick a rainbow-colored dress for her wedding. *Sophie, where are you?*

A shadow descended over the rainbow silk. Jessie looked up to see Tanner standing in front of her.

"I rang the bell, but I guess you didn't hear it. I missed you, Jessie. I also apologize for browbeating your landlady. Listen, whatever I did, I'm sorry. If I said something I wasn't supposed to say, I'm sorry for that, too. Do you mind if I sit down? What are you doing?"

"Letting out the seams of this dress. Sophie is supposed to be getting married tomorrow but she isn't here. I don't think there's going to be a wedding."

"Then why are you doing that?"

"I might be wrong. I want to be prepared just in case. What are you doing here, Tanner? You hung up on me, remember."

"That's because I was upset about Irene. I'm sorry. I would have called, but Pop came back to the ranch after the funeral. Two days later he suffered a heart attack. It was touch-and-go for a few days but he's mending now. He wanted Resa and me with him every second. I think he's going to retire. I called your apartment a thousand times. There was never any answer. I called the house in

Atlanta, but they said you had left. They wouldn't give me the number for this house, so I went to your landlady. If Sophie isn't here, why are you here? I need to understand all of this, Jessie."

"She's my friend, Tanner. When I became so involved with you I let her down. I didn't return her calls, I let you convince me to take the phone off the hook. It's my own fault. I have a mind of my own, but I was so wrapped up with us I let her flounder. I knew she was going through a bad time. I feel like I betrayed her. I hate myself for doing that to her. I guess I thought if I came here, somehow, some way, she'd know it and come back. Too many bad things have happened to Sophie lately. I failed her. That's the bottom line. For years now I was the only constant in her life, and vice versa."

"Why didn't you just hire a private detective? Pop knows a really good one he uses when he wants to dig dirt on someone. I can get you the guy's name."

Jessie looked at Tanner as though he'd sprouted a second head. "I never thought of that."

"It shouldn't take long. They use computers. Most times those guys don't even have to leave the office. Forty-eight hours sounds familiar. Where's your phone?"

"In the kitchen."

"Do you have her social security number and driver's license number? The world revolves around those two things you know."

"No, I didn't know that. I'll get them for you."

"Whoa, there, little lady. You packed on a little weight since I saw you last. I knew Creole food was spicy but I didn't think it was fattening."

"It isn't. I'm pregnant," she said over her shoulder as she marched from the room.

"FREEZE RIGHT THERE, JESSIE!"

Jessie stopped and turned around, her face miserable.

"Say that again."

"I said, 'I'm pregnant.' What part of that statement didn't you understand?" How defiant, how defensive her voice sounded.

Tanner threw his hands in the air, his face registering total disbelief. "I understand, I just can't believe it. When were you going to get around to telling me?"

"I wasn't going to tell you. Period."

"Why the hell not?" Tanner blustered.

Jessie thought she saw the disbelief change to relief. "Because I know how you feel about kids. Remember the day that little girl was skipping rope. I saw your face, heard what you said. I can manage. Sophie will help me. You are under no obligation to me at all. Look, Tanner, I've had a lot of time to think since I found out I was pregnant. You don't love me. At least not the way I want to be loved. I'm not sure what my feelings for you are. We don't seem to have much in common. You didn't call me at graduation. A phone call takes only a minute. Three minutes to sign a card and drop it in the mail. I don't think you're father material. I'm not even sure I'm mother material. However, I will learn. It's all very overwhelming for me. Plus, I'm worried about Sophie. Last but not least, let's not forget your mother's feelings toward me."

Tanner sat down on a bright red chair. "What do you want? Do you want to get married?"

"I don't want anything, Tanner. Need I remind you, you came to me, I did not call you. I planned to move on. You can't build a marriage and a life on sex. I need more, and I won't settle for less. I have to think of the child I'm carrying and what kind of life I want him or her to have."

"You aren't even working, Jessie. How are you going to support a kid and yourself? You need to be realistic."

"I can manage, Tanner. I have my degree now. I can get

a good job and hire a daytime nanny for the baby. Women do it all the time. I'm not afraid to work. Is there anything else? Oh, by the way, I'm sorry about the senator. Give him my regards."

"Is that your way of asking me to leave?"

"I don't have anything else to say. Do you? It is what it is. I can't change things. I'm willing to take all the blame here. Go back to your world, and I'll stay in mine. If you like, I'll stay in touch and send you pictures."

"You're making this sound like some goddamn cut-and-dried business deal. I need time to think. You can't just spring something on me like this and expect me to jump up and down with joy. A kid is a tremendous responsibility. I have to get used to the idea."

"No, Tanner, you don't. I'm letting you off the hook. I honestly don't want anything from you. You can go back to Texas and I'll decide what I'm going to do. I really can handle this. I want to hang up this dress, then I'll make us some coffee. We can sit here in the garden for a little while before you leave."

"Jesus Christ, Jessie, I just got here. You throw me a curve I'm still reeling from and then you want to boot my ass out of here. What the hell's gotten into you? We need to talk."

"No, we don't, Tanner. However, if you insist, I'm willing to listen. I have nothing to say, though."

In Sophie's bedroom, Jessie slipped the plastic liner over the rainbow-colored dress. She knew she was never going to get to wear the exquisite creation. Tears pricked at her eyelids. She sat down on the edge of the bed. She had to think about Tanner and what she was feeling, which was nothing. Her heart should be beating faster, her palms should be sweaty. She should be breathless with desire. She felt none of those things. What she felt was annoyance that the man she thought she loved was sitting down in the garden she'd just cleaned and pruned waiting for her to serve him coffee.

Jessie stared at the framed photograph on Sophie's night table. It was a picture of the two of them taken when they were seventeen and hamming for the camera. It was such a silly picture it was a wonder Sophie had kept it. The frame was from Tiffany's and probably priceless. Hot tears pricked her lids again. "You aren't coming back are you, Sophie? Why? I need to know why," she whispered. She looked around. Sophie and Jack had lived together for a short while, but there was nothing of his in the bedroom. Not a stray sock under the bed, no pictures, no extra toothbrush, nothing. Men, like women, tended to leave *something* behind. She'd read an article once that said men liked to mark their territory. She'd cleaned the room and had found nothing, not even stray hairs in the bathroom. All indications pointed to the fact that Jack Dawson had never inhabited this room at all. Did Sophie clean it? Unlikely. Later she would think about all this. Right now she had to deal with Tanner Kingsley, the father of her unborn child.

He looks at home, Jessie thought sourly as she carried a small tray out to the garden.

"Two sugars," Tanner said.

"Help yourself," Jessie said as she stirred cream into her own cup.

Scowling, Tanner poured his own coffee, added sugar and cream. The scowl stayed with him when he said, "We can get married at the end of the month. My mother will need a little time to prepare something. Pop will want to invite some of his cronies from the Hill."

"You are absolutely amazing," Jessie said. "You didn't hear a word I said, did you?"

"I heard everything you said. I'm trying to do the right thing here. A kid needs parents. As in a mother and a father. The kid needs my name. Do you want him growing up to be called a bastard?"

"That won't happen. I'll see to it. I don't want to get married, Tanner. Millions of women raise children alone. You seem to think I *need* you. I don't. You do not have to make an honest woman of me. That's what you think you're doing, isn't it?"

"I get it. Now that your friend Sophie isn't getting married, you don't want to either. Can't you think and act on your own? I'll never understand what the two of you have that makes you act like this. The only thing I can come up with is money. She has it, and you don't."

He was baiting her, waiting to see if she would say something. She could see it in his face, read it in his eyes. "Money has nothing to do with our friendship, Tanner. Sophie's friendship is more valuable to me than all the money in the world. If you don't understand that, I'm sorry."

"Are you refusing to marry me? Are you refusing to give the child my name? A lawyer might have something to say about that. My father knows the best of the best."

"That sounds like a threat. Are you threatening me, Tanner?"

"I have rights just like you have rights. The child, even though it isn't born yet, has rights, too."

Jessie schooled her face to blankness. He *looked* so sincere, *sounded* so sincere. Lawyers meant a whole new set of problems. Lawyers poked and pried and demanded answers. They might even find her parents and bring them back to testify to what a hateful daughter she was. It was true that Senator Kingsley had clout. "Then I guess I'll have to get myself an attorney, won't I?" She was surprised at how strong and cold her voice was. She'd learned from the senator how to bluff. If it came to that she would hire Sophie's lawyer, Arthur Mendenares.

"This is stupid. Attorneys cost money. In the end they're the only ones who walk away happy with their pockets full. I'm asking you to marry me, Jessie, for both our sakes and for the sake of the child. I'm trying to do the right thing here. Help me a little, will you?"

"What about me? What about us? If we were in love, it would be different. Parents who don't love each other will take a toll on the child. It isn't healthy for anyone. You're moody, thoughtless, and cranky—not to mention selfish. The only time you're affectionate is when we're in bed. We aren't even friends, Tanner. We're both too young to trap ourselves in a loveless marriage. I would never deny you your parental rights. You can see the child as often as you wish. We can trade off holidays and summer vacations. A child needs stability. As a mother, I can give that to our child. I'm sorry to say, Tanner, right now I don't even like you. What's best for our child is the only thing that's important. Do you agree or not?"

Tanner's voice took on an edge of anger. "What we had was good, Jessie. How can you deny that?"

"I don't deny it. In bed, Tanner. When we got out of bed it was miserable. You want everything your own way. Marriage doesn't work like that. It's give-and-take."

"It would appear we have a standoff here. I don't know what else to say, Jessie."

"There isn't anything else to say. Where do we go from here?"

"I don't know, Jessie. I guess I'll go back to Texas, and you'll go back to Washington at some point. I assume you'll get tired of waiting around here for a friend who seems to have forsaken you. I think, Jessie, we could make it work if we both try. I'd like the chance to at least try.

We'll be starting out even. Neither one of us has been a parent before. We can learn together if you're willing. I could turn out to be the best father in the world. How can you possibly deny me that chance? If you do, you aren't the woman I thought you were. I am sorry if I acted like a louse. I never thought . . . A baby wasn't something I had in mind. I dare say it wasn't in your mind either. You need to cut me a little slack here. I'll be staying at the Monteleone Hotel in the French Quarter tonight. If you feel like talking this evening, call me and we can have a drink in the Carousel Bar. If not, that's okay, too. I'll give you a call tomorrow before I leave. I hope your friend comes back, Jessie. I really do. I remember what it was like when I lost a friend. I left the name of the detective agency on the kitchen counter along with this number and your number back in Washington. One last suggestion—you could file a missing persons report. I'll see myself out, Jessie."

Jessie sat for a long time without moving, her brain whirling and twirling as she played Tanner's words over and over in her mind. He was right. How did she know what kind of father he would make? He might well turn out to be a better father than she would be a mother. He was right, too, about being in a state of shock just the way she was. Would marrying Tanner be best for the child? *Where are you, Sophie?*

It was midafternoon when Jessie, still in the garden, had her second visitor. She knew it was Jack Dawson immediately. Sophie had described him in detail on many occasions. He introduced himself. She did likewise. At his questioning look, she shook her head.

Jack Dawson was as handsome as Tanner Kingsley, but in a more effeminate way. His features were fine where Tanner's were rugged. He had the same piercing blue eyes and strong jaw. He combed his sandy hair to the left, Tanner combed his to the right. He was leaner than Tanner, but muscular. He was dressed casually for the summer heat in crisp khaki trousers and white dress shirt whose sleeves were rolled to his elbows. He wore expensive Italian shoes. "I guess the wedding is off," he said morosely.

"I guess so. I weeded the garden hoping . . . This is not like Sophie. I don't understand. Were specific wedding plans taken care of?"

"I don't know. Sophie said she was handling everything. She told me all I had to do was show up. My family arrived last night. I guess I'll show them the city and send them home. Sophie is the most efficient and conscientious person I've ever met. This is totally out of character for her. It's our wedding for God's sake."

"Did you argue? Did Sophie change? Did you do something that would have made her change her mind?"

"No to everything. We argued. Everyone argues. We never fought if that's your next question."

"Sophie said she was going to open her own business. What do you know about that?"

"She said she was looking into it. How long are you staying, Jessie?"

"Another day or so." *I don't like him,* Jessie thought. She'd bet her last dollar there was no family in town. So, what was he doing here? She stood and offered her hand. "I'll say good-bye then."

It was dusk when Jessie entered the house. She forced herself to go to Sophie's closet for one last look at her friend's wedding dress. Her heart aching, her stomach in knots, Jessie closed the closet door. She would close up the apartment and leave for Washington early in the morning. Perhaps she would be able to think more clearly back in her own apartment.

The loss she was feeling stayed with her all evening.

The following morning, Jessie tidied up the apartment,

drank a quick cup of coffee, and called the hotel to leave a message for Tanner saying she was on her way back to Washington.

Jessie took one last look at the house Sophie loved so much. She was drenched with sweat and it was only seven-thirty in the morning. She wiped at her eyes knowing she was only fooling herself if she blamed perspiration for the trickles on her cheeks.

Where are you, Sophie?

Chapter Fourteen

Jessie stared at the ringing phone knowing it was Tanner on the other end of the line. Should she answer it or not? She needed to go to the grocery store, needed to unpack her bags, needed to dust the apartment and open the windows. She needed to *think*. The moment the phone stopped ringing, she sighed. It had been her plan to think things through on the long drive from New Orleans. Instead she'd shifted her thought processes into a neutral zone and listened to the radio. Somewhere, somehow, on that long drive she had relegated Sophie's disappearance to a dark shelf in the back of her mind. She'd done all she could in regard to her friend. Now she had to think about herself and her immediate problem.

It was late, almost midnight when Jessie dried the dishes from her skimpy dinner. Now she was going to sit and drink tea and contemplate her life.

Tanner was right when he said a child needed two parents. Did she want a messy go-round with a batch of money-hungry lawyers? No, she did not. Tanner was also right when he said he could turn out to be the best father in the world, just as she could turn out to be the worst mother in the world. Anything was possible. Did she have the right to deny him the chance to prove it? Maybe yes, maybe no. Did she want to marry Tanner and become Mrs. Tanner Kingsley? Yes and no. Her heart, her mind, her gut told her Tanner wasn't marriage material. More to the point, was *she* marriage material? At one time she would have said yes. Now, she wasn't sure. Financially she was secure. Her child would never want for anything except a set of parents and a set of grandparents. If she married Tanner, the child would have an aunt in Resa. The senator would probably make a wonderful grandfather. The first Kingsley grandchild. Alexis didn't bear thinking about. If she did marry Tanner, she could always pull Alexis out on Halloween and dangle her as the Wicked Witch. The thought brought a smile to her face. It left almost immediately when the phone rang. This time she answered it.

"I'm sorry, Jessie, I forgot about the time difference. You sound like you haven't gone to bed yet. I was concerned that you made the trip home safely. Are you okay?"

He sounds like he cares, Jessie thought. "I'm fine. A little tired that's all. It's been a stressful few weeks."

"Stress isn't good, Jessie, for expectant mothers. Did you give any thought to our . . . situation?"

"I was doing that when you called."

"And?"

"Where would we live, Tanner? I told you, I will not live at the ranch."

"Would you consider a short-term arrangement until I can find us a place?"

"Define short-term."

"A month, five weeks. I didn't say anything to my family, Jessie. For some reason I didn't think you'd want me to. Will you give me some credit for trying? I'm the first to admit I'm no white knight. If I ever had any armor, it's full of holes."

"Yes."

"Yes what?"

"I'll give you credit. It's such a big step. We aren't in love. That's what bothers me."

"Jessie what does *in love* really mean? I care for you very much. It isn't just the sex thing either. I know you feel the same way. Look at your friend Sophie. You said she was crazy in love with whatever that guy's name is. Did that work out? She stood him up. And she wasn't pregnant. We can make it work, Jessie."

She was so tired. So weary. "Okay, Tanner. No planned wedding. You come to Washington and we'll get married by a justice of the peace. I don't much care if your mother likes it or not. I will not tolerate her interfering in our life. I want your assurances that you won't allow that to happen, Tanner. I will agree to live at the ranch only for five weeks. Not one day longer. One hour past that time, Tanner, and I walk away. Can you handle my terms?"

"I can handle it."

"I want it in writing."

"You what?"

"I want our terms in writing. I want a lawyer to look at the agreement. And I also want a prenuptial agreement."

Tanner blinked. "What's that?"

"A financial agreement that says what's mine is mine and what's yours is yours. Prior to the marriage. Anything we acquire during our marriage will be divided equally if we should divorce. That kind of thing. Lawyers work it up, and we both have to approve it. We'll set conditions for our child. In case something should happen to you or me, our child will be taken care of. Do you agree to that?"

"Yes, of course," Tanner said, reluctantly. "I'll have my attorney draw one up."

Jessie closed her eyes to ward off a wave of light-headedness. Her robust trust fund would be safe. "My attorney will look over whatever your attorney draws up. But I will have one drawn up for myself."

"That isn't necessary, Jessie."

"Yes, Tanner, it is necessary."

Tanner chuckled. Once she had loved the sound. Once she'd been breathless with the sound. Now the sound was sending chills up and down her arms.

"Then you're agreeing to marrying me. You know, Jessie, I always thought a proposal was supposed to be romantic. This is like a business deal. When do you want to get married?"

"How long will it take to draw up the agreement?"

"I'll go to the attorney's office first thing in the morning. When will you go?"

"First thing in the morning."

"That sounds good. They should be able to hash it out in a week's time. If you have a pencil, copy down the name of the law firm. Then the lawyers will do it all. We'll just sign the papers."

"To answer your question, ten days should give us enough time. I have some things to take care of. Is there anything else?"

"Is it okay to tell Pop?"

"No. All kinds of things can go wrong in ten days. I think I'd like to wait."

"Are you going to change your mind?"

"No. Are we going on a honeymoon?"

Tanner chuckled again. This time chills raced up Jessie's spine. "I think I can work that into my schedule. How about Key West, Florida? Or Key Largo?"

"How about a six-week cruise to wherever?"

Tanner's tone changed. "A week, Jessie. I can't be away from the ranch longer than a week. I have to think about Pop, too. We can plan a long vacation over the holidays or right after the new year."

"I'll think about that. I'm going to go to bed now, Tanner. Good night."

On a referral from Arthur Mendenares's offices in New York, Jessie walked into the prestigious law offices of Rupert, Rupert, Elton and Stennis to sign the final papers on Friday, five days later. She read the papers carefully, her index finger running under each word. Then she read them a second time.

The attorney was brisk, efficient, his eyes wary as Jessie held the pen in preparation to signing the stack of papers. "If you are having any doubts at all, Miss Roland, do not sign. If something's bothering you, we should discuss it. The child's welfare is at issue, and these papers have taken care of it."

"I want to be absolutely sure I am protected here. Whatever Tanner has in his name, whatever holdings or funds, at this point in time, I will have no claim on. Our child will, however, on his or her eighteenth birthday. Is that right?"

"Yes. If you and Mr. Kingsley venture into a business during your marriage, then both of you have a claim to it. Usually things are divided down the middle unless it can be proved otherwise."

"Where exactly does it say the same thing applies to me?"

The attorney's eyebrows shot upward. "Page four, second paragraph from the bottom. Your six thousand dollars will remain intact," he said tongue in cheek. "In fact, as you can see, no amounts of money are mentioned either by Mr. Kingsley or you. I thought it best."

"I'm afraid it's a little more than that, Mr. Rupert."

"How much more, Miss Roland?"

"Twenty-one million dollars. It's my trust fund. That's why *I* asked for the prenuptial agreement."

"I see. If your question is, is it safe, the answer is yes.

Mr. Kingsley will never be able to touch it. Do you have a will?"

"No."

"Then I suggest we draw one up right now before you sign those papers. It will only take about twenty minutes. Just give me a name of the person you want to take care of your child's finances in case anything happens to you. When your child is born you will call me and give me his or her name. We'll insert it at that time."

"Sophie Ashwood and Arthur Mendenares."

"Arthur's client? Arthur himself?" The attorney's eyebrows shot upward a second time.

"Yes."

"There's a very good restaurant on the first floor. Go down and have some coffee. When your will is ready I'll send my secretary down to fetch you. Later, you can update your will and be more specific with bequests and the like. This is for now. Do you understand?"

"Yes. Do you happen to know where Mr. Mendenares is?"

"I believe he's in Europe. Don't hold me to that."

"I'm trying to locate Sophie. I thought he might know where she is. Is there any way you can find out for me?"

"I'll put my secretary on it. He's a hard man to track down. We'll do our best."

"Thank you."

Jessie sat down at the small desk in the corner of the living room, the thick packet of papers in front of her. She read through every one. Satisfied that everything was just as Mr. Rupert said it was, she snapped a rubber band around the prenuptial agreement. She skimmed through her will before she inserted it between the rubber band. She carefully addressed a manila envelope to Sophie, writing in bold black letters, HOLD FOR SOPHIE in two different places. Ten stamps should do it. Before she could change her mind she walked up to the corner to drop the envelope in the mailbox. Done.

A week to close out her savings account, cancel the utilities, tidy up the apartment for the next tenant, and pack up her car. She also needed to buy an outfit to get married in. A tear rolled down her cheek. She brushed at it angrily. A second tear followed when she listened to the overseas operator speaking with Arthur Mendenares's Paris office, only to be told the attorney was on his way back to the States.

She had time on her hands now, so she might as well use it wisely and go for her wedding attire. She also needed to take out a marriage license and get her blood test. Tanner said he would take his test in Texas and bring the lab report with him. With the senator's office pulling the strings behind the scenes, Tanner would find a way for it all to work. She was sure if a waiting period was involved, there was a way to get around it. After that she would go to Rock Creek Park and sketch.

Four more days until she became Mrs. Tanner Kingsley. "It is what it is, Jessie," she murmured to herself as she made her way to Fourteenth Street to buy her wedding suit. "It is what it is."

Jessie sat on the stoop in the warm June sunshine. Earlier she'd loaded her bags into the cargo area in back of the Jeep. She'd said her good-byes to Mrs. Fisher earlier. Her car was parked at the curb. A glance at her watch told her she had a little over an hour until it was time to leave for the airport to pick up Tanner. They would get married in a five-minute ceremony and leave from the courthouse for Florida.

It was a quiet street, and she was going to miss it and the old brownstones that were so carefully tended. The trees on both sides of the street were full and beautiful, creating a tunnellike atmosphere. Umbrellas were never needed on a rainy-day walk to the corner to catch the streetcar. She looked up and down the street hoping to see someone she at least had a nodding acquaintance with. Someone to say good-bye to. There was no one. She felt like crying when she realized she would probably never return to this house. It wasn't that the house was special, it wasn't. Living here had given her a measure of independence. She'd paid the rent, cooked her own meals, cleaned the apartment. She'd gone to school and held down a full-time job. And now she was giving it all up. A strangled sound escaped her lips as she watched a man exit his car across the street. She frowned. He looked so familiar. He seemed to be studying the house numbers as though he were looking for someone. And then she recognized him.

"Mr. Mendenares! I've been calling for weeks. Do you know where Sophie is? You didn't have to come all this way. You could have called me. It wasn't an emergency. You know, a real emergency. Sophie and I always promised each other we would never be more than a phone call away. I thought you might know where she is. She was supposed to get married last week. I went to the house in New Orleans and waited. I got the garden ready and everything. I know I'm babbling here because I see something in your eyes I don't like. Why did you come here? Did something happen to Sophie? Is she hurt? I don't think I can handle any bad news, Mr. Mendenares. I really can't."

The moment the attorney started to speak, Jessie clamped her hands over her ears. A second later she was off the stoop and running toward the park. When she couldn't run any more she sat down on a wooden bench. Almost immediately she felt a gentle hand on her shoulder.

"I didn't want to put it in a letter. I knew you would have questions. I am so very sorry."

"What are you talking about? Where's Sophie? Why did she go into hiding?"

"Sophie's dead, Miss Roland."

"Don't tell me something like that. I don't want to hear that. Do you hear me? I don't want to hear that!" Jessie screamed.

"I'm sorry. There was no other way to say it."

"I'm getting married this afternoon. Sophie is only a year older than me. She's too young to die. Sophie . . . Sophie had things to do and places to go. She always said that. Tell me you're lying."

"For your sake, I wish I could. It was an accident. At least the authorities think it was an accident. Speaking for myself, I'm not sure."

"What kind of accident?" Jessie whispered.

"Sophie had a very hard time accepting her mother's death. She couldn't comprehend how such an accident occurred. She decided to drive the route herself, in the same kind of car, driving at the same rate of speed. At the precise area where her mother went over the cliff, she went over. The driving conditions were exactly right, the time of day was to the minute. The reason I say I think she planned it is because all her affairs were in order. Everything was taken care of."

"Not everything. She didn't cancel her wedding. She didn't call me or write."

"Oh, but she did, child. I was with her the day she called Mr. Dawson to tell him the wedding was off. She even wrote out a check for me to forward to him to cover what she considered his loss. She very conveniently left her handbag in my car when she started out. I was to clock her trip. It was all a ruse, and I was stupid enough to fall for it. I never thought . . . I should have . . . Anyway, inside her purse was her will, a letter to you, and a package of bubble gum. It's all in my car."

"You think Sophie killed herself. She would never do that. She came to terms with her mother's death. She said she loved Jack Dawson. She was going to open her own offices. When . . . when did she . . . ?"

"Two days ago."

"When is the funeral? I won't believe this until I see her . . . *laid out* with my own eyes."

The attorney waved his arms. "She's everywhere. She, like her mother, wanted to be cremated immediately. It was spelled out in detail in her will. She didn't want you to suffer through something like that. She told me once she thought funerals were barbaric."

Jessie's shoulders slumped as sobs ripped through her body.

A long time later she managed to say, "Why? I need to know why?"

"I don't have the answers you're looking for. I wish I did. Perhaps they lie in the letter she left for you. Sophie's will is a simple one. She left everything to you. It's all spelled out in the will. This is not the time or the place to discuss business. Whenever you're ready will be time enough. In the meantime it will be business as usual. I think I should tell you that Sophie opened offices all around the world. There aren't many, but they are scattered. She wanted something that was a little more than storefront. She opened such an office in the French Quarter. She bought the building outright. The taxes have been paid. If one were to enter the building, it could be anything. I know you don't want to hear this right now, but I feel compelled to tell you. There is a like building in downtown Corpus Christi. I've taken the liberty of writing everything down in longhand for you. I did it on the flight to the States. I'll be sending you a more formal version later on. I think it might be best if things went to the Atlanta house for now.

We'll use it as our base. Changes can be made later on. Where will you be living, Miss Roland?"

"Corpus Christi, Texas. I'm marrying Senator Kingsley's son Tanner."

"Yes, yes. Sophie did mention that to me."

"What . . . what should I do, Mr. Mendenares?"

"Grieve. It's all you can do. Time won't stand still, so we have to get on with the business of living. If there's anything I can do, call me. Walk back to my car with me so I can give you Sophie's purse. It's in my briefcase."

"Sophie was my best friend."

"And you were hers. She chattered about you constantly. She said you were in love. She was so happy for you."

"That's the second time in her life she was wrong. I'm not in love. I'm pregnant, but I'm not in love. The first time she was wrong was when she misjudged Jack Dawson."

"I see. She told me about Mr. Dawson and what a clever fortune hunter he was. She did love him very much. She thought she failed herself."

"You said she was paying him off. Why? How much?" Jessie asked, her eyes glazed.

"She said he worked so hard to con her, his efforts should be rewarded. A million dollars. To someone like Mr. Dawson I imagine it's a fortune. To Sophie it meant nothing. It was her slap in the face if you know what I mean."

Anger roared up Jessie's spine. "A million dollars as a reward for lying to Sophie. For cheating her of something she had every right to expect. Do not ever try to tell me it's the same thing as Sophie not telling him she was rich. It is not. I know how she agonized over the decision not to tell Jack Dawson. She's not . . . wasn't the liar. She chose not to advertise her wealth. Don't pay it. Rip it up. Another thing, find someone else to give her wealth to. I have enough problems as it is."

"It doesn't work that way, Miss Roland. I believe you heard me when I had this same exact discussion with Sophie a few months ago. If my memory serves me correctly, you looked at Sophie and said, 'it is what it is.' I now say that to you.

"I will rip up the check with great pleasure, Miss Roland. If you wait just one moment, I will give you Sophie's purse and my notes from the plane."

Jessie gulped back her tears when she reached out to accept the expensive Chanel purse. She brought it to her cheek. It smelled like Sophie. "I don't know what to do, Mr. Mendenares," she wailed.

The lawyer slid behind the wheel, but not before Jessie saw the tears in his eyes. "When I don't know what to do about something, I do nothing," he said. "I don't know if it's good advice or not. I'll be in touch. Be happy, Miss Roland. Sophie wanted you to be happy."

Jessie crossed the street to her own car and climbed inside. Her yellow wedding suit was mussed and wrinkled, a gray streak of dirt on the skirt. She waited until Arthur Mendenares's car was out of sight before she broke down completely, her body shaking convulsively, her hands beating at the steering wheel until they became so painful she had to stop. She reached for the black quilted bag and held it over her heart.

"I hate you, Sophie Ashwood, for doing this. Do you hear me! Now you are never going to see my child. I wanted you to be the godmother. Sophie, why? Why?

"I need someone to tell me what to do. I can't do this myself. My whole world is falling down around me. God, Sophie, why, why, why?" *Read the letter already. All you have to do is open it and read it.* Jessie looked around, certain someone had said the words aloud. It took her three tries before she could open the intricate clasp on the handbag. The scent of Sophie's perfume and the sweet smell of

the Bazooka bubble gum assailed her nostrils. She un-
wrapped one of the pieces and popped it in her mouth. She
chewed vigorously so she wouldn't cry, which was probably Sophie's intention from the git-go. First she read the
will. It was just as Arthur Mendenares had said. Sophie's
entire fortune was left to her with the exception of siz-
able bequests to numerous servants around the world who
had been pensioned off. She now owned everything—real
estate, yachts, planes, cars, islands, shipping tankers,
businesses. She got dizzy reading the list. For a simple
will it totaled fifty-six pages and was dated exactly three
weeks ago.

Jessie folded the will neatly before she slipped it back
into the legal sleeve. Her fingers struggled with the gummed
flap of the personal letter. It felt so thin. Thin meant only a
few words. Thin meant one piece of paper. "Oh, Sophie,
you owe me more than one skimpy piece of paper," she
blubbered. The bubble gum was sticky-sweet in her mouth.
She did her best to blow a bubble but couldn't.

Time lost all meaning for Jessie as she finally ripped at
the envelope and yanked the two thin sheets of paper free.
She forgot about her wedding, about picking Tanner up at
the airport.

Sophie's writing was small, cramped, supposedly a sign
of an introvert. Sophie had a knack for shooting down any
kind of myth that could even be remotely attached to her.

Jessie smoothed out the letter in her lap because her
hands were shaking too badly to hold the letter. She
chomped on the gum, her eyes wet.

> *Dearest Jessie,*
>   *If you're reading this letter, then you know
> I'm no longer on this earth. Hopefully, if God is
> in a kind, gentle mood, He'll let my spirit mingle
> with my mother's. Don't cry, Jess. Keep chewing*

that gum, and you'll make it through this letter. That's why I put it in my purse.

I don't want you beating yourself up asking the whys of it all. It is. Or, should I say, was? In no way are you to blame yourself. You are, I know it. It's all fucking bullshit, Jess. I've been on the edge too long. My mother's death pushed me right to the brink, and I tottered for a while. I might have been able to pull back if Jack had been who I thought he was. He had some scam, Jess, and I fell for it. I never let him know I found out how he set me up. When I bolted, he thought the wedding was still going to come off. I thought he would get in touch with you, so I faded out of your life in order not to put you in a position where you had to lie. If nothing else, I have true, loyal friends. Each and every one of them passed on your messages. Including Arthur. I know you went to Atlanta and New Orleans. I have the letters you left behind right here with me. I love you, Jessie Roland, for always being there for me. Guess what else I know. I know that you are expecting a baby. Yeah, I've had a tail on you since the beginning of the year. I think it's wonderful. You will, too, when you get over the shock. I know you're going to marry Tanner. If there's a way to make it work, I know you'll find it. I know also that you are going to make one hell of a mother. You're going to be the mother you and I never had. See, one of us got lucky.

I want you to have a good life, Jessie. I know you're going to miss me, but time will help. I'll always be with you in spirit. You know that. What you have to do now is believe it. You know what we always said, it's not enough to persevere, you must prevail, which is just another way of saying it doesn't matter where and what you came from, it's where you're going and how you get there that's important.

Jessie, I am giving you one whole day to grieve for me. Not one second longer. It's one of my last three requests of you. That was number one. Number two is that you go back to New Orleans and do that Sophie and Jessie thing. Every single thing we did after my graduation. I want you to make a day and a night of it. Laissez les bons temps rouler. The last thing I want you to do is a little more taxing. Blow me a bubble and stop the wailing.

I don't know if I have the right to ask this of you. I want you to do something for me that I never got to do. It doesn't have to be now, anytime will do. Build me a bridge, Jess. I know I'm leaving everything in good hands. Be happy, dear friend.

Gotta go now, Jess. My mother's waiting for me.

All my love and affection,
Sophie

In a daze, Jessie reread the letter. *Laissez les bons temps rouler.* Let the good times roll. In spite of herself, a smile tugged at the corners of Jessie's mouth. She proceeded to blow the biggest bubble she'd ever blown in her life. "It was for you, Sophie," she whispered as she picked the sticky gum off her cheeks.

Jessie fit the key into the ignition. She was about to pull into the street when she cut the engine and ran into the brownstone. "Mrs. Fisher, do me a favor please. If a young man comes here, will you tell him I went to New Orleans. Tell him if he wants to marry me, he can find me there. "

Jessie made one stop at the post office to send off Sophie's purse and Arthur Mendenares's notes in a large envelope she purchased at the counter. She wrote HOLD FOR JESSIE ROLAND on the envelope after she addressed the envelope to herself. According to Sophie's will, the household help would stay on till the end of the year unless she made other provisions.

In the car, she turned the radio on as loud as it would go. She continued to chew the bubble gum, which had lost its flavor.

"You just watch me, Sophie Ashwood, I'm going to build you a bridge that will blow your socks off if you're wearing any. I'll do it, too. I promise." The bubble she then blew was the size of a grapefruit.

Laissez les bons temps rouler, Sophie Ashwood.

On a sultry, steamy Monday morning, Jessie Roland married Tanner Kingsley for all the wrong reasons.

The five-minute nuptials took place in the exquisite garden of the house that once belonged to Sophie Ashwood. The bride wore a rainbow-colored afternoon dress and a small white veil. If the judge or the groom thought it strange that the bride chewed bubble gum throughout the brief ceremony neither mentioned it.

Jessie leaned back in her sand chair, her eyes on her husband. "I want to thank you, Tanner, for going along with . . ."

"Hey, it's okay. I really enjoyed those twenty-four hours. We did everything your friend wanted. It was nice in a sad kind of way. You'll hold on to your memories and in time you'll stop blaming Sophie for cheating you. That's what you're doing even if you don't realize it. Sophie didn't cheat you, she cheated herself. It takes guts to make it through the days. We don't live in a perfect world. There are no perfect people. We're all human. I'm speaking for myself here."

"I know all that. Sophie loved jazz, the rich Creole food. She was so . . . earthy. She never let on to anyone about how rich she was. She was always doing good things for people and never, ever, took credit. I don't know if I'll ever understand the why of it. Life is so precious."

"Who inherits? Did Sophie leave you anything?"

"Her favorite black Chanel handbag full of bubble gum. I'm sure one of these days we'll hear about it all. This is a nice place you picked out. I like the little villas as opposed to a hotel room."

"Are you saying I did something right?"

Jessie smiled. "When are you going to tell your parents?"

"I'll call later. I wanted you with me when I did it. Are we hoping for a boy or a girl?"

"It doesn't matter to me. What about you?"

"I just want it to have all its fingers and toes."

"We did the right thing, didn't we, Tanner?"

"I think we did. I'll try to be the person you want me to be. I'm sure I'll falter along the way just the way you will. Nudge me if that happens. I'll do the same to you. Neither of us is perfect, Jess. There are no guarantees. I can handle it. Can you?"

"I believe so. Tanner, I just want to be happy. I don't want to stand on the edge like Sophie did, believing there were no other options. I want us to be a family. My own wasn't all that happy. I suspect yours wasn't either. I want our child to be loved by both of us, and I want him or her to love us. It's all I want."

Tanner moved his sand chair closer to Jessie's. He reached for her hand. "You look as tired as I feel. We partied for twenty-four hours, slept ninety minutes, and drove here nonstop. I say we take a snooze under this beach umbrella and make wild, passionate love when we wake up."

"I think that's a marvelous idea." Unable to hold her eyes open, Jessie murmured "Do you love me at all, Tanner?"

"I wouldn't be here if I didn't," he muttered sleepily.

"Why is it so hard to say the words?" If there was a reply to her question, Jessie didn't hear it.

"We're home, Mrs. Kingsley."

"*Temporary* home, Mr. Kingsley. Five weeks, Tanner."

"I hear you, Mrs. Kingsley. Ready to take on the lioness? She's had five days to get used to the idea that I'm married. Her roar will be on the dull side. I'm glad you gave in where the party is concerned."

"I agreed because of your father. I understand he wants to show off his only son's wife. It's important to him to have his friends from Washington come to the party. I'm glad he decided not to retire."

"The doctor encouraged it. Pop needs to be doing something twenty-four hours a day. He'll take it easy. That was one of the conditions. You'd look really beautiful if you'd smile."

Jessie flashed her teeth in a wild grimace. "Let's get it over with."

"They're here," Angus Kingsley shouted to his wife.

"So they are," Alexis Kingsley said.

The senator hugged Jessie and whispered in her ear. "I'm so happy for you, my dear. Irene said you two were meant for each other."

Alexis's voice was cool, on the verge of frost, when she said, "Welcome once again to the Kingsley ranch, Jessica."

"It's temporary, Mrs. Kingsley. Five weeks to be exact."

Alexis's eyes narrowed. "What does that mean, Tanner?"

"It means we'll be here for five weeks. Not one day longer. Jessie and I want our own place."

"That's ridiculous. It's also a blatant waste of money when we have all this room. I already have contractors working on the second floor. You'll have your own suite of rooms. With the exception of a kitchen."

"Sorry, Mother. Jessie doesn't want to live here. Actually, I don't either. You won't like a child underfoot. It's settled, Mother."

"Angus, speak to your son. It is not settled."

Before the senator could speak, Jessie voiced her opinion. "Yes, Mrs. Kingsley, it is settled. I know you don't like me. I have no intention of walking on eggshells around you. Nor do I want to constantly watch what I say when I say it. I want a small house that I can make comfortable and cozy. I don't like this house. It reminds me of a space museum. I'm not comfortable here. I'm sorry if that offends you. If I had a choice, I'd choose a hotel for the five weeks. If you don't mind, I'd like to take a shower."

"Well, I never . . ."

"Guess she told you, Alexis. The girl has grit. That's why I hired her in the first place. I warned you they wouldn't want to live here. Did you listen to me? No, you did not. Now, that slip of a girl has made a fool of you." The senator chuckled. "Space museum. I never knew quite how to describe this house. She's right. By, God, she's right. Better call off those contractors."

"Shut up, Angus!"

The senator turned his back on his wife.

"You're enjoying this, aren't you? She's a nobody, a nothing your son had the misfortune to impregnate. She worked in an office for a paltry salary. It won't last. Tanner has a roving eye like you, Angus."

"You are one hateful woman, Alexis. How do you stand yourself?"

"You made me what I am, Angus. You made me the laughingstock of Corpus Christi. It was and still is all I can do to hold my head up in public. Everyone in this county knows you carried on an affair with Irene Marshall all our married life. Don't ever tell me I'm a hateful woman again. If you do, I'll see that you regret it."

"Go to hell, Alexis."

"Where do you think I've been all these years?"

"You made your own hell. I'm warning you, Alexis, don't interfere in our son's life. You already alienated our daughter and me. Tanner is all you have left. If you get your claws in him, you will come to rue the day. If that happens, I'll sell this ranch to Luke Holt, and you'll be out in the cold. I'll do it, too."

"Don't threaten me, Angus. I won't tolerate it."

"As I said, Alexis, go to hell."

"Bastard!" Alexis shot back

"Bitch!"

Jessie's eyes were wary when she opened the door to admit her mother-in-law. She waited.

"Tanner and his father are downstairs. I was wondering if you would like to wear my pearls this evening. If they don't go with your dress, I'll understand."

Jessie blinked. Was this a peace offering? If it was, she was woman enough to meet Alexis halfway. "You tell me, Mrs. Kingsley, do they go with this dress?"

Alexis cast a critical eye over the designer dress Jessie had chosen for the evening's festivities. "I think so. It's a lovely dress. You hardly show at all."

Jessie smiled. "I feel like a blimp."

"Here, let me fasten the pearls. Yes, they look wonderful. Shall we go downstairs and have a cocktail before our guests arrive?"

"How many people are coming, Mrs. Kingsley?"

"About 150." Her eyes glittering, she said, "Think about all those presents you'll get to open."

"Presents? People are going to bring presents!"

"Of course. I just love gaily wrapped presents. They're so mysterious until they're opened. Be prepared for at least a dozen toasters. Not to worry, we can exchange them for something else. Would you mind terribly, my dear, if I made a suggestion?"

"Not at all."

"Do you have other shoes? This is just my opinion, but I don't think the shoes you're wearing go with your dress. They seem so . . . *cloppy* if you know what I mean. The dress calls for something, vampy, strappy, a higher skinnier heel so they look more sexy. Your shoes are a pump with a fat heel. Shoes are very important. What size are you?"

"Six and a half."

"My size exactly. Wait here. I have just the thing and I've never worn them."

Jessie kicked off her pumps. She was right, they didn't go with the dress but were comfortable.

Alexis returned waving a pair of satin sling-backs. "What do you think?"

"What I think is I'll probably break my neck."

"You'll be sitting most of the evening. Later on you can come up and change if they start to bother you. Ah, that's perfect! You look stunning!"

"Ah . . . thank you. You look"—Jessie struggled for just the right word—"elegant."

Alexis smiled. "We are our own admiration society, aren't we. Come, it's time to go downstairs. Be careful of that long skirt so it doesn't get caught in your heel."

At the top of the steps, Alexis called downstairs. "Gentlemen! Gentlemen! Allow me to present the newest Mrs.

Kingsley. Isn't she stunning! Curtsy, Jessie," she whispered in her ear.

Jessie smiled self-consciously as she prepared to curtsy. She felt Alexis's hand on her back, her eyes widening in shock as she lost her footing and toppled down the steps.

"Dear God! Angus, Tanner, call the doctor, the ambulance. Call somebody. Don't touch her, you could do more damage," Alexis screamed as she rushed down the steps.

"Jessie, don't move. Pop is calling for an ambulance. Everything's going to be okay. Just don't move, honey. Mother, what the hell happened? You were right there."

"She fell, Tanner. I never should have given her those shoes. They were perfect for the dress. She must have tripped on the carpet. I'll get a blanket. We don't want her going into shock."

"Jessie, look at me. Hold my hand. Jesus, Pop, look how white she is. She's going to be all right isn't she?"

"Of course she is, son. Jessie is a strong girl. Where is your mother?"

"She went to get a blanket. She said something about Jessie going into shock. How long before the ambulance gets here?"

"Ten minutes. Possibly less. Maybe more. I don't know, Tanner."

"Shouldn't we be doing something?"

"Keep her calm. Are you in pain, Jessie?"

"Her eyes are rolling back in her head. What does that mean, Pop?"

"Son, I'm not a doctor. What I do know is we need to keep her awake. Talk to her. I'll go and see what's keeping your mother."

"Jessie, honey, it's going to be all right. I promise. I don't want you to talk. Just blink your eyes so I know you understand what I'm saying. You might have a concus-

sion. That's why you have to stay awake. Blink, Jessie."
Jessie blinked. "Are you in pain?" Jessie blinked several
times.

"I hear the siren, honey. We're going to get you fixed up
in no time. I'll follow in my car with Pop. It's going to be
all right, Jessie. I promise. I know you want to talk. Whatever you want to say can wait.

"We'll be right behind you, honey," Tanner shouted.

"She wants to say something," the EMS attendant said.

"I know, she's worried about the baby. What, honey?
What are you trying to say?"

"She . . . pushed . . . me."

The ambulance door slammed shut. Tanner stood still
as a statue, his eyes wide with shock. Angus Kingsley
clutched at his chest.

"Go inside, Pop. I'll go to the hospital. Jessie is deliri-
ous. I was watching them at the top of the steps. So were
you. No one pushed Jessie. We would have seen that.
Calm down, Pop. You have a party to get through. Jessie is
young and healthy. She's going to be fine."

The senator's voice was harsh and flat when he said.
"This might be a good time to tell you I checked with all
the taxi companies after Irene's house was broken into at
your suggestion. At first I wasn't going to do it because I
didn't want to know. I have a photocopy of the driver's log
sheet back in Washington. It was your mother. Furthermore, in the downstairs hall closet there is a pair of boots
that belong to Irene. The driver described your mother
perfectly. Don't discount what your wife just said."

"We'll talk about this later, Pop. I have to get to the hospital."

"Jessie is not a liar, Tanner."

"I know that, Pop."

His shoulders slumped, Angus Kingsley walked back

into the house. His wife was standing in the doorway, a yellow blanket in her hands.

"I should kill you for what you just did."

"For getting a blanket. That medicine you keep gobbling is making you delusional, Angus."

"What about those boots in the hall closet? How would you ever get Irene's boots unless you were in her house? I found the driver who took you to her house and back to the airport. You are a sick woman, Alexis. I'm going to look into having you committed."

Alexis allowed her eyes to narrow to slits. "Do not ever make the mistake of threatening me again, Angus. I hear car engines, and I see headlights. Put on your party face. That's an order, Angus. Just remember this. I know where all your political bodies are buried."

"Bitch!" Angus snarled.

"Bastard," Alexis snarled in return.

Tanner grimaced at the array of Styrofoam cups lined up on the table next to where he was sitting. He was on his third ashtray. Each time he filled it up, he moved it and took a clean one from another table. The waiting room was empty, the hour late. He should have heard something by now. In his life he'd never been this worried. If he lived to be a hundred, he would never forget his wife's pale face filled with pain and her incredible last words.

He heard the scratching sound of the paper shoes doctors wore in the operating room before he saw the green-clad figure, the surgical mask dangling down his chest. Tanner leaped to his feet. "How is she?"

"She's going to be fine. We couldn't save the child. We did everything we could. It was a boy."

"Does Jessie know about the baby?"

"Yes."

"I can't be certain about this, Mr. Tanner, but I think your wife is going to have a short-term memory problem. It happens sometimes when the mind can't handle something this traumatic. I'm going to put in a call to a colleague to have her looked at tomorrow. I've arranged for a private-duty nurse for the night. We'll be monitoring her carefully. You can see her for five minutes. I want her to rest. She sprained her arm in the fall, and she has a cracked rib. Those will heal. She's resting comfortably right now. Please don't upset her. Follow me."

"Jessie, it's me, Tanner. Are you awake, honey?"

"I'm awake. What happened? They said I lost the baby."

"Yes. I'm sorry, Jessie."

"I am, too, Tanner. Where am I?"

"In the hospital."

"I know that. Which hospital? George Washington Hospital?"

"No, honey. You're at the local hospital here in Texas. We came home two days ago. Tonight was the party. Don't you remember?"

"I don't remember, Tanner. They said I fell. I'm not clumsy. How did that happen?"

"I'm not sure, Jessie. Look, honey, the doctor said I could only stay five minutes. They want you to sleep. A nurse is going to stay with you through the night. I'll be back first thing in the morning. Can I bring you anything?"

"Just yourself. Am I going to be okay, Tanner?"

"You'll be good as new in a week or so. That's a promise."

"Do you think Sophie is looking out for our baby?"

Tanner cleared his throat. His eyes started to burn unbearably. "I'm sure of it, Jessie."

"Things always happen for a reason, Tanner. Sophie always said that. She'll look after him. Knowing that makes it bearable."

"We'll have other children, Jessie."

"Is that a promise?"

"It's a promise, Jessie. Go to sleep now."

Tanner bent down to kiss his wife's cheek. When a tear rolled from his eye onto Jessie's cheek he kissed it away. "Sleep tight," he whispered.

Part III

Part III

Chapter Fifteen

Corpus Christi, Texas July 1981

The slight buzzing of a bluebottle fly circling the paddle fan caught Jessie's attention. She stared at the blades but was unable to pick out the fly caught in the swirling motion. If she raised the screen, it might fly out, she thought. However, that meant she had to get up off the chair and exert herself. It was much nicer just sitting here breathing in the scent of the newly mown grass. She loved the sound of the lawn mower almost as much as the sound of the oscillating fan. She craned her neck to stare out the window at the bright summer sunshine. A swarm of fat yellow bumblebees circled the flower bed beneath the window. It was all so normal. A perfect summer day. A day to do things. A day to feel alive and a day to be grateful for all the good things in her life.

It was almost eight o'clock, and already the ranch was buzzing with activity. Eight o'clock meant Tanner would be coming in for breakfast with three hours of work under his belt.

Jessie looked around the room she shared with Tanner. It was pleasant enough, comfortable, too, but she hated it.

There was nothing here that said Jessie Roland Kingsley lived in this room. It was her fault for falling apart after the accident. Everyone said she had a breakdown. Did women really have nervous breakdowns when they lost a baby, or did other people sedate that person so she believed it? The array of pills on her night table drew her attention. Pills to go to sleep. Pills to wake up. Pills for energy. Pills for depression. Pills to increase her appetite. Pills to calm her down. Blue. Yellow. Pink. Green and the fat red ones that made her sick to her stomach. She blinked when the bluebottle fly settled on top of the bottle of red pills.

In the beginning, someone, usually Alexis, doled out the pills and watched as she swallowed them. It was easier back then to just take the pills so they didn't force them on her. Alexis had no patience with her. Tanner, on the other hand, would try to trick her and put the pills in her food or in her drinks. Now she realized she'd lived in a stupor for the last year. She hadn't taken any of the pills in a month. Mentally and physically, she was feeling like her old self. She continued to play the game of the invalid and wasn't sure why. Every morning when the ranch settled down she did an hour of calisthenics in the dressing room. Each day she removed the pills from the bottles and flushed them down the toilet. Let the Kingsleys think what they wanted to think.

"Hi, honey. Beautiful day, isn't it? Are you coming down to breakfast?"

"Do you think I should?"

"Absolutely. Did you take your pills?"

"I took them with the orange juice you left for me," Jessie lied.

"I think you're looking a lot better. Lucille made waffles this morning and I'm starving."

"Tanner, when are we going to move?"

"Are you going to start that again, Jessie? Just stop and think for a minute. If we were off somewhere else, what do you think would have happened to you without my family? My mother hasn't left the ranch since the day you came home. She was afraid for you. I know that doesn't sound like her, but she was so concerned she took over your care. You don't remember those early days when you came home from the hospital. They were pretty awful. You were downright suicidal."

"Me!"

"You. It was Sophie's death and the miscarriage that pushed you over the edge. Before you know it, you'll be right as rain. In fact, my mother is so encouraged by your recovery, she's taking a few days off. She left this morning for Dallas to do some shopping at what she calls 'the finer stores,' then she's going on to Washington. Pop wants her there for some ceremony. I need to know you'll be all right here on your own."

"I'll be fine." Three whole days without Alexis breathing down her neck. "I might even take a walk. Have I gotten any mail? Has anyone called me?"

"No mail. No calls that I know of. Did you ask my mother?"

"No. I will when she comes back. Since I seem to be improving, does that mean we're going to move? The agreement was for five weeks, Tanner."

"Jessie, this is not the time to discuss moving. When you're fully recovered we'll talk about it."

"I want to talk about it now. I don't like living in one room. I want my own space, my own kitchen."

"Jessie, that was by your choice. You never wanted to come downstairs. You took your meals in our room. I had to beg you to go outdoors in the beginning. I'm happy to see that you've made such strides. Mackie told me you've been going riding. I'm glad you're up to it."

"For heaven's sake, Tanner, it was those pills. I'm not going to take them anymore. They dope me up. I had a terrible fear of falling down those steps. That's why I didn't want to go down those steps. That's past now. I feel fine. I'm stronger. I feel alert. I've even done some gardening. I want to do it in my own place. I want to putter in my own kitchen. Can't you understand that?"

"We'll work on the moving thing when the doctor gives you a clean bill of health."

"Are you having an affair, Tanner?"

Tanner stopped eating. "What the hell brought that on?"

"If you haven't been sleeping with me, then who are you sleeping with? You are a very virile man. You also look guilty."

"You pushed me away. I'm sorry, but this isn't going to sound right no matter how I say it so I'll just say it. We tried making love, but you just lay there like a log. A couple of times you said and this is a direct quote—'Just do it and get it over with.'"

Jessie cringed, knowing what her husband said was true. "So you did have an affair?"

"I won't lie to you, Jessie. It wasn't an affair. It was sex. It didn't mean anything."

Jessie felt her strong new world start to crumble around her. "Would it mean anything if I did it?" she asked in a shaky voice.

Tanner slammed his fork down on the table. "Your first good goddamn day and you have to pick a fight. What the hell did you expect me to do?"

"I expected you to be faithful. It's obvious that you subscribe to a double standard where marriage is concerned. Was it Bippity-Bop?"

"I'm not getting into this, Jessie. It happened, it's over. End of discussion. Just let me remind you that you were not a wife to me these past months."

Her shaky new world continued to crumble with her husband's harsh words. "I don't know if I can forgive you or not. Maybe if we're alone, on our own, it might be different. I want my own place. I want a garden. I want to do something. I *need* to do something. Where are my things, Tanner?" Her voice was so cold, Jessie felt a chill run through her body.

"It's not wise to rush into things. What things are you talking about?"

"The things I brought with me when we came here. Where's my Jeep?"

"I think all your stuff is in Resa's old room. Your Jeep is in the garage, where you would expect it to be. I have to get back to work. I'll see you this evening. How does a candlelight dinner and soft music sound?"

"Like a planned seduction to assuage your own guilt. I'm not interested. You admit to being unfaithful, and now you want me to . . . whatever it is you want. No thank you."

"This could get real old, real quick. You didn't want that kid any more than I did. I did the right thing by marrying you, so we could give it a name. Face it, Jessie, neither one of us was ready for parenthood. You know it, and so do I. We both put the best face we could on the deal. I don't believe for one minute that losing the kid was the reason you stepped over the edge. It was Sophie dying that threw you into a tailspin. That's past. We're in a different place this time around."

"I can't believe you're saying such cruel things to me. Who *are* you, Tanner Kingsley?" Jessie gasped, her eyes filling at what she considered his verbal cruelty.

Tanner stomped from the room, his face a mask of fury.

Jessie sat at the breakfast table long after Lucille had cleared it. On the housekeeper's last trip into the room

Jessie queried her. "Lucille, did you take any calls for me during the past year?"

"Several times. Mrs. Kingsley always spoke to the gentleman. He was quite persistent. Didn't you return his calls?"

"Do you remember his name?"

"It sounded Spanish or maybe Italian."

"Was it Arthur Mendenares?"

"Yes, that's the name."

"Did he leave a number?"

"Once. I copied it down and gave it to Mrs. Kingsley. Do you want me to look for it?"

"Yes, if you wouldn't mind. Lucille, don't mention this to Mrs. Kingsley."

"I understand. I'll look for it now. Would you like more coffee?"

"Yes. Yes, I would."

"I'm glad to see you're feeling better."

Twenty minutes later, Lucille was back with the slip of paper. Jessie thanked her and returned to her room. Should she call from here or go somewhere else? Instinct told her to call the operator and ask to make a person-to-person call and to charge it to Sophie's old phone number in Atlanta. Ten minutes later she announced herself to Arthur Mendenares.

"My dear, it is so good to finally hear from you. I trust your trip around the world was all you wanted it to be. You must have a very indulgent husband."

Jessie felt her heart thumb against her rib cage. Why would Tanner's mother tell such a blatant lie to the attorney? "I didn't take a trip around the world, Mr. Mendenares. I've been here at the ranch. I fell down the steps and suffered a miscarriage. This past year is one big blur. I'm assuming my mother-in-law is the one who told you I was on a trip. Why were you trying to reach me?"

"I see." The lawyer's tone of voice said he clearly didn't understand. "We need to set up a meeting. I have satchels full of papers for you to sign. I can be in Corpus Christi by noon tomorrow. We can meet at the office. Do you remember where it is? No. All right, copy this address down. Perhaps it would be advisable to continue this discussion tomorrow. You're well, Jessie?"

"I'm well, Mr. Mendenares. I wish there was a place to go to so I could visit with Sophie. I've thought about her so much these past two weeks. Why is it so hard on those left behind? I need a place."

"Then pick one, Jessie. Sophie is wherever you are. If a particular place is important, designate one, and her spirit will follow you. This is not insight on my part. It's the way Sophie explained it to me. She said her garden in New Orleans was the spot for her mother. Is there anything I can do for you, my dear?"

"No. I need to think. I'll see you tomorrow."

Jessie spent the remainder of the day walking around the ranch as she tried to reconcile Arthur Mendenares's conversation in her mind. She realized she felt fit and strong. There was no way in hell she was going to sleep with an unfaithful husband.

Late in the afternoon, Jessie moved her personal things into Resa's room. At four-thirty she sought out the handyman and asked to have a dead bolt installed on the door. She wasn't going to take a chance on the shiny brass lock. Somewhere there was a key, she was sure of it. At five o'clock she dumped all the colored pills into the toilet, the water turning into a rainbow of color. The empty vials went into the wastebasket. At five-thirty she was sitting in the garden room on a wicker chair, sketching.

The garden room was the only room at the ranch that Jessie felt comfortable in. The wraparound paned windows were tinted slightly to allow the sunlight to cover

every inch of the long, narrow room but not blind the oc-
cupants. Thanks to Lucille's green thumb, the plants that
lined the room were lush and healthy-looking, their leaves
emerald green, the planting soil dark and rich. She particularly liked the vibrant, floral chintz covers on the cushions. Resa had told her once that she had made the covers
because she, too, liked the room. She'd gone on to say that
counting the stars at night was her favorite pastime. As far
as she knew neither Tanner nor his mother ever sat in the
room.

Jessie heard him long before she saw him. Her stomach
started to knot itself the moment Tanner walked into the
garden room. "I won't be here for dinner. I don't know
what time I'll be home. I moved your things back into *our*
room."

Jessie pushed her back deeper into the cushions as she
watched her husband to see if she could gauge his mood.
His voice was friendly-sounding, a direct contradiction to
his angry face.

"I'd like to get a dog, Tanner," Jessie said quietly.

"That's out of the question. Both my mother and I are
allergic to animals. I'm sorry, but that's the way it is. Every
time you open your mouth, it's to say you want something. Why is that, Jessie?"

"I'd like to know why your mother told Mr. Mendenares you took me on a trip around the world. She had
no right to lie to my attorney like that. I have this awful
feeling, Tanner, that you and your mother are up to something where I'm concerned. Perhaps we should file for divorce. The only reason we got married was to give the
baby a name. Since there is no baby, there doesn't seem to
be any reason to stay together. I have no intention of living
the rest of my life with an unfaithful husband or a mother-
in-law who hates my guts and lies about my wellbeing."

Tanner pushed his Stetson farther back on his head.

"Now that's the Jessie I know and understand," he drawled. "Divorces are not acceptable in the Kingsley family. My mother was trying to help you since you were in no condition to deal with attorneys. That first month you couldn't even dress yourself. All she did was try to take the pressure off your shoulders. Yes, she told a lie. Yes, I knew about it. Obviously, you have talked to him and set him straight, so what's the big deal?"

"Really," Jessie drawled in return. "What do you call the document your father got in order to marry your mother? I hate liars more than anything in the world."

There was no time to move, no time to dodge the blow she saw coming. Caught off-balance, her head reeled sickeningly. Stunned at what her husband had done to her, Jessie could only shrink deeper into the cushions.

"It's called an annulment," Tanner said harshly as he strode from the room.

Jessie sat for a long time staring at the sketch in her hand. As hard as she tried, she couldn't stop the flow of tears. In her wildest dreams she never thought the man she married would strike her. All she'd done was ask questions of her husband, something she had every right to do. For every action there was a reaction. Tanner himself had told her Irene divorced his father. Resa had told her the same thing. No self-respecting man struck a woman, no matter what transpired between them.

Hurt, angry, and humiliated, Jessie went upstairs to her room to change her clothes. Later she could carry everything back to Resa's old room. Now she was going to go riding. She needed to feel the wind on her face, needed to feel *free*.

In the stable she walked down the row of stalls, trying to decide which horse to choose. With the groom's help she finally chose a spirited mare named Sunny.

"Just give her her head and let her go. She might be a

little frisky at first since she hasn't been ridden in a few days. She likes it when you sing to her. Take along these sugar cubes and an apple, and she'll do anything you want. The only thing that will spook Sunny is a dog, and since there aren't any dogs around, you shouldn't have a bit of trouble."

Sunny cantered out of the stable, her nostrils flaring at the prospect of a run. "Easy, girl, easy. I haven't ridden you for a while, so take it easy with me. I know I'm going to regret this, but Tulip is just too placid for me today. Tomorrow I probably won't be able to walk, much less sit down, so let's start out easy."

Nothing, Jessie thought, *has felt this good in a long time.* Her hair billowing out behind her, her face flushed, she started to sing "Yankee Doodle Dandy" because it was the only song she could think of at the moment. Sunny slowed her wild stride until she was stepping daintily across the field. Twice Jessie leaned forward to offer the sugar cube. They rode until dusk settled and it was hard to see.

Jessie heard the low, menacing growl just as a yellow blur streaked past her. Sunny reared back on her hind legs. Startled and confused, Jessie fell to the ground. She heard rather than saw Sunny thunder away across the field. Did she have any broken bones? She winced as she maneuvered her body this way and that way. Suddenly she felt something warm on her cheek. "Oh, and who are you? God, you're beautiful," Jessie said, as she struggled to a sitting position. The yellow dog allowed her to fondle his ears and rub his belly. She whirled around when she heard a sound to see a shotgun pointed directly at her heart. She looked upward to see the tallest, the meanest, the angriest man she'd ever seen.

"Can't you read? Didn't you see the posted signs? This is private property, and you're trespassing."

"You don't have to yell. There's nothing wrong with my hearing. Your damn dog spooked my horse. Do you see a horse around here? No, you do not. So how do you suggest I get home? Or do you think I can flap my wings and fly? Put that gun away. You should never point a gun at someone unless you're prepared to use it. That was the first thing I learned when I took a firearms class. I came out first in my class in case you're interested."

"I'm not. Pack up and get out!"

"It's getting dark. I've been riding for two hours. For all you know I could have broken some bones. I could sue you. Your dog scared my horse. I like your dog, mister. He has better manners than you do. Are you going to help me up or not?"

A long arm reached for her arm. Jessie's feet left the ground for moments before she was standing next to the man with the gun. "Obviously you live around here. Will you lend me a horse? I'll return him in the morning. Or if you don't have a horse to spare, will you point me to the road?"

Jessie's feet left the ground for the second time in as many minutes. In the blink of an eye she was on the man's horse and he was in front of her. "Hang on," he said.

"Are you always this mean, or do you just hate women?" She didn't expect a response and wasn't surprised when she didn't get one.

Fifteen minutes later, the tallest, meanest, angriest man she'd ever seen reined in his horse and slid to the ground. He offered her his hand. She felt like a midget standing next to him. The dog whined at her feet. "Don't you ever pet this dog? He looks like he's starved for attention."

"My dog is none of your business. Tell me who to call so they can come fetch you."

Come fetch you. It must be Texas talk. "There's no one

to call. I have to get home on my own. What happened to that Texas hospitality I'm always hearing about?"

"It's a myth," the man said gruffly. "I'll back out the truck and drive you home."

"Are you crazy? I'm not getting in any truck with you. I don't even know you. For all I know you could be some kind of pervert that preys on women who *you say* trespass on your land. I didn't see one sign posted. Where's the road?"

"Don't you ever shut up?"

Jessie clamped her lips shut. She stomped off, not knowing if she was going in the direction of the road or not.

"Get your ass back here and in this truck."

"Don't tell me what to do. I'm sick and tired of people telling me what to do. First they dope me up for months at a time, then they tell my lawyer lies, and then I find out my husband has been unfaithful. I've been through a lot today, mister. The only person who has been decent to me is your dog. I love that dog. Why don't you pet him? Or is it a her? You're too arrogant for a female dog." Her knees gave out then, and she dropped to the ground. A moment later hard, driving sobs shook her entire body. Within seconds the dog was all over her, licking her face, pawing at her arms. She hugged him so hard he yelped.

In the dim yellowish light over the stable door, Lucas Holt watched in horror as Jessie's eyes rolled back in her head as she screamed, "Jelly! Jelly! Jelly!" before she blacked out, her grip a stranglehold on the dog.

It took all Luke's strength to pry open Jessie's arms to free the dog. "I don't know what we have here, Buzz, but it's something. It's okay, boy. Calm down."

The yellow dog sat on his haunches as Luke picked Jessie up to carry her into the house. "It's okay, boy. We're going to give her a good stiff drink and take her home. I think I know where she belongs."

"Think again. You aren't plying me with liquor. What happened? Why are you carrying me? Put me down. I said, put me down."

Luke dumped her on the sofa. Buzz whined, then growled. "You blacked out. You almost strangled my dog. You scared the hell out of both of us. Do you want some jelly bread?"

Jessie struggled to sit up. "Why would I want jelly bread?"

"Because you were yelling your damn head off that's why. You kept yelling jelly, jelly, jelly, and then you blacked out. I thought you were a diabetic or something."

Jessie rubbed at her temples. "That's strange. Usually it just happens in the dreams. I'm sorry. I really am. I truly did not see your posted signs. I think I got off on the wrong foot with you. I'm sorry about that, too." She held out her hand. "I'm Jessie Kingsley."

"You're Tanner's wife! Well, I'll be damned. I heard he got married and the next thing I heard was the bride had a nervous breakdown." He clucked his tongue and shook his head to show what he thought of that information.

"You heard wrong," Jessie snapped irritably. "I didn't have a nervous breakdown. If that's what people are saying, it's a lie. Furthermore, I don't expect to be Jessie Kingsley much longer. I'd really like to go home. Such as it is."

"If you aren't in a hurry, why don't you stay for dinner. You look like you could do with some good, nourishing food. A stiff drink might also be in order."

Jessie looked at him and then at the friendly dog. What was there to go home to? She did feel wobbly, and suddenly she was ravenous. "I don't want to impose."

"Like you said, we got off on the wrong foot back there. Shall I tell my cook you're staying for dinner?" he asked gruffly.

"I'll stay if it isn't too much trouble.. What I'd really like is a nice cold, as in very cold, beer right now."

"I didn't think women drank beer these days. I thought they liked fancy drinks with those little umbrellas."

"Maybe they do, but I don't. I like to swig it right from the bottle. My friend Sophie taught me to drink it that way. Especially on a hot summer day." Her eyes filled with tears at the mention of Sophie's name. She couldn't blink them away.

"Let me tell the cook I'll be having a guest for dinner. I'll bring the beer, and we can talk about Sophie. She's the reason for the tears, right?"

Jessie nodded. Why was he being so nice after being so hateful to her earlier? According to Tanner, Luke Holt was the Kingsleys' number one enemy. Was it some kind of trick to get back at the Kingsleys? She didn't care if it was. She needed to talk about Sophie. She swiped at her wet eyes with the sleeve of her shirt. The yellow dog watched her, his tail swishing from side to side. Jessie held out her hand. Buzz rolled over for his belly to be scratched. Jessie smiled. He was a beautiful animal and one she thought she'd seen somewhere before.

Luke returned carrying two beer bottles in one hand and a plate of crackers. "The stuff on top of the crackers will clean out a cavity so take it easy until you can handle the chili peppers. What should we drink to?" he asked, holding his bottle toward her.

"Peace, this beautiful dog, and . . . and Sophie," Jessie said clinking her bottle against his.

"You got it. To peace, to Buzz, and to Sophie." Luke watched as Jessie's eyes filled again. She blinked them away. "I'm a good listener."

"The Kingsleys don't like you," Jessie blurted. "On my first visit here, Tanner warned me never to set foot on your property. He said you'd shoot and ask questions later."

"That's half-true," Luke drawled. "I have no quarrel with you."

"I like your dog. I sketch a lot. I always seem to draw the same dog. All my sketches look just like Buzz but more detailed. Whoa, you weren't kidding about those peppers." Jessie finished off her beer in two long gulps, tears rolling down her cheeks. She gasped for air, her hand fanning her mouth.

"Milk! Consuela, bring some milk," Luke bellowed.

A roly-poly little woman with rosy cheeks and a tremendous braid of gray hair waddled into the room with a glass of cold milk and two bottles of beer. She smiled happily. The wide smile showed two winking gold teeth.

"Swish it around your mouth before you swallow it," Luke ordered. Jessie did as instructed.

"Don't ever give that to me again. What does it do to your insides?"

Luke laughed.

Jessie reached for the second beer.

"You aren't going to get crocked on me, are you? You still look a little rocky to me. What's your limit?"

"Four. Sophie could . . . Sophie could drink six. Without going to the bathroom!"

"No!"

"Yes."

Luke leaned back in his comfortable chair, his eyes steady on the young woman across from him. "Tell me about Sophie."

Jessie looked into Luke Holt's eyes. They were kind, gentle eyes, she decided. Enemy or not, she needed to talk about Sophie. "She died. She didn't just die. She . . . what she did was . . . was . . . she took her own life. Her mother died in a terrible car accident not long before . . . I thought she was over it to some degree. She acted like she was. Mrs. Ashwood was the third richest woman in the world.

Sophie inherited everything. She was in love with this man who was some kind of scam artist. Sophie found out he was after her for her money. She hadn't told him who she was, but he found out somehow. She was devastated, so she called off the wedding. They cremated her. I didn't find out till it was done. There's no place . . . you know, to visit, to say a prayer. People need to do that. Mr. Mendenares said her spirit is in the garden in New Orleans. I think I'm going to go there soon to see if he was telling me the truth. Do you believe in spirits?" She wound down then like a broken clock as she waited for her host's comments. God in heaven, did she just spill her guts to a total stranger, a man who supposedly was her husband's family's worst enemy?

Luke Holt shifted incomfortably in his chair as he debated how to respond to the tormented young woman across from him. At his feet, Buzz whimpered. "I don't know if I believe in spirits or not. I've never personally come across any. My mother believed in them. If you need a definite answer, then I'd say I have an open mind. I understand what you're saying about a place. A place is comforting."

Consuela appeared with a tray holding two more frosty beer bottles. Jessie reached for one at the same time Luke did. A bolt of electricity shot up her arm. She jerked it away to Luke's amusement.

"Sophie was my friend from the time I was little. She was the smartest person I know. She could do anything, legal or illegal. No matter what the problem was, Sophie could solve it. She knew everyone. She used to network, as she called it. Sophie could fix anything except her own life."

"She sounds like a saint. I find it hard to believe someone could be that perfect. That is the word you think of in

regard to your friend, isn't it? Did you ever, even for a few
minutes, consider that she was a controlling person?"

Jessie sniffed. "I hope that wasn't a trite remark. You're
right, she is . . . was a saint. I hope she's an angel now. Sophie would make a beautiful angel. She was the most important thing in the world to me, and I let her down. In all
our years, Sophie never let me down. She was always there
for me one hundred percent."

"I don't believe for one minute that you could have
stopped her, and I don't think you do either. Your friend
would have done what she did regardless if you were there
or not. You can't take the blame for someone's suicide."

"That's what Mr. Mendenares said. He told me to call
him Arthur."

"Who is Arthur?"

Jessie wondered if she was drunk. She felt drunk, and
she knew she was talking too much, but she couldn't seem
to stop herself. "Arthur is Sophie's lawyer. He runs everything. Everything is a lot. When are we going to eat? You
invited me for dinner, didn't you?"

"Hear that bell? If you will allow me," Luke said, holding out his hand. "Dinner is being served."

"What are we having? Do you know or is it always a
surprise? When you have your own kitchen you always
know what you're having when you sit down. Sophie
was the wind beneath my wings. Did I tell you that? I eat
most anything. That beer went to my head. Am I . . . you
know, sloshed? You don't seem like a bad guy, you know,
the enemy type. Except for that shotgun. I really like
your dog."

"You're on your way," Luke said, turning away so she
wouldn't see his grin. "Ah, let's see, mashed potatoes, roast
beef, salad, fresh peas and carrots, corn, fresh bread, and
probably cherry pie for dessert."

"This is certainly a lot of food," Jessie said squinting at the table. "Don't give me any more beer, okay?"

"Okay."

"Do you eat alone every night?"

"Yes."

"It's lonely, isn't it. Even if you're having just a sandwich, it's better to eat it with someone. Sophie and I always ate together when she was in town. She was an architect. She passed all nine parts of the test the first time around."

"Amazing."

"Not just amazing. *Fucking amazing.* Sophie graduated *summa cum laude.* Sophie loved to swear to shock people."

Luke chewed industriously so Jessie wouldn't see his smile. "You must miss her very much."

Jessie stirred the food on her plate. "If I could just understand, it might be easier to handle. I don't think I will ever understand. I didn't even wash my hands. I have to get home. Is this wine or iced tea?"

"Wine."

"Oh. In that case, I'll drink it."

"You should eat first."

"I don't like rare meat. I hardly ever eat meat. Killing animals is terrible."

Luke pushed his plate away. He leaned across the table. "Tell me about Jessie Kingsley. I'm up to here with Sophie," he said, touching his forehead.

"That's what Tanner said. Too bad, Mr. Holt. You said you were a good listener. You aren't. I am not any of your business. Besides, you're the enemy. I'm just Jessie, and Jessie is dull and boring."

"Where are you from, Jessie?"

Jessie gulped at the wine in her glass. "Here, there, everywhere. Why?"

"Just curious."

"It killed the cat you know. Who is Luke Holt?" Jessie asked craftily.

"Luke Holt is just a hardworking rancher who lost his fiancée to a terminal disease a while back."

"Where's your family?"

"They're gone. I live here with Buzz and run the ranch. We do just fine. Next year it will be different, when my stepbrothers come here to stay. For now it's just Buzz and me."

"You don't like the Kingsleys, do you?"

"No, I don't."

"They don't like you either," Jessie said smartly. "How drunk do you think I am?"

"I think you just crossed the line from tipsy to crocked. You aren't going to get sick or anything like that, are you?"

"Lord no."

"That's good."

"You should be married. I'm sorry your fiancée died. You never get over death. You have nice eyes and a nice smile when you aren't scowling. You need to pet that dog more often. I really like him. Do you think he'd sit still for me to sketch him?"

"Probably if you give him Fig Newtons. He loves Fig Newtons. Does that mean you're coming back? I'd welcome the company, but I don't think the Kingsleys will approve. My advice is to be careful."

"I'm not supposed to come here. You are off-limits. Maybe I could meet you somewhere."

"That probably isn't a good idea either. I'll take you home now. Drink some of that coffee before we leave."

"That's not my home," Jessie snorted. "I'm just staying here. Tem-por-ar-ily. I shouldn't be telling you all this personal stuff. I'm going to leave."

"I see."

"No, you don't. People always say that when they don't know what else to say. Oh, oh, why is this room spinning around?"

"Because you're drunk. Let's go outside in the fresh air. I can't take you home in this condition."

"Why not? No one is there. *Mrs*. Kingsley went away and *Mister* Kingsley is in town with Bippity-Bop. He's been having an affair with her, but he won't admit it. I moved out of the room. I shouldn't tell you these things. Don't tell anyone, okay."

"I promise not to tell. Is the world still spinning around? How about if I drive you to Resa's house?"

"Resa moved away. She's the smart one. She won't tell anyone where she is, so Alexis can't screw up her life again. Don't tell that to anyone either, okay?"

"I promise not to tell. Get in the truck and put your seat belt on. Hop in the back, Buzz."

"Am I taking his seat? C'mon, Buzz, you can sit on my lap. I really love this dog. I asked for a dog, but Tanner said he and his mother are a-lergic. When I move I'm getting a dog. Does Buzz have any puppies?"

"Nope."

"Too bad. If he gets some, will you give me one? I'll really love it. I'll rub his belly and scratch his ears all day long. I need somebody. I miss Sophie. Sophie is the only one who loved me. You can't count my mother because she was . . . emotionally sick. "

Luke stared at Jessie, a helpless look on his face. In his life he'd never seen a more miserable, unhappy human being. He wanted to say something, but the words wouldn't come. He reached for her. Until that moment he had no idea how thin she was. He held her while she cried. When she finally sat up and dried her eyes, he said, "If you need a friend, Buzz and I are offering up our friendship. Come by anytime you want. If you just want to talk, I'm listed in the phone book. Friendship, Jessie."

Jessie's head bobbed up and down. "I'm really sorry about upsetting your evening. Sometimes things get a bit overwhelming. Sophie always said for every action there is a reaction. I reacted."

"It takes time to heal, Jessie. I know, I was in your place not too long ago. You have to take it one day at a time."

"I know, but before you can heal you have to understand. What if I never understand? On top of all that, the whole thing is mine now. Damn, the world is spinning again."

"Take a deep breath. Do you want me to pull over to the side of the road? What whole thing are you talking about?"

Jessie turned to stare at the man across from her. She took a deep breath. "I mumble and mutter sometimes. Don't pay any attention to me."

"Should I keep that to myself, too?"

Jessie's head reeled. Did she just say what she thought she said? She wanted to cry all over again. "Yes, please," she whispered.

"Okay, Miss Jessie, this is your road. I can't drive you to the door, because the Kingsleys and I have restraining orders on each other. I have to stay on public land. Buzz will walk you to the door. Remember what I said about being your friend."

"I remember everything that's important. I truly value friendship. Thank you for dinner and for bringing me home."

"It was my pleasure," Luke said gallantly.

Jessie wobbled down the rutted road that led to the ranch. She jabbered nonstop to the yellow dog, who walked at her side. When she reached the back door she dropped to her haunches so that she was at eye level with the dog. "I wish you were mine. I don't know why that is, but I know I could love you. I just know it. I think I'm okay. Go back to Luke now."

"Woof."

"Woof, yourself," Jessie giggled as she hugged the dog. "Go on now, Luke's waiting."

The big dog turned and growled deep in his throat as a dark shadow approached the young woman at his side.

"Tanner!"

Chapter Sixteen

"What are you doing out here, Jessie? Whose dog is that?"

Jessie didn't need to see her husband's face clearly to know he was in an ugly mood. Her hold on Buzz's collar was secure. She could feel the big dog start to tremble. "I went riding and something spooked Sunny and I fell off. This wonderful creature brought me home." God, was this flat, fearful-sounding voice her own? When and how did she become so fearful?

"Whose truck is parked out on the road by our driveway?"

"What truck?" Jessie asked, stalling for time.

"Don't play games with me. Why is the dog still here? Do I smell liquor on your breath?"

"You absolutely do. I've been drinking. Three beers, maybe it was four, *and* a glass of wine. What do you think of that, Tanner?"

"Easy, boy, easy. Go home now. Go. God, please go," Jessie whispered to the dog. The big dog growled deep in his throat, his ears going flat against his head. Jessie, still on her haunches, tried to get in front of the dog, but he moved and she toppled over to roll on her stomach. She watched in horror as Tanner picked up his booted foot. If the dog didn't move, he was going to get kicked in the head. She rolled over, exhausting the last of her strength as she reached out for Tanner's leg, knocking him off-balance. Buzz barked loudly, the sound rolling across the pasture and on out to the road. When Jessie opened her eyes a moment later the big dog had his two front paws on Tanner's neck. In the moonlight she could see Buzz's bared teeth, his massive head just inches from Tanner's face.

"Get this fucking dog off me before I kill him."

Her legs wobbly, Jessie managed to get to her feet. "Isn't it the other way around, Tanner? What kind of person tries to kick an animal in the head? Not someone I want to know."

"Enough is enough, Jessie. Get this dog off me."

"He's not my dog. He isn't going to listen to me. I wouldn't move if I were you. He was defending himself. He knew what you were going to do. Animals have instincts, and they never forget."

"Get him off me. He weighs a fucking ton. I swear to good Christ if I ever see this mutt on my land, I'll shoot him."

Suddenly, Jessie was stone-cold sober. She dropped to her knees to peer at her husband in the light spilling through the kitchen door. Her voice was as full of menace as Buzz's deep growl. "If you ever raise a hand to this dog, I'll be forced to shoot you myself. That's not a threat, Tanner, it's a promise."

"Yeah, yeah, yeah. Now get him off me."

"C'mon, Buzz, good boy. Get off him." The dog ignored her and growled again before he sat down on Tanner's chest.

"Buzz, good boy, come here."

Tanner strained to raise his arm. Buzz's mouth opened,

and Tanner's wrist was clamped tight. "Okay, okay," Tanner gasped.

"Want a Fig Newton, Buzz? Attaboy. Come on. I'll get you one." The big dog leaped from Tanner's chest to race after Jessie, who was running out to the road where she collapsed against the truck. "Give him a Fig Newton. It was the only way I could get him off Tanner. If you love this dog, take him home and don't ever let him on this land. Tanner threatened to shoot him. He will, too. Buzz protected me. Thank you for allowing him to walk with me. Tanner's in an ugly mood," she gasped, sweat dripping

"Are you going to be okay? Listen, I know all about Tanner's temper. Here's my phone number," Luke said, handing over a business card from the glove compartment. "If things get out of hand, call me and come out to the road. I'll pick you up."

Jessie nodded as she jammed the card down her bra before she sprinted down the road. "Don't forget to give him the cookie," she called over her shoulder.

Luke fumbled in the console for a new package of Fig Newtons. "I don't have a good feeling about this, old boy. Jesus, I wish you could talk. I think we'll just sit here for a little while and eat this whole package of cookies. No, no, you aren't a lapdog. You weigh 80 pounds. You did good tonight, Buzz. Help yourself," he said, dumping the cookies out on the dog's seat. "You eat those cookies, I'll smoke my pipe, and if we don't see or hear anything by the time we're finished, we'll head home.

"She was kind of nice. She's got some hangups, but then don't we all? Living in that zoo will just give her more. However, that's none of our business. She needs a friend, Buzz. I'd consider lending you out on an hourly basis if it was anyone but the Kingsleys. You stay off those boundary lines, and we both know you know where they are."

Sensing his master's strange mood, the golden dog stopped chewing to lay his massive head on Luke's knee. He whimpered as Luke massaged his silky head. "Okay, c'mon up, but it's going to be a tight squeeze with the wheel. I know you're worried. Do you know how I know you're worried? There's still six Newtons on the seat. I'm worried, too, but I think we're both overreacting."

Man and dog sat quietly until the moon was high in the sky. Once, Buzz jerked his head upright to listen to a strange noise. Luke reached for the dog's collar when he thought the animal was going to bolt. The fine hairs on his own neck moved in the summer breeze wafting through the open windows of the truck. "I don't think it was her, Buzz. Voices carry clearly in the night air. It was probably one of the horses." The big dog whimpered again as he pawed Luke's knee, as much as to say, *Either we check it out or we go home.*

Luke turned the key in the ignition. "Tomorrow's another day, Buzz. We did our good deed. Let's go home. If you aren't going to eat those cookies, I'm throwing them out for the birds." Buzz made no move to eat the treats he adored. "That bad, huh?" Luke shivered in the warm night, the fine hairs on the back of his neck still standing at attention.

A weight settled on Luke's shoulders that he couldn't explain.

"What the hell was that all about?"

Jessie hoped her voice wasn't as shaky-sounding as she felt. "What?"

"That business with the dog. Where did you take him?"

"Out to the road. I'm tired, Tanner. I'm going to bed."

"I felt bad about leaving you, so I came home, and you let that goddamn dog attack me. I smelled liquor on your breath. What the hell is going on here?"

"I explained it to you once. I'm not going to do it again. Just for the record, I did not let the dog attack you. He did it on his own. You were a threatening presence. I'll say good night."

"Not so fast. Who was that out on the road?"

"I'm not clairvoyant. You came down the road, why didn't you ask who it was? The road is public property. I'm going to bed."

"Are you coming back to our room?"

"No."

"Why did you put that lock on Resa's door?"

"To keep you out. Let go of my arm, Tanner. Don't do something you'll regret."

"Is that a threat? You're getting awfully brazen all of a sudden. Why is that?"

"I said, let go of my arm, Tanner."

"You're my goddamn wife. Don't tell me what to do."

"You don't own me."

"I have a piece of paper that says I do," Tanner snarled.

"You have a piece of paper that says we're married. That piece of paper didn't stop you from screwing around while I was . . . sick. You do not own me. This is the last time I'm going to tell you to take your hand off my arm."

Jessie felt rather than saw the sneer on her husband's face. "And what are you going to do about it."

"This!" Jessie said, bringing up her knee into his groin. The moment Tanner doubled over, releasing his hold on her, she sprinted around the corner of the house, heading for the garage. The keys to her Jeep were in the ignition. All she had to do was open the door and drive the Jeep out to the road. Were the garage doors open? She simply couldn't remember. Did they work with a remote control? She had no idea about that either. Where was the side door? Was it kept locked? She lost precious time as she tried to lift the doors with no success. She didn't even know where the light switch was in the garage. A sob built in her throat as she ran around to the side door. The knob turned under her touch.

Jessie offered up a small prayer of thanks as she fumbled on the wall for the light switch. Finding nothing beneath her fingers but smooth plaster, she felt her way to the Jeep and climbed in. The keys were still in the ignition. "Thank you, God. Thank you, God," she gasped.

Blinding whiteness engulfed her as the fluorescent lights overhead came to life. The sound of the engine turning over in the close confines of the garage sounded like a turbojet to her ears. She twisted to the left when she saw Tanner so that she could lock the door. When she heard the sound of the lock snicking into place, she shifted from Park to Drive just as the back door of the Jeep opened. A second later she felt Tanner's arm around her neck, choking off her air supply. Her right leg stiffened as she pressed down hard on the accelerator. The four-wheel drive crashed through the garage door, dragging Tanner with it. He was forced to loosen his grip on her neck so he could get all the way into the backseat. Ripe curses filled the air.

Gasping and choking, Jessie let go of the wheel to massage her neck, the Jeep coming to a halt at the end of the driveway. *Go! Go! Go!* Her mind shrieked. Bruised and battered, her body refused to obey her mind's order. All she wanted to do was sleep.

"Get out of the car, Jessie."

Jessie climbed from the car, her shoulders slumped. She didn't fight when Tanner reached for her arm and dragged her across the yard, through the house, and upstairs to the room where she'd spent the last year. She was beaten and she knew it, just the way she knew what was coming next. Without a word she stripped off her clothes and climbed into the high four-poster.

A long time later she said coldly, "Are you finished?"

When there was no response, she slid from the bed and walked naked out to the hall and into Resa's room. She locked the door behind her. In the bathroom she looked at her thin body and winced. The massive bruise on her neck and shoulders brought tears to her eyes.

She talked to herself as she lathered her body, then washed her hair. "I have to get out of here. I have to leave now." She didn't know how she knew but she knew that Tanner had taken the keys from her Jeep. Did she have an extra set of keys? If she did, she had no idea where they were.

As she dressed she tried to formulate a plan in her head. If she weren't so tired, things would come together. What would Sophie do? Sophie wouldn't give up, that's for sure, she told herself. Terror gripped her then when she remembered Luke Holt's card that she'd stuck in her bra. A lump the size of a walnut lodged itself in her throat. She had to go back and get it. *Then what are you going to do?*

Her heart thumping wildly in her chest, Jessie tiptoed down the hall to Tanner's room. She listened for any sound that would alert her to Tanner's wakefulness. Satisfied that all was quiet within the room, she opened the door and crept in. The card safely in her hand, she backed her way out of the room, pulled the door close to the jamb but didn't close it completely. She managed to get to the bottom of the steps and out to the stable, where she led Tulip into the cobbled stable yard. This time she didn't bother with a saddle but leaped on the horse and muttered, "Go, Tulip!" She held on to the mare's mane, certain she was going to black out any second. The moment she saw the Holt ranch in the moonlight she heaved a mighty sigh. "Whoa, girl, easy now." The animal whickered softly. Jessie slid off, then tapped the horse's rump. "Go home, Tulip!" She watched as the mare trotted off the way they'd come.

Jessie eyed the distance to the house. *I can do this. I know I can do this. I have to do this. Put one foot in front of the* other *and* go forward. She almost fainted when she saw the back door looming in front of her. How was she to get in? Should she bang on the door and wake up Luke? Maybe she should go to the barn and sleep there. She saw it then, Buzz's doggie door. She dropped down and crawled through. She almost fainted a second time when she saw Buzz waiting for her. "Shhh," she said. "I'm just going to sleep right here on this nice braided carpet."

Buzz stared at the sleeping girl, circling the carpet, his tail swishing furiously. He whimpered as he tried to nudge her to wakefulness. He licked at her face and then her arms. When she didn't move he tried using his snout to wake her. When she still didn't move, he raced from the room to Luke's room and bounded onto the bed to tug at the pillow Luke was sleeping on. When it was free of his master's head, he pushed it onto the floor. With no regard for Luke's comfort he started to tug on the light quilt.

"Buzz, what the hell are you doing? Jesus, the things I put up with. Come back here! Where are you going with my pillow? The quilt, too! Okay, what did you do? It's okay, accidents happen. Consuela will get it in the morning." He watched as Buzz dragged both the quilt and pillow to the top of the steps. With his snout he pushed them and then dragged them to the bottom of the steps. He stopped once to look at Luke. "Woof!"

"Woof, my ass. It's three o'clock in the morning. Okay, okay, let's see what you did."

In the kitchen he stopped short, his eyes widening, his jaw dropping. "I see her. Yeah, yeah, I see her. How the hell did she get in here?" His eyes went to the latch on the door and then down to the doggie door. "One more pound and she wouldn't have made it. You did good, Buzz. Let's put the pillow under her head. The quilt is good, too. Oh, oh, what have we here?" he whispered to the dog. The ugly bruise on Jessie's neck forced Luke to rear back. He looked again at the marks on both her arms and then he cursed, making up words as he went along. Buzz whim pered.

"Shhh, she's sleeping. She's okay. Look at it this way, she was smart enough to make it here. That has to mean something." He bent over a second time to see a small corner of white paper sticking out of Jessie's blouse. He recognized his card. Something welled up in him, something he hadn't felt for a very long time. Something he didn't want to think about.

"Stay, Buzz. I'm going to take a shower and dress. I'll be in the office."

Before he went upstairs, Luke checked all the locks. Satisfied that the doggie door was the only entry, he climbed the steps.

Tanner rolled over, his arm snaking out to the left side of the bed. Bright sunlight speared into the room, making him aware of the headache that pounded behind his eyes. He squinted once to look at the clock. Eight o'clock! In his life he'd never slept past six-thirty. The previous hours rushed at him like a runaway train. He cursed bitterly because he couldn't think of anything else to do.

Swinging his legs over the side of the bed, he rose to a sitting position. He was forced to cup his head in both hands as the headache hammered away inside his skull. He needed aspirin and hot coffee. He headed for the bathroom, stepping over Jessie's discarded clothing. He wasn't going to think about *that*. Stupid bitch. Who the hell did she think she was?

At the door to his sister's room he stopped to look inside. The room was neat and tidy and the bed looked as though it hadn't been slept in.

"Lucille!" he bellowed.

The housekeeper came to the bottom of the stairs. "What is it?"

"Where's my wife?"

"I don't know, Mr. Tanner. I didn't see her this morning. I thought she was upstairs. Your mother is on the phone."

Tanner bounded down the steps. "Tell her I'll call her back." He raced to the kitchen window. Jessie's red Jeep was right where she'd left it hours ago. The driver's side door hung open. The sight of the splintered garage door made the pounding inside his head more intense. He looked toward the stable and was stunned to see Tulip nibbling on grass. What the hell was the mare doing loose at this hour of the morning? As if he didn't know. He reached for the coffee cup Lucille was handing him with one hand and the phone with the other.

"Good morning, Mother. What can I do for you?"

"I just want to know how Jessica is."

"She's gone."

"What do you mean?"

"Just what I said. Yesterday she had a good day. She said she was feeling fine and wasn't taking the pills anymore. She flushed them. She accused me of having an affair, and we had a fight. I left, and she went riding. I regretted the fight and came home early and she had this dog with her and had been drinking. We had another fight, and when I woke up this morning she was gone."

"Did she take her things?"

"I don't know. I took the keys to her Jeep. I think she went somewhere on Tulip and sent her home. And how is your day, Mother?"

"It was fine until I called you. What exactly do you mean by a fight?"

"She drove the Jeep through the garage door. That should give you some kind of an idea."

"Did you strike her? What would make her leave? What did you say?"

"I said a lot of things. She said a lot of things. I grabbed her, got a choke hold on her, but I didn't . . ." Too late he remembered the sickening slap he'd given her earlier in the evening.

"She doesn't know anyone. Where would she go?"

"How the hell should I know. There was a truck out by the road when I got home last night."

"Was it Luke Holt?"

"I don't know, Mother, and I don't care."

"Get her back, Tanner. This is not good. You're just like your father. You get yourself into a mess and expect me to get you out of it. I didn't come here to Washington because I was dying to see your father. It seems he's gotten himself into bed with some rather shady lobbyists. A special counsel has been appointed to *look into things*. There is every possibility that they might want to talk to Jessie. I suggest you find her and make nice. I know you know how to do that. Are you listening to me, Tanner?"

"Half the state of Texas is probably listening," Tanner snarled.

"The only place she could have gone is the Holt ranch. Go there now."

"And get my head blown off? It was your idea to get a restraining order. Luke did what you did."

"Jessica has nothing to do with that. If you tell him she isn't stable, explain the circumstances, he'll listen. There are no alternatives, Tanner."

"I can't believe I'm hearing this. You actually want me to go to Luke Holt of all people and pretend my wife is a nutcase. Luke Holt! If she is there, Christ only knows what she said to him. Just who the hell do you think he'll believe?"

"Do it, Tanner. Or, call the police and tell them she's

missing. That in itself will make headlines. Headlines this family cannot afford with what's going on here in Washington. I have to go now. I'll call you again at noon, your time."

Tanner gulped at the scalding coffee.

Forty-five minutes later he screeched to a halt in the front of the Holt ranch. With no desire to get his head blown off, he leaned on the horn but didn't get out of the truck. He sucked in his breath when the front door opened to reveal Luke and the huge dog. His mouth went dry when he heard the hammer of the shotgun that was pointed at his chest. He poked his head out of the window and said, "Hold on, Luke. My wife seems to have wandered off. The mare she was riding came back to the ranch. I was wondering if she came here."

"That's about the funniest thing I ever heard. Almost as funny as those bankers telling me they couldn't approve my loans because your daddy said I wasn't a good risk. Get the fuck off my land, Tanner, before I shoot a hole right through your stupid head."

"You aren't answering my question, Luke. Did my wife come here or not?"

"Sure I did, you asshole. I said that was the funniest thing I ever heard. If you aren't out of here on the count of three, I'm going to shoot right through that windshield, and if your head is in the way, oh, well. You're trespassing. One! Two!"

Tanner shifted into reverse, his foot pressing the accelerator to the floor. A cloud of dust sailed upward.

Luke closed the door. "Let's see if our guest is awake, Buzz."

Jessie was sitting at the kitchen table with a cup of coffee, Consuela hovering close by. Jessie looked up, her eyes filling. "I'm sorry. I didn't know where else to go.

Tanner took the keys to my car. Buzz let me in. I hate to impose, but do you think you can give me a ride to town?"

"Tanner was just here."

"I know. I heard. I'm so very sorry. I don't want to involve you in this mess, and it is a mess. If you aren't comfortable driving me, could you call a taxi from town for me?"

"It's not a problem. I'll drive you. It might be a good idea if we had a little talk, Mrs. Kingsley."

"Don't call me that. It's better if you don't know . . . it's not that I don't want to talk about it, I do, but it isn't wise. I'll be fine once I get to town."

"Do you have a bag or a purse? Do you have any money?"

"No, I don't have any money, but that's not a problem. I can have some wired to me in a few hours."

"What about your clothes and personal belongings?"

"I left everything behind. They packed away everything. I'm not sure, but I think I lived in a bathrobe this past year. The clothes I have on aren't mine. I rather think they're Resa's that she left behind. It's not a problem, and it's the least of my worries right now. By any chance do you know how to pick a lock?"

"No," Luke drawled. "Do you?"

"No, that's why I asked. I have to meet someone at noon. I guess I can wait outside. Can we go now?"

"Did anyone ever tell you you can run, but you can't hide?"

"Sophie used to say that. At the end she tried to do it but I guess it didn't work for her. I'm not trying to hide. I'm not exactly running either. I'm leaving. At one time I had a very good life. I want that life back, and I'm going to get it."

Luke looked at the determined jut of her jaw and at his dog, who was allowing himself to be tickled and scratched.

It was clear that Jessie had Buzz's seal of approval, and everyone knew dogs were the shrewdest judges of character in the universe.

"Then let's go, Jessie. Did you have anything to eat?"

"No. It hurts to swallow. I'll get some soup in town or something soft."

Luke waited to see if she would offer up an explanation for the deep purple-and-yellow bruise on her neck. He watched as she lightly massaged her neck. "It might be a good idea to have someone take a picture of those bruises."

"That's something Sophie would say. Do you have a camera?"

"Yes. I take pictures of Buzz all the time. It's a Polaroid."

Jessie posed self-consciously as she pulled her shirt away from her neck and then rolled up her shirtsleeves as Luke focused and snapped, the pictures shooting out of the camera, one after the other. "Would you mind keeping them for me for the time being?"

"Sure. Just let me put the pictures in my safe and the camera in my office."

They spoke only once on the ride into town. It was Luke who broke the silence. "Who are you, Jessie?"

"I wish I knew. I'm going to find out, though. It seems that I've been marking time to get to this place in my life."

"I'm a good listener."

"I'll remember that. Do you know the address I gave you?"

"It's along the waterfront. Prices are high there. Is it a business?"

"More or less. I'm going to have to find a place to live. I don't know the area. Can you recommend something?"

"Are you interested in a house or a condo?"

"Either or."

"Ocean Drive is beautiful. It's a long, bayfront residential avenue of large, older homes with the best views in town. That's if money is no object. I know for a fact that the Arkansas Princess has several units available either to rent or buy. Pricey but nice. The access road is off Road 1A, if you're interested. There are all kinds of apartments for rent if that's more to your liking. Until you make up your mind, a hotel might be the short-term answer."

"The area is lovely. I liked it when I came here the first time to visit Resa. This might be the place where I put down roots. Then again, maybe not. I also like New Orleans. I have a lot to think about. I hope I didn't intrude too much on your life. I truly appreciate your coming to my assistance. I don't know how to thank you."

Luke nodded.

Thirty minutes later, Luke said, "This is the address you gave me. It looks like a relatively new building. I can't read the sign by the door."

"It says Ashwood Designs," Jessie said quietly. "You can just drop me off. I'll find a coffee shop and wait inside until noon."

"You don't have any money," the ever-practical Luke said.

"Water's free."

"Here," Luke said, reaching into his pocket to withdraw a crumpled ten-dollar bill. "You can owe me, okay?"

"Okay." Jessie smiled as she tweaked Buzz's ear. "Your owner is some kind of guy," she said as she stared directly at Luke and winked. She backed out of the truck, aware of Luke's flushed face. Buzz barked and barked. "See you."

"Yeah, see you. Will you call and let me know you're okay? Buzz doesn't like things that hang loose. He's like me; we like things all tidied up."

"I'll call you."

Jessie stood on the corner watching until Luke's truck was out of sight. She looked at the ten dollars in her hand.

Did she really want to go into a public restaurant, where people could see the awful bruise on her neck? She could do without the soup or coffee. What she really wanted was a cigarette and a cold soda. She looked up and down the street to see if there was a drugstore or a small convenience store. Surely one of the office buildings had a snack bar or lunchroom. Looking both ways, she crossed the street to enter one of the buildings, where she purchased a bottle of Coca-Cola and a pack of cigarettes from a concession stand in the lobby. She walked back across the street to take a seat on a bright green bench two buildings down from the one where she was to meet Arthur Mendenares. She smoked one cigarette after the other, sipping the soft drink in between hard little puffs on the cigarettes until the attorney arrived fifteen minutes ahead of schedule. Jessie ran to him, her arms outstretched. This kindly gentleman was her only link to the past and Sophie. She started to cry immediately.

The attorney handed her a pristine white handkerchief. "Come inside, child. We'll talk where there aren't any ears and eyes."

Jessie watched as Mendenares punched in a series of numbers. She was surprised when the door swung open. "Sophie designed the lock and the building. The building in New Orleans is just like this one. She said she didn't want to get confused. The code to the lock is Sophie's birthday." The moment the door swung shut behind them, the room came alive underneath bright fluorescent lighting. "It's an art gallery," Jessie said in awe.

"Not just any art gallery," Mendenares said gently. "Take a better look."

"They're my sketches. Where . . . how . . ."

"From the house in Atlanta. She told me you left pads and pads of sketches. She thought they were wonderful and deserving of wall space. They're beautiful. Do I dare ask if you at one time had such a beautiful animal? They all appear to be the same dog."

"No, I never had a dog. I always wanted one, though. What a wonderful job she did. The frames are exquisite, the matting superb. Did Sophie do all this?"

"Yes. When she designed the building, she marked the front walls for just this purpose. It seemed to give her great pleasure. She worked tirelessly, around the clock actually. What this room is is a front. The offices are in the back and in the small loft overhead in the rear. Let me show you."

Jessie watched as he pressed more numbers on a second keypad beside a heavy mahogany door. "The code to this door is your birthday. Copies of everything pertaining to Sophie's estate are in this room. A lot of the files have been placed on a disc. We have the latest computers here. Very high-tech. Sophie thought it was wonderful. She did love electronic gadgetry. We can talk about this later. Right now I need you to sign some papers. As soon as everything is signed, I'll have them input and placed on a disc. You will be able to peruse them at your leisure and offer any suggestions or changes you might want to exercise at that time. The last page in the green folder sums up your net worth."

Jessie flipped to the end of the green folder. She gasped aloud. "My Lord!"

Arthur Mendenares smiled. "I take that to mean you're pleased."

"I'm speechless."

"Consider it a temporary condition," the attorney smiled. "Now, Jessie, let's go upstairs to the loft Sophie designed for you. It has eighteen hundred square feet. You could actually live up here if you wanted. There's a kitchenette, a full bath, sitting room, and an extra room that Sophie designated as a bedroom. Sophie used the color red because she said it was your favorite. If you look downstairs over the railing, you have a clear view of the small gallery.

"On more than one occasion Sophie told me your views were the same as hers when it came to wealth. Are you comfortable with all this?"

"I don't know. What is it I'm supposed to do?"

"Familiarize yourself with all your holdings. I would truly appreciate input from you in regard to your different investments. Sixty days from now I will consult with you before any decisions are made. You can call me at any time of the day or night to ask questions. My office will always know where I am. I would appreciate the same from you. This last year has been very taxing, and I would like to discuss it right now."

They talked then, like two old friends. A long time later, when Jessie leaned her head back against a plush red chair, she felt tears prick at her eyelids. "Now, Mr. Mendenares, you know everything there is to know about me right down to my awful nightmares and the fact that my husband manhandled me last night. I'd like to file for a divorce and would like you to handle it for me. I don't know anything about Texas law and property settlements. Every piece of paper, every document that has come into my hands is at the house in Atlanta. To my knowledge, the Kingsleys know nothing of my inheritance. I guess my next question is, could Tanner have found out I inherited Sophie's estate? Please remember, I lived in a fuzzy world for a year. It's true I was grieving for Sophie, and it's also true that I lost my baby. I don't want to believe I teetered on the edge. I don't believe I'm the type to have a nervous breakdown. A whole year is gone out of my life. I can't get it back. Right now my head is buzzing, and I need time to think and plan. I'll stay here, but Mr. Mendenares, I have no vehicle and I'm going to need money."

"You're going to call me Arthur—remember? Mr. Men-

denares was my father. I can have a vehicle of your choice
here within the hour. As to money, a bank account that is
quite robust was set up in the name of Ashwood Designs.
The bank itself is within walking distance. If you'll give me
a moment, I will give you the checkbook and bank state-
ments. To answer your question, I suppose it's possible
your husband or his family checked out Sophie's will.
However, in order to do that they would have to know
where the will was probated. With the senator's connec-
tions, I suppose it's possible, but I would say unlikely. The
will was entered into probate in Athens, Greece. You might
want to give some thought to updating your own will. As
it stands, you inherited Sophie's estate before you were
married. Your husband has no claim on it."

Jessie sighed with relief. "How long did it take Sophie
to set all this up, Arthur?"

"Not long. She knew what she wanted, and she had the
money to pay out to set everything up. The only things
money can't buy, Jessie, are happiness and good health.
Sophie used her money to make things happen. I don't
think the child ever slept. Now that I think back to the
ways things were, I think she had a time schedule of sorts.
Do you plan on staying here in Corpus Christi?"

"For now. I need to regain a little more strength. I think
I'd like to take a trip to New Orleans or maybe Atlanta.
Not necessarily right now, but soon. I need some time to
come to terms with the events in my life. I feel like I've
been blindsided. I left everything at the Kingsley ranch.
I'm wearing someone else's clothes. Can you get me a
credit card?"

"I can have one here for you in twenty-four hours. In
the meantime, cash works."

Jessie smiled. "I think I'd like an all-terrain vehicle. A
Land Rover would be nice. Dartmouth green if that's possible. Where will I keep it?"

"Consider it done. In the garage. You simply drive around the back. The door is electronic. There's a laundry room also. The chute is in the bathroom. You can access the garage from the office part of the building. Sophie thought of everything. I have time for a quick cup of coffee before I leave. I'll make some calls now, if you don't mind."

"Is there coffee?"

"In the freezer. Sophie said it lasts forever in the freezer. I myself didn't know that. There's also a fancy machine that grinds the coffee, then drips it. Quite remarkable."

Jessie laughed at the amazement on the attorney's face. "I'll make the coffee."

Ninety minutes later, the attorney wrapped Jessie in his arms. "Remember now, call me at any time of the day or night. I want your promise. If you take any trips, let me know your whereabouts. Now, think, is there anything you want me to do other than file your divorce papers?"

"No. That's it for now. I'll see you out, then I'm going shopping."

"Your car will be here at four. I told them to drive it around the back and to leave the keys under the floor mat. Don't forget to garage it when you get back."

"I want to take back my maiden name, Arthur."

"Absolutely. Take care of yourself."

It was six-fifteen when Jessie, with the help of a taxi driver, let herself into Ashwood Designs. Bags, boxes, and groceries filled the small gallery. Jessie tipped the driver generously before she closed the door. She was safe in her own nest, thanks to Sophie. It took her seven trips to climb the eight stairs to the loft and another hour to put her groceries away and to unpack all her new clothing and hang it up. It was nine o'clock before she parked her new truck in the garage, showered, brewed coffee, and fixed herself a dinner of scrambled eggs, which she wolfed down while she watched a mindless television show. At ten o'clock she called Luke Holt. She didn't realize she was holding her breath until she heard his deep resonant voice.

"Where are you, Jessie?"

"I'm here at Ashwood Designs, the building where you dropped me off. It seems there is a really nice loft here that I can live in, so I'll be staying here for the time being. I just wanted to thank you again for all your help. When I'm settled, I'll call and invite you and Buzz to dinner. Will you come?" she asked anxiously.

"Do I have to get dressed up?"

"No. Does that mean you'll come?"

"I never turn down a free meal. Can you cook?"

"Not well, but I manage. Do you want me to send you your ten dollars?"

Luke chuckled. "I think I can wait it out."

Jessie smiled. "Okay, I'll call you when I'm settled. Thanks again."

"My pleasure. Are you going to tell anyone where you are?"

"God, no!"

"Okay, just so I know."

"Good night, Luke."

"Good night, Jessie."

Jessie sat for a long time, hugging her pillow. For the first time in a very long time she felt good. All thanks to Sophie. "I miss you, old friend," she whimpered.

Squaring her shoulders, Jessie dialed the ranch. Tanner picked up on the second ring. "It's Jessie, Tanner. I'm calling to tell you I won't be coming back to the ranch. I consulted an attorney today and am filing for divorce. Whatever I left behind, throw out."

"What the hell! Jesus, all we had was a spat. You're filing for a divorce because of *that*?"

"I'm not getting into the whys and whats of anything with you, Tanner. It is what it is. You can keep my six thousand dollars as a going-away present."

"Wait just a damn minute, Jessie."

"No, Tanner, you wait just a damn minute. I'm going to charge you with assault and battery. I have the bruises and the pictures to prove it. I don't want anything from you or your family. We'll keep it neat and tidy. If you provoke me, things will change. I'll add rape to the charges."

"I didn't rape you."

"You would have if I hadn't taken off my clothes and gotten into bed. To me it's the same thing. Good-bye, Tanner."

Chapter Seventeen

Alexis looked around her husband's office. At one time, when Angus first came to Washington, the offices were neat and tidy, newly paneled with rich furnishings. Back then she'd had the mistaken idea that she could take her place here in this city and work alongside her husband even if it was just in a social way. That idea had never gotten off the ground, thanks to Irene Marshall.

She hated thinking about Irene Marshall. Even though the woman was dead, she still managed to insinuate herself into her thoughts.

What in the name of God was she doing here anyway? She'd risen at four-thirty, unable to get back to sleep. Her intention had been to head to the airport for the first available flight back to Texas. Halfway to the airport she'd had the driver turn around and bring her here, to Angus's office. Whatever she hoped to find was not forthcoming. Did she dare open Angus's safe? Why not. On one of Angus's trips back to Corpus Christi she'd managed to go through his wallet and had come up with the combination to the safe. For years she'd carried the little slip of paper in her wallet. It was wrinkled and frayed, the ink faded, but she could still make out the numbers.

Payback time, Angus.

The moment she heard the click of the dial, Alexis yanked at the heavy door before she could change her mind. Thank God she'd had the presence of mind to lock Angus's door. She crossed her fingers, hoping she would find stacks and stacks of currency. There was no way in hell she was going to live in a cracker-box house and eat Hamburger Helper. She wanted to cry when all she saw were neat piles of papers in rubber bands. No money. Not even a stray dollar bill. She carried everything to the desk where she carefully examined each piece of paper.

Twenty long minutes passed before she snapped the rubber bands back into place. She used up another few minutes stuffing the packets into her purse to read more carefully on the long plane ride home. She wanted to cry with the injustice of it all. Instead, she swallowed the last of the coffee the young man in the outer office had prepared on her arrival. She closed the safe and then the built-in cabinet door.

Alexis sat down in her husband's chair—the chair that his body had molded over the years. It smelled like Angus. She looked around and felt sadness well up in her. She clearly remembered how proud she was the first time she came to this place. She'd even been proud of Angus way back then. How short-lived that small window in time had been. The urge to cry again rushed through her. "You made me what I am, Angus," she whispered.

She found her gaze going to the rich paneling that was dull now with greasy streaks and swirls where dust had settled. The plants were full of yellow leaves, the soil dry and grainy. The carpet was dusty, and so was the desk and all the rest of the furniture. Angus had always been so proud of his staff's housekeeping abilities. Obviously this new crew needed a refresher course. She raised her eyes to look at a picture of Angus and John F. Kennedy, Angus's

idol. The opposite wall held a picture of Abraham Lincoln, Angus's second idol.

"You were such a fool, Angus," she said, her voice
breaking. "Didn't you see this coming? Didn't you care? I
won't let you do this to us. I will not. I will not let you destroy everything. The ranch belongs to us, no one else. I
will not move into one of those prefabricated buildings
and wear housedresses with zippers down the front. I will
not buy my cosmetics from a drugstore, nor will I color
my own hair. I will not allow you to rip my life out from
under me." She cried, not caring if her mascara smeared.
"I'm so tired of pretending I don't care. I'm sick to my soul
at what I've become. Just once, Angus, couldn't you have
patted me on the head and said something nice? I longed
for a smile or a pat on the head from you. And now, when
it's all coming down around your head, you want me here
at your side to present a united front. And like a fool, I
came because you asked me to. I tried, my God, how I
tried in the beginning. All you did, Angus, was rub salt in
my open wounds. You flaunted Irene for the world to see
in my face and my children's faces. Acting like I didn't care
was my only defense. I can't even fault Resa and Tanner
for succumbing to Irene's coziness. It was the only way
they could get next to you. You dangled Irene like a carrot
for them, and they had no other choice but to nibble at it."

How was it possible that her husband had succumbed
to temptation? All that money people were saying he collected from illegal foreign sources boggled her mind. Who
were the slimy lobbyists he was in bed with? When exactly
did he sell out? If one were to believe the newspaper stories, it was when Irene Marshall's husband become ill so
many years ago. The papers in her purse were proof that
Angus had paid for astronomically expensive experimen-
tal treatments in Mexico for Henry Marshall. He'd also
paid for a costly villa for years so Henry would be com-

fortable while Angus cuckolded him. Add Irene's medical bills to the list, and it was easy to understand why the mortgages and trust funds had wiped out the ranch accounts long ago. The ranch was now down to zero monies. Zero accounts meant a cracker-box house, Hamburger Helper, and housedresses with zippers.

"Like hell!" Alexis muttered.

A discreet knock sounded on the door. Alexis wiped at her eyes before she stirred, gathering up her purse in preparation for leaving. Standing in front of her was one of the tallest, shaggiest men she'd ever seen in her life.

Alexis Kingsley stared at the man standing in front of her, then at the credentials he held out for her inspection. Joseph Delbert Long. Special prosecutor. Her nostrils flared as her nose went up a notch. "Is this supposed to mean something to me?"

"I'd like to see Senator Kingsley, please."

"He's not in yet. You're welcome to wait. I stopped by to pick up some personal things," Alexis lied. "The senator should be here shortly."

Alexis walked over to the young man who had replaced Jessie Roland. She dropped her voice to a low murmur. "Under no circumstances are you to allow that man into my husband's office. I don't care who he says he is."

"Yes, ma'am."

Alexis's nose went up another notch as she sashayed from the office, her heart beating so fast she could barely manage to take a deep breath. Her face a mask of fear, she rode the elevator to the ground floor without once glancing at her fellow passengers.

Outside in the pouring rain she raised her umbrella. Directly in front of her, walking like he was crippled, was her husband. He was soaked and from the obvious strain on his face he didn't appear to realize it was raining. "Angus, step out of the way. I need to talk to you," she said gently.

"There's a man upstairs named Joseph Delbert Long. He's a special prosecutor, to what I have no idea, and he wants to have a talk with you. I want you to listen to me and I want your total, undivided attention. If you like, you can step under this umbrella. It's pouring rain, Angus. You're soaked. Even summer rains will give you a chill."

Alexis's voice changed to a low-voiced hiss. "I want you to look at something, Angus, and I would advise you not to make a scene." She opened her purse to reveal the packets of papers from the safe. "I have it all right here. As soon as you get rid of that shaggy bear in your offices, you will call the financial planners who set up these trust funds for Irene Marshall's twins. You will revoke them or do whatever it takes to put those monies into the ranch accounts. If you don't do this, I will drag both Irene's and Henry Marshall's names through every court in the land. Then I will move on to the twins. I always suspected you were their father, and now I have the proof. I will destroy them, Angus. You had no right to take what was ours and give it to that family. You destroyed me, but I will not allow you to destroy Resa and Tanner's inheritance. How dare you disgrace us like this. How dare you, Angus! If you think for one minute those twins are going to take you in, you are sadly mistaken. You're tainted now. They're just starting their life. They aren't going to want reminders of this horrendous scandal. Give them all that money, which by the way is enough for several lifetimes, and they won't need you anyway. Why? I need to know why you did this?"

"It's not important. I did it, and that's the end of it. I'd do it again, too! You are a vicious, hateful woman."

Alexis started to cry. Her voice was weary and choked with tears when she responded. "I never should have believed all the lies you told me. I did, though, because I was young, foolish, and I loved you. If you remember correctly,

I did not want to marry you. I was prepared to move on as long as you supported the child. You wouldn't hear of it. Irene wouldn't hear of it. Then Irene goes all noble and divorces you so you can marry me while I protest all the way to the altar because I wanted to believe you. You promised me many things, Angus, and none of those promises ever came to pass. I had every right to expect you to be faithful. Were you? No, you were not. From day one you carried on an affair with Irene. Her marriage to Henry was a sham. You probably arranged for that marriage, too. Paying his medical bills was his payoff, I suppose.

"Now listen to me very carefully. I am prepared to live out my days under the disgrace you created, but I am not prepared to do it in poverty. You will revoke those trust funds and that's final. Irene's twins don't even know you're their father. How are they going to handle your disgrace and the scandal that's erupting? You paid for their college, they'll inherit their mother's house, mortgages and all, and get on with their lives. They will not become part of our lives. Is that clear, Angus?"

"No! I can't do that to them. They expect the trust funds. Irene and I talked to them about it. They are my children."

"Your first obligation is to our family. This is all your doing, Angus. You created this mess, and you're just going to have to get out of it. The first step is the trust funds. Know this, Angus, I meant ever word I said. I will destroy them, and if you get in my way, you will feel my wrath, and it won't be anything like what you're experiencing now. It's payback time, Angus. One last thing: Take the twins' names off the deed to the ranch. I want this all taken care of by the end of business today. I will not give you one hour longer."

"Alexis?"

"What?"

"I never loved you."

"I know that, Angus. I hoped that some way, somehow, you would learn to love me as much as I loved you. I guess I knew even then that it wouldn't happen. Hope springs eternal. That's why I didn't want to marry you. Put the blame where it belongs, on Irene."

"She wasn't perfect."

"Neither am I. You aren't either. We're talking about our financial survival here. I think I can handle the scandal and the disgrace. I cannot handle poverty."

"I have a press conference this afternoon to announce my resignation. I'd like it if you were there with me."

"Yes, I can see how you would want me at your side. I don't owe you anything, Angus, not even consideration. You, on the other hand, owe me my life. How do you expect me to forgive all those years of disgrace and neglect?" Alexis choked back a sob. "What time is the press conference?"

"Four o'clock." Angus felt his shoulders stiffen. "I imagine you prayed for me to die when I had my heart attack."

"On the contrary. I prayed you would live. I even went to church to light a candle."

"That's probably the biggest lie you ever told."

"Believe what you like. I'll be here at your side, Angus. Where are you going to live when this is all over?"

"What do you mean where am I going to live?"

Alexis looked at her husband with clinical interest. She saw the fear in his eyes and played to it. "Forget the twins. They won't want any part of you. Resa and her husband went off God only knows where. Tanner lives at the ranch. I live at the ranch. Do you intend to stay in that studio apartment with the press and the authorities breathing down your neck?"

"The ranch is mine. It's been in my family for genera-
tions. It doesn't belong to you."

"It belongs to us, Angus. The children and I are not prepared to share our half. Any fool can see you aren't well.
Meet me halfway, Angus, and you can come back to the
ranch. I'll take care of you. I'll devote my life to you if necessary. I think you should go inside now and get out of
those wet clothes. Remember what I said. I'll call Tanner
to pick us up at the airport."

Angus Kingsley stood in the pouring rain, watching his
wife walk away. He was oblivious to the curious stares of
people rushing indoors to get out of the rain. He knew he
would do as she asked. His options were all used up, just
as his health was. The best he could hope for was to live
out his remaining days at the ranch, a place he'd once
loved.

As he shuffled forward he felt a hand squeeze his chest.
He struggled for a deep breath. He'd do it all over again.
He wouldn't change a thing. By the time the hearings and
indictments got under way, he'd be with Irene. Probably
the only thing he'd ever done right was not telling the
twins he was their father. As much as he hated to admit it,
Alexis was right about them, too. They no longer returned
his phone calls. What he did know for certain was they
would both take the trust-fund monies once he was gone if
he didn't do what Alexis wanted. Sometimes life just wasn't
fair.

"What will be will be," he muttered.

Jessie watched the evening news as she chomped on a
sour green apple, her eyes watering at the tartness. She
watched the man she'd once adored as he tried to stand
tall in front of the microphones and cameras, his wife at
his side, her hand protectively on his arm. He looked ill,
like a wounded warrior who knows the end is near. She

couldn't help but wonder why his children weren't standing next to him. Did she dare call him? Did she even *want*
to call him? What could she say? I'm sorry you betrayed
your constituents and your family? She bit into the apple,
juice trickling down her chin. Some things, she decided,
were better left alone. Whatever the senator did or didn't
do was none of her business. Just because she was married
to his son didn't mean she belonged in their fold.

Jessie continued to listen to the news as the announcer
and his colleagues put their own spin on Senator Kingsley's breaking scandal. Why did they have to go on and on
about it? Why beat a dead horse? She was ready to turn
off the television set when the news anchor announced
they would go live to Dulles International Airport, where
Senator Kingsley and his wife were set to depart for Corpus Christi, Texas. Did she want to see this? No. The immediate silence thundered in her ears the moment she
turned off the set. Later that evening she would read the
paper. In her opinion, it was easier to read something horrible and sad than to see it front and center.

In the kitchen, Jessie stared at the phone. Should she call
Luke Holt and invite him to dinner? No. Maybe. No. She
certainly had enough spaghetti. In the end she threw her
hands in the air. "What kind of life is this? I'm not doing
anything. I'm not contributing. All I do is walk from room
to room or go to the grocery store. I must be desperate to
want to invite someone to dinner I just met. This is simply
existing; this is not living."

Jessie backed up until she was once again staring at the
telephone. The urge to reach out and call someone was so
strong, she clenched her hands into tight fists. Whom
could she call? Her parents, Luke Holt, Tanner, Arthur?
"None of the above," she muttered through clenched
teeth.

Minutes later, Jessie reached into her closet for a cherry

red canvas bag and started to fill it with some of the new clothing she'd just purchased. The bag almost full, she stopped. What was the point in going to Atlanta or New Orleans? There was nothing there for her. Why torture herself. She unpacked and replaced the bag in the closet. "I need to put down roots. I need to do something. I need to get a job. I need to live my life. If I leave, there won't be anyone to sign for all the things I ordered. It's part of my new life. I need to stay here. I need to make sense of my life. From now on it's what Jessie wants." She hated it when she muttered to herself. Her mother always said her father was addlepated when he walked around muttering under his breath.

Jessie slammed her palm against her forehead as a brilliant idea surfaced. She raced to the offices, punched in her birthday code. A moment later she was sitting in front of the computer scrolling down the list of companies she owned. She continued to scroll until she found the firm she wanted—International Designs. One-of-a-kind collectibles, with an address in Milan. She continued to scroll through the financials and the operating offices until she saw the name of the store's general manager as well as a list of collectibles sold since the beginning of the year.

Jessie pushed her swivel chair back against the wall as she let loose with a sharp whistle. International Designs was certainly a money-maker with astute management. She couldn't ask for a better outlet to send her pieces once she crafted them. Maybe she should think about a glossy catalog. She was excited now, her thoughts carrying her in all directions. Importing, exporting, catalogs for domestic use and possibly internationally. All she needed was the talent to make it all come true. How hard could it be to sculpt what she sketched? A second thought struck her. Before she acted on the thought, she copied down the address for International Designs and then turned off the computer. She raced to the entranceway of the building where she walked from picture to picture. She could remove the pictures from the frames, airmail them in rolled containers to be framed in Milan to hang in the gallery of International Designs. If she attached outrageous price tags, they were sure to sell. Anyone foolish enough to pay fifty thousand dollars for a snuffbox would surely pay five thousand dollars for one of her pictures. Think big, Jessie told herself as she removed the pictures from the wall. She had thousands of these sketches. Big ones, little ones, medium-sized ones, poster-size, and miniatures, but she would have to go to Atlanta to get them out of storage. There were hundreds of them in her old playhouse back in Charleston. There were even some sketches that she'd left behind in Sophie's house in New Orleans.

Jessie struggled to remember the last time she'd been this excited, this exuberant about *anything*. Never, that's when. She'd been excited about leaving Charleston, getting away from her parents, and being on her own. She remembered the feeling well, but it was nothing like what she was feeling now. That alone had to mean something. Had she finally found her niche in life? Was this what she was supposed to do? "Who cares!" Jessie shouted, her voice ringing with pure joy. "I'm doing it!"

Maybe she would pack that red canvas bag after all.

Luke Holt snapped the newspaper on the side of his chair, a sign that Buzz was to lie quietly until he was finished watching the early news, at which point they'd go for a walk.

Calm by nature, Buzz was definitely off his routine. First he'd growl, then he'd flop down on his belly, only to get up, his tail swishing angrily against his master's ankle. He whined now, his paws scratching at the carpet under Luke's rocking chair. "Shhh, I want to hear this, Buzz. It looks like the Kingsleys' chickens are finally coming home to roost. You know what they say, 'What goes around comes around.' Right now I'd say the senator looks like a tired old dog who has finally given up. Okay, okay, let's get to it, Buzz."

Luke's glasses came off and the newspaper dropped to the floor. "I give up. What the hell is eating you? You've been *antsy* all day. What do you want? You already had two chews, a bone, and all those Fig Newtons. No more treats. You're going to get sick with all the junk I give you. It's almost suppertime, and you're getting dog food. You're making me crazy. Stop looking at me like I cut off your tail. I need a clue, something to go on. Jesus, I wish you could talk. Show me!"

The big dog ran to the kitchen, looked around, then sat down by the stove.

"Yeah, it's almost dinnertime. Dog food. Okay, okay, we'll go for a walk. Come on."

Instead of running to the door like he usually did, the yellow dog raced back to the den and then up the steps to the second floor. Luke followed him, cursing as he went along.

"You better not be showing me a spot where you lifted your leg, or you're sleeping in the barn tonight."

Buzz barked as he leaped onto Luke's king-size bed.

"You've been doing that since you were two months old. If this is your clue, it doesn't mean much. It wouldn't even pass as a good trick. Okay, okay, I think I'm starting to get the point." Luke watched as his pillow was pulled from underneath the spread and nudged to the floor.

"Why don't I make this easy on you since it's going to take you an hour to tug that cover off the bed." Luke yanked at the coverlet and dropped it to the floor. "Now what?"

Buzz sat back on his haunches, his head tilted to the side. "Woof."

"You liked her, didn't you? Yeah, yeah, I get it. She said she'd call and invite us to dinner. It's too soon. I suppose we could, you know, sort of drive by her place and maybe she'll be outside cleaning the windows or something. I don't see how doing something like that would hurt anything. We could even knock on the door. We could say we were in the neighborhood, that kind of thing. It's probably a really bad idea, but I'm game if you are."

Buzz barked as he dived under the bed, where he kept his stash of toys. Luke listened to him rummaging to find his favorite squeak toys. When he finally bellied out from under the bed he had a latex miniature of himself in his teeth. He dropped it in Luke's lap.

"I know this is supposed to mean something. Clues, Buzz, I need clues."

Buzz pushed and nudged the small toy until it was in Luke's hand. He gave it a playful squeeze. Buzz barked and barked as he pushed the toy into the crook of Luke's arm.

Luke sat down with a thump, his back pressed against the bed, his eyes on the panting dog. "Whoever it was that said dogs are dumb sure as hell didn't know about you. You want us to get her a dog and take it there. That's my best guess. What, no barking? Am I right?" Buzz licked Luke's face, his tail swishing so fast Luke got dizzy. "Okay, let's do it! It will be a reason to knock on her door. That business of us being in the neighborhood wasn't going to fly anyway. How about a puppy *and* Chinese?"

Buzz was a streak of golden light as he raced from the room. He was outside and in the truck before Luke got to the kitchen. "Forget the pork chops, we're dining out tonight," he said to his housekeeper. "Next stop the Corpus Christi Animal Shelter!"

Buzz chomped on a leftover Fig Newton.

Thirty minutes later, gravel spurting up behind his back wheels, Luke ground to a halt. "Hey, Alvin, hold on. Don't close up yet."

"Luke, what brings you way out here? Hey, big guy, how's it going. Biggest mistake I ever made was giving you this dog."

"Your loss, my gain. I'd part with the ranch before I'd give him up. Listen, I'm looking for a dog for . . . a friend. This particular friend, in my opinion—and Buzz's, too—is in need of a dog. I could be wrong, but I don't think so. Look, I know what you're going to say. If it doesn't work out I'll take the dog. Deal."

"I call this divine intervention. You stopping by like this," Alvin said. "Dave Palmer came in here on Monday with this dog he found on the side of the road. She was barely alive, and she had a pup with her. I got her fixed up, and she's doing real good. The pup, too. I can't separate them, Luke, because the pup is still nursing. I'd say she was well taken care of until just recently. God, some days I wish they could talk. No collar. She's been groomed because her nails have been clipped. I called all the local vets but didn't get anywhere. Is this . . . friend the type to take care of a dog like I'm talking about?"

"I think so, Alvin. Like I said, I'll take them both if it doesn't work out. What breed?"

"She's a full retriever. Beautiful animal. She's young, too. This is a guess on my part, but I'd say she's only had one heat. She doesn't like the cage and she sure as hell hates the dog food I've been giving her. I think whoever owned her gave her table food because she gobbles that down lickety-split."

"Let's see her."

Buzz backed up until his backside was touching the

truck. He started to whine. "You remember, don't you?" Luke said gently. "It's a good place, Buzz. You wait here."

"So what do you think?" Alvin asked.

"I think that's one good-looking dog, Alvin. The pup is just as good-looking. Boy or girl?"

"Boy. Let her get a good whiff of you. I wish Buzz would come in. She's skitzy when it comes to her pup, Dave said. Weak as she was, she put up a fight when he tried to get her into the truck. She'll make someone a hell of a companion. I was thinking of taking her myself."

"I'll take her, Alvin. Go outside with Buzz while I talk to her. I don't want her to be afraid. Do your best to get Buzz in here, okay? Does she have a name?"

"The girls have been calling her Silky. The pup is Sam. They don't respond to either name, so you can call them whatever you want. They have all their shots. I gotta charge you, Luke."

Money changed hands. "Buy some extra dog food for the rest of these guys. Can't you find homes for them?"

"In time. You know we don't put them to sleep. By next week most of them will be in new homes. The people around here always come by once I go on the evening news. I'll see about getting Buzz in here."

Luke opened the kennel door and reached in to stroke the silky head, his voice low and gentle. He talked for a long time before he reached for the pup. "C'mon, girl, we're going someplace where you're going to be happy. I don't know how I know this, but I do. We're not going empty-handed either. We'll stop for some real food, some gear, and I'll present you with a big red bow. Nobody in their right mind would turn down a deal like that." He turned when he felt his leg being nudged. "This guy is Buzz. Okay, let's get this show on the road."

"Fixed a bed with some old towels in the back of your truck, Luke. I'd let Buzz sit back there with them."

"You don't think she'll jump out?"

"Hell no. First of all her primary concern is the pup. She's taken to you, I can see that. She's still a little wobbly. A few more days with some good food and she's going to be raring to go. She knows how to walk on a leash, too. I think she got lost is what I think. Probably some tourists passing through stopped and she wandered off. Put the pup in first, then you lift her in. Buzz goes last. If you're nervous, I can ride along with you, but I think she'll be fine. Buzz will watch out for her."

"We'll manage, Alvin. Thanks."

"Tell your friend to call me if she has any problems. Is your friend a woman?"

"Yeah."

"It's a lock then. Female dogs bond with females. The little guy will go with the crowd. See you around, Luke."

Luke felt something burning his eyes when he picked up the mother dog. Just before he lowered her into the bed of the truck she raised her head to lick at his cheek. "Watch them, Buzz. I'll go slow, but we have to make a couple of stops."

It was seven-forty when Luke pulled the truck to the curb outside Jessie's building. He checked on the dogs before he rapped sharply on the door, his brow furrowed at the intricate digital lock. When the door opened he grinned. "I was going to make up this excuse about being in the neighborhood, but I didn't think you'd buy it. Buzz wanted to come here. It's really a very long story. However, I come bearing gifts. It's . . . ah, what it is . . . is the kind of gift you have to see. It's in the back of the truck with Buzz. He really did want to come here. You did say you would invite us to dinner. I was going to buy Chinese, but the time got away from me."

"It's okay. I almost called you myself, but I thought it

was too soon. I have a whole pot of spaghetti. Does Buzz like meatballs?"

"Buzz eats anything. So do I. Do you want to see your gift? Now listen, it's the kind of gift that can't be returned. If you don't like it, I guess I can keep it. You are very pretty. I like that color you're wearing. What do you call it?"

Jessie flushed. Thank God she'd brushed her hair and washed her face. For some strange reason she'd also splashed on some perfume. "It's called plum. I'm glad you stopped by because I really don't like eating alone. Can I see the gift now?" How breathless she sounded. Did he notice? Of course he noticed.

"Uh-huh. You bet. I mean, yeah, it's waiting for you."

"Oh! Oh! I . . . Oh! Is she for me? Is it a girl? A puppy! Is she for me, too? Oh! You did this for me! You dear, sweet man!" Jessie threw her arms around Luke's neck. A moment later, her face brick red, she backed away. Buzz howled. The pup made a snarling sound that sounded like meow, meow. The mother dog struggled to get to her feet.

"I'll carry her in for you. The mother is a girl, the pup is a boy. I guess that's kind of obvious." He was babbling. "All this other stuff is for them. It will take six trips. We even brought some food. It's the kind of stuff I gave Buzz in the beginning until I more or less weaned him off it to dog food."

"She's scared. Look how she's shaking. What if she doesn't like me?"

"She's going to love you. All you have to do is . . . bond with her. She's had a rough time of it this past week, maybe longer for all I know. You carry the pup and go first. That way she'll trust you."

"I don't know what to say."

"Then you'll keep her?"

"Just try taking her away! He's adorable."

"Didja hear that, Buzz? She said the pup is adorable."

"Well, what have we here?" Luke said as he plopped the last of the dog's gear in the small gallery.

"My pictures. Actually, they're sketches my friend Sophie had framed for me."

"Did you have a dog like this?" Luke asked, going from one picture to the other.

"I never had a dog. My parents wouldn't allow it. I had tons of picture books when I was little, though. Most of them were dog books. There must have been one in particular that I liked more than the others. I seem to draw the same dog over and over. I took the pictures off the wall right before you got here. I'm sending them to Milan to a shop that has a gallery. Where should we put all this stuff?"

"Let's look around. Where do you think you'll want her to sleep?"

"In my room. On my bed with me. I always wanted to have a dog sleep with me. You know, at the bottom of the bed to keep my feet warm. Where does Buzz sleep?"

"On my bed. He started out at the bottom but worked his way to the top. He has a pillow, and so do I. My housekeeper tells me he snores louder than I do." Jessie laughed as she gathered up a load of stuff to carry to the second floor.

"Spread out that bed. It has a shearling lining. Completely washable. Okay, good. Now I'm going to put her down and you catch that pup and put him next to his mother. A few toys, a warm fuzzy or two and I think they'll both go to sleep. Ooops, a water bowl. This is a ceramic bowl made by an Indian in Santa Fe. If you take it back to the store later, they'll stencil the dog's name on it. A dog's name is very important, so you might not want to rush into just any old name. Buzz and I will go out to your living room and wait for you. You need to spend a little time with her so she understands that she's safe and has a new home. Stroke her head and talk softly."

"Listen, I'm sorry about what I said that night about you not taking care of your dog. I was in a very bad place that night," Jessie said.

"Sometimes appearances are deceiving. Did you see the news this evening?"

"As a matter of fact, I did. I don't want to talk about the Kingsleys. You can set the table if you don't mind. The kitchen is small, so just look around and you'll find everything."

Jessie closed the door behind Luke and Buzz. She sat down next to the oversize dog bed to stroke the animal's silky head. The pup was sound asleep. Tears welled in Jessie's eyes. "I know there's a sad story behind you, but you don't ever have to worry about anything ever again. I'm going to take care of you. Forever and ever. Your pup, too. This is just a guess on my part, but I think you're going to make up for a lot of things that haven't worked out in my life." An overwhelming urge to pick up the dog and cradle her in her arms and squeeze her till she yelped was so strong Jessie beat her hands on the floor. The weary dog opened her eyes and whined softly. Jessie crooned to her as she stroked her head. "Sleep now. Everything is going to be okay. I won't close the door."

In the open doorway, Jessie turned for one last look at the sleeping dog and her pup. "Thank you, God," she whispered. "Thank you for sending Luke, too." Later, when Luke was gone, she'd think about what he'd just done for her.

"This looks festive," Jessie said.

"It's the red napkins."

"I love red. Purple, too."

"Buzz has a red neckerchief we use on holidays. Are you a holiday person, Jessie?"

"I am now. I'm starting a new life. You're serving me, too!"

"You cooked it. It's the least I can do. I don't do dishes, though."

"I hate cleaning up. It goes faster when two people do it. Is it good, or is it just okay?"

"Tasty. I washed off a couple of meatballs for Buzz. Dogs shouldn't have tomato sauce. Did you know that?"

"No, I didn't."

"We brought you two question-and-answer dog books. I put the chicken in the refrigerator. It will take about two weeks to build her up. I say give her lots of vegetables mashed up in the chicken. That is not in the books. It's what I did for Buzz, and look at him now. I can't take credit for it, though. Alvin told me to do it. He has a dog that's nineteen who has never eaten anything but vegetables and fruits. Alvin is a vegetarian. The dog is in perfect health aside from his age and he's slowed down."

"Amazing."

"Nice place you have here. What's behind the gallery? Are you going to work in the gallery or what?"

Or what? Jessie set her fork next to her plate. "This is my building. There's an office behind the gallery. I'll show it to you later. It is absolutely mind-boggling to me at times how things work out. I have a feeling, Luke, that you and I are going to become good friends, so I don't want to start off on the wrong foot. If I'm wrong about our friendship, that's okay, too. I'm going to tell you who I am and what I'm all about. I hate lying, and I hate subterfuge. I hate always being on guard, of being afraid I'll say something that will . . . will blow my cover. I don't want a cover. All I want is to be me. I can't even do that because half the time I don't know who me is. This is a long story. Do you want to hear it?"

"Yes I do."

Jessie talked steadily for almost an hour. She watched Luke carefully for his reactions to what she was saying. When she didn't see anything to alarm her, she finished up with, "and that's the way it is."

"You never told Tanner? Why?"

"Instinct. Sophie's warnings. My own lack of confidence. I wasn't sure if I loved him or not. I didn't think it was a good idea to marry him. It was all a big mistake. It's behind me now. All that money is an albatross around my neck. I'm working on it, but it certainly isn't going to be my life's work if you know what I mean. Now, tell me about you."

Luke frowned. "It doesn't compute. Tanner not knowing, I mean. Tanner makes it his business to know everything."

"He couldn't have known. Sophie was the only other person who knew. I don't like what I'm seeing on your face. Do you know something I should know?"

"I don't know if I do or not. It was common knowledge, so it isn't as though it was a secret."

Jessie's face settled into hard lines at the prospect of what she was about to hear. "I want to hear."

"During my high school years, Angus brought young kids to the ranch. City kids. Fresh air, wholesome food, animals, space, that kind of thing. They stayed the whole summer. The first time was in our freshman year. The kids were different each summer, except for one kid who came every year. I don't know if this is true or not, but the rumor was Angus paid for his college education. That's one plus in Angus's favor. Anyway, the night of our high-school graduation there was a big party at the Kingsley ranch. I was there. It got rowdy, and there was a lot of beer. We were sitting around a big bonfire toasting weenies and marshmallows and the talk got around to girl talk. It was late, and the girls were already gone because

Mrs. Kingsley heard Bop say she'd play Lady Godiva.
There was a big discussion between Tanner and this kid
about how their life's agenda was to find and marry a rich
girl. Someone started a pool, and we all put money into it.
The first one to snag a rich girl got the pot. I think there
was eighty bucks in it. That whole summer until we went
off to college, Tanner and the kid schemed and plotted. I
stopped going to the ranch about then because they became obsessive about it. Especially J.J. I think they spent
the entire summer at the library. J.J. was one of the
smartest kids I ever met. He knew how to research and
network. In that respect he was a lot like your friend Sophie. When we parted at the end of the summer, they had
a list of eligible young women and profiles of those women.
Tanner had his own car and plenty of money. All they did
was tool around doing their research. About two years
ago, maybe longer, it's kind of hazy right now, I heard
from one of the guys in town that J.J. had a lock on a
really big fish that was going to be the answer to the
lifestyle he and Tanner had always dreamed of."

This was not what she wanted to hear. In spite of herself, she asked, "I thought Bippity-Bop was wealthy." She
hated the warm flush creeping up her neck to her face at
her words.

"She's more than comfortable from what I hear, but her
parents, like all the other ranchers, had problems. Most of
the money was gone years ago. They keep up a front. I'm
not talking about simple rich if there is such a term. I'm
talking about the kind of wealth associated with Aristotle
Onassis."

"Oh." The only person she knew who ever had that
kind of wealth was Sophie Ashwood. And now that wealth
was hers. She suddenly felt sick to her stomach.

"I know what you're thinking, and as much as I hate to

say it or even think it myself, I tend to agree. I am not a big fan of coincidence."

"What . . . what was J.J.'s name?"

"I don't know if I ever knew it. If I did, I forgot it. It was a long time ago. The guy wasn't someone I wanted as a friend any more than Tanner was at that point in time. I don't like talking about this. At least now you know a little more about Tanner. For all I know it could have been a pipe dream. To my knowledge J.J. has never been back here. Someone in town would have mentioned it. Now, to get back to your question, I'm pretty much an open book. Where's Buzz?"

"Maybe he went to check on my new roommates. Let's go see." Later, when she was in bed she would think about what Luke had just told her.

In the doorway, Luke clapped his hands over his mouth so he wouldn't laugh aloud. Jessie did the same thing. Buzz was sprawled on Jessie's bed, his big head resting on one of her pillows. The second pillow was under the mother dog's head. All were sleeping peacefully.

"Buzz has this thing about pillows," Luke whispered. "I wasn't kidding when I said he wanted to come here." He told her about Buzz's antics back at the ranch. The story brought a smile to Jessie's face.

Back in the kitchen, Jessie filled Luke's coffee cup. "Now, tell me about you. I'd like to know what happened between you and the Kingsleys."

"For starters, I never wanted to be a rancher. I had no other choice when my dad and stepmother were killed. I studied forestry at Penn State. I'm a ranger but never got to work at it. I managed to get my master's by going nights later on. My mother died when I was fourteen and my father remarried a few years later. I have three stepbrothers. Ted will complete his master's in December, Joe will finish up in April and both of them are going to come back here to run the ranch. Steve has been helping out summers the past two years to get a feel for it all. Come January, I'm going back to Penn State to teach. Summers I'll work at Black Moshannon State Park doing what I love to do."

"You're leaving!" Jessie asked in dismay.

"Yes. I wasn't cut out for this. I stayed on because I knew it was what my father expected me to do. My brothers love it. It's the best possible solution for everyone. The ranch is doing well. We brought in a few new wells a few years ago that will tide the ranch over if bad times come up. As to the Kingsleys versus the Holts, it's a long story. All the ranchers in these parts had a bad six-year run. We all had a lot of paper at the bank. Angus was pretty flush at the time. When our notes came due, he managed to wheel and deal to buy up the notes so he could foreclose. I was the only one who held out. My stepmother had a very generous insurance policy, with her children as beneficiaries. I didn't even know about it until the boys told me. They turned it over to me, and I was able to hold off our creditors and the bank. I then went to Dallas and borrowed money from a friend to sink a well. We lucked out and brought in two real gushers. I paid off my friend, set up my brothers, and paid off our mortgages. There's quite a bit left, but to my thinking, the boys own the ranch even though my name is on the deed. I don't want them to have to worry if another bad time comes. When I walk away from here it's going to be with Buzz and my truck, although I think I'm going to have to get a new one before long. I am not, nor have I ever been, a material person. I am a peace-of-mind person. Your wealth doesn't bother me, and it doesn't scare me, Jessie.

"The reason Angus wanted my land so badly was because I've got the water, and the underground cables are on my property. I would never deny any rancher water or electricity, not even Angus. I do charge a fair price, though. Does that tell you who I am? Do you still want to be friends?"

"Sure I do. It's going to be hard, though, if you're living in Pennsylvania and I'm here."

"That's true."

I miss you already, Jessie thought. "Tell me about you and Tanner."

"We were friends once. I went one way, and he went another way. He wasn't the person I thought he was, and I imagine he thought the same thing about me."

"That's it. Tanner led me to believe there were deep, dark secrets buried somewhere."

"Speaking for myself, I don't have any deep, dark secrets. I'm a what-you-see-is-what-you-get kind of guy."

"Is that another way of saying you don't want to talk about Tanner?"

"Yes. I'm not one to look back. I deal with today, and I think about tomorrow. Yesterday is gone and there's nothing I can do about it. I have an idea, let's go get an ice-cream cone. Simple minds, simple pleasures. Buzz can baby-sit. We'll bring one home for him. He loves strawberry."

"You just want to get out of doing the dishes. I'd love an ice-cream cone."

"Then let's go, lady."

Jessie felt *antsy,* in control but out of control. Her back ramrod stiff, she paced the confines of the small, narrow kitchen. Without stopping to think, she reached for the telephone behind her. She made a flurry of calls to the information operator and then another series of calls to her parents' bankers. When she had no success in obtaining their numbers she dialed Arthur Mendenares's private number. Forty minutes later she had her parents' phone number.

A cigarette found its way to her lips. She puffed furiously as she placed her overseas call, at the same time wondering why she had such an overwhelming urge to call her parents. She also made a mental note to quit smoking the moment her life settled into something resembling normalcy. She waited patiently, her heart pounding in her chest. What in the world was she afraid of? The moment she heard her father's voice, her own voice became confident and strong.

"Daddy, it's Jessie. How are you?"

"Dear girl, I'm fine. How are you?"

"At the moment, I'm fine, too. Can we talk, Daddy?" The implication was clear: Can Mama overhear you?

"Your mother is in the garden. As a matter of fact, she's sleeping. She isn't well, Jessie."

"I'm sorry to hear that. Daddy, I need to talk to you. I want your help. That's not quite true, I desperately *need* your help. Please, Daddy."

"Darling girl, I'll help in anyway I can. Now, tell me what it is that's troubling you."

"I'm going to go backwards from the present to the past. I'm in Corpus Christi, Texas. I got married to Senator Kingsley's son. Not because I wanted to, but because I was pregnant. The child needed to carry the name of his father. I miscarried and for a year I was out of it. I can't even remember it. I finally came out of my stupor a few weeks ago and moved out. I realize now I never should have married him. Mr. Mendenares is going to handle my divorce. I'm sure you know Sophie . . . Sophie took her own life. I still have a hard time with that. Anyway, she left her entire estate to me. I'm having a hard time with that, too, but I accept it and will not shirk my responsibility or the trust Sophie placed in me. Are you listening to me, Daddy?"

"Yes, child, I am. I am so very sorry about Sophie. I

adored her as you know. Some of my fondest memories are of you two scalawags running around the yard. Arthur sent us a note a few days after it happened."

"Daddy, why wasn't I allowed to have friends? Why was Sophie my only friend? Was there something wrong with me? Did you ever take me to the doctors to see why I had those awful dreams?"

"Your mother was overprotective, Jessie. When your . . . sister died at such an early age she became . . . fearful. She never got over her death. We did speak to your pediatrician, and he said all children have nightmares. He wasn't concerned and said you would outgrow them. There was nothing wrong with you, dear child. You were a healthy, robust little girl. I'm sorry to say your mother didn't think any of the other children were good enough for you. She only wanted you to associate with people she approved of. Unfortunately she didn't approve of anyone, even her old friend Janice. It wasn't right and I never approved of what she did. Does that . . . help?"

"No, Daddy. Time is supposed to heal all wounds. I lost a child, too. I have to start making sense of my life. It seems there is a part of me that's missing. I can't explain it any better than that. In view of the things that have been happening, I've made the decision to go to a psychiatrist to try and make sense of it. They can hypnotize me. I'll do whatever it takes. I can't and won't live like this any longer."

"I see," Barnes said.

"You sound funny, Daddy. Do you really see, or are you just saying that? Do you think I'm making a mistake?"

"Some psychiatrists are charlatans. I wouldn't rush into anything."

"Sophie said, and I agree, that something awful must have happened to me as a child. If you don't know what it is, then the only way to find out is to have myself hypnotized. Maybe nothing happened, and Sophie and I were both wrong."

"I suppose that's what you'll find out in the end. I hate to see you put yourself through more trauma."

"I have to know, Daddy. I've always known something was wrong, but I never knew what to do about it. I fell off a horse a few days ago and had the strangest reaction. It was like the nightmare but during the day. I took it to mean I am getting closer to whatever it is that's been such a stumbling block. I hope I haven't upset you, Daddy."

"I'm upset for you. I just wish there was something I could say to make things right for you."

"There is. Don't tell Mama I called. You sound so strange, Daddy. Are you sure there's nothing wrong?"

"I think it's the long-distance call. I am halfway around the world, honey. Take care of yourself."

"I will, Daddy. Enjoy the sunshine."

"Don't you mean moonlight?"

"And the moonlight, too." Jessie waited for her father's chuckle. When she didn't hear it she said, "I'll call and let you know the results if I do go through with it."

"All right. Good-bye, honey."

"Bye, Daddy."

Jessie sat for a long time staring at the phone. It wasn't her imagination that her father had sounded strange. Knowing him as she did, she didn't think he'd lied to her, but he certainly hadn't told her the whole truth. Why was that, and how did she know?

"Instinct," she mumbled.

It was almost midnight when Jessie walked on tiptoe into her room. She smiled at the sleeping dog and her pup as she brushed her teeth quickly, washing her face and hands before she undressed and slipped into a nightgown. Still watching the dog, she turned down the bedcovers and fluffed up her pillow. In the dim bedroom light, she could see the big dog watching her. In her bare feet, with her pillow under her arm, she walked over to the dog, dropped to her knees, and whispered, "I'd like it a lot if you let me sleep here with you. I'm a quiet sleeper. What I'd really like to do is sleep behind you, but I think you want to keep your eyes on me so I'll lie right here." Later, she swore the big dog sighed when her head finally hit the pillow and curled into the fetal position. She woke once during the night, aware of the dog's body warmth and the fact that one of her paws rested on her shoulder. At the last second before drifting into sleep she remembered that she hadn't told her father about the dog. She sighed as sleep claimed her weary body.

Barnes Roland stared at his sleeping wife. She was so thin, so fragile-looking. A part of him filled with love and another part filled with anger. The two emotions warred against each other as he gently shook her shoulder.

"Wake up, Thea. We have to pack. We're leaving."

"I don't want to take a trip, Barnes. What time is it?"

"The time doesn't matter. Jessie called."

"And you didn't wake me! You are so cruel, Barnes. What did my sweet love say? Is she coming for a visit? Is she going to call back? I knew she would come to her senses sooner or later. Oh Lord, we have to get the house ready. When is she coming, Barnes? You wanted to surprise me. It's all right. I forgive you. I have to plan. This is so wonderful. Did she tell you to give me a kiss and a hug? She loves me, Barnes, I know she does."

"Thea, listen to me. Jessie is not coming here. I want you to listen to me very carefully because I will not repeat any of this a second time. Jessie is going to go to a psychiatrist and have herself hypnotized. Do you understand what that means?"

"No, Barnes, I don't. Why would she do that?"

"So she'll remember what happened. She said she fell off a horse and she had one of her nightmares in the daylight. At least I think that's what she meant. We have to leave, Thea. I told you there was a possibility we would have to move on someday. If she remembers, she can tell the authorities where we are."

"But the pool, the gardens, the tennis court . . . We did that for Jessie."

"You insisted on doing that, Thea. I told you Jessie would never come back."

Thea's feeble voice rose to a shriek. "But she did come here. She brought Sophie with her. You lied to me just the way you're lying now."

"Jessie is going to remember, Thea. I'm not planning on being here when the authorities come for us. Now, are you coming with me or not?"

"If we go to Argentina, Jessie will never be able to find us. That's where you're planning on going, isn't that right? That's where all those Nazi war criminals went to hide out. We'll be just like them if we go there."

"We are like them. What we did was unconscionable. We're too old to go to jail, Thea. What's it going to be?"

"Can we leave a note for Jessie?"

Barnes watched as his wife's eyes glazed over. "I have her phone number. When it's safe perhaps we can call her."

"Give it to me, Barnes. I'll do whatever you want if you give it to me. I swear. I promise. I just want to talk to her. Just once, Barnes. My prayers have finally been answered. She's sorry for all the misery she caused us. I forgive her. It's so easy to forgive someone you love. Oh, Barnes, what should I pack?"

"Nothing but essentials. We'll pay off the servants, close up the house, and pretend we're leaving on an extended vacation. All I need for you to do is to remember your new name on your new passport."

"Do you think Jessie will visit us in Argentina? You must be happy, Barnes, you've been planning this for so long now."

"It's a good thing I did. Everything I said is starting to come to pass. Please hurry, Thea."

"You didn't answer my question. When will Jessie visit us?"

"Ninety days. Three months," Barnes lied, sweat beading on his brow. "You'll need every one of those ninety days to get things ready for Jessie. You do want it to be perfect and beautiful, don't you?"

"I think we'll do her room in blue and silver this time. Silver is pretty, don't you think, Barnes?" Thea asked dreamily. "We should buy her some nice jewelry, too. Maybe a new car."

"Whatever you want, Thea. Don't forget your pills."

"Is Jessie really going to visit us in Argentina?"

"Yes," Barnes lied again as he ushered his wife into the house.

Thirty minutes passed before Barnes heard the feeble cry. He slipped twice on the marble floor, righted himself, his breathing harsh and ragged in his struggle to get to his wife.

"Thea! What happened?"

Thea, her face ashen, could only gasp and clutch her chest.

"Lie still, Thea. I'll call the doctor to send the ambulance. Don't try to talk."

Thea's hands flapped in the air, her eyes rolling back in her head. "Give me the number, Barnes. Please," she gasped.

Barnes stuffed a crumpled piece of paper from his pocket into his wife's hands.

The sound of the wailing siren sent tremors through his body. He should follow it, but first he had to think, to make some kind of plan. Argentina was out of the question for now.

What should he do? Should he forsake Thea and go off alone? He still had a good number of years left if he took care of himself. Thea, on the other hand, could die in a matter of hours or days. She could also recover and continue to live in her zombielike state for many more years.

Barnes closed his eyes as he roll-called his life.

Then he cried.

Chapter Eighteen

"The senator has no comment," Alexis Kingsley said as she slammed the receiver back into the cradle so hard it bounced onto the table. She slammed it again. "We need to disconnect this phone and get an unlisted number. When are they going to give up? It's been three months!" Her angry voice turned gentle. "Did you take your pills this morning?"

"They'll never give up until the day I die, and I'm working on that. Go away, Alexis. Cut the damn wires, disconnect the phone, rip it out of the wall. Do whatever you want to do. It's none of your business if I took my pills or not. Why do you care anyway? Which brings me to my next question, why are you being so nice?"

Alexis sat down opposite her husband. "Your problem, Angus, is that you're upset because everything I said came to pass. I am truly sorry the twins left you to flounder. I know their disdain for you was devastating, especially as you are their father. However, they showed that side of themselves *before* you revoked their trust funds. They are bright, intelligent young people with solid educations behind them, thanks to you. They inherited their mother's farm and sold it for close to two million dollars. That gives them very nice nest eggs to start their lives."

"I don't want to talk about this, Alexis. It's over and done with."

"It's never going to be over and done with. If it was over and done with, why do those lawyers come out here every single day? Why do you look like death warmed over when they leave? What's going to happen? I have a right to know, Angus."

"I'm going to die is what's going to happen. When I go, this mess goes with me."

"Is there any way . . ."

Angus's voice was a cold bark. "No. You'll be fine, Alexis. The ranch will stay in the family. Resa and Tanner will be fine, too."

"That's not what I was going to say. How can you talk to me like this, Angus? We don't even know where Resa is for God's sake. Tanner's wife is suing him for divorce. More papers came for him today. The boy is not fine."

"He should have thought things through. He's like you, Alexis. All he wants to do is destroy all the good things that come his way, just the way you did and still do. You are both selfish and ungrateful. Jessie is a wonderful woman. I had hopes she could make something of our son. For all our differences, Alexis, I never, ever laid a hand on you. Why aren't you worried about *that* getting in the papers. Our son, the physical wife abuser."

"I have to blame you for that, too. All those children you brought to the ranch were a bad influence on Tanner. Especially J.J. Tanner is still friends with that . . . that leech. I will never forget the year you brought his whole family here for two whole weeks. I lost count of the children they had. They were slovenly white trash, Angus, and it rubbed off on Tanner. I swear I think he thought that was what a family was supposed to be like. I couldn't do it all, Angus. I made mistakes, some worse than others but at least I tried. Did you ever offer to help me? No, you didn't. Irene and her family were your priorities. It's in the past, and we can't undo it."

"If you believe that, then you are beyond hope. I agree that J.J. was an opportunist. The family was poor. God says we're supposed to help our fellow man. I'd do that over again, too, Alexis. I'm going to take a nap now, so leave me alone. Go back to your cage and don't interfere in Tanner's life. Let him handle his divorce on his own. It should be a simple one; Jessie doesn't want anything."

"Go to hell, Angus, but take those pills first," Alexis said as she left the bright, sunny room where her husband sat shivering underneath a plaid blanket. She cried all the way back to her room. Her husband was dying, and still he wouldn't say one kind word to her. Just one kind word. Was it too much to ask?

Jessie parked in the driveway behind the office, pressing the remote control to open the garage door at the same time she switched off the ignition. The dogs ran to her, pawing her legs for attention. In a daze, she petted them, urging them back into the garage. The heavy door dropped back into place with a loud thud. Her eyes glazed, Jessie looked around the room she'd spent so much time in the past three months as she dropped to her knees to cradle the dogs to her chest.

Sensing the change from her earlier mood, the dogs tried to climb into her lap as they struggled to lick her face. They were her lifeline now, and she clutched at them, holding them as tightly as she could. "It's not the worst thing in the world. The worst thing in the world would be finding out I'm pregnant without you two guys in my life. It's going to be okay. We'll be a family, just the four of us. A child needs a dog. Two dogs are even better. You'll look out for him or her, and I'll look out for all of us. I think we're going to have to move, though. Maybe a minifarm or someplace with lots of property so you can run. I don't want Tanner to know this time. I wonder if you understand anything I'm saying. It's okay if you don't. What's bothering me the most is telling Luke. I don't know why that is. We've become such good friends. Whatever will be, will be. I'm taking the view that God is giving me a second chance and maybe, just maybe, He means me to be a mother after all. The last time I was scared and unhappy. This time, this time . . . I feel like it's meant to be."

Jessie's eyes wandered to the shelf above her worktable to the neat line of sculptures that were drying. They were good, even Luke said they were good, and each one was getting better, which to her meant the first ones were exercises. It didn't matter. She loved sculpting the miniature golden retrievers. Her gaze swiveled to the far corner of the garage, where a mound of clay sat under a wet towel. She was sculpting a life-size figure of Buzz to give Luke as a going-away present when he left for Penn State. It was the kind of conversation sculpture people set outside their front door so guests would oooh and aaah over it once they met the flesh-and-blood model.

Jessie rubbed the big dog's belly as her pup sniffed out the front corners of the garage. "It is what it is, girl. I'm not going over the edge like I did the last time. This time it's one day at a time. We aren't going to look back because, like Luke said, yesterday is gone. We don't know what tomorrow will bring. All we have is today and a lot more of them to come." The golden dog woofed her approval.

Jessie dusted her hands dramatically. "I'm going to change my clothes and get to work. But first we have to call Mr. Gabriel Montoya in Milan and fire him."

In the kitchen, Jessie placed a person-to-person call to

Milan, Italy. She popped a cola while she waited for the call to go through. It was late with the time difference, but she knew from Arthur that Montoya rarely closed the gallery before midnight.

Jessie's hand trembled when she reached for the letter Montoya had sent a week ago. It was an ugly, demeaning, cruel letter. Would he have written the same letter if he had known she was the owner of the gallery? Probably.

"Mr. Montoya, this is Jessica Roland. Yes, the owner of the gallery. Yes, at the moment I reside in the United States. Yes, it was business as usual. The situation changed when your letter arrived several days ago. I'm sorry to say I don't agree with your decision not to hang the animal sketches in the gallery. As the owner of International Designs, my decision is the final decision. What that means, Mr. Montoya, is this, you will mat and frame the pictures I sent you, and you will hang them immediately. If you can't see yourself doing this, I am prepared to accept your resignation, effective immediately. I found your letter to be unnecessarily cruel and very unprofessional. I can't help but wonder if the tone of your letter would have been different had you known the pictures were mine. They are mine, Mr. Montoya. Furthermore, they are not crude, nor are they amateurish. And yes, they do have a place in my gallery. It's obvious to me you are not an animal lover. I can accept that. What I cannot accept is your haughty attitude. When can I expect your resignation, Mr. Montoya?"

Jessie listened to the gallery manager's sputtering denials as he blamed his assistant Philip for everything. She interrupted him once to say, "I'm not interested in all this bullshit, Mr. Montoya. As the owner of International Designs I can do anything I please, and it pleases me to sever our relationship. If you want to bad-mouth me to your client base, do so. I will then sue you for slander. Put Philip on the phone. Now!

"Philip, this is Jessica Roland. I want you to escort Mr. Montoya from the gallery. As of tomorrow morning, you will operate the gallery. Your first order is to mat and frame the pictures I sent. Cluster them on one wall. Understand this. I do not care if anyone buys them or not. Put outrageous price tags on them. Whatever the traffic will bear. Mr. Montoya seems to think the sketches are childish, poorly drawn, and improper for your high-class clientele. Obviously, I don't agree. Miss Ashwood herself is the one who suggested these pictures hang in the gallery. Is there anything I've said that you don't understand? Fine. Mr. Mendenares will be in touch with you. Of course your salary will increase. It was nice speaking with you again, Philip. Good night."

Jessie clapped her hands. She would know soon enough if Montoya was right or not. In the meantime she had other things to do and think about.

Pregnant. With Tanner's child. Motherhood. What was Luke going to say, and why was his opinion so important to her? As Scarlett said, I'll think about that tomorrow. Life is going to go on no matter what I think or say. The alternative doesn't bear thinking about.

"Okay, guys, time to go to work."

Jessie watched the frisky pup as he bounded down the stairs and out to the garage. The big dog walked at her side, her tail swishing happily. In the garage, the pup sought out his basket of squeak toys, scattering them everywhere. The moment Jessie perched on her stool, the mother dog dropped to the floor, her head on her paws, her eyes on the pup who was frolicking from one corner of the garage to the other.

Jessie eyed the small collection of animals Sophie's housekeeper had forwarded. She'd lined them up next to the small animals she'd been making the past few months. Her first creations resembled her early-childhood endeavors.

Each brought a memory of a time when life was happy for her and Sophie. Tears pricked her eyelids. She would never part with these small, endearing statues. She would save them for when her own child was ready to venture outside the parameters of storybooks and toys. If she became successful at what she was doing, perhaps one day it would become a mother-son/daughter business.

Jessie reached for a bag beagle Sophie had named Elroy. It brought a smile to her face as she let her fingers caress the little statue. One ear was crooked and one paw was shorter than the other three. All the more reason to love and treasure it. She wondered why she wasn't crying. Was it possible there were no more tears left in her? Was she finally moving beyond her grief, or was this just a stalling measure so she wouldn't have to read the mail containing Tanner's response to the divorce? Probably a little of both, she decided. *Get it over with. Open it and put it behind you,* she thought.

Every curse she'd ever learned from Sophie spewed from her mouth when she read the papers saying Tanner was contesting the divorce. If he found out about the baby, what would it do to the divorce proceedings? Thank God she'd had the presence of mind to use Sophie's name when she'd had her checkup. It had all been so strange. When the nurse asked her name she'd rattled off Sophie's name without hesitation. That meant there was no record anywhere of Jessie Roland Kingsley having visited a doctor. What exactly did contesting a divorce mean? Did it mean she and Tanner had to agree on things, or did a judge make the final decision? She had to call Arthur. There was no way she could work or enjoy Luke's visit later on if this was hanging over her head. Her gaze dropped to the pile of crisp, crackly papers. Why did legal papers always crackle? It was such an ominous sound. She crunched the papers into a tight ball before she tossed it across the room.

The frisky pup had it in his paws within seconds. When she looked at him again the papers were in shreds.

My address was on those papers. In the blink of an eye, Jessie was off her stool and running to the garage door, where she yanked and pulled until the heavy mechanism that was an added security measure snapped it into place. She secured the internal locking mechanism, testing it. Satisfied, she slapped the wet towel over the clay she'd planned to work on. Now she had other things to do.

Jessie raced into the house and into the office, the dogs nipping at her heels, where she grappled with the phone as she tried to remember Arthur's number without having to look it up. The moment she heard his voice she started to babble incoherently.

"Jessie, Jessie, slow down. It's not the end of the world. We can handle this. I'll abide by whatever decision you make. I just want you to be cautious. Tanner has rights, Jessie. A father always has rights. He's also within his rights to contest the divorce. That doesn't mean he will prevail. It will be your word against his. I'm sure Mrs. Kingsley and Tanner will both offer supporting evidence about how they took care of you while you were ill. A doctor will no doubt agree with whatever they say. Once you enter Luke into the equation, it starts to get sticky. You need to know that. Yes, you can run, but you can't hide. Someone, somewhere, will always know where you are. You only have to think about Sophie to realize what I say is true. If you think going back to your family's home is your answer, then do it. Just be sure you're doing it for the right reasons. A child does need roots. So do you, Jessie. There's a place waiting for you. I just don't know where that place is, but I suspect before long you'll find it. I would be honored to be the child's godfather, but I think we're a little ahead of ourselves here. No one can come after you for using Sophie's name at the doctor's. That was rather astute of you, my dear. Sophie would have approved. Now, tell me, how are those wonderful dogs of yours doing?"

Jessie sighed. "They *are* wonderful, Arthur. They're at my side all the time. You would not believe how protective they are. They sleep with me. We eat at the same time. The pup is a handful. He's into everything. By the way, he chewed up those papers you sent me. If Tanner comes here, should I talk to him?"

"That's entirely up to you, Jessie. When most people are faced with a situation like this they have a tendency to make a last-ditch effort, which is what I suspect your husband is doing. I wouldn't worry about it until it happens. I don't know of any specific law that says you have to tell Tanner you're pregnant at this time. Take it one step at a time. Your phone number is unlisted so he cannot harass you over the phone. Don't make any rash decisions or decisions you will have difficulty living with in the future. I'll send you a new set of papers. Go on with your life, Jessie. How's the sculpting going?"

"Very well. I fired Mr. Montoya. I think I'm going to go back to Charleston. That's where my life began. I know they say you can't go home again, but I won't be going to that home. I'll make one of my own. An hour from now I'll probably change my mind. There are days where I feel like a gypsy."

"Take your time making decisions you can live with. I suspect you could be happy there if you lay your old ghosts to rest. If there's nothing else, my dear, I'll say good night. Remember, if you decide to leave, call me so I'll know where and how to reach you. By the way, have there been any further developments in regard to Senator Kingsley?"

"Luke heard a rumor at the Cattleman's Club that the senator's health is very fragile, and his prognosis is not good. That's all I know."

"I'm sorry to hear that. Good night, Jessie."

"Night, Arthur." Jessie shook her head. "I guess it is night-time in England right now," she said to the dogs. Both animals were sound asleep at her feet. She felt calm now.

Calm enough to make reasonable decisions.

Tanner Kingsley parked his car across the street in the office-building parking lot. He sat for a long time staring at the building where his wife now lived. A newly renovated building. An impressive building. Was there an apartment over the office part of the building? Obviously, since he could see that the whole top floor was lighted. All he had to do was walk across the street and knock on the door. Or, he could walk around back and see if there was a side or back door to the second floor. What would he do if his wife didn't answer the door? Go home with his tail between his legs? "Uh-oh, what have we here?" He watched as Luke Holt's truck pulled into the narrow alleyway that led to the back of the building. "You sly little witch," he seethed.

Tanner was out of the car in seconds. He looked both ways before he sprinted across the road to the alley. He cursed ripely when he heard the heavy garage door slide down. The sound of a second bolt shooting home made him curse again. He kicked at Luke's tires as he continued to curse. "Son of a fucking bitch!" He ran back to his car, popped the trunk for the tool kit he always carried with him. Five minutes later he was back in the alley gouging all four of Luke's tires. His face turned ugly as he listened to the air hiss from the tires. "That will teach you to mess with my wife," he muttered.

The quiet night was shattered with the sound of a dog's ear-piercing barks. He moved then, faster than he'd ever moved in his life, his breathing ragged as he catapulted into the front seat of his car. He slouched down in the seat immediately, afraid that either Jessie or Luke would look out of one of the top-floor windows. He'd just done an incredibly dumb, stupid thing, and he knew it. J.J. would never approve. J.J. liked to think ahead, to plot and destroy. Well, J.J. wasn't exactly batting in the big leagues these days.

"Should I stay here in the car and watch the building? Why? To see what time Luke Holt leaves. If he's fucking my wife, I want to know about it," he fumed. He fired up a cigarette and puffed furiously. When the inside of the car filled up with smoke he opened all the windows. He smoked cigarette after cigarette until the pack was empty. Twice he got out of the car to stretch his legs, his anger continuing to build.

His watch told him it was 12:10 when he stepped from the car for the third time. The light spilling from the second-floor windows looked the same. Luke wasn't going anywhere unless he wanted to ride his rims. His face contorted into an ugly grimace as he envisioned his wife and Luke in bed together. There wasn't one damn thing he could do right now, and he knew it. He climbed back into the car and turned on the ignition. Tomorrow was another day. He'd root J.J. out of bed when he got home. J.J. better have a few answers since this was all his doing.

"I thought the pepper steak was pretty good. What did you think, Jessie?"

"I guess I have a lot on my mind today. It was nice of you to bring dinner, Luke. It was very good. I guess I just wasn't hungry. I talked to Arthur this evening. I think I'm going to go back to Charleston. It's going to be Thanksgiving in a few weeks, and I'd like to get settled before the New Year. As each day passes, I realize more and more how rootless I am. It preys on my mind all the time.

Charleston is the only place I truly know. Just because I wasn't happy with my family living there doesn't mean I can't be happy living there now with the dogs and . . ."

"And . . . "

"Tanner doesn't know where I used to live. He won't be able to follow me. Arthur will see to forwarding my mail. This address can still be used. I have such terrible feelings about Tanner. At some point I became afraid, and that's so unlike me. Maybe it's an intuitive thing. You'll be leaving right after Christmas. You're the only friend I have here, so there's no point in my staying here. I can sketch and sculpt anywhere."

Luke stared at Buzz and Jessie's dog as they tugged at a braided rope, the pup chasing his mother's tail as they cavorted around the kitchen. "Buzz is going to go into a tailspin when you leave. I think he's in love. You really need to give those dogs names, Jessie."

Jessie's hand started to twitch. "I . . . I more or less . . . sort of . . . if I tell you, will you laugh?"

"Me? No."

"At first I was going to call her Rosie. I tried it out on her, and she didn't pay the least bit of attention. Then just before I woke I had that bad dream again and did my usual number with the screaming. I might have scared her, I'm not sure. In my half trance I started to call her Jelly, and she responded. Isn't that strange?"

"No. Did you try calling her by name after that?"

"Yes, and she responded. Maybe she likes the sound of it. I'm calling the pup Fred. He sort of knows his name."

"I approve. More wine, Jessie? We should drink a toast. Something else is bothering you. Do you want to talk about it?"

"Actually, I don't. However, I wouldn't feel right if I didn't tell you. I'm pregnant. It . . . it happened that night when I ran to your house. At first I tried to . . . to fight him off. I'll understand if you . . ."

"If I what, Jessie?"

"If you don't want to come here anymore. If you don't think I'm a worthy friend. I don't know if it's my imagination or not but I thought . . . I had this feeling that we were moving toward . . . something else. I've been honest with you from the beginning. I don't like hiding things. I've had enough of that in my life. Does it . . . does it make a difference?"

"Of course it makes a difference but not in the way you think. I can't believe you would think it would change our friendship. You're right, too, about us moving closer to something with more meaning. Hell, I can't wait to get here in the evening. I didn't think I was ever going to get past my grief, but you and the dogs—along with Buzz—brought me out of it. Buzz is a basket of worms until he hears me start up the truck. I've never been around anyone who was pregnant. I know diddly-squat about babies. Someone told me babies are like puppies: They cry a lot, eat a lot, and poop a lot."

Jessie burst into laughter. "That's a pretty fair assessment."

"Is that why you want to move?"

"One of the reasons. For now I don't want Tanner to know. Later, when I'm settled and when I feel my roots have taken hold, I'll tell him. Right now I don't think I can handle an ugly divorce with a child as a bargaining tool. Tanner, in my opinion, is not father material. I also don't think he cares about children. He'll just use it against me. I can't believe I was stupid enough to fall for his line. I was so . . . so *needy*. Good Lord, what are those dogs barking at?"

"You stay here, Jessie, I'll take a look. They want into the garage? Did you lock the door?"

"You saw me lock it, Luke. The security lock is in place, too. Be careful."

Luke was back in the kitchen within ten minutes. "I have four flat tires with no spare in the truck. They were slashed. When Buzz sniffed the tires his hair went straight up."

"Who would do such a thing? No one knows you come here."

"Obviously someone does. All four tires, Jessie."

"This address was on the divorce papers. It would be like Tanner to do something like this. I'm sorry, Luke. You can drive my truck home or you can stay the night. Your choice."

"Do you realize I never even kissed you? I thought about it. A lot."

"I realize it. I thought about it, too. A lot. It's not our time, Luke."

"Do you think there will be a time when it is 'our time'?"

"I think so. I don't know when, though. You have commitments now, and I have things I have to take care of. I made mistakes, and I don't want to make any more. I'm not saying you would be a mistake, what I'm saying . . ."

"I know, Jessie. Are you one hundred percent committed to Charleston?"

"Not a hundred percent. I diddled with the idea of Atlanta or New Orleans. Neither one feels like it could be *home*. It's a place to start. That's what I have to do, Luke, find a starting place."

"Is there any possibility you would consider Pennsylvania?"

Jessie's heart skipped a beat. She nodded. "There is that possibility."

"I could see both of us pulling a child on a sled in the snow. It snows there in the winter," Luke said brilliantly.

"Does it?" Jessie said just as brilliantly.

"My brothers are coming home next week. I'm free then. I could go with you to, you know, check it out. I was," Luke cleared his throat, "looking forward to spending the holidays with you. For the past few years I slept late and opened a present I bought for myself and then went back to bed."

"That's pitiful," Jessie said. She told him about her last Christmas with Sophie. "Four weeks isn't much time."

"You call ahead to a realtor and tell them exactly what you want. It eliminates a lot of that looky-look stuff. That's how I found my apartment. If you put down a robust deposit, most times you can move in before the closing."

Jessie leaned across the table and reached for Luke's hand. "What about my pregnancy. If I take a step like you're suggesting, I need to be clear in my mind that you won't at some point, you know, decide it does matter after all."

"Look at me, Jessie. Who are you looking at right this second?"

"You. Luke Holt."

"Right. My name isn't Tanner Kingsley. I don't look like Tanner Kingsley, and I do not act like Tanner Kingsley. I am Luke Holt and Luke Holt has been falling in love with you for three months now. Hell, my dog's already in love with your dog."

"And all my money?"

"Give it away, spend it, it doesn't matter to me."

My God, he means it, Jessie thought. She felt dizzy and disoriented. "But you never even kissed me," she blurted.

"A sorry state of affairs."

"Are you going to remedy it?"

"Did I hear you say the choice was mine to spend the night or take your truck home?"

"I did say that."

"I made my choice."

Jessie's heart was pounding so loud in her chest she could barely hear the words she uttered. "What's your decision?"

"I'm staying. I'll sleep on the couch."

"I wish . . . it just . . . it isn't our time yet, Luke."

"I know. I just want to be close to you so that when our time does come, I'm ready."

"You really mean that, don't you?"

"I never say anything I don't mean. I'm a patient man."

"I'll remember that, Luke."

Luke grinned. "See that you do."

Jessie woke slowly to total silence. Where were the dogs? In her raspy, unused morning voice she called, "Jelly! Fred!" Both dogs bounded into the room, Buzz right behind them. The three of them sniffed the bedcovers and her pillow. If Buzz was here, that had to mean Luke was close by. Maybe he was outside with his truck assessing the damage in the bright light of day.

Ordinarily she would have tussled with the dogs for a few minutes, but not today. A feeling of panic rushed through her as she made her way to the kitchen, a towel draped around her naked body. The relief she felt at the sight of the note on the kitchen table left her weak in the knees.

> *Dear Jessie,*
>
> *The last thing in the world I wanted to do was leave. However, if we're going to head for Pennsylvania tomorrow instead of next week as we discussed, I think it best to get my own house in order. I'll be back late this afternoon. Don't be alarmed when you see a tow truck in the back. I want you to get spiffed up. I'm taking you to the*

fanciest restaurant in town and we're leaving the dogs home!

I looked out the living-room window when I got up and saw something I didn't like. Be aware that someone is either watching or observing your building. From this distance I can only say they look official. My advice would be to not open the door to anyone but me. I left Buzz as you can see. He can be downright ornery when he wants to be. Besides, like his master, he's in love.

Luke

Jessie kissed the small piece of note paper like a lovesick teenager before she clutched it to her chest. A contented smile on her face, she poured coffee. She leaned against the counter, her eyes dreamy. She read the note over and over until she had it memorized. He was in love. Like Buzz. In love with her. Was it possible? It wasn't until the ninth or tenth read that she raced to the front window. She peeked through the vertical blinds but didn't see anything out of the ordinary.

What did Luke mean by the word official? A detective possibly hired by Tanner? Someone from the senator's world? The word official bothered her. Don't open the door, Luke said. If she didn't open the door, how was she going to go shopping for a new dress? Plus, she had no vehicle if Luke took hers. She ran to the garage. The Rover was there. Luke either hitched a ride or called someone from the ranch to pick him up.

Jessie looked at the clock—8:25. The stores didn't open until ten. She had time for a nice leisurely breakfast and a quick shower. Surely Luke wasn't serious about her staying inside. Didn't he know she would want to buy a new dress? She couldn't help but wonder what he would look like in a suit. A real buttoned-up guy, she thought.

The gallery bell rang as she was scooping scrambled eggs and crumbled bacon onto the dogs' plates. She let it ring even though the dogs raced down the seven steps to the main floor. The scent of the food brought them all back on the run. They gobbled the food and ran back down the steps. Buzz's bark was loud and ferocious sounding. Fred's squeaky protests brought a smile to her face while Jelly sniffed the doorsill, emitting ugly growling sounds.

The doorbell continued to ring as she ate her breakfast, stacked the minidishwasher, and took her shower. She ignored it, singing at the top of her lungs. *Nothing* was going to ruin her day.

It was nine-thirty when she heard rather than saw activity outside the garage. She ran back to the front of the loft to peer out the window. She saw the tow truck with Luke's truck on the flat bed being wheeled onto the main road. At least now she'd be able to back out the Rover for her shopping excursion. At the same moment she spotted the empty, dark blue sedan that definitely looked *official,* the doorbell chimed. Her heart took on an extra beat as she craned her neck downward to see if she could see who was ringing the bell. The dogs barked and howled, sniffing the doorsill, the barking going from curious to ferocious to downright bloodcurdling when the bell continued to ring.

If the person really was official, it must have something to do with Senator Kingsley. She thought then about all her predecessor's logs and the ones she herself kept that were now in Atlanta. Did she dare go there to get them? Should she destroy them? Did she want to be a part of an ongoing investigation concerning Senator Kingsley? She absolutely did not. If she stopped in Atlanta on her way to Pennsylvania, would someone follow her? Should she burn the logs? A paper shredder, she thought. The phone was in her hand a second later as she dialed the house in Atlanta. Her instructions were brief and curt. Order a paper shredder to be delivered to the house no later than tomorrow morning. Have it installed in Sophie's bedroom. "I can do whatever I want with my own property," she muttered. "Ditto for my predecessor's property that was given to me." A cautionary voice whispered in her ear. *Maybe you shouldn't be so quick to destroy those logs. You might need them in the divorce settlement.* She argued with herself. *There really isn't anything in the logs other than things you observed, visits that were in the daily office logs.* The cautionary voice niggled again. *What about all those after-hour visits when the senator wanted you to stay late and told you to forget about the office log? Don't be rash.* She continued to argue. *Tanner knows about Sophie's house. So does the senator. But, do they know you inherited Sophie's estate? Do they know the Atlanta house belongs to you? Think in terms of search warrants. Maybe you should open the door the next time someone rings the bell. Forewarned is forearmed.*

A headache started to form at the base of Jessie's skull. *Perhaps a phone call to Tanner might shed some light. I can always say I'm calling to see how the senator is. Or, I could drive out to the ranch and ask in person.*

Jessie looked at her watch—10:10. If she hurried, she could scoop up a dress and shoes and drive straight out to the ranch. Luke probably wouldn't like what she was contemplating. "I'm in charge of my own life, no one else, and that includes Luke," she muttered.

Jessie gulped down three aspirin before she headed for the garage. The dogs lined up to stare at her. "I'll bring you a chew. Watch the house and don't let anyone in." She knew she was seeing things when Buzz moved his head up and down. She secured the garage door with the special key that came with the elaborate security mechanism. The official-looking car was still parked in front of her building. It was still empty, and there was no sign of pedestrian traffic. She barreled out to the road, thankful that there was no oncoming traffic. Every ten seconds she checked her rearview as well as side-door mirror for a sign of the dark blue sedan. If it was behind her, she couldn't see it. A tenseness settled between her shoulder blades as the headache pounded away inside her skull.

Being a perfect size seven, Jessie had no trouble finding a dress. She whittled down her choice to two and couldn't make up her mind, so she asked for both, one a tangerine silk and a swirling creation in electric blue. She grabbed a pair of strappy shoes with a medium-size heel from a display, asked for them in a size six and a half. If she used Sophie's Chanel bag, she was in business.

Twenty minutes later she was on her way to the Kingsley ranch, her purchases in the cargo hold of the Rover. The headache was still with her but less intense. She wondered if she was making a mistake. Time would tell.

Jessie glanced at her watch. Tanner would be arriving any minute now for lunch. That had to mean Alexis and the senator would be in attendance. She brought the Rover to a standstill in the paved area behind the kitchen. She diddled around for a few minutes, waiting to see if anyone would come to the door. She knew in her gut she was being watched from the breakfast-room window.

How quiet it was. She knocked smartly on the door, her head high, her shoulders thrown back. When the house-keeper opened the door, she smiled. "Miss Jessie, it's nice to see you."

"I came to see the senator, Mattie. Is he up to seeing visitors? If not, I'd like to see Tanner."

"Who is it, Mattie?" Alexis called from the breakfast room.

"It's Miss Jessie, Mrs. Kingsley. She came out here to see the senator."

"For heaven's sake, don't keep her standing in the kitchen. Bring her in. Set another plate. You'll stay for lunch, won't you, Jessica?"

"Thank you for the invitation, but I had a bite to eat before I came out. I'm going away for a few weeks and wanted to see the senator before I left. Is he up to visitors?"

"He really isn't seeing anyone these days, my dear. However, he was always so fond of you so I think he might make an exception. He doesn't look the same, Jessica, and he's very frail. He has good days and bad days. I'm so glad you stopped by. I'm sorry, though, that you can't stay for lunch. Tanner will be in soon."

She looked different. Thinner. Bony actually. Her face was drawn, and she had on too much makeup. The diamonds were in place, and the designer clothing hadn't changed. "Sit down, Jessica, while I tell Angus you're here. Please, help yourself to coffee and perhaps one of Mattie's muffins. She made them fresh this morning."

Jessie nodded. She perched on the edge of the chair, ready to bolt at a moment's notice. Minutes went by until Alexis beckoned her from the doorway. "Just go up and Angus is in the room at the end of the hall. He likes to look outside at the fields and he has an excellent view of the stable. He used to be an exceptional equestrian. Don't stay too long, my dear, as he tires very easily."

So she wasn't going to stay and listen. Relief washed through Jessie until she remembered the heating vents.

Alexis was being kind when she said the senator was frail. He was emaciated. His eyes were dark and glittering, set into deep sockets. His once-craggy features were gone, to be replaced with deep hollows in his cheeks, his chin loose and sagging. His nose dripped. He wiped at it constantly. The urge to cry welled in Jessie. "Senator, it's me, Jessie. I came out to see how you were doing. I was going to call, but I didn't want to intrude. I'm going away for a while and wanted to see you before I left. Is there anything I can do for you?"

"I wish there was. I remember the day you came to me. I knew you were one in a million."

"Thank you, Senator."

"They're after me, girl. I blew it. I thought I was infallible. Being on the Hill so long makes you think in those terms. By the time they nail everything down, I'll be gone, so it makes me no never mind. They pester me all day long. I miss Irene."

Jessie wasn't sure how she should respond so she said nothing, merely nodding to show she understood.

"They want to talk to you. They think you know things. Do you, child?"

"No. Everything's in the logs. Are you going to be . . . can they . . . do anything to you?"

"It all came down to money, Jessie. Irene and Harry needed it, the twins needed it. I knew how to get it, so I did. I made deals, cut corners, sold out my votes to the almighty dollar. I say I'd do it again, but I wouldn't. There can't be anything in the world worse than dying in disgrace for all the world to see. No one will remember the good things I did for this state. All my colleagues stopped returning my calls around the same time the twins stopped. That's what hurts the most. What are you going to tell them, Jessie?"

"I don't know, Senator. I guess it depends on what they ask me. Everything is in the logs. My memory is hazy at best."

The senator nodded. "Irene's farm was worth a fortune. It fetched over two million dollars. If she had sold it when all this started, I wouldn't be in this position. Why didn't she sell it, Jessie? Why did she let me put my ass on the line the way I did?"

"I don't know, Senator. Maybe back then the farm wasn't worth as much as it is in today's market. Maybe she wanted something to leave her children. I just don't know."

"They don't tell me much around here anymore, but I do know you filed for a divorce. You would have been good for this family, Jessie, but I'm not blind to my son's faults. I hate to say this, but I'm relieved. For you."

"Senator, who is J.J.?"

"Tanner's old friend from school days. He was one of the city kids that came out here every summer. Luke didn't like him. I wish Tanner had turned out like Luke. I screwed Luke over too. Could never look him in the eye again after that."

"What's J.J.'s real name?"

"Can't remember. It was a long time ago. I haven't seen him in years and years. Why don't you ask Tanner? They were like two peas in a pod. Always in one scrape or another. Alexis bailed them out so many times I lost count. He was smart, that one. He had brains and dreams."

"What kind of dreams, Senator?"

"You know, kid stuff, young-buck stuff. He was going to find the richest girl in the world and marry her so he'd never have to use that fine brain of his. He and Tanner were forever betting on one thing or another. Seems to me, old J.J. finally landed the big one and then it fell through. Tanner was mighty upset over that. He had his own thing going on. If it's important to you, Jessie, I'll try and find out."

"It's not important, Senator. You look tired. I should leave now."

"You said you were going away. Why, child? Is it because of Tanner?"

"Partly. I need to put down some roots. Tanner and I weren't meant for each other. I think you know that. All the wishing in the world can't make something out of nothing. I'm going to move on, and so will Tanner. Are you sure there's nothing I can do for you, Senator?"

"Don't tell those bastards anything, Jessie. Let them forage for whatever they think they can dig up on me. Think kindly of me once in a while."

"I will, Senator. Take care of yourself."

A strangled sound Jessie thought was laughter followed her from the room. One down, and one to go. Or was that one down and two to go?

"Jessica, please, sit and have a cup of coffee with Tanner and me. We get so tired of talking to each other. It will be nice to hear another voice for a change. I meant to tell you earlier how wonderful you look. Am I mistaken or is what I'm seeing the glow of pregnancy? You do glow, Jessica."

Tanner stopped eating long enough to say, "Pregnant? Are you, Jessie?" Tanner asked, a wistful look on his face.

Jessie's world started to crumble in that instant. Damn Alexis to hell. She wondered if she looked guilty. She tried to smile, shaking her head as she picked up a muffin, more to have something to do with her hands than anything else. She should never have come here. Mother and son looked like vultures to her. Lawyers wouldn't be able to lie about something like a pregnancy. Would they? Oh, God, why had she come here? How was she going to explain all of this to Luke? Her back stiffened. "Tanner, were you at my apartment last night?"

"I don't even know where the hell you live. Look, Jessie, I don't want this divorce. I'm contesting it. If you are pregnant, you better tell me now. A judge won't view an omission like that in a kindly way."

"Do I look pregnant to you, Tanner? A baby by you is not something I even want to think about. I'll say good-bye now. Thank you for the muffin."

The Rover blazed down the access road to rocket onto the highway leading into the city. Jessie didn't take a deep breath until she was safe in the garage.

Drained of all her emotion, she led the dogs to the loft where she curled up and was asleep almost immediately. She knew the hateful, ugly dream was going to surface but she didn't care. All she cared about was sleeping to blot out Alexis's gleeful face.

Chapter Nineteen

The look-alike golden dogs sat at attention, their gaze unwavering, as the restless, sleeping woman tossed and turned. The pup sat at the side of the bed, industriously chewing one of Jessie's loafers. Buzz whined deep in his throat, while his companion made a hissing sound of distress.

Jessie rolled over, her face contorted, her arms flailing as she sought the pillow next to her. The hair on the back of Buzz's neck stood straight up when a bloodcurdling scream ripped from her throat. Jelly was on the bed in an instant, Buzz close behind.

"Mommieee, Mommiee! No, no, take it off. Mommieee! Jelly! Jelly! Mommieee! Not mommie, not mommie!" Both dogs pushed and tugged at Jessie's arms as she rocketed from one side of the bed to the other.

Buzz barked once and then again, the sound so loud, Jessie bolted upright. Disoriented, her eyes glazed, she fought to take deep breaths as tears streaked down her cheeks. When her vision cleared, she flopped backward onto her pillows, her heart thundering in her chest. The dogs licked at the tears on her cheeks.

"I scared you, didn't I?" Jessie mumbled as she cuddled

the huge dogs. "It's okay, I scared myself this time, too." She stroked their silky heads while she waited for her heartbeat to return to normal. Ten minutes later when her heart had resumed its natural beat, she swung her legs over the side of the bed. "Okay, treats for everyone. Coffee for me. Oh, Fred, another shoe! Where's that sneaker I gave you?" The pup cocked his head to the side, waiting to see if his treasure would be taken away from him. When his mistress shrugged, he followed the crowd to the kitchen.

Jessie measured coffee into the basket, handed out rawhide chews to keep the dogs busy. A headache clawed at the base of her skull.

While she sipped at the hot coffee she replayed the ugly dream over in her mind. This dream was so much worse than the others, yet different. She'd never screamed for her mother before. Take what off? Possibly one of her sweaters. A coat? Tight shoes? A hat? She closed her eyes as the headache forged its way deeper into her skull. She reached for the aspirin bottle and gulped down four, washing them down with the coffee. From past experience she knew they wouldn't help. The headache would stay with her until she was totally relaxed, the dream fading. Maybe if she thought about Luke and the pleasant evening they'd spent together, she could unwind.

The doorbell to the gallery rang just as Jessie started to pour a second cup of coffee. Should she answer the door or not? It wasn't Luke. Luke always came to the garage door. Did she even have the energy to walk down the stairs and then have a conversation with whoever was ringing the bell? Her head continued to throb. For some strange reason the ringing bell wasn't bothering the dogs. Friend or foe? Foe of course. She had no friends other than Luke and Arthur Mendenares.

Jessie snorted, a sound of utter disgust, when the bell

rang for the third time. Coffee cup in hand, she marched down the steps, the three dogs behind her. She opened the door, stretching her leg across the narrow opening so the pup wouldn't scoot out. "Tanner!"

"I want to talk to you, Jessie."

"This is not a good time. I have a raging headache. We just spoke a few hours ago. I have nothing to say to you."

"I'd like to come in, Jessie. Are you hiding a secret lover or something?"

Jessie sighed. "Or something," she mumbled as she held the door for Tanner to enter. All three dogs sniffed his legs, circling him like Indians preparing for an attack. Despite her raging headache, she laughed aloud when Fred, unsteady on his feet, tried to lift his leg, then squatted and peed on Tanner's right shoe.

"I'll get you a paper towel. That wasn't nice, Fred. You're supposed to go on the paper. Now, Tanner, what do you want to talk about? I can give you ten minutes. I have plans."

Tanner looked around. "What is this place?"

"It's a small gallery for me to hang my sketches. The loft is where I live with the dogs. It's really quite wonderful. You were saying."

"Jessie, I don't want a divorce. I don't think you do either. I did a stupid thing, and you reacted to it. I'm really sorry. It will never happen again. I don't want us to throw away our marriage for one stupid mistake."

"It won't work, Tanner. I don't love you, and you don't love me. That's the bottom line. A marriage based on anything less can't possibly work. I'm getting on with my life, and you need to get on with yours."

"It's Luke, isn't it? Did you sleep with him? I knew it! I can tell by the look on your face."

"Were you here spying on me last night, Tanner?"

"Now why would I do a stupid thing like that? Were

you doing something you weren't supposed to be doing? You look guilty, Jessie, and you didn't answer my question?"

"What I do or don't do is no concern of yours, Tanner. I filed for divorce. We're separated. Why can't you understand that? Luke is a friend."

"If that's true, what's his damn dog doing here and where did you get those other two?"

"I don't think that's any of your business, Tanner. You need to leave now."

"I don't want a divorce, Jessie. I'm contesting it. When a judge hears how I took care of you when you didn't know what day it was, with my mother's help, of course, who do you think he's going to listen to? We had the best doctors in Texas for you. For Christ's sake, I spoon-fed you. My mother helped you take a shower and dressed you. That has to count for something. Then you betray me with Luke Holt!"

Jessie's brain raced. Would sexual allegations harm Luke's job at Penn State? Didn't Tanner's infidelity count? Of course not, he was a man. "What is it with you, Tanner? Spell it out."

"I want you. I want our marriage to work. I want us to have children together."

Jessie felt a sick feeling settle in the pit of her stomach. "It's too late. I don't want this to turn into something ugly. Can't we part with some semblance of friendship? As it stands right now, I don't like you. Don't make me hate you."

"Are you pregnant? If you are, it changes everything. Any lawyer in the world will tell you that. Are you, Jessie?"

"Tanner, it's time for you to leave. Your lawyer should talk to my lawyer. You shouldn't even be here. I'm not going to play your games. If you come back here, I won't open the door."

"All lawyers do is eat up your money and turn both parties against each other. My father can attest to that. Which brings up another point, where are you getting the money to pay rent here and to pay a divorce lawyer? I hope you aren't planning to stick me with the bill when we have luxurious accommodations at the ranch."

"That goes under the heading of my business, not yours. Tanner, we are not going to get back together. The sooner you understand the better off we'll both be."

Jessie walked to the door, the dogs at her side. Fred raced to the newspaper and tried again to lift his leg only to topple over. He peed a stream across the paper. "Good boy, Fred."

"Stupid dog," Tanner snarled. "I'm sending you the bill for these shoes."

"Fine."

At the door, Tanner turned. "This is a big mistake, Jessie. We belong together. If Luke is involved in your life, you're going to be one sorry young woman."

Jessie sighed. She didn't mean to ask the question but she did. "What does that mean? Are you threatening me?"

"It means he won't love you the way I do. It means I'll name him in the divorce proceedings. Adultery is not viewed kindly around here. Luke has always been a loner. If his fiancée hadn't died, he would have found a way to get out of marrying Allison. He's not marriage material. If that sounds like a threat, then I guess I am threatening you."

"I don't take kindly to threats, Tanner. And you are marriage material, is that what you're saying? If you are, then why were you unfaithful to me? Don't bother to answer that because I don't care. How will the courts view *your* infidelity? Go back to the ranch and don't come here again."

"Uppity, aren't we?" Tanner said.

"Tanner, who is J.J.?"

Tanner turned to stare at his wife, his face blank. Jessie thought she saw a trace of fear in his eyes.

"I never heard you mention him. Yet he seems to be a very good friend of yours. What's his real name?"

"What do you want to know that for? I think his name is John James or James John, something like that. I never called him anything but J.J. Pop used to bring city kids to the ranch in the summer and we hit it off. Guess old Luke was shooting off his mouth. He never liked J.J."

"I thought maybe he was the friend that died in the car accident on the way back to school."

"Yeah. Yeah, that's what happened. I told you, I don't like to talk about that."

"You're such a liar, Tanner," Jessie said as she pushed him through the door and then locked it. *And he was lying,* Jessie thought as she herded the dogs to the loft. The question was why would Tanner lie about an old friend? Her scalp started to prickle as an idea began to form in her mind.

Jessie sipped at her cold coffee, her mind racing. Without stopping to think she picked up the phone. Ten minutes later she had a plane reservation for Atlanta. Her flight left at seven o'clock, with a return reservation for eight o'clock the following morning. She didn't need to pack anything since she had clothes in Sophie's closets. All she needed was for Luke to agree to watch the dogs until she returned. She called him. The housekeeper told her he was on his way into town.

Jessie raced to the bathroom, where she washed her face, brushed her hair, and changed her clothes. The last thing she did was change her brown leather purse for Sophie's black Chanel handbag. She was in the garage nestling Elroy into the corner of the bag when Luke arrived. She started to babble immediately. When she finally wound down she stared at Luke before she kissed him, so hard he started to shake.

"I'll be back by noon tomorrow."

In a voice quivering with emotion Luke said, "Does this mean we aren't going to Pennsylvania tomorrow?"

"That's pretty much what it means. The day after is good. Is it good for you?"

"Do that again."

She did.

"I can drive you to the airport," Luke said, his voice still quivering.

"No. I need time to think, and I can't think when I'm around you. Are you going to stay here or go back to the ranch?"

"I think I'll stay here. Are you sure it's okay?"

Jessie smiled. "More than okay. I'm going to miss you."

"If I tell you something, will you remember it?" Luke asked gruffly.

Jessie's face turned solemn when she nodded, her eyes puzzled at Luke's tone.

"Remember that I love you."

Jessie thought she could feel her blood start to sing at that precise moment. "I think I can remember that."

"And," he prodded.

"I love you, too. Don't you forget it."

"Go on before I decide to do other things. Will you call me to let me know you arrived safely?"

"Of course. Luke, don't answer the door or the phone. I'll ring twice, hang up, and ring again so you'll know it's me."

"Gotcha."

Tanner paced, the phone wire stretched to its limits as he waited for his call to go through. He refused to meet his mother's angry gaze. When his friend finally picked up the phone, Tanner said, "You know, J.J., you are so full of shit your eyes are turning brown. I told you it wasn't going to work. I don't think there's a whole brain between you and my mother. This Jessie is not the Jessie I married. She's different and, yeah, she's probably screwing around with Luke. I could see it on her face. Just because my mother *thinks* Jessie's pregnant doesn't mean she is. She could cut and run at any moment, and where does that leave me? Hanging by a thread, that's where. All she has to do is call a few of Sophie's friends or that lawyer, and it's over. Somewhere in this world she has a set of parents. You aren't listening. I did that nice-guy shit, and it didn't work. I say we pack it in. Get yourself a legitimate job and work for your money. That's what I'm going to do. I wasted too many years of my life on this crap, and I'm fed up. I'm a rancher. I can build this place back up to the way it was years ago. Don't call me, I'll call you."

Alexis winced when her son slammed the receiver back into the cradle.

"Whatever you're planning on saying, don't," Tanner seethed. A moment later, he was in his mother's face. "I've had it with this crap. Pop took care of the ranch business. So we aren't millionaires, so what. We'll be comfortable. The garbage with Pop will blow over when . . . at some point. If it's money you're worried about or grandchildren, Bop is mine for the taking."

"I wish you wouldn't call her that. Her name is Barbara."

"It's a joke. That doesn't matter either."

"I think you need to do one last thing, Tanner. You agreed to that ridiculous prenuptial agreement, so you have no claim on her money. But if Jessica is determined to go through with the divorce and she's as rich as we've been led to believe, then if she's pregnant—as I suspect—perhaps she'll settle with you. I know you aren't interested in a child. Giving up all parental rights for a princely sum of money is something worth thinking about. *Demand* that Jessica go for a medical checkup. I believe you are within your rights to ask for that. If she has nothing to hide, there should be no problem. If she is pregnant, *demand* liberal visitation rights, holidays, summers, weekends. Call your attorney and *demand* they make a motion or whatever it is lawyers do so Jessica doesn't leave the state. Do it now, Tanner, before she gets away from you. Judge Rickle will have it in place within an hour, and Jessica will be served. I think that's how they do it. If your wife is carrying on an affair with Luke and plans on leaving or possibly marrying him, she'll want to settle with you. I wouldn't advise telling J.J. Do it *now*, Tanner. I want to hear your end of the phone conversation."

Tanner called his attorney and barked orders into the phone. When he hung up the phone he glared at his mother. "I feel like a lowlife piece of scum. I want you to know that, Mother. Just for the record, I regret all this bullshit. I regret ever laying eyes on J.J., and I damn well regret the bad time I gave my wife. Do you want to know something? In my own cockamamie way, I do love her. She's honest, she's got a good mind, she's loyal, and at one time she did love me. I screwed her over for the almighty dollar. I hate what I've turned into. I realize now I don't want her money. I never wanted it. What kind of man lies, cheats, and steals from a woman? Guys like J.J. because they are too goddamn lazy to work for a living. Do you have any idea of how much I hate that son of a bitch? If I ever find out he was the reason Jessie's friend took her life, I swear I will kill the bastard. If there was a way for me to make this all come out right, I'd do it in a heartbeat. I absolutely refuse to end up like you, Mother."

Alexis flinched. "I'm afraid you are going to have to get over it," Alexis said "I tried to warn you about J.J., but you refused to listen. I think you should go up and see your father. He's having a bad day."

"I can't right now. I'll play chess with him this evening. In case you forgot, I have a ranch to run. Don't hold dinner for me."

Alexis stared at her son's back as her brain clicked into high gear. How badly did Jessica want a divorce? What was an unborn child worth on the open market? Tanner was just talking off the top of his head. She had the rest of the day and evening to figure it out.

Jessie's watch said it was one o'clock in the morning. Would she frighten the old housekeeper if she just opened the door and walked in? Should she ring the bell and wake her? She finally opted for the bell. Moments later the light over the back door came on. The old woman peered through the curtains. "Lord have mercy, child. Is something wrong?" the housekeeper asked as she opened the door.

"No. I'm sorry I woke you, Anna. My plane was late getting in. I just need to get some things. I won't be staying long. I plan to leave first thing in the morning."

"You didn't wake me, Jessie. I don't sleep much these days. Catnaps is more like it. Are you sure you want me staying on here, paying me for baby-sitting a house that's all closed up?"

"Is it too much for you?"

"Goodness gracious, no. All I do is tidy up the kitchen and my room. The rest of the time I watch the soap operas. I don't want you to feel you have to pay me out of pity."

"It's not that at all, Anna. I wanted someone here. I couldn't bear to close up the house for good. You were part of Sophie's world for so long. You belong to this house. I really want you to stay on for as long as you can. The money has nothing to do with it."

"Sophie left me well provided for. That child was so good and kind. It breaks my heart that she's gone. Are you hungry, Jessie? I can fix you a nice dinner. I made a roast chicken. All I have to do is warm it up."

"That would be nice. Leave it in the oven, and I'll come down and get it later. I would like a soda."

The housekeeper uncapped a bottle and handed it to her. "I'll be in my room if you need me."

Jessie walked through the antebellum mansion, turning on lights as she went along. Memories engulfed her as she walked up the magnificent staircase, remembering how Sophie had screeched at the top of her lungs as she sailed down the polished banister to land on her rump.

"You're here, I can feel you," Jessie whispered as she entered Sophie's room. She grew so light-headed at her old friend's scented room she had to hold on to the doorjamb for support. When she felt ready to continue, she opened the Chanel bag and withdrew the clay figure of Elroy. She clasped it tightly in her hand as she made her way to the closet. Here, in Sophie's walk-in closet, the scent was almost overpowering. She dropped to her knees, Elroy still clutched in her hand, to pull back the long, narrow carpet covering the floor safe. With the aid of the overhead light she was able to twirl the knob to open the safe, amazed that she remembered the combination. When she heard the click of the dial she sat back on her haunches. She bit down on her lower lip, drawing blood. *I'm afraid to open it,* she thought as she looked at her shaking hands. This safe had been Sophie's pride and joy. The one place where she could hide things, store things, *safeguard* things.

Senator Kingsley's safe in Washington had been large on the outside but very small on the inside, with two small shelves. This safe was three or four times the size of the senator's. What did Sophie keep in it? She yanked at the heavy door, pulling it upward. A loose, single sheet of white paper sailed upward with the draft from the door. Jessie reached for it. A letter to her from Sophie. "Oh, God," she wailed.

Dear Sweet Jessie,
I guess things must be pretty damn sticky for you if you've opened this safe. I hope whatever is in here will make things right for you. I know you're crying. Stop it right now. That's a god-damn order, Jessie. The past is prologue. I wish I was there to make things right for you. As things draw to a close for me, I now realize each of us has to find our own peace in our own way. You can do it, Jess. I know you don't understand the path I chose. That's okay, too. What you have to do now is kick ass and take names later. There's some bubble gum in the bottom of the safe. It's probably stale, but what the hell. You were the only constant in my life, and I love you for that. Have a good life, Jessie. Don't forget your promise to me.

All my love,
Sophie

Blubbering like a baby, Jessie fumbled in the depths of the safe for the Bazooka gum Sophie had been addicted to. It wasn't stale at all, she thought as she chomped and chewed. "Get on with it, Jessie," she mumbled around the wad of gum in her mouth.

Jessie carefully removed the contents of the safe. Jewelers' boxes, deeds with rubber bands around them, the deed to the Greek island crunched into a ball lying near the bottom like it was nothing more than scratch paper.

How that deed hurt Sophie. Stacks of brown-manila envelopes with red-wax seals. There was only one envelope with the seal broken. Sophie's investigative report on Jack Dawson. "I'm so sorry, Sophie, but I need to read this. I don't want to, but I have to. I guess you knew someday I would be doing this. Well, here goes."

Jessie howled her misery and grief when she finished the last envelope. Her back to the wall, she sobbed until there were no more tears left. She felt like a robot as she struggled to her feet a long time later.

It was four o'clock when Jessie closed the safe and positioned the carpet the way she'd found it. She reached for a tired-looking gym bag on the top shelf, stuffing three of the manila envelopes, the deed to the Greek island, the Chanel bag along with Elroy, and the jewelers' boxes inside. In the small office off Sophie's bedroom, she turned on the paper shredder and proceeded to shred all the journals she'd kept over the years, along with those of her predecessor.

When she walked out of Sophie's room Jessie took a moment to savor her old friend's scent one last time. It was mind-boggling that this room could still smell like her old friend after all this time. "I know you're here in spirit, Sophie. I know it in my heart," she whispered. Jessie inhaled deeply before she blew a magnificent bubble. "On your best day you never blew one this good, Sophie," she whispered again. She knew if she ever came back here, it wouldn't be for a very long time. Perhaps one day she would return with her son or daughter. Then again, maybe she wouldn't come back. The pain she felt was all-encompassing as she made her way down the steps.

In the kitchen, being as quiet as she could, Jessie ate the dried-out chicken and a crusty potato that had no taste.

She gulped down two more sodas as she smoked half a pack of cigarettes before it was time to leave for the airport.

She left the house quietly and didn't look back, her pain and grief riding her like a wild stallion.

Sophie was right. The past was prologue.

Chapter Twenty

"You look as tired as I feel, Jessie," Luke said. "I'm going to leave, but I'll call you in the morning. Buzz needs to be back home among his things. If you want me to come back, I will."

"No, that isn't necessary, Luke. You're right, I am tired. The dogs need my attention, and the pile of mail looks important. It was a nice trip, Luke. I'm glad I checked it out. I still don't know if Pennsylvania is a place where I want to put down my roots. We'll talk about it tomorrow."

When the heavy garage door slammed against the concrete, Jessie slid the security bolt home. "I'm trying to postpone the moment when I have to deal with the mail and the answering machine, guys," Jessie said to the dogs. She refused to look inside the Rover, knowing the gym bag she'd taken from Sophie's bedroom was still on the front seat where she'd left it on her return from Atlanta. She had to deal with the contents very soon, just as she had to deal with the mail and the answering machine when she entered the apartment. If she didn't, she wouldn't be able to sleep.

At the top of the four steps leading down to the small gallery, Jessie looked at the pile of mail Luke's housekeeper had piled on the foyer table. Legal-looking envelopes, air-mail envelopes, legal-looking manila envelopes. She gathered it all up, dropping some of the envelopes in her haste, snatching envelopes from Fred.

In the kitchen, Jessie dropped the mail on the kitchen table. She debated fixing herself a strong, stiff drink versus making a pot of coffee. She finally opted for the coffee knowing she wasn't going to be able to sleep anyway. So much had happened in the last ten days. If anything, she was more confused than ever.

While the coffee perked she thought about the last ten days and how happy she'd been with Luke in the small college town. But, could she live there? Luke said he wanted to marry her when she was free. He said he would adopt her child, and they'd live happily ever after. Was it possible? She wondered what it would be like to make love to the handsome, craggy man who had once threatened to shoot her on the spot. He was a good, kind man. A man who loved animals. A what-you-see-is-what-you-get person. He said he didn't care about her money, and she believed him. He said he loved her, and she believed that, too. She believed him when he said he would give her her own space to do whatever she wanted with her life.

All of the above on one condition. As Sophie always said, there were always conditions. Settle your life, Luke had said. Find out why those ugly dreams plague you. Make peace with your parents. Find out why you think you hate your mother. Since I have no parents of my own, I want your parents at our wedding. Cut the Kingsleys out of your life so they don't invade our lives once we marry. Do what you have to do, then walk away. "One condition, my butt," Jessie muttered. "That's six conditions, or five if I don't count my parents being at the wedding."

Jessie poured coffee before she attacked the mail on the table. She sorted through it first according to the postmarks.

When she finished, her shoulders were stiff, her face expressionless as she ran to the Rover parked in the garage. She yanked at the battered gym bag, unzipping it as she raced back to the kitchen. She slammed the manila folders on top of the legal papers from Arthur Mendenares. Her heart racing, her adrenaline at an all-time high, she sorted and sifted until she had the papers exactly the way she wanted them. Then she stared at them. For a very long time.

Jessie continued to stare at the piles of papers with unblinking intensity all through the long night, her brain sorting and collating, sifting and memorizing. Occasionally her index finger moved one pile to another and then to still another.

When the twelve-cup percolator was empty and the velvety night gave way to the lacy lavender shadows of a new day, Jessie picked up the phone. She dialed the Kingsley ranch. Tanner picked up the phone on the second ring. "This is Jessie, Tanner. I want to see you. Now. That means within the hour. Thirty minutes is good. Yes, I always rise early. You're wasting time, Tanner."

Jessie broke the connection before she placed a person-to-person call to her parents' house in Barcelona. She took a deep breath, surprised at the clarity of her mother's voice when she picked up the phone. "Mama, it's Jessie. I'm fine. How are you? And Daddy? Why am I calling? To invite you to my wedding," she lied. "I plan on getting married as soon as my divorce is final. It won't be long. It was a terrible mistake. I should have known better. We all make mistakes, some more serious than others. I am pregnant, though. I'm due in the spring, when the flowers bloom. I'm looking forward to being a mother. Luke wants to meet you and Daddy. He asked me to extend an invitation to you and Daddy to visit the ranch," she lied a second time. "This weekend would be good. Yes, Mama, I know you've missed me. Is Daddy sleeping? Will you wake him and see if it's okay for you to make the trip? Luke will want to do some planning, and it is short notice. Christmas! Yes, being together for the holidays will be nice. Will you wake Daddy from his nap? Please, Mama. I have so many things to do today. I don't want to tie up the phone even though it is early in the morning here."

"Daddy. Did Mama tell you why I called? She did. Good. Daddy, what do my dreams have to do with you coming to my wedding? Luke wants to meet my parents. I never asked you for anything, Daddy. This is important to me. Mama said she was fine. Surely you can hire a nurse to make the trip with you. It isn't as though you can't afford it. I'm pregnant, Daddy. Of course I'm happy. Luke is wonderful. I'm going to give you my phone number and Luke's, so you can call me with your flight information. Luke and I will meet your plane. You sound strange, Daddy. Is something wrong? Then I'll wait for your call. Think of the holidays, Daddy. Yes, I can hear Mama in the background. I'll say good-bye for now."

Jessie looked at her trembling hands. Her stomach heaved, then settled down when her breathing returned to normal. She stared at her reflection in the glass door of the wall oven. Her eyes looked glassy, her hair on end. She stepped over the sleeping dogs to make fresh coffee. While it perked she washed her face, brushed her teeth, then ran a comb through her hair.

Back in the kitchen, Jessie sat down at the table, her gaze going to the different piles of papers lined up like yellow soldiers. Ten minutes later the doorbell rang. Neither dog moved. This time, Jessie ushered Tanner up the steps to the loft and into the kitchen.

"I hope this is important, Jessie. Before you say whatever it is you got me here for, I want to say something to you. I want you to hear me out, and I don't want you to interrupt me until I say what I have to say. I'll probably never get the guts to do it again so just listen, okay, I'm sorry about everything. I don't plan on causing you any trouble. I was pissed when I called my attorney to make all those demands. My mother and J.J. were pressuring me, and even I know that's not a valid excuse. It took me all of ninety minutes to realize what an ass I'd become. I stayed in one of the line shacks that same night, thinking about my life, about Pop and J.J. and what I'd allowed myself to become. The following day I called my attorney and canceled all the demands I'd made the day before, but the legal paperwork was already in the pipeline. I came by to tell you in person, but you were gone. Some woman spoke to me through the door and said she didn't know when you'd be back. I won't contest anything. You were right, there's no point in dragging this crap out. We need to get on with our lives. It's not a trick," Tanner said wearily.

"Why don't I believe you, Tanner?"

"I didn't give you much reason to believe me. I'm sorry I ever allowed myself to get into this position. I guess I'm more my mother's son than I thought. I know it probably doesn't make much sense to you, but it's better if you don't know . . . certain things. Jesus, when I think back, I could puke. I'm sorry for everything, Jess. I mean that, and I'm just not mouthing words here. Do you need anything? Is there anything else I can do?" At Jessie's negative nod, he said, "I didn't think so. You were always pretty self-sufficient. I admire that trait. In my own way, I'm very fond of you. I don't really know if we could have made it work or not. Part of me wants to believe we could have. The other part of me says no. As much as I hate to admit this, Luke's a decent guy. I think he might be good for you. I don't know if you're pregnant like my mother suggested or not. I don't want to know. The truth is, I don't deserve to know. I'll be at the ranch, Jess. That's if you ever need me for anything."

Jessie stared at her husband, her jaw dropping when he held out his hand. Was it a trick?

Tanner shrugged. He jammed his hands into his pockets.

"I know everything, Tanner. It's all there on the table. Your folder is the third one. Take a look."

Tears blurred Jessie's eyes as she watched Tanner's stricken face. "Where did you get this?" he asked gruffly, a look of shame on his face.

"Sophie left it for me. She never opened it, though. I found it last week when I went to Atlanta. Do you have any idea how I felt when I read that report? I felt like a slab of beef on the auction block. How could you set me up like that? All that plotting and conniving. My skin is crawling just thinking of it. What about Sophie, Tanner?"

Tanner sat down at the table. *He looks like he's in shock,* Jessie thought.

"Sit down, Jessie. I need to look at you when I tell you about . . . this," Tanner said, pointing to the envelopes and the files on the table. "You deserve to know the truth. All of it. I hope you can handle it better than I did."

"All I want is the truth, Tanner."

"Pop brought J.J. and a bunch of other kids to the ranch the summer we were juniors in high school. J.J. was slick, fast on his feet. He had an answer for everything. He was so goddamn smart it was sickening. I was a mediocre student at best. I thought he was the best thing since sliced bread. I wanted to be like him. It all came so easy to him. He had goals and dreams. Big goals and even bigger dreams. Girls fell all over him. If they didn't have money, he wasn't interested. Our senior year he came up with this idea to seek out and find the richest girls in America and make them fall for us so we would never have to work a day in our lives. He made it all sound so believable, like it really could happen. At first it was fun. I don't think I believed for a minute that it was really going to work. J.J. became so obsessed it started to make me nervous. I don't know if you know this, but Pop paid for his college education. Poor Pop, he didn't know the half of it. He does now, though. I'm so ashamed I find it difficult to look him in the eye. It's a pretty damn sorry state of affairs when your old man is ashamed of you. It's my own fault, and I'll live with it. Pop loved you like a daughter, Jessie."

"I was and still am very fond of your father. He was always very kind to me."

"He made mistakes, too. I always thought he'd die in the Senate. You know, go out in a blaze of glory. If there was a way for me to help him, I'd do it in a heartbeat. He doesn't have long to live . . . days really."

"I'm sorry to hear that. I'm glad I got to see him one last time."

Tanner fired up a cigarette. "Anyway," he said, blowing a stream of smoke, "J.J. convinced me we could make his plan work. We spent days in the library. One night we hid in the men's room and stayed through the night working with a flashlight. J.J. was like that. He had a plan, and he was going to make it work. He found your friend Sophie, and Sophie just happened to have a friend named Jessie Roland. We spent an entire year getting the lowdown on your friend. As a rule, women found J.J. irresistible, and Sophie was no different. She fell for him. He had it in the bag, megamillions, and Sophie was head over heels in love with him. J.J. was so convinced he was going to pull it off, he got cocky where Sophie was concerned and then he switched his attention to you and me. Sophie liked pillow talk. J.J. and I knew more about you than you know about yourself. When you showed up at Pop's office looking for a job, I thought J.J. was going to have a heart attack. I can't tell you what went wrong between Sophie and J.J. To this day I don't think he knows. If he does, he hasn't shared it with me. He switched up then. I was to be the savior. You had the money. Sophie told him about your trust fund, about your family. As I said, she liked pillow talk."

"This is . . . is reprehensible. Sophie's dead because . . . God, Tanner!"

"You're right, it is reprehensible. That's when I wanted to pack it in, but J.J. wouldn't hear of it. When you said you were pregnant J.J. thought we had a lock on it. I tried to wiggle out. I didn't want to . . . marry you under those kinds of circumstances. We had fun. The sex was great. You were right, we weren't in love. J.J. said your money would make up for all that. At that point my mother was working on her own agenda. She could literally *smell* your money. By the way, it was a three-way pot. J.J. was to get a third, I was to get a third, and my mother was to get a third. This isn't going to go down well, Jess, so hold on. You said my mother pushed you down the steps that night you lost the baby. It was the last thing you said to me before you blacked out. She denied it, of course. That would have made her a murderer, and I couldn't believe that of my own mother. You didn't remember any of it, so I left it alone. When we brought you home from the hospital, I kept waiting for you to say something, to remember what you'd said, but you never did. Without telling him anything in particular, I asked the doctor what his opinion was, and he said it was possible you had some short-term memory loss. He also said you were in shock. Obviously, you still don't remember, which leads me to think the doctor was right and you really were in shock. I wanted to take you away after that, but the dark stuff hit the fan with Pop. You were so depressed, and then I got depressed. My mother doted on you. She made sure you got dressed, that you got outside in the fresh air. She had the cook make you tempting dishes to try and get you to eat. She'd go into town and buy you trinkets, send you flowers. She seemed sincere to me. The two of you got along very well during that time. It was a god-awful time for all of us. I wanted to do the right thing. I even tried. I just want you to know that. For whatever this is worth, Jessie, I don't think Sophie killed herself over J.J. I think her suicide had something to do with her mother."

Jessie stared at her husband as she tried to comprehend what he'd just told her. "I wish you hadn't told me that, Tanner. My mind is totally blank when it comes to that accident. It's just one more thing I have to deal with now."

"I'm really sorry, Jessie. I did tell Pop, though. If you ever remember, I want you to tell me. I think about it all the time. Greed is . . . ugly."

Jessie shook her head to clear her thoughts. Later she would think about what Tanner had just said. "In the end, Sophie knew about Jack Dawson. That is J.J.'s real name, isn't it?" Jessie asked in a harsh whisper.

Tanner nodded.

"Where's J.J. now?"

"Probably lurking in the bushes somewhere. He's one sick bastard, I can tell you that. I'm not much better, but I did come to my senses. I don't know J.J. anymore. I don't know what he's capable of. I've cut him loose. Go away from here, Jess. Go as far as you can. Lose yourself somewhere. You have the resources to do that."

"What about you, Tanner?"

"I'll run the ranch. I'll probably end up marrying Bop. Maybe we'll have kids, maybe we won't. Everyone thinks she has money. She doesn't. Neither does her family. They keep up appearances, that's about it. We've always had a 'thing' for each other."

"What will happen after your father . . . goes?"

"That will be the end of it. No more headlines, no more lawyers, no more scandals. Of course they'll dredge it up every year on the anniversary date. I'll just have to live with it. I'm in no position to cast stones, Jess. Pop took care of everything at my mother's insistence. After Irene's death and the twins' cutting him off, he just gave up. The thing he found hardest to deal with was Irene's failure to sell the farm during her lifetime. If she had done that, Pop wouldn't be in the mess he's in. Resa seems to think it was Irene's way of getting one last jab at Pop for having the affair with my mother. I don't know what to think. The ranch is in Resa's and my names, with a provision that my mother live out her days there. Resa wants no part of it and is going to sign over her share to me. She's happy. She wants to start a family. She'll never come back here."

"Mr. Mendenares gave me a check Sophie wrote to Jack Dawson for a million dollars. She said he earned every penny of it. I tore it up."

"Good for you, Jess. Listen, I have to get back to the ranch. I've taken care of everything on my end with my attorney. There won't be any glitches along the way. What should we do here, shake hands, wave, kiss each other on the cheek? What?"

Jessie's smile was tired and wan. "What do you feel like doing?"

"Hugging you."

Jessie opened her arms.

"You feel good, and you smell nice," Tanner said.

Jessie laughed. "So do you. I am pregnant, Tanner."

"I'm going to pretend I didn't hear that."

"At some point, I'll bring him or her back to see you. I don't know when that will be. I'll tell the child about you. It may take a long time, Tanner. If it's a girl, I'm going to call her Sophie."

"Sophie's a nice name," Tanner said with a catch in his voice.

"If it's a boy I don't know what I'll name him. Something strong-sounding."

"Do you forgive me, Jess?"

"No. Someday I'm sure I will, but not right now."

"I can handle that. What are you going to do with all that money you inherited from Sophie?"

"I have no clue. I'll think of something."

"Take care of yourself, Jessie."

"You too, Tanner."

Jessie sat quietly for a long time after Tanner left, her eyes on the sleeping dogs. It was midmorning when she reached for their leashes. "I need some fresh air. How about a nice long walk and a run in the park. We'll get an ice-cream cone on the way home."

It was cool with a hint of rain. Jessie shivered inside her windbreaker as she trotted along behind the dogs. In the park, she sat down on a bench to remove the dog's leashes. They ran then, coming back to check on her every few minutes. She smiled indulgently as she looked around. There were few people in the park today. *Too gloomy and overcast,* she thought. *Parents only like to go to the park when the sun is shining.*

Two hours swept by before the dogs returned to the bench one last time for the liver treats Jessie carried in her pockets. They were docile and tired from all their running when she hooked the leashes to their collars. "Time to go home."

Coming toward her was a mother with a stroller and a toddler holding on to the side of the stroller, a magnificent German shepherd next to the little boy. The dogs eyed one another as they came abreast on the narrow path. A rosey-cheeked baby slept soundly in the stroller. Farther down the path a young man was jogging toward the little family, a box of popcorn in his hands.

"Feed the ducks, Daddy, feed the ducks," the toddler squealed.

"I'm sorry," the young mother said. "We seem to be taking up the whole path."

"That's okay," Jessie smiled. "Fred isn't used to other dogs. He just wants to smell your dog who, by the way, is beautiful."

"Thank you. You look like you have your hands full. Posy is gentle. She's wonderful with the children."

"How old is the baby?" Jessie asked. "I'm pregnant," she blurted.

"Congratulations," the young mother said. "This is it for us. Two kids and a dog are about all I can handle."

"What's your name, big guy?" Jessie asked the toddler.

"Harry. Scary Harry. Right, Dad?"

"He used to love to play peek-a-boo when he was little. It was a game," the father grinned.

"What's your sister's name?" Jessie asked.

"Hers name is Hannah. Hannah Banana," the toddler squealed.

Jessie stared at the little family, her eyes rolling back in her head. A moment later she was on the ground, the dogs barking shrilly in her ear. When she came to, Fred and Jelly were licking at her face. "What happened?" she mumbled.

"You failed asleep on the ground," Harry said importantly.

"You fainted," the young mother said. "I used to faint when I was pregnant with Harry. I never had that problem with Hannah, though. I wasn't taking my prenatal vitamins. Be sure to tell your doctor. Don't dwell on it either. Pregnancy is a wonderful thing. We're going to drive you home. No, no, it's fine. Besides, it's going to rain any minute now. A nice cup of hot tea or some hot soup will fix you right up. The color's back in your cheeks. How are your feeling?"

"A little wobbly," Jessie said as she held on to the father's hand. The toddler was eating the popcorn from the ground. "Things have been rather stressful lately," Jessie said as she eyed the sleeping baby. Something tugged at her memory but refused to surface. "I would appreciate the ride if you're sure it isn't too much trouble."

"No trouble at all. What's one more person and two more dogs?" the father said, a worried look on his face.

"That's what I always say," the young mother chirped. "We'll just manage. It's that simple."

I have to get home. I have to get home. I need to get home, Jessie's mind shrieked as she climbed over the dogs, the stroller, and Scary Harry, who was squealing about sleeping on the ground without pajamas.

Jessie's nerves were stretched to the breaking point when she tried to punch in the numbers on the intricate lock and at the same time offer effusive thanks for the ride home. Did she have the couple's name and address? She vaguely remembered holding a business card in her hand at one point.

What in the name of God was wrong with her? Was she losing her mind? Was she on the verge of a nervous breakdown? Was it her pregnancy that caused her to faint or was it Tanner's visit?

None of the above. It was the baby. The baby in the stroller.

The dogs raced up the steps to the loft, their leashes clicking and clacking on the steps. Jessie ran after them to remove the leashes. She handed out rawhide chews before she inched her way to the corner of the kitchen where she slid to the floor, cowering. Tears puddled in her eyes and ran down her cheeks as her heart pounded inside her chest.

She was still sitting in the corner, hours later, when Luke let himself into the garage. He called her name as he climbed the steps to the loft.

"Jessie? What's wrong? Are you all right? Look at me, Jessie. Tell me what happened." He dropped to the floor to take her in his arms. "Tell me everything. Between the two of us we can make it right. You're safe. The dogs are here. Everything is fine."

The words rushed out of her mouth like speeding bullets. "One minute I was standing up with the dogs, and the next thing I knew I was on the ground. The woman said I should be taking prenatal vitamins. I have them but haven't been taking them. I meant to, but I didn't. It wasn't Tanner. That's a closed chapter. I didn't hit my head or anything. I was looking at the baby. That was the last thing I remember until Scary Harry said I was sleeping on the ground without pajamas. They were such a nice family, Luke. They brought me home in this junky station wagon full of dog hairs, kids' junk, and groceries. They were so happy. I could tell they're having a hard time making ends meet. I have to do something for them. I will, too, as soon as I figure out what's wrong with me. It must have something to do with the baby. I was fine until I . . ."

"What's wrong? You were fine until what?"

"It must not have been the baby because I was looking at her the whole time we were talking. She was in a rickety stroller and facing me. It wasn't a baby carriage with the front closed up."

"What were you talking about? Maybe someone said something that triggered something in your mind."

"Small talk. They were going to feed the ducks. The toddler said his name was Scary Harry and his father explained that he liked to play peek-a-boo when he was a baby. Then he said . . . he said his sister's name was . . . was . . ."

"What was it, Jessie?"

"Hannah. Then he giggled and said, 'Hannah Banana.' I guess that's when I fainted."

Luke laughed. "You have to admit, it is kind of funny. Scary Harry and Hannah Banana. They sound like a wonderful family. Did you ever know anyone named Hannah?"

"No, but my heart is racing. It's hard for me to breathe, Luke."

"It's okay, Jessie. There's nothing wrong. Relax, take deep breaths. Nothing is going to hurt you. I'm here. The dogs are here. Everything is fine. Come on now, deep breaths. One, two. That's it. Relax."

Jessie's voice rose until it turned into a wild shriek. "I can't breathe. I can't breathe. No! No!"

"You *can* breathe, Jessie. Take a deep breath. Nothing's going to hurt you. I'm here. Everything is fine, *Hannah,*" he crooned, his tight grip on her arms relaxing. "It's all right, *Hannah.* "

Dumfounded, Luke watched as Jessie calmed immediately at the sound of the name Hannah. He brought her close to his chest, stroking her head as he whispered words he couldn't remember later.

"I have an idea. Why don't I make us a nice omelet. You clear the table. What is all this stuff, Jessie?"

She told him.

"Do you believe him?"

"Yes. That part of my life is over. The divorce will go through without any problems. I'll call Arthur this evening and tell him everything. You called me Hannah a few minutes ago? Why?"

"I don't know why, Jessie. You calmed down immediately. Somewhere in the back of your mind the name is important. What is *this* stuff, Jessie?"

"I guess you could say it's my life. Sophie was big on doing investigative checks on everyone in her life. My life, too, as it turns out. There's a report here on my parents that I don't understand. By the way, Luke, I have a confession to make. I called my parents and asked them to come here. I invited them to your ranch. There's something in the report I don't understand. You read it, and I'll make the omelet."

"Are you sure you want me to read this, Jessie? I don't know if I have the right to read something so personal about people I don't even know. It's such an invasion of privacy."

"I want you to read it, Luke."

"Then I'll read it."

"Hannah is a pretty name, isn't it?"

"Yes, it is."

Chapter Twenty-One

Thea Roland swallowed the handful of pills her husband handed her. She looked so pitiful, Barnes looked away. There were days when he thought he loved his wife and days when he knew he hated her. Today was one of the days when he hated her.

"How can you sit there like that, Barnes? Aren't you even the least bit excited to be going to the States to meet Jessie's beau? She called us, Barnes. After all this time she must have finally realized how much we love her. She wants us at her wedding. Her beau wants to meet us. It's just so wonderful. I prayed for this. Day and night, Barnes, I prayed for her to do this. In just a few days it will be Christmas. That makes it all the more wonderful. Why am I talking to myself, Barnes? If you're worried about me, don't be. I did everything you said, I quit drinking and smoking. I take all my pills. I've been eating three meals a day and I take a half-mile-long walk and a nap. I'm fine. I'm up to the trip. I don't need a nurse, and I don't want a nurse. Get rid of her. I don't want my daughter thinking I'm an invalid. I feel vibrant. I feel alive. I feel loved. If you don't say something, Barnes, I'm going to throw this book at you."

"It's the beginning of the end, Thea. I don't for one minute believe the story Jessie told us. I think she has finally remembered, and it's all going to come crashing down around us once we return. It seems like I've been warning you about this forever, and now it's finally coming to pass. You need to open your mind, Thea. What will you do if we get there and Jessie knows? What will you say? How will you defend what we did?"

"That isn't going to happen. Our daughter would never . . . I want you to stop thinking like that. Jessie loves us. She was too little to remember. You're worrying needlessly. She wants us there, so you can give her away at her wedding. The father of the bride. It sounds so wonderful. Almost as wonderful as mother of the bride. Do you think I'll be able to dance with the groom at the reception? Maybe once around the floor. Did anyone ever go in the pool, Barnes?"

"No, and no one has ever played tennis on the court either. Thea . . . do you . . . do you ever feel any remorse for what you did? How can you tune it out like this? Every day of my life I think about it. I have never been as fearful in my life as I am right now. Can't you see what is happening?"

"No. I don't think about it. How can our daughter's invitation make you fearful? It's the sun, Barnes, it makes you overreact. It was a long time ago. Jessie is mine. Finders keepers, Barnes. Anyone who leaves a child alone deserves whatever happens. It's a good thing I was the one who *found* her. Look at the wonderful life we gave her. Jessie is my daughter. That's the end of it, Barnes."

"What if I'm right, Thea? What if Jessie remembers, and this is all a trick to get us back in the United States so we'll be arrested? Thea, you have to listen to me. I know she's remembering. I know it as sure as I'm sitting here."

"No one will take her seriously. We'll say she was always a troubled child, and we did everything we could for her during her early years, hoping she would outgrow what she perceived as her troubles. A child of two cannot possibly have a clear memory of *anything*. We have all her papers, her adoption records. I told you, I don't want to discuss this any longer. You *paid* for her, Barnes."

Barnes's shoulders started to shake. "For God's sake, will you listen to me. Everything was forged. It was never real. You have to face the truth. Thea, do you have any idea at all of what I've gone through all these years? Do you have even a clue about what it was like for me?"

"You're just nervous. It happens to all of us as we get older. We paid for her, Barnes. That's the end of it."

"I kept a scrapbook, Thea. I have every single article that was ever written about the kidnapping."

"Stop using that word. We adopted Jessie. You should never have done that."

"We kidnapped her. We did not adopt her. I had to do it. It was my way of punishing myself every day of my life. Every damn day since that hateful day, I've gone to the library to look for articles. I copied them. Then I'd go home, paste them in the book and get sick. Every goddamn miserable day, Thea."

"I didn't tell you to do that. Stop it right now, Barnes. No one knows but us. We paid tens of thousands of dollars for her."

"I'd be willing to bet my last dollar Jessie's parents never spent a penny of that money. If you think for one minute Janice Ashwood didn't know, then you are a fool. She put two and two together early on. She didn't buy into that adoption business like you thought she did. Why else do you think she cut her ties with you?"

"As young girls, Janice and I were dear friends. When each of us married and went our separate ways, the friendship deteriorated. She was a loose woman, Barnes. I couldn't tolerate something like that. I felt sorry for Sophie. Now they're both dead. What kind of mother leaves her child in the care of a nanny and a housekeeper? Not someone I want to call a friend. None of our other friends kept up the friendship with her either. You know as well as I do that if she was home three days out of the year, it was a lot. She had no morals, Barnes. If she knew, as you seem to think, she would have told Sophie, and Sophie would have told Jessie. You're worrying needlessly."

"I'm telling you, she knew," Barnes insisted.

"She's dead, so it doesn't make any difference. When we left to go to California I dropped her a note. Then I wrote again later and told her about the adoption. If all our other friends believed it, why wouldn't Janice? I was ill then, and they all accepted the fact that you were taking me away for a change of scenery. You're just a worrywart. I'm getting sick of this conversation, Barnes. How many times do I have to say it?"

"Forever. I have never been able to reconcile what we did. There is nothing worse in this world than guilt. I think I would have killed myself a long time ago if it wasn't for the knowledge you couldn't survive without me. Do you know how many times I dialed Jessie's parents' phone number? I never told you about that, did I? I'd call, listen to the hope in their voice, then hang up. I cried, Thea. I cried for them. I always did it from a phone booth so the calls could never be traced back to us. We robbed them, Thea. We stole their child and claimed her as our own."

"I *found* her, Barnes."

"Goddamnit, Thea, you did not find her. You stole her, and I aided and abetted you. You need to look this full in the face before we return to the States. You need to be prepared."

"I am prepared to meet my daughter and to spend Christmas with her. Do we have all the presents? Do you think Luke will like the Rolex watch we bought for him? I know my sweet love is going to love the diamond pendant with matching earrings. I think we should buy them a summer home on St. Simons. What do you think, Barnes? A large house with a connecting suite so we can visit as often as we want."

"Look around you, Thea," Barnes said wearily. "Carry the memory of all the bright flowers, the golden sunshine, and the sparkling blue water with you. When they cart us off to jail, everything will be gray and institution green. There won't be any flowers or sunshine. We'll have to wear prison garb and eat greasy, starchy food. There will be no hairdressers or manicurists. We'll be living in a cell with bars and locks with a toilet and a sink. You'll have to work for six cents an hour. I'll be making license plates and you'll be washing other people's dirty underwear. The inmates do awful things to you in prison. You need to listen to me, Thea. We will not be together. We will be separated. We won't even be near one another. If you have one of your spells, I won't be able to help you."

Thea jerked upright in the chair she was sitting on as she listened to her husband's desperate-sounding voice. For the first time in her life she felt fear. "Why . . . why are you saying these things? Did Jessie say something? Is it just a feeling? Did you call *those people* again? Does Christmas have something to do with it?"

"It's what Jessie didn't say, Thea. To my ears she sounded like she was lying. It came so out of the blue. The last time she called she said she was going to seek help for the dreams. She has a dog. I heard it barking in the background. That alone might trigger her memory. Now, do you understand?"

"A dog! Jessie has a dog! What kind of dog, Barnes?"

"Probably the same kind of dog that was with her that day. I told you, Thea, she's starting to remember." The naked fear Barnes saw in his wife's face tore at his heart.

"Listen to me, Thea. I have an idea. I know you aren't going to like it, but hear me out. Please. Since the doctor said you were well enough to travel, I suggest we go to Argentina. I still have all the papers to make that possible since we were going to do it once before. We can get lost there. No one will ever find us. But, before we go, we have to call the Larsons and tell them where their daughter is. Or, we call Jessie and tell her the truth. We can do so much good, Thea. Maybe in some small way we can make up for what we did. We have a lot of money. We can volunteer our time in orphanages. We're too old to be parents, but we can be grandparents to a lot of parentless children. Children no one wants. You can buy them things, Thea. You can play with them and love them. Those places are drab and colorless. We can bring sunshine into their lives. Somehow, some way, we need to atone for what we did. Please, Thea. I need some peace in my life and so do you. If you don't agree for our sake, do it for Jessie. She deserves to know her real parents."

"We'll never see her again, Barnes," Thea said tearfully.

"A just punishment we both deserve. If we go to prison, we'd never see her anyway. I don't see that we have a choice, Thea, truly I don't."

Thea continued to cry. "What about the presents, Barnes? It's almost Christmas."

"When Jessie left us, she didn't take anything we'd given her. She won't want them, Thea. If we leave today, we can make a wonderful Christmas for many, many children. We can make it Christmas every day of the year if that's what you want. I need to try and cleanse my soul, Thea. So do you."

"Can we at least call to say good-bye?"

"No, Thea. Let's decide now how we're going to do this. My suggestion would be to ship all the scrapbooks to Jessie. Phone calls can be traced too easily. I can take them to the airport and have them put on the flight we were going to take. If we leave this afternoon, we'll be in Argentina by the time Jessie gets her packages. Close your eyes, Thea, and imagine the look of wonderment on her face and her parents' faces when they finally meet. Think of it as Jessie's Christmas miracle. Well, Thea?"

"We'll never know about her baby, will we? Will God forgive me, Barnes?"

"No, Thea, we'll never see Jessie's child. I don't know if God will forgive either one of us. I pray that He will."

"When Jessie finds out, she's going to hate us."

"She already hates us, Thea. The poor child just doesn't know why. We have to live with it, Thea."

"All right, Barnes. Will you pray for me, too. I don't think God will listen to me."

Barnes felt his voice crack. "God listens to all His children, Thea. You have to be sure, my dear. Once we decide, there's no turning back."

"I know, Barnes. My heart feels . . . so empty. I don't know if I can love a strange child. I wanted to love Sophie, but I couldn't. I blamed her for everything."

"It was a mistake, Thea. You weren't thinking clearly. Sophie's gone now. God is taking care of her. I think we should travel light. We can buy whatever we need when we get to Buenos Aires. I'm going to package up the scrapbooks and take them to the airport. I'll cancel our flights to the States and arrange our new flights while I'm there. I'll have to stop at the bank and make some new arrangements. I shouldn't be more than a few hours."

"Is this truly the only way, Barnes?"

"It is the *only* way."

"I'll be ready to leave when you return."

"Thea?"

"Yes."

"I feel . . . I feel peaceful all of a sudden. Do you?"

"No, Barnes. Perhaps I don't deserve peace. Time will tell. Go now, take care of your Christmas miracle. I'll be fine. I'm just going to sit here in the sun and count the petals on the flowers. It will help to pass the time."

"I won't be long."

"Take your time. Even I know miracles don't happen in seconds."

Thea leaned back in the comfortable chair she always sat in. She rang a tiny silver bell before she unclasped the locket she was never without. "Bring me some cigarettes and a double shot of Jack Daniel's. Fetch a clean ashtray, too, Dolores."

Thea sat for a long time in the warm sunshine. She didn't touch the drink with the melting ice cubes or the fresh package of cigarettes. She only had eyes for the miniature picture of Jessie in the gold locket. "Finders keepers, my sweet love. Finders keepers." When the pain came she didn't bother to clutch her chest. She knew the end of her life was upon her. She kissed the small picture one more time before she drew her last breath.

Thea Roland was cremated six hours later. Barnes carried the square metal box that was wrapped in coarse brown paper and tied with string. The box was still warm when he boarded his midnight flight to Buenos Aires. He placed it gently on the first-class seat next to his own; Thea's reserved seat.

He slept deeply and peacefully with the knowledge that the ugliest deed of his life was finally going to be made right.

Jessie stood back to survey Luke's handiwork. "It's a beautiful tree, Luke. It smells wonderful, too. Wherever did you get these gorgeous ornaments?"

"My mother collected them. Some belonged to my grandparents. Each year she added a few new ones. She saved all the stuff I used to make in school. They're kind of brittle, but I guess macaroni wreaths can survive anything as long as you spray paint them. I always hang them front and center. I think I was in the fourth grade when we made jewelry boxes for our mothers at Christmastime. First we painted a cigar box, then we laid out the macaroni shells to spell our mother's name, glued them, and sprayed them red and green. We glued velvet on the bottom. My mother kept her jewelry in it until the day she died. Not the dime-store stuff, the real *jools*. My dad gave her an emerald bracelet that year. She put it right inside. As I got older, I'd often go into her room to see if her stuff was still in it. Each time a piece of macaroni fell off, she'd glue it right back on."

"How wonderful. That's such a nice memory. I don't have any like that. Christmas was always . . . I don't know . . . there was always *so much*. Half the time I didn't open everything until days later. We made things in school, but my mother just put them in a drawer. One Mother's Day we planted a marigold in a milk carton. The flower was really pretty, like soft butter. I saw it in the kitchen trash a day or so later. My best memories are the ones where Sophie and I were together. I miss her so much. Do you think there will ever come a time when I don't get all choked up at the mere mention of her name?"

"In time. Everything takes time, Jessie. You have to open yourself up, though. So, do we do tinsel or garland?"

"Tinsel. It makes it all shimmery when the lights are on. Tell me what's in the present. I'll tell you if you tell me," Jessie teased.

"Oh, no. You have to wait till Christmas Eve. That's how we do things around here. I don't think Buzz ever got so many presents. Jelly has quite a few, too. I see two for me, two for you, and umpteen zillion for the dogs. It does look festive, I'll say that."

Jessie laughed. "The paper and the ribbon cost more than the gift. One year Sophie gave me seven pairs of underwear with my name and the day of the week on them. I used to go into the bathroom at school to change into them because my mother thought they were tacky. I loved them. I was devastated when I outgrew them. Phone's ringing," she said cheerfully.

"I'll get it. Don't even *think* about climbing that ladder to put the star on top. I'll do it."

"You're pretty bossy today. It must have something to do with all those watered-down spirits we've been consuming." Jessie giggled as she hung a glass ball with a hand-painted old-fashioned Santa on it that was so beautiful it took her breath away.

"Jessie."

"Uh-huh. I hope you're going to tell me that was my father on the phone with his flight information. I thought they'd be here by now."

"I don't think they're coming, Jessie. That was the airport. They said a large package addressed to you at this address was put on their flight this morning. Your parents did have reservations, but canceled them. I'll pick up the package if you want me to."

"They're not coming? But . . . my mother said they were. Daddy agreed. Maybe something happened. Do you think I should call? It's probably a box of Christmas presents. I would appreciate you picking it up if you don't mind. I'll finish the tree and, no, I will not attempt to hang the star. I think I will call my father as soon as I can locate his number. I must have my address book with me in my purse."

Jessie's mood of exuberance changed to one of trepidation when she finally located her address book and placed a person-to-person overseas call. She felt nervous and jittery when the call took longer than anticipated. When the operator came back on the line to say the phone was disconnected, Jessie said, "Are you sure?"

"Yes, ma'am."

"Can you find out when it was disconnected?"

"I'll try, ma'am."

Jessie waited, her heartbeat quickening at the silence on the other end of the line.

"Ma'am, it was disconnected at two o'clock Barcelona time."

"I see. Thank you. Have a nice holiday."

Jessie sat down on the bottom step of the ladder. Her mind whirling, she watched the dogs sniff and scratch at the pile of presents under the tree. *What time is it in Barcelona now? Five hours ahead of us*, she thought. That meant it was one o'clock in the morning in Barcelona. "Such a brilliant deduction, Jessie," she muttered to herself.

A small worm of fear started to crawl around inside Jessie's belly. Nothing short of a catastrophe could keep her mother from coming to the States. Why would they disconnect the phone if they were still there?

Something was wrong.

It was nine-thirty when the front doorbell rang. The dogs leapfrogged to the front foyer as Jessie opened the door. "Western Union, ma'am. I have a cablegram that was routed to our offices for Miss Jessica Roland Kingsley. Sign here."

Her heart thundering in her chest, Jessie signed for the cable. Her hands shook so badly she could barely open the envelope. The message was short and concise.

Mrs. Dorthea Roland died today at noon. Her body was cremated at four o'clock.

Jessie gasped as she reached out to the banister for support. She looked at the cable a second time. It was signed "Barnes Roland." There was no "Dear Jessie," no "Love, Daddy." Why did he say "Mrs. Dorthea Roland"? Why didn't he say, "Your mother passed away"?

Jessie lowered herself to the steps, the dogs at her feet. She was still sitting there when Luke returned an hour later, a large cardboard box under his arm.

"Ho! Ho! Ho! I come bearing Christmas presents. I hope the tree is done. Jessie! What's wrong?" Luke said dropping to his knees at the bottom of the steps.

Jessie handed him the cable.

"I'm sorry, Jessie. Do you want to go over there? If you do, I can make the arrangements. It might be a little rough with the holiday flights, but a death takes precedence. I'm sure we can get you an emergency flight. Or, you could charter a flight."

Jessie shook her head. "I knew something was wrong. I felt it all day. Actually, I've felt it for a long time now. I don't feel anything. I want to feel sadness, but I don't. My mother died, and I don't feel anything. That certainly doesn't say much for me as a daughter. I did try to call, but the operator said the phone was disconnected. That must mean my father left to go somewhere. As much and as often as they squabbled, they were lost without one another. He had Mama cremated so she would always be with him. What am I supposed to do, Luke?"

"Whatever feels right. I think you're in shock right now. I'll make some tea. My mother always made tea when things weren't . . . right. Tea was always a magic word in our house."

"When I spoke with Mama she said she was fine. She used to . . . when she wanted more attention than I was willing to give, she'd plead illness to throw guilt on me.

Daddy would have said something. People don't just . . . die. Well, I guess they do, but I never thought it would happen to my mother. She was really excited about coming back to the States. Why didn't Daddy call me? This cable is so strange, so unlike him. He must be in shock, but he usually has a handle on things. Luke, don't you think the wording in the cable is strange? It sounds like a stranger wrote it, not my father. Why did he sign it 'Barnes Roland?' Doesn't he consider himself my father any longer?"

"Why don't you open the box, Jessie. Maybe they wrote you a letter to send along with the gifts. I'm sure your father was in total shock. He did what he had to do. Men aren't good at things like that—in my opinion. Do you want me to open the box or make tea first? We'll sit in front of the tree with the dogs, drink our tea, and open the box. How does that sound?"

"It sounds *grim*, Luke. Shall I give each of the dogs a present? Will you listen to me? I sound like things are . . . normal. My mother just died, my father had her cremated, and he's nowhere to be found. I don't feel any kind of emotion, and I'm going to sit here, drink tea, and open presents. What's wrong with this scene? What's wrong with me?"

"Nothing's wrong with you, Jessie. Stay put till I come back."

Luke stood in the doorway, the tea tray in his hands, staring at Jessie and the dogs. How lost and vulnerable she looked. He felt his chest swell as an overpowering protectiveness washed over him. He had to do something to wipe the stricken look from her face. Just when things were starting to look up for her this had to happen. Death was never easy, as he well knew, but death at this particular time of year was always more traumatic.

"It's hot, Jessie, be careful," Luke said, setting the tray on the floor. He sat alongside of her, a kitchen knife in his hands. "It's taped and tied. Are you ready to open it?"

"I guess so. Mama did love to shop."

Luke's jaw dropped when he folded back the stiff flaps of the cardboard box. "There aren't any presents, Jessie. Just some scrapbooks."

Jessie sighed. "Mama loved to take pictures. I guess they're the family albums. Daddy must want me to have them. I don't want to look at them, Luke. My mother was incredibly photogenic. Daddy, too. I always looked so . . . *round.* "

"If you let me look at your baby pictures, I'll let you look at mine. Why do mothers always want to take that bare-assed photo of you they pull out to show your girl-friend the first time she visits?"

"I'd love to see your baby pictures, but I have none to show in return. Mama said Daddy didn't know how to work the camera or he'd run out of film. She wasn't good about taking baby pictures. Then when I was two or so they took me to a studio for portraits. From that point on there are all kinds of pictures. Sophie was always grum bling that we didn't have baby pictures to compare. It would have been nice, though, to have some, so when my own baby arrives, I could, you know, compare."

Luke poked around the box. "There are four of them. Once your dad got the hang of the camera, he must have gone wild. Let's look at least one of them."

"All right. Remember now, I look *round.* That's another way of saying I was chubby until I was in my teens."

"Look at you now! These aren't photo albums, Jessie. Look, they're full of newspaper clippings. Old ones. They seem to start around 1957. Jesus!" Luke slammed the photo album closed and tossed it back in the box.

"What do the clippings say? Are they about my dismal dance recitals, my tinny piano recitals, my command birthday parties?"

"None of that. They . . . they're about a kidnapped child named . . . named Hannah Larson."

"What? Let me see that! I don't understand," Jessie said flipping through the pages. "Why would my parents keep something like this? Who is Hannah Larson?"

"I suspect she's you, Jessie. These are your missing baby pictures." Luke's arm went around her shoulder.

Jessie shook off his arm. "Are you saying I was kidnapped and that I'm Hannah Larson?"

"That would be my assumption. It certainly would explain the dreams, and look at this. The Larsons had a dog named . . . Jelly. Read this article, Jessie, it will break your heart. You always scream for Jelly in your dreams. I guess when you were snatched, for lack of a better word, the dog broke loose and ran after the car."

Jessie wrapped her arms around her knees as she rocked back and forth, tears rushing down her cheeks. "They kidnapped me! They stole me from my parents! Oh, Luke!"

"Shhh, it's going to be all right."

"I thought I was adopted. Sophie ran this investigative report on my parents. She was always doing stuff like that. There really wasn't much in the report. My parents lived in Atlanta. Then they moved to California after my sister died. We moved to Charleston, South Carolina, the year I started kindergarten. There was no record, according to the report, of my birth in California or of an adoption. It could have taken place somewhere else, I suppose. I had this cockamamie idea I was adopted, and that's why I tried to trick my parents into coming here. I was going to confront them. Kidnapped!"

"This is what we're going to do. You read through the

first scrapbook, I'll read the second one. You do the third, and I'll do the last one. When we're finished we'll compare notes. I want you to think in terms of a Christmas miracle. Think about it, Jessie. I can take you there. You can walk right up to the door and . . . and . . . say who you are. In my eyes that's a miracle."

They read silently, the dogs snuggled between them for over two hours. When they packed up the box, Jessie turned to Luke. "My father used to call me Hannah Banana. I still don't remember."

"It doesn't matter anymore if you remember or not. It's all here. Trust me when I tell you, your parents will know you the minute they lay eyes on you. Do you have any pictures of yourself when you were little?"

"No, but Sophie had albums in her room of the two of us together. I could call the housekeeper and have her pack them up and take them to the airport for the first flight out. She's probably still awake. She told me she only cat-naps. I could . . . pick them up and . . . how long will it take to drive to Tennessee, Luke?"

"A long time. I don't think either one of us is in a condition to drive. We could charter a plane. You can afford it, Jessie. You could be there for Christmas Eve. Jesus, what a whopper of a miracle. Do it, Jessie. Call the housekeeper."

"Okay." Ten minutes later, she said, "She's going to do it. We'll have the albums by ten o'clock. What if they don't remember me? What if they stopped loving me? Maybe I need more time to think about this. What if they moved away?"

"They didn't move away. They still live in the same house. They have a dog named Jelly, third generation. Your mother says each time the phone rings or the doorbell sounds, she thinks it might be news of you. There are all kinds of things about you in those articles. You can read them on the plane, line by line, word by word. Your parents sound like wonderful, loving people."

"We're taking the dogs," Jessie hiccuped.

"Damn right we're taking the dogs."

"Is it okay then that I don't feel any grief for . . . for Mrs. Roland?"

"Yes, Jessie, it is."

"I guess that's why my . . . Mr. Roland worded the cable the way he did."

"I imagine he's gone underground. There's no statute of limitations that I know of on kidnapping. He could still go to prison if they find him. I'm glad he had the good sense to send these scrapbooks to you before he left."

"So many years, so much lost time. How will I ever get that back? God, I wish Sophie was here."

"You can't get it back, Jessie. You have the rest of your life to look forward to."

"God, Luke, I can't wait. Do I look okay? What should I wear? We have no presents to take."

"I don't think you're going to need any presents. You look beautiful. You could probably show up in a bathrobe, and it wouldn't make any difference."

"I need a red sweater, Luke. I can't go without a red sweater."

"Then we'll get you a red sweater first thing in the morning."

"Luke, I just realized something. I have a home. A real home. All my life I've felt rootless, like I was a guest wherever I was. I really have a home. Do you realize what a wonderful word that is? Home is where you belong. Until now I never belonged." Hard, driving sobs tore at her throat. "How could they do that? Why? I want to hate them."

"No. Let it go. Don't look back. You have a whole new

life ahead of you. Don't spoil it with ugly memories. I'm going to call the airport now to see about chartering a plane. I want to go with you, Jessie."

"And I want you with me. I'm going to sit here with the dogs and drink this wonderful, delicious tea."

"Good girl. Hey, Jessie, I love you."

"Guess what, Luke Holt, I love you, too."

A light snow was falling when Luke opened the door of the rental car for Jessie. Dressed warmly, she shivered, not with cold but with anxiety as she fixed the leashes on Jelly and Fred. "It looks so cozy, so *Christmasey*, with the colored lights and the wreath on the door. We never had any kind of outdoor decoration, not even a wreath. The tree was always artificial. It's so warm-looking. Oh, Luke, I don't remember it at all."

"No one said you have to remember."

"Maybe I'm not Hannah Larson. Maybe this is all some horrible mistake. I should remember *something*. Just one little thing. I want so bad to remember something. I *need* to remember, Luke."

"When you're inside, something may strike you. It will take time, Jessie. It's Christmas Eve, a time of miracles. Be open. Shift into neutral. Take deep breaths. This is going to be the best ever Christmas for all of you. Ready?"

"No," Jessie wailed. "Maybe we should look in the windows or maybe we should walk around a little, you know, to get the feel of it."

"No, we don't need to do that. We need to walk up to the door and ring the bell. I hear a dog barking. That has to mean he's picked up our scent and knows we're out here. It's going to be everything you ever dreamed of, Jessie. All you have to do is put one foot in front of the other and walk up the steps to the porch. I'm right beside you, the dogs are here. *Do it!*"

Minutes later, Jessie jabbed at the bell with shaking fingers. She took a step backward, her hold on the dogs' leashes secure.

She's a pretty woman, and she looks like a mother, Jessie thought. There was a smile on her face as she wiped her hands on her apron. "Goodness, I didn't expect carolers so early. I just finished the supper dishes. Would you like to come in? It's snowing, isn't it. I always think snow on Christmas Eve is kind of special. Please, come in. Don't worry about the animals. I have one of my own."

"We . . . we aren't carolers, *Mama.* I think my name is Hannah and these are my dogs Jelly and Fred and my friend Luke. Are you my mother?"

"Bennnnnn!"

Jessie looked at the man coming toward her. "I think you used to call me Hannah Banana. You are my parents, aren't you?" she pleaded, her eyes filling with tears.

"Dear God," was all Grace could say.

Ben struggled with what he was seeing, his arm around his wife. "And what was it you always said in response?" he asked, his voice so strangled-sounding only Jessie understood what he was saying.

"Mash 'em up, Daddy," Jessie blurted, drawing the words from somewhere deep within her.

"Dear God," Grace said again.

"There was a whistle hanging on my bed. To call all the good fairies if I had a bad dream. Jelly had a blanket of his own. I had one just like it. You made them for us."

Grace started to sob as she opened her arms to her daughter.

"We never gave up hope," Ben said as he gathered his wife and daughter close.

Luke smiled. The dogs eyed each other warily.

"Do I have brothers or sisters?" Jessie asked, her eyes brimming with tears.

"You have two brothers. They're at their girlfriends' houses for Christmas. They'll be home for New Year's. We have no manners, Ben. Please, give me your coats. Can I fix you something to eat. I have a wonderful ham and homemade bread with some special relish I make myself."

"I'd love some," Luke said.

"Me too. We didn't have time to buy presents."

"Shucks, no presents are needed. Your mom bought you a red sweater. This year it was a cashmere one. It's soft as a feather," Ben said proudly. "Every year at Christmas she buys you a sweater, wraps it, and puts it under the tree. Then after New Year's we take it up to the attic. There's a bunch of them just waiting for you."

"I love red sweaters. Was I wearing one that . . . day?"

"Yes. You had a cold. I wanted you to stay warm."

They talked all night long.

In church the next day their eyes shone with tears when the minister announced to the congregation that Hannah Larson had finally returned to her parents.

In the driveway, on their return from church, Ben said, "Do you remember what we used to do in the snow?"

"You bet I remember," Jessie said, flopping down in the snow. "Snow angels! Little ones and big ones. Oh, God, this is so wonderful. I hate to leave."

"Leave?" the Larsons said in unison.

Jessie dusted the snow off her coat. "Yes. I have to leave. I have a promise to keep. I don't think you'd be very proud of me if I didn't honor it. Luke, I . . . you're going to have to go to Penn State alone."

"What do you have to do, honey?" Grace asked.

"I have to build a bridge for someone I loved with all my heart. I don't know how long it's going to take me to do it or even how I'm going to do it or where I'm going to do it, but I am going to do it. I'd like to leave knowing my child and I will be welcome when I return. Luke . . . tell me you understand. I don't want any promises because I can't make any in return. I want you all to know I love you, and you will be in my heart every single day until I return."

"Each of us has to do what we think best. Your mom and I aren't going anywhere anytime soon. We'll wait. Forever if necessary," Ben said. Grace nodded.

"Sophie would be so proud of you, Jessie," Luke said. "Do what you have to do. Trains, buses, and planes can take you to Penn State every day of the week. What about the dogs?"

"They're part of my family. They go with me. Merry Christmas, everyone."

"Merry Christmas!"

Epilogue

The man astride the chestnut mare shielded his eyes from the sun as he watched the mailman pack the ranch mailbox with a hefty amount of mail. Bills, catalogues his mother no longer ordered from, ranch bulletins, and more bills. He reached down for the mail to rifle through it. Who in the hell would be writing him from Nairobi, Africa? From the feel of the packet it had to be someone wanting something. He almost tossed it into his saddlebag with the rest of the mail and then decided, *What the hell, I need a laugh today. It's probably from stupid J.J.*

Tanner's eyebrows shot up to his hairline as he pushed the Stetson farther back on his head. Jessie! What the *hell* is Jessie doing in *Africa?* He ripped at the envelope, aware that his hands were trembling. After all this time.

Dear Tanner,

I hope you're well and everything is working out satisfactorily at the ranch. I also want to send my condolences on your father's death.

We have a son, Tanner. He's three now. I talk to him about you on a daily basis. I call it our quality time. To my dismay, he looks exactly like you. He adores this country and has more playmates than he knows what to do with. He already knows his letters and numbers. He's a sturdy little boy. He's warm, loving, polite, and caring. I told him when we return to the States we'll visit his daddy.

I'm doing my best to honor Sophie's last request. It hasn't been easy, but you know me, I never give up. Once you asked me what I was going to do with all of Sophie's money, and I told you I didn't know. Now I know. I'm building a bridge. It's a hell of a bridge, Tanner, and it costs a bloody fortune. When it's completed, and I don't know when that will be, I'm calling it the Sophie Ashwood Bridge. Knowing diddly-squat about building a bridge, I'm amazed I got this far. Determination and love I guess. I did manage to hire the best engineers and contractors I could find. For all I know, my life's work may be building bridges. Wish me luck.

If you have time, drop me a line. Send along a picture of yourself and your parents for our son. I named him Angus Tanner Larson Kingsley. The enclosed clippings will explain everything. I finally met my real family. It was so wonderful, there are no words to describe the feeling. They're all coming over here this summer. I have two brothers. I have definitely been blessed. Sometimes I think it's all a dream.

I wanted to make a settlement with you before I left, but my life got in the way. The enclosed is from my heart, Tanner. I want my child's father to have as good a life as he and I have.

I haven't heard from Luke in months. I guess he likes teaching and working summers being a ranger. I think life is getting in his way, too. I suppose some things are just not meant to be. Give my regards to your mother. I'm enclosing a picture of Angus with a baby elephant he calls Polly. We're happy, Tanner.

Affectionately,
Jessie and Angus

"I'll be a son of a gun!" Tanner said slapping his Stetson on his leg. He stared at his likeness so long his eyes started to water. The picture went into his shirt pocket as he picked through the papers. A deed to a Greek island. "Well, hey, I can handle that," he chortled. The deeds to two Greek shipping tankers, an art gallery in Milan, and a bank account in a Swiss bank with so many zeros it made him dizzy.

Tanner looked out across the dry, dusty fields and the few head of cattle that remained. Then he looked toward the horizon, wondering how many miles it was to Africa and how long it would take to get there.

Angus Tanner Larson Kingsley. It was a hell of a name. "Way to go, Jessie."

Visit our website at
KensingtonBooks.com
to sign up for our newsletters, read
more from your favorite authors, see
books by series, view reading group
guides, and more!

BOOK CLUB
BETWEEN THE CHAPTERS

Become a Part of Our
Between the Chapters Book Club
Community and Join the Conversation

Betweenthechapters.net